The Final Kiss

by
Dashawn Taylor

ISBN 10: 0-9800154-5-6
ISBN 13: 978-09800154-5-4
Next Level Publishing LLC. trade paperback first edition

10 9 8 7 6 5 4 3 2 1

Printed in the United States of America

Marketing and Promotions: Aleasha Arthur, Co-Owner/ COO of Next Level Publishing

For information regarding wholesale and publishing information, contact:info@nextlevelpublishing.com

Cover Layout and Design by: HotBookCovers.com

Editor and Book Layout: Jassi Wright {jassiwright@gmail.com}

www.TheFinalKiss.com
Facebook.com/TheRealDashawnTaylor
Twitter.com/dashawntaylor

This Book is for My Father

I would give anything to have one last
conversation with you.
Love you, Dad…
Miss you more than words could ever express.

Michael L. Taylor (Rest In Peace)

Thank You...

First and foremost, I thank GOD for continuing to bless me with the strength, wisdom and patience to share my gifts with the world.

- *My Family*

To my beautiful mother, Joann Smith. Thank you for always having my back and reminding me to never give up and keep pushing forward no matter the obstacles that lie ahead.

To my brothers, Michael Taylor, Steven Taylor, DJ Symphony, Bryan "Ca$h" Staton. To my sisters, Alika and Bria Taylor, and to my beautiful niece, Harmony Taylor.

To Ruth Taylor, I will miss you always, Grandma. Your wisdom will always remain with me, and I promise to continue to make you proud. Rest In Peace.

I can't move forward without mentioning my extended family: The Smith Clan, The McClinton's, The Taylor's and The Townsends. I would have to write another book to express my undeniable thanks to my entire family for always being there for me. Special thank you to my grandmother, Rosetta Smith, to my grandfathers, may you both rest in peace, Horace "Boy" Smith and Benny Taylor. To my uncles Jon, Roosevelt, Herbert, Leonard, Uncle JR (Rest In Peace), Uncle Kenny, Uncle BeBop, Uncle Robert, Aunt Martha and Uncle Richard. Thank you to my aunts Cynthia, Marie, Estelle, Patricia, Dorothy (Rest In Peace), Aunt Ronia (Rest In Peace), Aunt Mary and Aunt Betty. To my cousins and extended family: Simone, Stephanie, Nicky, Sebanya, Pam, Cookie, Leon, Robert Ponton, Anthony, Alvin, Reese, Junior, Kim, Chucky, Dennis Fowler, and Kisha Taylor.

- *My Team*

To Aleasha Arthur, the smartest and hardest working woman in this industry. Thanks for being a dynamic business partner, an undeniable mirror and most of all…a great friend. Let's continue to power forward and #WIN

To Jamise Dames, my editor for life and probably the biggest reason I didn't give up on this game when the "beast" started stealing…lol. Thanks for helping me regain my voice, and what more can I say…but Thank you.

To the staff of Next Level Publishing, thank you for all of your hard work and great ideas. We have so much more to do. Let's continue to move flawlessly as a unit and make history.

- *My Power Circle and Living Angels*

Kyle Newsome, Lee Harris, Shaleik "Lavish Look" Murray, Felicia Newsome, Allison Purvis-Smith, Jon Kurpis, Tressa "Azarel" Smallwood, Shawna Grundy, Jamil Newsome, Samar and Salisha Newsome, Sonja Simmons (Rest In Peace), Tanisha Malone, Carl and Chandra Cole, Shannon Phillips, Erica Murray, Big 7, K'Wan, Wahida Clark, Isadora Douglas, Cynthia Anderson, Brittani Williams, Melinda McKenzie, Tia Rudd, Toni Ciullo, Norma Vandemark, Erick S. Gray, Jen and Robbie Zumsteg, Deborah Cardona, Cynthia Strickland, Ericka Williams, Kisha Green, Martinique Moore, Tobias A. Fox, George Sherman Hudson, Sisi Cummings, Hakim & Tyson (Black and Nobel Bookstore), Lesslie Moore, Sandi & Maria and the entire Literary Ladies Book Club, JM Benjamin, Felicia Waters, Treasure E. Blue, DC Bookman, Tra Verdejo, Sylvia Cole, OOSA Bookclub, Go On Girl Bookclub, Black Expressions, Mahogany Bookclub, Sidi, APOOO Bookclub, Classy Readers Bookclub, Divas of the Serengeti Bookclub, Bridget O. Davis, Source of Knowledge Bookstore, TLJ Bookstore, Urban Knowledge, Vicky Stringer, Carl "Mann" Johnson, Capone Lee, Olivia Fox, Elaine Edwards, Bob Sumner, Pamela Smith, Athena Parker, Tina Graham, Trizonna McClendon, Jennifer Pruitt, Trice Hickman, Jana Wilson, Shawon, Nikki Turner, Roger Maloney, Indria Britt, T. Styles,

Shannon Holmes, D'Erica Flowers, Mack Mama, Michelle Edwards, Theresa O'Neal, Zahir and Tiffany (Empire Books), Lil' Mo, TuRae Gordon, Simply Monica, Justzo, Anwan Glover, Tamika Newhouse, Al Saadiq Banks, Tiffany Turner, Mother Rose, Alexander Bookstore, Expressions Cultural Center, Horizon Bookstore, RM Bookstore, Angela Beverly, Wendy Williams, Vibe Magazine, Reggie Rouse, Rashad, Jermaine Wilson, Phillip Bryant and the Honey Child Team.

If you don't see your name, blame it on my mind and not my heart. Feel free to add it here____________________!

Love Ya!

“The eyes are the windows to the soul…but no one really knows what treachery lies deep within the hearts of men.”

– Heidi Kachina

Prologue...

Sunday, November 4, 2007
East Orange, New Jersey
1:49 a.m.

Heidi Kachina violently burst out of the back door of her mother's house. She stumbled onto the back porch and barely escaped being murdered. She held a black briefcase full of money tightly in her left hand, and a shiny chrome gun in her right. Her terrified heart thumped in her chest as she ran down the stairs. The foul stench of death was in the air. The devil was on her neck, and she only had a few seconds to escape with her life.

She frantically rushed through the backyard. Her best friend, Faith, had just gotten killed in the house, and the horrific images flashed in her mind. Heidi stumbled through the tall grass and struggled to keep her balance. She held the money tightly and raised the gun behind her, then looked behind. No one was following her. She continued running, and almost reached the front of the house. A large figure appeared in front of her from the shadows. Heidi stopped in her tracks, then raised her gun toward the dark silhouette, which appeared to be male. "Who's there?" Heidi shouted as her hands shook.

The figure never answered. Heidi focused her eyes to get a good look as it slowly moved toward her. The silhouette was definitely male.

"Who are you?" Heidi yelled again. "What do you want?"

"I'm sorry, Heidi," the man responded coldly.

Before she could get a better look at him, he let off five thunderous gun blasts in her direction. Heidi's body was viciously lifted off her feet as three bullets entered her chest, pushing her down to the ground with a thud. She screamed out in pain toward the heavens. Heidi started coughing up blood and cried as her assailant hovered over her. She finally got to see his face. It was a man she had known for nearly a year. Aaron Smith.

"Aaron?" she whispered. She couldn't believe Aaron had shot her. She'd trusted him with her darkest secrets, and had believed they were building something special together. Never once would she have suspected that she would be killed by the hands of a man she'd trusted with so much, especially her life.

Aaron coldly looked down at her like she was a lifelong enemy. He kicked the gun out of her hand and sadistically stared into her eyes. Heidi's body trembled with fear and agony. The hot bullets mutilated her body from the inside. Aaron reached down and grabbed the briefcase out of her hand. "I'm sorry Heidi," Aaron softly spoke. "I can't let you have my money." He scowled, then appeared to smirk as she struggled to breathe. Aaron peered around the dark neighborhood, then aimed at her. He was ready to finish her off.

"Please don't kill me," Heidi called out to Aaron, then struggled for breath again. Before she could open her mouth to speak, Aaron fired two more shots mercilessly into her chest. Her body rattled from the heavy shock. Heidi tried to breathe. The blood spilled from her chest like a river. Heidi never made another sound. Aaron's bullets flat lined her.

"Goodnight princess," Aaron coldly whispered.

Heidi's body shut down, momentarily dying, but her mind stayed active. She heard a slight rumbled just over her body, and knew Aaron had run away from the scene. The backyard fell silent. Her brain raced and she struggled to stay alive. She mustered all her inner strength to keep her mind active. She refused to die tonight. She turned her concentration away from the bullets in her chest and focused on the revenge in her heart. There was no way Aaron would get away with this. Heidi's faint pulse continued and she never gave up. As she laid on her back preciously clinging to her life, she vowed that if she lived, Aaron would pay dearly for betraying her.

Chapter 1

Friday, October 4th
7:21pm
Grand Ballroom – Marriott Hotel
Newark, NJ

TWO YEARS LATER

"I have witnessed a lot of death in my life. There is no question about that. People look at me sometimes, and they are amazed when I tell my story. It's not a pretty one. I still have nightmares to this day when I reminisce about losing people who were close to me. People like my former fiancé, Jayson…God rest his soul. And people like my best friend, Faith, who died at the hands of street thugs who tried to tear apart my family. And most of all, the man who was dearest to my heart, my brother, Lamar, who bravely died while trying to save my family that same horrific night. I miss my brother so much that I feel real pain when I see his face in my mind. My soul aches every time I think about the people who were torn from me, and for many years it was hard for me to stand on a solid foundation and move on. Rage and fury filled my heart, and for the longest time I was unable to trust another person at all, let alone trust another man. But something magical happened to me a few years back, something that I can't explain. A man came into my life and changed the way I felt about everything in my past and the way I felt about myself. Tonight, I want to introduce you to that amazing man."

At the podium stood a very elegant and beautiful woman. Her emotional words captivated the standing-room-only crowd in the grand ballroom. Her stunning five-foot-eight frame towered over the microphones, and her mature features were both regal-like and alluring. Almost everything about her was sophisticated. From her platinum floor-length evening dress to the sparkling accessories on her wrists and neck, the woman shined like a polished diamond. She illuminated magnificence and style to the crowd. Everyone had their eyes fixed on her, and not a soul in the room could turn away from the fascinating woman. Her name was Heidi Kachina.

A slightly emotional Heidi took a quiet moment to gather her composure. The sensitive topic of family and death began to twist her inside out. She thought about her colorful past and the drama she had experienced in her life. Losing her closest friends and family members was never easy to handle. The memories would always bring her to tears, and tonight Heidi found herself fighting hard to hold back the waterworks. She looked out into the crowd and scanned the waiting faces. Her stare was lifeless, failing to blend in with her luminous aura. Heidi's eyes were deadened from shielding the immense pain that was locked away deep in her heart. Like dark tinted windows, it was hard for other people to see inside them. But those who were close to Heidi were well aware of her haunting demons. They all knew about her daily battle for inner peace and the strength to move on.

Heidi looked down at her prepared speech and regained her poise. She raised her head again with pride and continued to address the audience. "I said all of that to simply say that...I am a walking, living and breathing testament of the integrity that this man has deep within him," Heidi started to raise her voice. "He genuinely cares about people and will always go the extra mile to take care of someone who is in need. This city needs a man who knows what it means to get his hands dirty, and do the necessary work that many of us shy away from. This city needs a man who will put the good people first and not fall into the selfish cycle of corruption. And this city needs a man who is fearless, determined and focused on the goal to make this a better place for us to live, work and raise our families. This wonderful man has earned my trust, and I am positive that he is deserving of your trust as well. So without further ado...I introduce the man of the hour, my loving fiancé, Mr. Tycen Wakefield!"

A thunderous roar of cheers and ovations erupted in the ballroom. The large crowd applauded wildly as Tycen emerged from the rear of the stage and walked toward the podium. Heidi smiled like a young schoolgirl as Tycen approached her with open arms. The audience applauded louder as the two warmly embraced and exchanged a passionate kiss for all to see.

"Real Deal Wakefield! Real Deal Wakefield!" The crowd chanted like they were at a rock concert.

Tycen smiled at Heidi, then turned his attention to the microphones. The audience continued to scream his name, and Tycen humbly received the praises. He watched as Heidi left the stage area and blended into the crowd. He slowly raised his hands in an effort to calm his army of supporters. "Good evening ladies and gentleman." Tycen smiled and glanced out into the audience. "My name is Tycen Wakefield."

The audience erupted with loud cheers as they finally heard from the man they had been waiting to see all evening. They continued to chant his name. A few photographers began to snap pictures of the crowd.

Tycen raised his hand again and continued to speak. "I thank everyone who came out to support me this evening." Tycen smiled and surveyed the audience. "Thank you to the members of the media and to the high-ranking officials who came to oversee my announcement. I also thank the resilient residents of Newark who continue to push forward, and who give me the strength and the confidence to make a positive difference in their lives and the lives of their families." Tycen noticed a few familiar faces in the crowd and pointed toward them with a smile. He paused for a moment as the audience cheered on. "Finally, I have to give special thanks and gratitude to the woman who has kept me grounded throughout this process. You know there is an old saying that I will never forget. They say behind every successful man there is a woman with a frying pan waiting for him to screw up."

The audience laughed and applauded at the timely joke. Heidi shook her head and smiled at Tycen, who gave her a wink from the podium. He nodded his head toward her and continued to address the elated crowd.

"Believe me, guys...without this woman being there to show me the light during my darkest hours...there is no way that I could have made this decision with good conscious," Tycen lowered his voice as his tone became more candid. "Her strength to battle on no matter the obstacle has rubbed off on me, and I'm forever grateful to have her in my life. So before I make my official announcement, I would like everyone to give a well-deserved round of applause to my beautiful fiancée, Heidi Kachina."

Everyone in the room turned their attention to Heidi and clapped their hands. Heidi bashfully covered her mouth and gracefully waved to the crowd. Tycen smiled at his gorgeous fiancée. He gave her a warm expression, then once again turned his attention back to the audience.

"So, tonight, we are here to begin a new chapter in our illustrious history," Tycen began to raise his voice. "Tonight we are here to ensure that the future of this wonderful city is put in the hands of people who will work together every day to move us forward and undo the harm that those in our wake have forced upon us." Tycen paused for a moment. The audience cheered him on and he continued to speak. "I battled over this decision for some months now. And every time I came to a feeling of doubt...I reminded myself of the story of little Lexi Hamilton. For those who are not familiar with the story, Lexi Hamilton was the beautiful sixteen year-old girl from Newark, who was abducted on her way to school. Lexi was missing for over a week before her story gained a single headline. Her family cried out for help, and those in power abandoned them. And now, after five years, the current mayor is finally bringing national attention to this story and trying to benefit off of Lexi Hamilton's tragic legacy. But I say, no more. I say, it is time for the corrupt powers down at city hall to be removed. We need to replace selfishness with inclusion. We need to replace exploitation with progress. And we need to simply replace lies and empty promises with the truth and accountability. So it is with a humble heart, a focused mind and a compassionate spirit that I announce my candidacy to be the next Mayor of this great city of Newark, New Jersey!"

An explosion of cheers cascaded from the crowd in the ballroom. The room was suddenly immersed in chants and praises from the enthusiastic audience. People started waving signs and screaming Tycen's name. Music blared from the speakers. The groovy sound of Etta James' version of Oh Happy Day put everyone in a festive mood. People began to dance and mingle, and all Tycen could do was smile and marvel at the large group of energized supporters.

Heidi looked around the electrified room and was overwhelmed by the sight. It was no secret that the battered city of Newark was in desperate need of new leadership and a change in social values from the local government. A grassroots movement was growing larger and the call for action was becoming louder throughout the suffering neighborhoods. People were growing increasingly frustrated with the current mayor, and the public perception of city hall was becoming worse with each passing day. Judging by the excitement in the room this evening, people believed that her fiancé could be that person to change it all.

Tycen gave his closing remarks and waved to the crowd. People cheered and danced in the ballroom sensing that change was coming soon to the city. Tycen reveled in the praises for another quick moment and confidently headed off the stage.

Heidi walked over and greeted her fiancé. "That was an amazing speech honey," she whispered in Tycen's ear as she embraced him. "You are definitely made for the spotlight."

"Thank you sweetie. Your introduction was perfect," he responded, and then gave Heidi a quick kiss on the lips. He gently grabbed her by the hand. The adorable couple headed out of the ballroom and into the luxurious lobby of the event hall.

Cameras flashed from a small group of reporters as Tycen and Heidi slowly walked toward the exit. A few onlookers made their way over to the couple and clamored to get a second of Tycen's time. Heidi took a step back as more supporters began to flock to her fiancé. He was unexpectedly hit with dozens of questions, but Tycen stayed patient and answered each one. Heidi gazed at Tycen, watching as he handled himself like a seasoned politician, and felt a strong sense of pride and gratitude to be a part of his complicated life.

They were growing closer every day, and Heidi felt a deep affection for him that she hadn't had for the men in her past. Her attraction to Tycen was far beyond physical and emotional. There was something magnetic about their connection, and Heidi felt like Tycen could potentially be the last man she would ever love. Every second that she spent with Tycen made her feel stronger, and just the mere thought of losing him made her miserable. Despite her drama-filled past, Heidi vowed that she would never let her former life skeletons ruin her future. Every day she tried to let go of her distrustful ways and give Tycen the fair chance to fully enter her heart. Heidi knew it would not be an easy task, but looking at her fiancé tonight reminded her that Tycen was well worth the risk.

"Okay guys, I can only answer one more question and then I have to say goodnight," Tycen raised his hand and spoke loudly to the crowd of onlookers.

"Just one quick question, Mr. Wakefield," a tall reporter yelled from the back of the group.

"Go ahead, sir." Tycen nodded.

"Some people can look at your resume and conclude that you may be a bit unqualified for the position of Mayor of this city." The reporter gave Tycen a hard stare and continued his statement. "What do you say to those people who believe you lack the experience to accomplish all of those great things you promise?"

Tycen squared his shoulders. "The people who currently occupy the offices on Broad Street are career politicians. They have years of experience throughout this state of sitting on boards, running local wards and even unions. I believe those past relationships are the root of the problem of this city." Tycen looked around the small group as people continued to snap pictures and reporters jostled to hold up their recorders. "I want to use my inexperience, as you would call it, to my advantage. As Mayor of Newark, the people can rest easy knowing that they will finally have a man in office that will represent their needs. The people need to be reassured that their mayor will not waste their time and money trying to do favors for people who don't need it. Believe me, now is not the time for greed and corruption. Now is the time for change and hope. And I believe tonight is the beginning of a new day for this great city of Newark."

The small group in the lobby cheered the powerful response. The tall reporter closed his mouth and looked at Tycen as Tycen waved goodbye to the small group of journalists. He gave them one last photo opportunity, then reached out for Heidi's hand. People continued to shout Tycen's name as the couple politely pushed their way toward the exit, then headed out the building.

"What was that about?" Heidi asked as she latched on tightly to her fiancé's arm. "Why was that reporter so rude to you?"

"Who knows?" Tycen responded. "I'm positive that some people in this city don't like the fact that I'm running for mayor."

Heidi looked over to her fiancé and decided not to press the issue. She could tell that he was irritated by the reporter's question, but she was impressed by the way Tycen had handled himself. She squeezed him tighter as they walked over to the white limousine parked in the front of the building.

"So where do you want to go for dinner tonight?" Tycen

asked. They eased into the backseat of the plush vehicle.

"Baby, I was hoping we could skip dinner tonight." Heidi smiled as her fiancé closed the limo's back door. Tycen looked over at Heidi as she moved closer to him. She softly grabbed him by the face and began to slowly kiss him on the lips and cheeks. Tycen was caught off guard by Heidi's sudden change of mood. He playfully jumped when he felt Heidi's hand reach down between his legs. She slowly started to massage his strong thighs and Tycen started growing excited. "You looked so damn good on that stage tonight," Heidi sweetly groaned and moved her hands up to his chest as the limo pulled off. "I wanted to attack you in front of all those people."

"Good thing you didn't," Tycen joked and continued to kiss his fiancée.

"Earlier I told the driver where I want to go," Heidi whispered. She gave Tycen a frisky glare, calmly looking him up and down. "I just want you to relax, baby. You deserve it. Tonight is your night, Mr. Mayor."

Tycen smiled at Heidi's command and sunk deeper into the leather seat. He felt her warm tongue began to graze his neck, and he closed his eyes. Heidi let out an anxious moan and grew excited when she felt Tycen's heart begin to race. She was ready to please her man in every way possible. The limo started to pick up speed, and Heidi knew they would soon be at their destination. She continued to seduce Tycen. The back of the limo heated up with every passing second. She couldn't wait to finally spend a sexy evening with the man she loved.

Chapter 2

Friday, October 4
8:28pm
Beth Israel Hospital
Newark, NJ

"Ma'am, please...try not to move your head too much. You have been unconscious for a few hours now, and you may feel a bit groggy. We have reason to believe that you were assaulted this evening. You have suffered a serious blow to your head, but you're currently in stable condition right now at Beth Israel hospital in Newark, New Jersey. There is a police detective here who wants to briefly ask you a few questions about the incident tonight. It will only take a few minutes. Is that okay with you?"

A thirty-year-old woman struggled to stay conscious. Her eyes were bloodshot. Her fragile body felt hollow and gravely empty, as she lay motionless in the hospital bed. Her beautiful face was now swollen out of proportion due to the gash on the side of her forehead and a large bruise on her chin. The woman struggled to stay awake as the pain started to slowly seep into her body again. Never in her young life had she been a victim of a violent crime, but tonight she was involved in a vicious carjacking that had almost killed her. Her name was Kimberly Moore, but those close to her affectionately knew her as Kimi.

A dull beeping noise and the sound of medical equipment made Kimi become increasingly nervous. She slowly scanned the bright room, and then closed her eyes again as another sharp pain punished the base of her forehead. She moaned.

The lead nurse on duty hovered over Kimi's battered face

and gently squeezed her palm.

"You're probably going to feel some pain and some slight discomfort, ma'am," the nurse tried her best to console the aching Kimi. "You're scheduled for another round of medication in a few minutes. Just hold on a little bit longer if you can."

A million thoughts flooded Kimi's mind as she tried to remember what took place earlier that evening. She tried to figure out how she ended up in the hospital in so much pain. Brutal images of a black steel object smashing against her head made her tighten her eyes. She started to have choppy memories of her bleeding face pressed against the freezing sidewalk. A quick flash of the brake lights on her SUV haunted her thoughts, and Kimi opened her eyes wide.

"Niko…!" she cried out.

The female detective in the room quickly jumped to her feet. She rushed to the opposite side of Kimi's bed and pulled out a small recording device. "Thank God she is finally awake," the detective blurted, her overzealous presence scaring Kimi. "Okay nurse, do you think she will be able to talk now?"

The nurse glanced over to the investigator in frustration and twisted her face. "Please keep your voice down. She just woke up," the nurse whispered.

"My name is Detective Bell," the woman announced to Kimi and ignored the nurse. She quickly showed Kimi her shimmering badge and continued speaking. "I've been investigating a number of carjackings in the city, and we have reason to believe that you may have been one of the victims of a long string of robberies."

Kimi's face didn't budge. She continued listening to the detective and gave her a blank stare.

"I hate to do this right now," Detective Bell said. "But the sooner you can answer just a few questions…the sooner I can get out of your hair and let you get some rest. Does that sound good?"

"Yes," Kimi said and tried to clear her dry throat.

"What's your name?" Detective Bell asked.

"Kimi Moore," she nervously whispered.

"You had no identification on you when they brought you in tonight," Detective Bell added. "It may have been in the car, perhaps?"

"Yes," Kimi responded. "I think my purse…and a few of my bags were in…the backseat."

"Okay." Detective Bell turned around and pulled out a few black and white photographs from a stack of folders. She showed one of the images to Kimi. "We were able to download the red light camera pictures from the department of transportation, and I think we have identified your vehicle. Is this it?"

Kimi took a look at the still image of her BMW X5 and nodded. Another jarring memory of the carjacking flashed in her mind again and caused Kimi to shake.

"Do you remember anything about tonight?" Detective Bell asked. "Anything that could help us find out who was behind this?"

Kimi closed her eyes and tried to remember the tragic episode. The nurse squeezed Kimi's hand again as she noticed Kimi struggling to recollect the incident. "I know I was driving down Avon Avenue," she said. "I'm not sure which corner I was at, but I had to stop at a red light, and that's when a truck sped up behind me. I think one truck was in front of me, too. I remember all of them had guns when they got out and ran over to my vehicle."

"Okay good." Detective Bell nodded and tried her best to sound encouraging. "So it was more than just one of them?"

"Yes," Kimi said.

"Did you get a good look at them?" Detective Bell asked.

Kimi thought for a moment. The expression on her face changed as she started to remember more about the carjacking. She tried to recall the faces, but her mind continued to draw a blank. The vivid image of a pistol being pointed at her car window circled in her mind.

"I'm sorry, I don't remember looking at their faces. I only remember the guns," she lowered her voice. "I was scared that they were going to kill me." Kimi's eyes started watering, and she unconsciously squeezed the nurse's hand.

"I understand," Detective Bell responded. "Do you remember anything else?"

"Yes, I do," Kimi whispered. "One of them...pulled me out of the car...and beat me with his gun," she stuttered as the tears began to trickle from the sides of her eyes. The memories were becoming more vivid, and Kimi's heart started to race faster. Kimi pushed her mind even further, and tried to concentrate on the man who pulled her out of the car. Another clear image of the incident flashed in her mind. The memory of a gun blast shook her. Kimi slowed down the image in her mind, and then looked up to the detective. "There was something on his wrist," Kimi whispered.

"Something like what? You mean like a watch or bracelet?" Detective Bell asked.

"No," Kimi quietly responded. "I think it was a tattoo or some kind of mark. But I can't remember what it was. I remember him pointing the gun at my window and a mark on his wrist, but I can't see exactly what it is. I'm sorry." The hospital room fell silent as Kimi tried her best to recall her attacker's wrist. She closed her eyes tighter, but the image never became clearer. Her mind continued to concentrate on the dangerous threat of the gun, and Kimi slowly opened her eyes. She looked up to the detective and sluggishly shook her head in disappointment.

Detective Bell gave Kimi a sympathetic expression. She was hoping to get a more detailed description of the mark, but she decided not to press Kimi at this time. "I understand. Maybe it will come to you later. And believe me, I know this is tough," Detective Bell lowered her voice. "But this is important. Do you remember hearing anything from the men? A name, perhaps? Any code words? Or anything that seemed out of place?"

"No, I'm really sorry. I can't remember much," Kimi said. "It happened so damn fast, and I was really scared."

"I can understand that, Kimi. And no need to be sorry, you are doing just fine," Detective Bell said. "Was anyone else in the car with you?"

"Yes, my boyfriend," Kimi whispered and looked up to the detective. Both of her eyes were filled with tears now. "My boyfriend was in the car with me."

"Wait! There was another person in the car?" The detective's eyes lit up. She looked over toward the nurse. "Is he here at the hospital?"

"No, we only had one victim from that scene," the nurse informed.

"Are you sure?" The detective snapped.

"I'm positive," the nurse fired back.

"I think they took him," Kimi whispered.

"What?" Detective Bell dropped her jaw. "What do you mean?"

"He was in the car, and I don't think he ever got out." Kimi cried as she recalled the X5 disappearing down the street. "I think they took him."

Detective Bell scrambled to get a pen from her jacket pocket. Kimi's revelation put a new twist on tonight's case. The carjacking had just turned into a kidnapping, and the detective knew she had to act fast. "What's your boyfriend's full name?" Detective Bell asked.

"Niko Stanton," Kimi whispered.

Detective Bell looked up from her pad and glared at Kimi for a moment. Her eyes became wide and slightly tense as Kimi's revelation swirled around in her mind. The detective looked like she had seen a ghost. "Niko Stanton?" Detective Bell blurted. "The lawyer from the Stanton Law Firm?"

"Yes." Kimi's face froze.

"Let me get this straight, your boyfriend is Niko Stanton, and he was in the car when you got jacked?" The detective tried to piece the story together correctly.

"Yes," Kimi repeated and the tears continued to flow.

"I'll be damned!" Detective Bell gasped, and then turned around. She reached for her phone and started dialing frantically.

"What's going on?" Kimi cried out. She noticed the detective's demeanor had dramatically changed. "What does that mean?" she quickly asked.

Detective Bell walked to the other side of the hospital room and made a few calls. The nurse tried her best to calm Kimi, who was now raising her voice and demanding answers.

"Excuse me," Detective Bell turned her attention toward the nurse. "I need this woman moved to a private room. If possible, we need to get her as far away from the emergency area as possible. I also need you to grab two security guards and have them posted right outside the door, okay?"

"Okay," the nurse responded and turned back to Kimi.

"I need you to do it now!" The detective bluntly ordered.

The nurse spun around and looked at Detective Bell. She sensed the urgency in the detective's voice, then swiftly headed out the door. Kimi's heart started pounding harder. She looked over toward the far side of the room and stared at the detective.

"What's going on?" Kimi asked again.

"Now I need you to trust me, Kimi," Detective Bell lowered her voice. She sent out one last text message, and then walked over to Kimi's bedside. "I'm going to make sure the hospital keeps you here overnight for your own protection."

"Protection?" Kimi gasped.

Detective Bell turned her attention to the front door of the hospital room. She wanted to make sure no one was in earshot of her conversation. "What I am about to tell you is extremely important." Detective Bell looked at Kimi. "Although I am not working directly with the case, I am familiar with Niko Stanton's involvement with an ongoing investigation of Leon Marquez."

Kimi's face stiffened. "Judging by your expression, I'm assuming you heard the name before?" Detective Bell asked.

Kimi slowly nodded her head. Her boyfriend Niko had spoken the familiar name on a number of occasions. And Kimi knew Leon Marquez was the ruthless boss of the most dangerous crime family in Newark, but more importantly, he was a former client of Niko's. After Leon Marquez and his thugs threatened Niko's life, Niko had decided it was time to turn his back on his most treacherous client. A few months later, Niko closed his law firm and cooperated with the authorities. He worked closely with the FBI and the local police department to bring down Leon Marquez and his crime family. It didn't take long for Niko to have a target on his back and a price on his head. He and Kimi were heading out of town when the carjacking abruptly interrupted their plans of starting a new life. Kimi thought about Niko's face and closed her eyes. She sadly realized that things were going from bad to worse, and could only imagine what her boyfriend was going through.

"I don't want to alarm you, but I feel obligated to take this precaution for you," Detective Bell said. "If the Marquez family targeted your boyfriend for this, it is possible that your life can be in danger too."

"And you think it was really a kidnapping?" Kimi asked.

"Most carjackers just want the car," Detective Bell responded. "Rarely do they want the people that are in them. We have no choice but to assume that this was a deliberate and calculated kidnapping."

Kimi closed her mouth and shook her head. The pressure of the traumatic evening was getting the best of her. Detective Bell looked down at her phone as another text message came in. An uneven grin came to Detective Bell's face, and Kimi felt uneasy when she noticed the detective's mood changing again. She decided to ignore her suspicions.

"I don't want you to worry, Kimi. We are going to keep the guards next to your room all night so you will be safe." The detective nodded toward Kimi. "I have contacted my partner, and we're going to make sure you are relocated safely."

Kimi didn't say a word. She nervously looked at Detective Bell as the detective reached into her pocket.

"I actually have to go now...but...I'm going to leave my business card with you. My partner is going to call me back, and then we will figure out how to safely move you out of the hospital." Detective Bell carefully put the card on a silver tray next to Kimi's clothes. "If you think of anything else about tonight...please call me. No matter what time it is, don't hesitate to call me. I want to be the first to know."

Kimi nodded her head and looked at the business card for a moment.

"And don't worry, Kimi. We are going to find your boyfriend," Detective Bell assured. "Believe me."

Kimi had no choice but to take comfort in the detective's promise. Her brutal night quickly turned into her worst nightmare, and Kimi felt helpless. She closed her eyes and tried to remember any other details about the carjacking that could help the authorities find her boyfriend Niko.

Chapter 3

Friday, October 4
9:37pm
West Orange, NJ

A few miles away, in the back of the white limousine, a warm bead of sweat dripped from Tycen's forehead. He let out a quiet moan as his lustful fiancée relentlessly seduced him. Heidi pressed her hot body against him hard as he lay awkwardly across the back seat of the vehicle. Tycen was so engrossed in the feeling of Heidi's hands all over him that he never noticed the driver heading to one of the most talked about resorts in the state. Heidi moved and kissed Tycen one last time as she felt the limo slowing.

"Wow that was fast," Heidi whispered. She raised her head and took a quick peek out the window. The limo turned onto a long driveway and slowly crept up the steep hill. The bright lights started to shine through the window as the vehicle reached the top of the driveway. Heidi crawled off of her fiancé and moved to the other side of the limo. She gathered her things and gave Tycen a suggestive expression. Tycen recognized the look and returned the gesture.

"I think we're here baby." She pointed out the window.

Tycen pushed himself up by his palms, then turned around and looked outside. A smooth grin came to his face when he laid eyes on the illuminated sign in front of the extravagant hotel.

"The Venice Cove?" He asked as he turned back to Heidi. He was clearly impressed.

"Yes, baby. It's time we step our game up." Heidi giggled.

"Now baby, if you're going to be the Mayor, we can't have you being spotted in those raggedy ass hotels no more. You deserve the best from now on, sweetie."

Tycen looked around as the limo parked in the front of the establishment. The hotel sat boldly on top of a large mountainside. The majestic vibe was a direct contrast to its surroundings. The resort reminded Tycen of a place that belonged in the middle of Las Vegas. "Damn, this is nice," he uttered.

"You ain't seen nothing yet, baby." Heidi continued to gather her things. "Let's go. I need to show you something."

Tycen stepped out of the limo first, and then reached out his hand to Heidi. He watched her sexy body as she slowly emerged from the back seat. Heidi felt Tycen's warm hand slide across her waist and a slight tingle between her thighs. She couldn't wait to get Tycen alone. The cold air whisked by the couple and forced them to rush into the building. Heidi's eyes lit up as they entered the palace-style foyer of the resort.

"Oh shit," Tycen said in sheer amazement.

"Told you." Heidi gazed on.

The couple surveyed the warmly lit hotel lobby. Two large Greek-style pillars set on each side of the room, only outdone by the magnificent ceiling mural of seven cherubim. Tycen gazed at the gold and silver trimmings on the walls, and felt like he had entered another world. The Rosa Aurora marble floor that stretched out beneath his feet was unlike anything he had ever seen. Heidi clutched onto her man's arm. She smiled knowing he was taken aback by the scene.

"How the hell did you find this place?" Tycen continued to look around.

"The Real Housewives of New Jersey show." Heidi giggled.

Tycen looked down at his fiancée, and shared a laugh with her as the couple walked over to the hotel concierge.

"Reservation for Kachina." Heidi smiled and pulled out her credit card. The hotel clerk politely browsed through her computer and beamed at the couple. Heidi waited for her information to be processed and looked up to Tycen. "Do you have some of those campaign stickers with you?" Heidi asked.

"I sure do," Tycen replied and reached into his coat pocket.

A devilish smile came to Heidi's face as her fiancé handed her two button-sized stickers.

"Thanks sweetie." Heidi smiled and looked around the hotel lobby. She started to get excited knowing she had an even bigger surprise for Tycen tonight.

"Okay, Ms. Kachina you are all set. I have you on the top floor in the sky loft." The clerk handed Heidi a gold access card.

"Thank you." Heidi smiled and grabbed the card. She handed the clerk one of the campaign stickers. "He's trying to act modest tonight, but this man is going to be the next Mayor of Newark," Heidi proudly announced and nodded toward Tycen. "Please vote for him if you can."

"Oh thank you, ma'am. I sure will," The clerk politely responded and looked at the sticker. "Do you guys need anything for the room?"

"Does it have a bed?" Heidi joked.

"Yes it does." The clerk smiled.

"Then that's all we need. Ain't that right, big daddy?" Heidi giggled and cuffed Tycen's ass.

The shocked clerk tried to hide her embarrassment as she pointed the couple in the direction of the elevator.

"Okay, time to go." Tycen chuckled and playfully grabbed Heidi by the arm. The couple stumbled away from the front desk and headed down a long hallway. Tycen was still in awe of the beautiful resort layout. He gazed at the magnificent artwork on the walls as they reached the end of the bright hall. "This is a very nice place," Tycen said, then pressed the elevator button.

"I'm glad you like it."

The heavy metal doors parted. Heidi took one look inside the empty car and smiled. A sexy thought came to her mind, and Heidi nibbled on her bottom lip. She slowly walked to the back of the elevator and watched Tycen as he pressed the button for the top floor. Another rush of excitement ran through Heidi's body as the doors closed. They were finally alone. Without warning, Heidi dropped her bag to the floor and quickly pushed up on her fiancé. She pulled him close to her and kissed him wildly. Her eager tongue searched for his, and she quivered when she finally tasted him. "Damn baby," Heidi let out a girlish moan.

The elevator started rising along with the budge in Tycen's pants. Heidi pulled him even closer and ran her hands down by his waist. Her aggressive nature turned on Tycen. Heidi could feel his growing dick calling for her attention.

"I wanted to do this to you all night," Heidi whispered.

"Do what?" Tycen asked, his tone barely audible.

Heidi quickly backed away from her fiancé and gave him a deep stare. Tycen's heart skipped a beat. Her expression made him slightly nervous and caused his loins to throb in anticipation. He didn't know what to expect. Heidi playfully showed Tycen the campaign sticker, then laughed like a devious schoolgirl. She reached just above Tycen's head and placed the sticker over the surveillance camera.

"Baby, what the hell are you doing?" Tycen gasped.

Heidi never answered him. She looked at the control panel on the wall, then slammed her palm against the emergency stop button. A deafening alarm rang out. Tycen's heart dropped to the floor when he felt the elevator slam to a violent stop. Heidi quickly caught her balance and looked at her fiancé. Despite the blaring alarm, Heidi's lustful face was surprisingly calm. She moved her lips closer to Tycen's ear and spoke softly to him.

"Just relax baby. I got this," Heidi whispered.

The words danced around Tycen's mind, and he felt Heidi's hands reaching down between his legs. "Damn," he said.

Heidi carefully unzipped his pants. She kissed him passionately on the lips again, pulling him to the middle of the elevator, then exposed his swollen dick. His body weakened with every soft stroke from Heidi's hands, and he grew stiffer with every pull.

Heidi became more excited. She grabbed his dick tightly and rubbed it against her silk dress. "Ooooo fuck," Heidi moaned, mistakenly plucking her clit with his hardness. She quivered from the sensation and dropped to her knees.

Tycen's head fell back when he felt her wet tongue begin to tease his chocolate skin. Heidi didn't waste another second as her hot mouth engulfed all of his throbbing manhood.

"Damn Heidi," Tycen moaned, grabbing the back of her head.

Heidi closed her eyes tighter as she opened her mouth wide for her fiancé. Tycen's dick was at full mast, and Heidi had never felt him so hard. The fear and adrenaline made his dick seem even bigger tonight, making her question if she could handle all of him. She forced him deep inside her mouth, and clutched on tight to his thrusting thighs. Tycen became more animated, and she could hear him moaning her name, even over the loud alarm. Wildly, she bounced her head back and forth against Tycen's crotch. She stroked and sucked on her fiancé like this was the last time they would be together. The sounds of her wet tongue caused Tycen to moan out loud. Heidi loved to please her man, and tonight her mouth made love to his dick like never before.

Tycen became lost in the moment. Fire alarms and surveillance cameras were the furthest thing from his mind. Heidi was in full beast mode tonight, and he loved it. She jerked Tycen's dick and watched his face twist with pleasure. He called out her name again. Heidi reached under her dress and grabbed a handful of herself. A lustful moan vibrated from her throat. Her pussy was dripping like sweet fruit, and Heidi vibrated with excitement. She was beyond horny. The thought of Tycen being deep inside of her gripped her imagination. She could almost feel Tycen's thickness spreading her wide open and touching every tender spot in her wet walls. Her body quivered again, and Heidi felt close to climaxing on her own fingers. She looked up to her fiancé and felt another rush. She slowly stood to her feet and looked Tycen directly in the eyes.

"We gotta go." She gave him a desperate look.

She reached behind her fiancé and slammed her hand against the emergency button. The elevator started to rise again, and the alarm ceased. Heidi looked at Tycen and watched as he frantically zipped up his pants. She grabbed her bag as they finally reached the top floor, and the heavy metal doors parted. Heidi grabbed Tycen by the hand and rushed out the elevator. Her hot body yearned desperately to be pleased, preventing her from walking straight. She squeezed her thighs together as she pulled Tycen faster. He shook his head with a smile and let Heidi lead the way. Her rushing and stumbling to get to their hotel suite, caused him to laugh. It was a hilarious sight, albeit sexy. Heidi slowed as she finally laid eyes on the sky loft near the end of the hall.

She exhaled. "Dammit." Heidi fumbled, adjusting the gold card so she could slip it into the slot. Heidi quickly opened the door, and then playfully shoved her fiancé inside. She dropped her bag down onto the plush carpet and turned on the lights. "Finally," she whispered as the door to the loft slammed shut. Her hands were on Tycen again, pushing him against the wall. She kissed him and quickly unbuckled his pants. She didn't give him the opportunity to marvel at the luxurious room, and he didn't attempt to, instead he took off his jacket and started to undress.

Heidi reached down between his legs and started to massage his growing dick again.

"I want you baby." She panted and ran her tongue up and down the side of Tycen's neck. She felt his dick rising, and another rush of adrenaline ran through her body. She turned around and pressed her ass up against Tycen's waist. "Unzip me baby. Please," she whispered.

Tycen clutched Heidi by the shoulder. He slowly grabbed the metal zipper and pulled it down to the small of her back. Heidi kicked off her sexy heels and stepped out of the falling dress. She seductively strolled to the bed and Tycen followed her naked body.

"Lay down baby," Heidi whispered as she sat down.

Tycen didn't say a word as he took off the rest of his clothes. He smoothly slid onto the bed next to his fiancée. He turned on his back, giving Heidi a full view of him. His dark skin was all Heidi needed to see to turn up her juices. She crawled on top of him and put her lips softly on his chest. She loved the taste of his ebony skin. It drove her wild.

"Baby, you smell so good tonight," Tycen whispered. He grabbed onto Heidi's thighs as she mounted him like a stallion. Tycen ran his warm hands up and down the sides of her body and Heidi moaned again. She rocked back and forth until her thirsty pussy found the tip of Tycen's dick. She gripped his chest in pain as his large rod entered her without an apology.

"Owww baby," Heidi whined like a little girl. "Don't hurt me...baby."

Heidi's words only excited Tycen more. They both knew Heidi loved the pain. She loved to feel Tycen's dick pounding her with authority, knowing an explosion of pleasure was just on the other side. She bounced on top of her fiancé until his diamond-hard dick plunged deep as it could. Tycen watched Heidi close as she started to lose control. He loved to see her beautiful face tightened with a mix of lust and anguish. The sight was beyond stimulating.

"Baby...don't you stop," Heidi cried out.

Tycen gripped her hips tighter, and then forced himself deeper. He could feel her sweet honey leaking all around him. He knew she was getting close. He rocked his hips to her sexy rhythm. Heidi leaned closer and thrust her breasts in Tycen's face. She yelled out when she felt his hot mouth suckling on her nipples. She bounced even harder and felt a wet orgasm rushing from her stomach. Heidi covered her mouth. She was too embarrassed to tell her fiancé she was climaxing so soon. But Tycen knew. He could feel the soft walls of her pussy squeezing tightly around his dick, announcing her flow.

"Damn Heidi," Tycen moaned as his own body started to react to her sweetness. He fucked her harder.

Heidi came all over his throbbing dick. She held back her screams and looked at her fiancé in amazement. Something felt different about tonight. Tycen's full attention was on pleasing her body, and every thrust felt divine. Another warm sensation rushed from the back of her neck and traveled down to the top of her ass. She was coming again. She yelled out and gripped onto Tycen's chest. "Oooh baby wait—" Heidi could barely speak. Her body gyrated like a bucking horse. Another forceful orgasm hit her like a lightning strike, and Heidi cried out in pleasure. Tycen was fucking her like never before, and Heidi couldn't believe how good the sex was tonight. She gasped in pleasure and looked her fiancé directly in the eyes. For a moment Tycen thought he saw a tear. "Don't move," she whispered.

Tycen watched as his fiancée switched positions. She placed the bottom of her feet flat on the bed. Heidi made a hissing sound as she slowly squatted on his dick and spread her legs like butterfly wings. Tycen got a full view of his dick sliding in and out of Heidi's now drenched pussy.

"Yes baby," Heidi moaned as she felt Tycen begin to slip even deeper into her. She leaned back and grabbed Tycen's legs. She held on tight and started to ride him harder.

"Yes, baby. Do it like that," Tycen moaned. All he could do was relish in the moment.

Heidi turned the tables on her fiancé and started fucking him with authority. Tycen moaned and called out her name again. Heidi got more excited and started twisting her pussy on him. "You like that baby?" Heidi moaned.

"I love it," Tycen quickly blurted.

Heidi bounced her horny body on her fiancé. She felt his dick becoming harder and knew he was close to climaxing. She leaned up and placed her palms on her knees. The move forced him to go even deeper, and Heidi felt herself coming again. She screamed out and bounced her caramel ass wildly on his dick.

"Yes baby," Tycen called out.

Heidi stared at his face. She loved to see the lustful gaze in his eyes as she pleased him. Tycen noticed Heidi was growing more excited. He couldn't hold on any longer. The gushing of her sweet pussy had finally gotten the best of him. The room fell silent as Tycen held on tight for what was coming next. Heidi noticed his face twisting and she braced herself. Tycen yelled out her name. A boiling orgasm shot from his loins. Heidi cried out in ecstasy. Her body jerked and pulsated. Tycen's multiple orgasms made her climax again.

"Oh my God...Tycen!" Heidi yelled out and dropped her head.

She felt his dick throbbing from the sensation. Tycen moaned as the heavenly feeling engulfed his body. Heidi collapsed on her fiancé and kissed him on the lips. The episode was one she wouldn't soon forget. Tycen embraced her as their warm bodies stayed as one. Heidi moaned and slowly rubbed her face against his chest. She could still feel his heart pounding from the sex. Heidi squeezed his body and decided to remain silent. She didn't want to ruin the lovely vibe. The couple sunk deep into the soft pillows on the bed. Heidi and Tycen slowly caressed each other and shared a peaceful moment inside the quiet sky loft.

Chapter 4

Saturday, October 5
12:30 am
Newark, NJ

"Stay right there...I'm on my way! Don't do nothing stupid! You hear me? I'm just five minutes away. We can talk about this when I get there."

The chrome rims of a late model Maserati slowed down to a crawl as the gaudy vehicle approached a dark intersection. Sitting watchfully behind the wheel was a fresh-faced man in his mid-twenties named Asad Banks. His smooth demeanor didn't match the agitated expression that was painted on his face. He disconnected the call, then slammed the cellphone down in his lap.

"What the fuck," Asad whispered, clearly frustrated by the call.

His vigilant eyes cut from left to right as he scanned the desolate streets for anything unusual. Despite the late hour, Asad was wide-awake and ready for anything. He waited for the traffic light to change. Living in the carjacking capital of the world always kept Asad mindful of his surroundings, and tonight he was especially on edge. Thirty minutes earlier he had received a frantic call from his best friend who rudely disturbed his peaceful night. Just thinking about the call made his blood boil. Asad glanced at his watch, and he noticed he only had a few minutes to reach his best friend before things spiraled out of control. He surveyed the dark area once again, then punched the gas. The screeching of the tires echoed off the buildings. Asad blew through the red light and sped up the street. He was en route to his friend, who needed him.

A few miles away, a loud thump rumbled from inside Ruth's Soulfood Restaurant. A woman's furious voice could be heard coming from the parking lot as a distraught man paced back and forth inside the building, near the glass front door. The man's feet stomped with authority through the empty restaurant. He was in his late twenties, but his scarred and scruffy face made him looks well past forty. The stressed out scowl belonged to Dante Harper.

Another loud scream came from the parking lot, and Dante yelled again. He was gripping a metal baseball bat in one hand and holding his cellphone in the other. His disturbed face was near madness as he angrily kicked over a bar stool and a few tables near the window. A few seconds later, Dante seemed to attack everything that was within striking distance. The woman in the parking lot yelled again, and Dante rushed over to look out the glass door. He noticed a black and white police car quickly pulling up directly in front of the restaurant.

"This fuckin' bitch called the goddamn police," Dante yelled out. "Fuck!" He took another violent swing at the liquor bottles behind the bar. The sound of the shattering glass echoed throughout the small dining area as he walked from behind the bar. He headed to the door, then looked outside again. The woman was rushing over to the squad car and pointing toward the building. Dante's heart started racing faster. He walked away from the entrance and headed back into the dining room. He realized things were about to escalate in a hurry.

Outside the restaurant, the woman was yelling and screaming for the police to help her. Two cops quickly exited the vehicle and went to question to the hysterical woman. "Calm down, ma'am. What is going on?" A policewoman rushed over.

"Officers, I'm Ruth. I own the restaurant. One of my ex-employees locked himself inside and he is refusing to leave," Ruth yelled. "I don't know what the hell is wrong with him. He's crazy."

"Who's crazy, ma'am? His name? What happened?" the second cop asked calmly.

Before the restaurant owner could say another word, a jet black Maserati pulled up behind the cop car and came to an abrupt stop. Asad Banks quickly jumped out the vehicle and rushed over to the police. "Good evening, officers. I'm Asad Banks." Asad quickly raised his hands and held up his credentials to the police. "I'm the mayor's brother."

The police recognized Asad and nodded toward him. "Okay," one said.

The restaurant owner took one look at Asad, then rolled her eyes. "I just knew he would call you." Ruth gave Asad an ugly expression. "Every time he gets into fuckin' trouble, he calls his goddamn flunkie."

Asad ignored Ruth's hateful words and kept his focus on the officers.

"Can somebody tell me what the hell is going on?" One of the officers looked at Asad, then turned his attention to the restaurant owner.

"I can tell you what's goin' on," Ruth shouted. "I called in one of my workers today and told him that I had to let him go. I had to fire him, and he went berserk. He locked me outside. Now he's inside tearing up my restaurant. I think he is fuckin' drunk or maybe on drugs—"

"No wait," Asad quickly butted in, cutting the woman short. "Officers, that is my best friend inside. I'm positive that he is not drunk, high or under the influence of any illegal substance."

"How do you know?" Ruth shouted.

"I just know..." Asad looked at her. "Why did you fire him? What did he do?"

"It doesn't matter." Ruth gave Asad a funny look. "It's my restaurant. I had to let him go."

Asad looked at the restaurant owner with a suspicious glance. Something about her explanation didn't sit well with him. Asad turned his attention back to the officers. "Listen... like I said...that's my best friend inside," Asad kept his voice low. "I'm pretty sure he's just upset. If you give me a second to go inside and grab him, I will get him out of there, and then this young lady can have her restaurant back. It's that okay?"

The female officer looked over to her partner, who shrugged his shoulders. Asad Banks was the brother of the most powerful man in the city, and he was also the chief of the mayor's security detail. Asad had a lot of friends on the police force, and he was notorious for doing favors for the officers and their family members. His reputation and connection to city hall was all he needed, in most cases, to avoid any problems with the police. Tonight, he hated to throw his brother's name around, but he needed to squeeze his best friend out of a tight jam. As the officers' demeanor changed, Asad realized they would grant him the favor.

"You got five minutes, Mr. Banks." The male officer nodded. "If he doesn't cooperate with you...believe me...he will be arrested."

"Understood." Asad gave the officer a calm look, then headed toward the restaurant, cursing his best friend's name with every step he took to the front entrance. Asad could see his best friend's shadow pacing back and forth. Asad simply shook his head. "Dante, it's me. Man, you gotta let me in," Asad shouted out as he gently tapped on the glass. "The cops are out here now, and we need to do this fast, Dante. Come on, man, open the door for me."

Dante heard his best friend's voice and felt relieved. He rushed over to the front door and let Asad in. "C'mon."

"Dante, what the hell is wrong with you man?" Asad shouted the second he got into the restaurant. He quickly closed the door behind himself and locked it.

"Man...she has no right to do what she did," Dante shouted, looking at Asad.

"What are you talkin' about?" Asad looked around the empty restaurant. "Ruth just told the cops she had to fire you."

"Exactly! Fire me for what?" Dante yelled. "Man...I been here for almost three years. This is all I got."

"Damn. So what did you do?" Asad asked.

"Nothing!" Dante quickly responded. "I come here every day and do my job. I wasn't drinking on the job. Wasn't late. Nothin'. She told me she had to cut back."

"Cut back? What does that mean?" Asad twisted his face. "This restaurant is always busy. Everybody knows she's making good money in here. If anything, she probably needs to hire more people."

"That's the shit that I said to her," Dante raised his voice. "And if she needs to cut back...then why the fuck is she only firing me? Man this is bullshit," Dante yelled again, then swung the metal bat at the wall.

Asad hated to see his best friend like this. He had known Dante since the second grade, and he loved him like a brother. Although they started to head down different paths in life, Dante was still his closest friend. There wasn't a favor Asad wouldn't do for his longtime friend. Tonight, Dante was pressing his luck. With the police in front of the restaurant and itching to make an arrest, Asad knew he only had a few minutes to convince Dante to leave quietly and without incident.

"Listen Dante, I know you pissed off, but we got to get out of here." Asad peeked outside.

"Man...what the hell am I supposed to do now?" Dante shouted again. "I need money."

"I know. But tonight is not the night to do this," Asad said. "I got you, fam. We can figure out something. Just give me a couple of days. I may be able to work out something for you. But now...we got to get out of here."

Asad's voice sounded serious. He looked outside, and could see that the police were getting restless. He looked back to his best friend, Dante, and nodded toward him. "Seriously, bro. We need to make a move." Asad pointed outside. "You know

Newark's finest has no problem making the paper tomorrow morning for causing a scene here."

Dante thought about Asad's words, then nodded his head. He didn't want an already bad night to turn worse. Dante tossed the bat to the floor, giving in. Asad stepped in front of Dante as they approached the front of the restaurant. Asad opened the door, and then waved his hands toward the officers. Dante followed Asad, stepping out onto the walkway and slowly heading away from the building. The angry business owner ran by the men and darted into the restaurant. She was anxious to see what kind of damage Dante caused.

Asad kept Dante close as he approached the police. "Thank you, officers," Asad politely said as he walked with Dante to the Maserati. "I won't forget this."

"Not a problem," the male officer said. "You know overtime season is coming up, so don't catch amnesia when it's time to make that schedule Mr. Banks."

Asad read between the lines and gave the officers a reassuring gesture. He got into the car, and Dante strapped himself into the passenger seat. Asad didn't waste another moment as he fired up the engine. He threw the vehicle into gear, and then pulled off down the block. The speeding car disappeared into the thickness of the night.

Chapter 5

Saturday, October 5
4:26am
West Orange, NJ

Heidi's eyes flashed open wider than two headlights. Her heart burned as she awakened from a wicked nightmare. Tears dripped down the side of her face, and she realized she had been crying in her sleep. The reoccurring dream replayed in her mind. Heidi tried to catch her breath and shake the scary images out of her conscious. She'd awoken in Tycen's comforting arms, yet she'd never felt more fragile. She slowly sat up on the edge of the bed and tried to stop shaking. The daunting nightmare was tearing her apart inside. She looked back at a sleeping Tycen, then slowly rose off the bed, careful not to wake him.

Heidi walked to the other side of the hotel suite. Her naked body caught a quick chill, making her tightly hug herself. The large window gave way to a marvelous picture of the night sky. She strutted toward the view. The beautiful stars and thick clouds began to calm her. Her breathing became even, and she warmed her arms with her palms.

"This is ridiculous," Heidi whispered in frustration, then rubbed the back of her neck, thinking about her lack of sleep. This was the fifth night in a row that she was stirred by the harsh nightmare. The images consumed her thoughts, making it impossible for her to sleep peacefully. Heidi tried to figure out why she was having the same dream every night. She pondered for a moment, then slowly turned around and looked at Tycen again. He was resting like a toddler. Heidi gazed at his handsome face and pressed her lips together. She thought about all the good times they shared as lovers. From the moment she'd met him, Heidi knew her life was going to change forever. She was in love with Tycen. There was no doubt about that. But Tycen was not the only man on Heidi's mind tonight.

Lately, Heidi found herself thinking about a man from her past, Aaron Smith. It had been a few years since she'd laid eyes on Aaron, and she'd tried to forget him, badly wanting to move on with her life. Her relationship with Tycen was growing, but no matter how hard she tried to push them away, the memories of Aaron were never too far away. Her once trusting friendship with Aaron had turned into something dark. A feeling of confusion, betrayal and anger came over Heidi every time she pictured Aaron's face. She wanted to bury him in the past, but couldn't. There were so many questions left unanswered. How could Aaron do what he did to me with no remorse? Where the hell is he now? Will I ever see him again? Heidi's curiosity, and her burning need for clarity kept the memory of Aaron alive and well. Aaron had betrayed Heidi in the worse way. The physical and emotional pain he'd inflicted still hurt. Heidi wanted answers. She wanted to see Aaron's face again and fix the damage he'd done. Even tonight, Heidi felt pressed to find Aaron and finally put an end to one of the darkest chapters in her life.

Heidi glanced over to Tycen one last time. She walked over to her bag and grabbed her cellphone. She took one look at the time, then shook her head. She couldn't believe the hour.

She sat down on the soft sofa near the window. She fumbled with the phone as the bright smartphone light illuminated her face. She quietly tapped the buttons, then scrolled through her photo gallery. Her heart buckled when she pulled up her only picture of Aaron. A rush moved through her. The old photo reminded her of a time in her life when she was vulnerable and confused. She'd trusted Aaron. She'd believed they were building something special, though they'd only shared one kiss. And she'd never forgotten that brief moment of affection. The kiss had opened up an unfamiliar and deep emotion within her soul. She felt a similar feeling resurfacing tonight as she looked at the photo. She stared deep into Aaron's eyes, lost in the moment. She could only imagine why Aaron had betrayed her the way he did. Heidi couldn't wait for the day she could finally confront the man who'd torn her world apart.

"What are you doing?" Tycen's rough voice interrupted the silence in the room.

Heidi turned around and almost screamed when she saw Tycen standing over her. She never realized the bright light from her phone could wake him. Startled, she dropped her phone, then tried to pick it up, but it was too late.

Tycen's expression froze. "What are you doing?" he repeated, looking at a naked Heidi, sitting with the phone in her lap. He instantly became suspicious.

Heidi didn't know what to say to her fiancé. She turned off the phone, then looked up to him. "I couldn't sleep," Heidi mumbled.

"Everything alright?" Tycen whispered, giving her a close onceover.

"Yeah, I'm okay," Heidi quietly responded.

"So why are you crying?" Tycen asked, tightening his expression.

Heidi reached up to her face and wiped away a few tears. Heidi never realized Aaron's photo had made her weep. Tycen's eyes judged her. She dropped her head for a brief moment. She knew Tycen had questions, and he deserved an explanation. She gathered up the courage to speak. "I had another nightmare tonight."

"The same one?" Tycen asked.

"Yes," Heidi said. "That's why I got up. I couldn't go back to sleep. I'm so sorry for waking you."

Tycen gave her a weary look, then walked over to the bed, slid on his pants, then grabbed a sheet. He turned on the bedside lamp, then made his way back to her. "Here you go." Tycen handed the linen to Heidi. He was bothered. "You want some water?"

"I could use some. Thanks," Heidi responded, wrapping the warm sheet around her body.

Tycen headed to the mini bar, then poured his fiancée a cup of water and himself a glass of wine. He walked back to Heidi. "We need to talk," he said, handing Heidi the glass.

"About...?" She whispered and took the water.

"We need to talk about what's going on with you." Tycen sat down across from Heidi. "You know I respect your privacy. I'm not trying to make a big deal about this. But, right now...I really feel like you're keeping me in the dark about all of this. What's going on with these goddamn dreams? Talk to me, baby."

Heidi quietly groaned, then sipped the water. A flashback of the nightmare entered into her mind, forcing her to close her eyes. "I'm sorry you feel like you're in the dark, baby," she whispered. "I know I don't talk about this a lot."

"So why keep it to yourself?" Tycen quickly asked. "You don't have to keep running from this anymore. Talk to me."

The seriousness of Tycen's words made Heidi look away for a quick moment. She thought about the dream again and looked back to her fiancé. "I don't know why this is happening," Heidi admitted. "The nightmares are coming all the time now. Like every night. And I don't know why it feels so damn real."

"Sometimes it's just a dream...and that's it," Tycen tried to empathize with her. "Maybe if you talk about it...you can see why you keep having it over and over again."

Heidi made eye contact with her fiancé. She appreciated his willingness to always stick by her side while she was going through her struggles. She gave Tycen a warm expression. How could she not tell him everything that she was going through? Tycen tried to make it easy on Heidi to express herself. He always understood, but, tonight, Heidi could tell his patience was wearing thin. She recognized his blank expression. Heidi slowly nodded her head and decided to share the tense details of her dream. "It always starts in my old house in Newark. The one I grew up in," Heidi gently cleared her throat and continued to speak, "I hate that goddamn house. Every time I see it in my dreams, I get the same feelings about it. I never remember exactly how the dream starts...but...I do know, I'm running out the front door like a bat out of hell. I can tell something big is behind me. I just can't see what it is. There's a bunch of people in the street, and when they see me running they all start to run too. They're more scared than I am. So that's when I realize it's gotta be something ugly, maybe even a monster that's behind me."

"A monster?" Tycen quickly mumbled.

"Yes...I know it sounds silly as hell," Heidi whispered. "But I think it's a monster."

"No, it's nothing silly about that. It's a dream. So let me ask you this, do you ever turn around to see what it is?" Tycen asked. He couldn't help himself. He wanted to know more.

"Hell no," Heidi fearfully responded. "I'm always too scared to turn around. Everybody is screaming and yelling in front of me, and I feel like I'm the last one in the pack." Heidi paused for a moment. "You know how you're dreaming about running...but you're moving slower than everybody else? That's how I feel every time. I want to haul ass, but I just can't. My legs won't move as fast as I want them to. So I start yelling and screaming like everybody else. Then something odd happens, other people see us running...and they start running too. The shit is crazy."

"Damn," Tycen said.

"Then, for some strange reason, I can feel whatever it is starting to gain on me," Heidi dropped her tone. "I can't hear it... but I can feel it...it's like something is breathing on me. It's scary. It's like a heavy feeling that comes over me every time. Almost like the feeling of...."

Heidi stopped herself and looked down for a moment. She

was growing emotional.

"A feeling of what?" Tycen asked.

"It's like a feeling of not being here anymore," Heidi whispered in a grim tone. The loft fell silent as the couple reflected on Heidi's words. She slowly rubbed her eyes and shook her head. "I'm too scared to turn around, but I know it's something close to me," Heidi continued to describe her nightmare. "So I keep running...and for some reason...the people in front of me have nowhere else to go. It's like a huge brick wall in front of everybody, and we're all trapped. So everybody turns around, and they're yelling and pointing and screaming like crazy. And I just know that it's over for me because I'm the slowest bitch in the group and there's no way I can get away. So I start to scream too, and that's when I wake up. Every single time...it's the same thing. The dream always ends with me screaming like a damn idiot." A few tears bubbled in Heidi's eyes and she wiped them away.

Tycen felt for her. "Damn, baby... Stop calling yourself an idiot because you have nightmares. It's okay. I would be more nervous if a dream like that didn't scare the hell out of you."

Heidi didn't respond. She simply wiped away a few more tears and tried to make sense of the dream.

"How old are you?" Tycen asked.

"Huh?" Heidi grunted. She was caught off guard by the question.

"In the dream? How old are you in the dream?" Tycen asked. "Are you a young girl in the dream or are you a grown woman?"

"I don't know," Heidi quietly said as she took a moment to think. "I mean, I feel like I'm grown in the dream. But why am I back at my old house? Maybe I am a little girl."

"Can you see yourself in the dream?" Tycen asked.

"No, not really," Heidi replied. "I mean...I do look down at my legs, but everything is so damn fuzzy. I don't know if I'm young or grown. I don't know."

"It's okay," Tycen said. "I think it might have something to do with your past, since you're dreaming about the house you grew up in. Maybe there's something from your past that's trying to catch up to you."

"Yea, I thought about that too."

The room fell silent once again as Heidi rubbed her forehead. Old images of her childhood swirled around in her head as she tried her best to make sense of everything in her reoccurring dream. Heidi had had a typically rough time growing up, just like just about every other young girl she knew living in the inner-city of Newark. Being surrounded by poverty, drugs, crime and violence didn't stop her from being the bright light of her family. Her mother would always put her only daughter first and make sure Heidi had had the best. Even as a young girl, Heidi knew she had to be different when she grew up. Her mother had made sure that Heidi would not be like the other lost souls in her neighborhood, those who were headed down a destructive path.

Tonight, Heidi thought back to those delicate days of her youth. She couldn't deny the fact that the growing pains of her early years had played a big part in making her a stronger woman today. Heidi thought for another moment, then shook her head. She could not think of anything from her childhood that would have her scared enough to emotionally cripple her dreams while she slept.

"Can I be honest with you?" Heidi asked softly.

"Of course," Tycen responded, taken by Heidi's tone that told she was deep in thought.

"Baby, I can't remember anything that happened when I was younger that's haunting me right now," she whispered. "I think about that all the time, especially now since I started having these nightmares again. Now, don't get me wrong, I know my childhood was crazy. But I can't think of nothing that happened when I was a young girl that would have me running like that in my dream."

"What about now?" Tycen quickly asked. "Are you running from something now?"

The words froze Heidi. Tycen's question hit her deep, causing her bloody memories to resurface. He waited for her reaction, making her feel like he could see the flashbacks of her past few years whirring in her mind. Her thoughts turned to Aaron Smith. Heidi's life had taken a violent turn after being betrayed by Aaron. Heidi tried her best to shield her latest love from her darkest secrets, but Tycen's stare told her he could tell there was much more pain behind her exterior.

As their relationship grew stronger, Tycen found himself becoming more curious about Heidi's past. Tycen continued to stare at Heidi. He waited for an answer, but she didn't say a word. She thought about the question, and couldn't bring herself to tell Tycen about all the dreadful details of the past few years. Heidi never shared that she had been deceived by a very dangerous past lover. She never told the gory details of losing her best friend and her brother. Tycen had no clue how Heidi had come close to being killed on a number of occasions. She wanted desperately to reveal her secrets to Tycen, but she was afraid of his reaction. She didn't want to lose her fiancé, and she knew that one day he would need to know the truth.

"Are you going to answer my question?" Tycen asked and twisted his face.

Heidi didn't respond.

"What about that guy on your phone?" Tycen grew annoyed. "Who is he? And why the hell were you looking at his picture? Huh? At four in the morning...why are you looking at his picture?"

Heidi's heart raced as Tycen blasted her with questions. She put her head in her hand, and then took a deep breath. She never answered him.

Tycen looked over to Heidi and closed his mouth. He calmly stood to his feet, then walked to the other side of the room. He fixed himself another drink. Heidi sensed his attitude rising. She watched as he downed a half-shot of vodka, then poured another one.

"It's not what you think," Heidi slightly raised her voice,

finally speaking. "Believe me, Tycen. It's not what you think at all."

"Whatever," Tycen snapped.

"What does that supposed to mean?" Heidi quickly asked.

"You keep holding back, when it comes to me, Heidi," Tycen whispered and looked down into his glass. "I don't know why you just can't tell me what's really going on with you."

"I'm not holding back," Heidi replied. "I just don't think it's the right time."

"See...that's exactly what I mean," Tycen raised his voice. He downed the second shot, the turned around and glanced at Heidi. "It's like you got this whole other side to you. And I have no clue how to accept that. I hate feeling like I don't know you completely. I get frustrated when you hesitate to tell me what's really going on with you."

Tycen's honest words humbled Heidi for a moment. "I know I haven't told you everything about me," Heidi said in an apologetic tone. "And I don't want you to think I don't trust you because I do."

"But right now, it's not about trust," Tycen said. "This is getting bigger than just me and you."

"Huh?" Heidi asked. "I don't understand."

"Baby, I'm running for the highest office in the city," Tycen said. "Right now, and I mean literally as we speak, somebody is digging in my past, trying to find something to use against me. And when they get through with me, they're gonna move to the next person in line. And that's you." Tycen's words started to sink into Heidi's mind. "You see where I'm going with this?"

Heidi didn't respond. She thought about all the drama in her life and how Tycen's new enemies would try to use her sketchy past against him.

"Believe me baby, I trust you," Tycen said. He headed back near Heidi, and sat down across from her. "I hate to bring the election into this, but it's a serious reality we need to consider.

People are going to start asking questions, and we can't dodge them forever."

"I understand," Heidi whispered, looking over to Tycen.

"Do you really?" Tycen asked. "I hate to put this on you, but sooner or later we need to have a real conversation, and you need to tell me everything, Heidi. You can trust me. I'm not here to hurt you, sweetie. I want to marry you one day. So you should know that I love you and I respect you. Whatever happened between you and that guy is in the past. I get that. But I don't want you to feel like you can't talk to me. Okay baby?"

Heidi gave her fiancé an uneven expression. She slowly nodded her head. Tycen had an uncanny knack of making her see the bigger picture of things and keeping her spirit at ease. Heidi put her phone away. She stood up and walked over to Tycen. She sat on his lap, then put her arms around him. Heidi gave her fiancé a deep kiss on his lips. "Okay baby, I do understand," Heidi whispered as she rubbed his hands. "Thank you for understanding. We'll talk about this soon, Tycen. I promise. Let's go back to bed. I know you have another long day tomorrow. I'll be fine. I think I just needed to calm down."

"Okay," Tycen whispered, deciding not to push her. He could tell that the topic was weighing heavy on Heidi's mind. Tycen returned the deep kiss.

Tycen's soft lips set off a trigger throughout Heidi's body. She rubbed his shoulders and looked at him, then stood. Tycen watched her as she headed back to the bed. Heidi dropped the white sheet to the floor and exposed her naked ass to him. Tycen became aroused. Their brief argument disappeared in the back of his mind. Heidi spread her limbs wide across the bed, then gave her fiancé a flirtatious invitation with her eyes. Her sleek fingers caressed her skin.

Tycen nervously chuckled. "You think you slick." Tycen stood to his feet, then walked over to the bed. "We still need to talk."

"I know, baby." Heidi smiled. "Just not tonight." She

grabbed Tycen's wrist, pulling him to the mattress. His hard body landed on top of her, and Heidi moaned out loud. She rubbed her hands across his smooth back. "I hate it when we argue," she whispered. She kissed Tycen's lips again, pulling him closer. Heidi moaned in Tycen's ear when she felt his body reacting to her seduction.

"Me too," Tycen admitted, pulling away just enough to slip out of his pants, then quickly grabbed her by the shoulders. He wanted her bad. The brief argument made his adrenaline boil.

Heidi felt his growing passionate aggression, and knew they were only seconds away from pure ecstasy. The couple proceeded to make love. Heidi looked into Tycen's eyes with total concentration. Just for tonight, she wanted to forget about Aaron Smith and the dark nightmares that continued to haunt her sleep.

Chapter 6

Saturday, October 5th
10:21am
Beth Israel Hospital
Newark, NJ

"News 12 New Jersey has just learned that the mayor of Newark is calling for an emergency public rally next weekend in Military Park. After a bloody week that claimed the lives of ten people throughout the metropolitan area, officials at city hall say this is a much needed gathering to call on the public to help curb the recent outbreak of violence that has crippled the streets of Newark. The rally will be held on the anniversary of the disappearance of Lexi Hamilton. The sixteen-year-old Newark girl was abducted on her way to school nearly five years ago, and hasn't been seen since. The story has recently received national attention as officials in Washington, DC call for stiffer child abduction laws. Please stay tuned to News 12 as we bring you up-to-the-minute developments on this and other breaking news stories."

The next morning in Beth Israel Hospital, the faint hum of the television caused Kimi to slowly awaken from a heavy slumber. She grabbed the front of her forehead with both hands, and let out a primal yawn. Her mind was still pounding from a massive headache. The bright lights in her room only made it worse. Kimi looked around and noticed she had been relocated to a private room. The strong medication had rendered her unconscious for most of the night, and Kimi was totally unaware that she was moved to a different hospital ward.

Kimi sat up on the edge of the bed, and then gently placed the soles of her feet on the floor. The cool sensation stimulated her senses. She was grateful to be alive. After the traumatic evening that had broken her down, both mentally and physically, Kimi knew she was lucky to see another day. She yawned again before shaking her head with a hint of disgust. She hated the smell of hospitals, and this one was no different. The pungent aroma of stale food, medical cream and disinfectant spray turned her stomach. She slowly rose to her feet, and then walked to the room's private bathroom. Her heart almost dropped to the floor when she turned on the lights.

Kimi barely recognized the battered face staring back at her in the mirror. Her jaw was still swollen, and the huge cut on the side of her forehead made her sad. She moved closer to her reflection, examining her wounds. She softly touched the fifteen stitches that ran across the deep slit, then exploded into tears. Kimi felt like her beautiful face had now been destroyed. She thought about the violent carjacking. Another image of her boyfriend Niko being kidnapped flashed in her mind. An ugly feeling came over Kimi, and she dropped her head in shame. Was this karma's way of paying me back for my shady ways?

Kimi was far from an angel. Before she met Niko, he was a happily married man and the proud owner of a thriving law firm in Newark. After fifteen long years, the fire in Niko's marriage started to fade faster than the images on his wedding photos. Niko was searching for an escape when Kimi slid into his life like a beautiful angel from the heavens. From the first day he met her, Niko knew he had to have her.

Niko and Kimi grew extremely close. They even contemplated starting a new life together. But there was a problem; Niko was still married. When secrets of his wife's own affair was uncovered, Niko and Kimi had set a deadly trap that would eliminate her completely from the picture. The plan had worked perfectly, and Niko's wife was dead a few weeks later. Kimi now had blood on her hands and Niko's murdered wife on her conscious. Kimi knew she would have to find a way to bury her fears and her emotions if she was going to find Niko and escape Newark forever.

Kimi slowly picked up her head, then stared into her own red eyes. A quick flashback of the carjacking suddenly hit her. She thought about the man with the gun who'd pulled her out of her BMW. The image of the large pistol came to her mind. Her heart skipped a beat when the mark on the man's hand suddenly became clear, making Kimi's face freeze. The man had a tattoo on his right wrist, and Kimi could now see it vividly in her mind.

The shocking thought brought her back to reality, and Kimi quickly left the bathroom. She rushed over to her pile of clothes, and then rummaged to find Detective Bell's information. A feeling of relief came over Kimi when she saw the white business card fall to the floor.

"Thank God," Kimi whispered, then grabbed the detective's information. She shuffled over to the hospital phone, and then quickly dialed the first number on the card. She couldn't wait to give the information to the detective, hoping that it would help find Niko.

"Dispatch!" A strong male voice answered on the other line.

"Yes…hello," Kimi nervously uttered. "I'm trying to reach a Detective Bell."

"Hold please," the voice responded quickly.

Kimi heard the line click, and she waited patiently. She looked at the clock on the wall and saw it was a few minutes before noon.

"Special Operations Division!" another male voice announced from the other line.

"Yes, good morning. I'm looking to speak with Detective Bell," Kimi said.

"Detective Bell is actually scheduled to come in today at one o'clock," the voice responded. "If you call back after one o'clock, I'm sure you can reach her then."

"Okay," Kimi said. "Is her partner available?"

"Detective Bell doesn't have a partner, ma'am."

Kimi's mouth fell open. The words shook her for a moment, and Kimi looked down at the business card. "Are you sure Detective Bell doesn't have a partner?" she nervously asked.

"I'm positive," the voice quickly replied. "No one down here at S.O.D. has a partner, ma'am. Is there anything else I can help you with?"

"Ummmm....actually....no, I guess," Kimi whispered. She hung up the phone, then sat back down on the edge of the bed. She thought about Detective Bell's face, and was sure she mentioned having a partner last night. Kimi started to grow nervous. A thousand questions swirled around in her head, and Kimi didn't know what to make of Detective Bell's lies. Why did she mention having a partner? Kimi's confusion started to grow into fear. She walked over to her pile of clothes, then started to dress. Regardless of the detective's motives, Kimi knew she didn't want any parts of her anymore. With every passing minute, Kimi realized she needed to make a move and make it fast. She had to leave before Detective Bell returned to the hospital.

Meanwhile, just outside of the hospital room window, a light rainfall started to accumulate on the streets of Newark. A blue Ford Crown Victoria slowly navigated through the slushy streets, making its way toward the entrance of the hospital. The unmarked police vehicle circled the area, then finally parked in the fire lane on the side of the building. Sitting behind the wheel was Detective Bell. The frustrated detective peered through the tinted windows, then located the person she was looking for. Jogging through the drizzle was a stout man in his late twenties. He wore a semi-professional outfit that clearly didn't match his rough face and unkempt hair. His name was Dennis Ryder, but he was known in the streets as Dent.

Detective Bell unlocked her door and watched as Dent quickly jumped in the passenger seat. He looked over to the detective, who was upset.

"I'm not late, am I?" Dent nervously asked.

"You're not late, but what the fuck are you doing here?" Detective Bell snapped.

"What do you mean?" Dent asked.

"I told them to send me somebody that can pass as my partner." Detective Bell shook her head. "Not somebody that looks like they're fresh out of a fuckin' prison cell."

Dent nervously chuckled.

"I'm not fuckin' jokin, right now," the detective said. "What's your name?"

"Dent," he quietly replied, now serious.

"Your real name, asshole," Detective Bell snapped again.

"Dennis Ryder."

"Okay, when you get up there, don't tell that girl that your name is Dent," Detective Bell ordered. "Say your full name."

"Okay." Dent slowly nodded his head.

"How long have you been working for The Marquez Crew?" the detective asked.

"Two years," Dent responded and twisted his face.

"And you wasn't with them when they pulled that carjacking on Avon Avenue last night, right?" Detective Bell asked.

"No, I wasn't there," Dent quickly responded.

"Are you sure?" Detective Bell raised her voice.

"I wasn't there," Dent uttered. "I heard about it this morning. They had me doin' some other shit last night."

Detective Bell stared at Dent for a moment, trying to read his demeanor. She knew she didn't have enough time to fully press him, so she decided to move on. "Okay, so let me remind you how this works." Detective Bell cut her eyes at Dent. "The staff in the hospital already knows you are here to pick up Kimi Moore and put her in protective custody. Just say that you are my partner and you work for the Special Operations Division or S.O.D., okay?" Dent nodded his head. Detective Bell reached under her seat, then handed Dent a shiny badge attached to a leather case. Dent took the badge and placed it in his pocket. "When you get her, just bring her down to the car, and I'll handle the rest, understand?" the detective asked.

"Yup," Dent replied.

"Now, if you get caught or arrested or anything crazy happens, you don't know me." Detective Bell gave him a hard stare. "You understand that, right? Don't tell a fuckin' soul where you got that badge from. Say you found it. But don't bring up my fuckin' name. Got it?"

Dent hesitated for a moment and nodded his head. "Yup."

"I'm serious. You do not know me if this goes bad," Detective Bell continued to bark out instructions. "Whatever happens up there, just shut your mouth and go along with the program. We will make sure you get bailed out if you get arrested."

"Okay, I understand that," Dent said with an uneasy expression on his face.

"And one last thing," Detective Bell continued. "Marquez wants her in one piece, so take it easy on her. Just bring her down here nice and quietly, okay?"

"Right...I got you," Dent responded. "What about my money?"

"You get paid when the job is done," the detective quickly replied. "Just concentrate on this shit right now, and worry about the money later. We got you."

Dent nodded his head, deciding not to protest. His orders were clear, and the job was easy enough. Five hundred dollars just to pose as a police detective and walk Kimi out of the hospital seemed like a task that was well worth the risk. He gave Detective Bell one last look, then hopped out of the car. He jogged around the building and headed toward the entrance to the hospital.

Detective Bell gazed out the tinted windows again. Although Dent made her nervous, she was hoping he could pull off this simple job without a problem. The rain started to pick up, tapping on her vehicle. Detective Bell relaxed deep into her car seat, keeping a watchful eye for anything that could ruin her plan.

Back upstairs on the fourth floor, the tension was building in the hospital room as Kimi labored to put on her clothes. The pain from her bruises started to get to her, but this was not the moment to dwell on her injuries, she told herself. Sensing she was running out of time, Kimi quietly prepared herself to leave without drawing any attention to her room. She was zipping up her jacket when she felt a throbbing pain coming from her scalp. She returned to the bathroom and noticed that the cut on the side of her forehead was bleeding again.

"Dammit," Kimi grumbled.

She knew she wouldn't get far with blood trickling from her forehead. Kimi scrambled around the bathroom and searched for more bandages. She felt relieved when she found a goldmine of gauze, tape and sterilization pads under the sink. Without another minute to lose, Kimi redressed the wound and stopped the bleeding. She grabbed a handful of medical supplies, including some she wouldn't need, like syringe needles, and shoved them into her pocket. She couldn't take any chances of her bruises giving her more problems along the way. She rushed out of the bathroom, checking the clock on the wall. The time was moving swiftly, and Kimi needed to get shaking, but her gut told her to grab the detective's information and try to call her one last time. She was curious to find out if Detective Bell had arrived at the police station yet. Kimi picked up the phone and put it to her ear. An eerie feeling came over the room as she carefully dialed the phone number.

"Hello, excuse me, are you Kimi Moore?" a burly sounding voice called out behind her.

Kimi spun around in a panic, dropping the phone to the floor. Her heart started racing out of control. She fearfully watched a stocky man walk into her hospital room. He deliberately approached her, and Kimi threw up her hand like a crossing guard. "Who are you?" Kimi nervously questioned the stranger.

"Oh...I'm sorry." The rough looking man stopped in his tracks. "My name is Dennis Ryder. I'm Detective Bell's partner."

The words froze Kimi. The blatant lie caused a tense chill to creep up the back of Kimi's spine. She didn't know what to do next. Her mind raced as Dennis looked around the hospital room. "What do you want with me?" Kimi whispered. Her voice cracked with fear.

"My partner asked me to escort you out of the hospital," Dent calmly responded as he picked up on Kimi's nervous vibe. "I heard about your incident last night, and we have decided to put you in protective custody for your own safety."

Kimi thought for a moment, and her hands began to nervously shake. She decided to say the first thing that came to her mind. "Can I see some identification?" Kimi asked.

"Sure," Dent responded with an uneven smile. He slowly pulled out the leather case and presented a police badge to Kimi. He nodded toward her and smiled again. "Don't worry about a thing. You're going to be fine." Dent bobbed his head, then pointed to Kimi's jacket. "So, I see you are all set to go."

Kimi felt the pit of her stomach turn. She couldn't figure out why Detective Bell was trying so hard to deceive her. As the man put the badge back in his pocket, Kimi noticed he didn't have a weapon on him. She realized that there was no way he was an officer of the law. He tried his best to act normal, but Kimi sensed something dark about him. She grew more nervous. Kimi didn't want to find out how this game of charades was going to end. She needed to get away from this man, and get away from him fast. Kimi started to calm herself so she could think clearer. She looked around the room, trying to figure out how to escape from Dent. He was clearly stronger than Kimi. She knew she had no shot of pushing by him to escape. An altercation with this man was out of the question. Kimi was in no mood for another beating.

"Do you need me to grab anything for you?" Dent asked.

Kimi shook her head and thought about the question. For the first time today, she realized that she was wearing everything that she owned. Her luggage and even her purse were stolen with her BMW last night. Kimi glanced around the room one last time. She pushed her mind to think quickly, knowing she was running out of options. An idea finally came to her, and she glanced over to the imposter. "So how long have you and Detective Bell worked together?" Kimi calmly questioned the man. She tried to buy some time to gather her thoughts.

"Ummmm. . .me and Detective Bell? Let's see, we have been partners for a minute now," Dent stuttered when he spoke. The question forced him to think fast. "I have to say that we have been working together for at least five years."

Kimi's expression never changed as she listened to the lies. She grabbed the phone off the floor and hung it up. Dent watched her closely as she put her hands in her pockets.

"You ready?" Dent asked.

The question hit her like a shot of adrenaline. Kimi was ready. "Where is Detective Bell now?" Kimi quietly asked.

"Detective Bell is outside of the hospital waiting for us," Dent responded and gave Kimi a crooked look.

"Okay let's go," Kimi mumbled.

Dent never turned his back on Kimi. He watched her like a guard dog as they both headed to the door. With every step Kimi took, Dent started to grow more excited. He knew he was getting closer and closer to his easy payday.

Kimi took one last look around the room before she reached the door. "Dammit, you know what..." Kimi suddenly stopped walking. "Can you do me a favor? Turn that television off for me?"

"No problem," Dent quickly responded.

Kimi stared at Dent as he turned around. His mind was locked in on his money, and he never suspected that Kimi was sizing him up. He stretched out his right arm, reaching for the television above his head. Kimi paid close attention, watching as his jacket sleeve dropped down his forearm, exposing his wrist. Kimi clinched her fist tightly in her pocket. She recognized the tattoo on the man's wrist, and had to stop herself from covering her mouth. The mark was eerily similar to the one she had seen on her attacker's wrist last night. Kimi wisely realized Dent was connected to the same gang that was responsible for kidnapping her boyfriend Niko. Another shot of adrenaline rushed through her as she realized her life was in danger. She needed to make a move. Kimi didn't hesitate for another second. She turned around and made a quick step toward the door. Dent reacted and lunged for her. Kimi screamed when she felt his strong hand grab her by the shoulder, and her hand dug into her pocket. As he forcefully spun her around, Kimi removed her hand from her pocket and wildly swung at Dent's head.

"Owwwww....shiiiittt!" Dent yelled out as he felt a piercing pain on the side of his face.

He stumbled backward, nearly falling over the hospital bed. Kimi shot out the door faster than a bullet. Dent helplessly watched her leave as he struggled to regain his balance. He yelled again from the sharp pain, reaching for his cheek. He carefully pulled a half-inch syringe out of the side of his face, then slammed the needle onto the floor. Kimi's clever move had slowed him just enough to give her a good head start.

Dent ignored the blood leaking from his face and bolted out the room. People in the hallway were screaming and jumping out the way as Kimi frantically ran for her life. Dent spotted the back of Kimi's jacket just before she hit the corner, then he ran after her. His stocky frame bumbled down the hallway. He was determined not to let her get away. He made it to the end of the bright corridor just in time to see Kimi enter the stairway located in the middle of the adjacent hall. Dent picked up his pace to catch up, but found that Kimi was shockingly fast. A few seconds later, a blaring alarm startled him.

"Shit!" Dent shouted, fearing the worse. He burst through the entrance to the staircase and quickly looked around. A noise made him look up, and he saw a large metal door swinging back and forth. It was just a couple of flights above him. He ran up the stairs, two at a time, guessing Kimi was going to the roof. The alarm she'd set off told him she'd gone through the emergency exit, and Dent knew she couldn't get far. He bull-rushed the metal door and ran out onto the roof. The cold rain whipped Dent in the face. He could barely see straight as he searched around for Kimi. He was near the center of the roof when he heard a faint noise behind him. He turned around just in time to see Kimi pulling on the metal door from inside. She had fooled him once again. Dent tried to reach the door before she closed it, but he was too late. Kimi slammed it shut. Dent kicked the door in frustration, realizing he was locked out of the hospital.

Now with Dent stuck on the roof, Kimi had enough time to sneak safely out of the building. She quickly darted down the stairs, making it to the bottom floor. The lobby was packed with visitors, patients and hospital staff. Kimi felt her heart racing as she eyed the exit. She composed herself, and then blended into the rush. The alarm was still buzzing, and people were scrambling to figure out what was going on. Kimi dropped her head to avoid eye contact, then quickly left the building. She hailed the first cab she could find and hopped in the back seat.

"Just go, Sir. Please!" Kimi screamed toward the driver.

A feeling of relief came over Kimi. She almost cried from the pressure. The cab drove off, and Kimi closed her eyes. She thought about Detective Bell, praying that they never crossed paths again. Kimi had to get somewhere safe and get her mind right. She needed to figure out how she could find her boyfriend Niko, then leave this dangerous city behind for good.

Just as the yellow cab sped away from the front of the hospital, Detective Bell was rushing into the main entrance. The loud alarm caught her attention. The veteran detective sensed that something was going terribly wrong with her plan. She raced inside the hospital, then twisted her face. There was too much commotion. She quickly approached the security desk near the rear of the lobby. "I'm Detective Bell from the S.O. Division of NPD," she announced, then flashed her badge to the security guard. "Where was that alarm set off from?"

A young and inexperienced security guard scrambled to scan his workstation. He browsed his console, then looked up to Detective Bell. "The alarm is coming from the fourth floor," the security guard stammered.

"Fuck!" Detective Bell barked.

"It's okay. We have a few guards already on it, officer," he said.

"Detective!" she boldly corrected the guard. "I'm a Detective! And I'm investigating one of your patients on the fourth floor. Tell your guards to back off. Let them know I'm heading up there and I will take care of this. Do it now!" Detective Bell's voice shook the young guard. He grabbed for his radio as the detective sprinted away from the desk. Detective Bell imagined the worst as she entered the main staircase, then bolted up the steps. She made it to the fourth floor in record time. "What the fuck is going on up here?" Detective Bell grumbled.

Her angry demeanor caused a few nurses and patients to move out of her way as she stomped down the hallway. She scanned every room looking for any sign of Kimi or Dent. The loud alarm continued to buzz. Detective Bell finally reached Kimi's room. It was empty.

"Goddamit," Detective Bell blurted. She looked around the hallway again, finally noticing a male nurse near the end of the hall. Detective Bell approached the man as he tried to calm everyone. "Excuse me, is there a patient on this floor named Kimi Moore?" Detective Bell asked and showed the nurse her badge.

"She was on this floor," the nurse shook his head. "We don't know what exactly happened. One minute she was in her room, and the next minute she was being chased by some man."

Detective Bell tightened her jaw as the nurse revealed the news to her. "And what happened?" the detective asked.

"One of the security guards was searching for them in that staircase." The nurse pointed down an adjacent hallway. "But I don't think they found Ms. Moore or the man."

Detective Bell's face grew serious. She turned away from the nurse, heading to the staircase. Her simple plan was quickly unraveling at the seams. The detective reached the middle of the hall, then angrily pushed the door open. She entered the staircase and looked around. The alarm continued to blare, but the staircase was empty. A few voices could be heard echoing from the bottom of the stairway, floors down, which Detective Bell assumed belonged to the security guards who were searching.

A loud thump of a door banging sounded from just one flight up. The detective's heart started racing. She quickly drew her weapon. The banging continued, and Detective Bell tilted her head, focusing on the noise. It wasn't a door banging, but a hand knocking. She rushed upstairs to the top floor, gripping her gun tighter. The noise was coming from the other side of the roof exit. She stilled her breath, preparing for what could be waiting for her on the other side of the heavy door. Another hard knock caused her adrenaline to rush. Detective Bell kicked the bottom of her foot against the emergency exit door, opening it with a boom.

"Oww fuck!" a male voice yelled as the door flew open.

Detective Bell raised her weapon and rushed outside. She saw Dent stumbling backward on the roof. The hard rain smacked her in the face. "What the fuck are you doing?" Detective Bell yelled out, approaching him. "Where is Kimi?"

"She got away from me," Dent uttered and held his head.

"You lost her?" Detective Bell shouted.

"That bitch fuckin' stabbed me in the face," Dent screamed, pointing to his still bleeding cheek.

Anger flooded Detective Bell. She was enraged. Dent seemed to be clueless to the amount of damage he had caused by allowing Kimi to escape. Detective Bell grabbed the stocky man by the neck and put her gun to his chest. "I should fuckin' kill you, asshole!" the detective yelled.

"What? Hold up! What are you...doin'?" Dent stuttered, raising his hands.

"What the fuck happened?" Detective Bell yelled, continuing to push Dent backwards.

"I went to her room and tried to walk her outside," Dent started talking fast. "She was cool at first, and then she just started trippin'. She slashed me in the face with a damn needle, then ran. I thought she was comin' to the roof, so I got stuck up here."

"What?" Detective Bell yelled. She couldn't believe what she was hearing.

"I swear that's what went down," Dent pleaded, stepping backward.

"What did you say to her?" Detective Bell asked sharply.

"Huh?" Dent mumbled in fear.

"Did you tell her that you was my partner? Did you say my name?" Detective Bell asked.

"Yes," Dent nervously responded. "I mean...that's what you wanted me to say, right? I told her that I was your partner. I told her that I was with you."

Detective Bell's eyes became even more intense. She was beyond angry with Dent, and knew, because of his actions, Dent had become a liability. Her connection to him would surely land her in prison. She restrained herself for a brief moment, looking at Dent. "So you basically fucked us both," Her tone was harsh.

Dent closed his mouth, not saying a word. The whole ordeal had shaken him, and the fire in the detective's eyes pushed him beyond nervous.

"Give me that fuckin' badge I gave you." The detective released Dent's neck, then held out her hand. She kept the gun barrel close to his body.

"Here...!" Dent stuttered again, then handed over the

badge. He looked at her, trying to read her eyes. Never in a million years could he have predicted what she did next.

Detective Bell placed the badge in her pocket. She looked up and glanced just behind Dent. The detective moved the heavy pistol away from his chest, then quickly smashed him in the jaw with it. The violent move caught Dent by surprise. Detective Bell attacked Dent like he was a murder suspect. She pistol-whipped him until he was barely conscious. Dent swung his arms and reached out for her. He tried to defend himself, but the detective's fury and combat training was too much for him to handle. She grabbed Dent again by the neck and pushed him backwards. Blood flew from his battered mouth as he yelled. In one swift move, Detective Bell placed her foot just behind the reeling Dent, then shoved him off the hospital roof. Her ruthless eyes never flinched. She watched him drop down five floors, and almost smirked. His helpless body reminded her of a bag of garbage flying through the air. The ground seemed to shake when Dent's body mercilessly collided with the concrete below. Now his crumbled form made her stomach churn. Detective Bell let loose a mouthful of spit, then turned. She looked around the roof, grabbing for her radio.

"This is Detective Bell of the S.O.D.N.P.D. I have a suspect down at Beth Israel Hospital," Detective Bell uttered. "Please dispatch paramedics of the facility to the north end of the building." Detective Bell clicked off her radio, and returned her attention to the street below. Her stare was cold as she watched the rain continue to dance on his lifeless body.

Chapter 7

Saturday, October 5
2:02pm
Newark, NJ

"One hundred and fifty thousand people die every day. Think about that number for a moment. One hundred and fifty thousand people leave this earth every single day, and most of them don't know where they are going. Some of them got a huge bank account, but don't know if God is even going to allow them to make another withdrawal. Some of them just got a shiny new car, but don't even know if The Father is going to let them start the engine again. What about you? Do you know where you are going when God calls your number? Where are you headed? Where will you spend eternity?"

Sixty-two-year-old Pearl Kachina sat solemnly on her sofa. Her mind was trapped deep in thought. The potent message from the evangelist burned into her emotions. Pearl unconsciously nodded her head toward the television, wiping away a few tears from her face. She wrung her aging hands tightly together as the pastor continued to speak, then turned up the television. She wanted to receive the next part of the speaker's message, loud and clear.

"I'm not here today to tell you to dwell on your past mistakes. Oh no. I'm not here to tell you to bog down your soul with the misguided actions of your former life. I am here to simply ask you not to wait to get prepared to meet your maker. For one doesn't know the day or the hour. Not the angels in Heaven...not even the Son, Jesus Christ. For only the Father knows!"

Pearl bowed her head and said a silent prayer. She squeezed her hands tightly together. Dark thoughts of death had been haunting her for some time now. With each passing day, Pearl found it more difficult to shake the ugly thoughts. She couldn't pull her mind away from the scary feeling of being deceased or what she could expect in the afterlife. Today, Pearl's mind was being harassed by images of caskets, flowers, cemeteries and blood. Her heart raced with anxiety, and she decided today was a good day to pray. She spoke passionately as the words spilled from her tongue. Pearl tilted her head back, and opened her eyes as she whispered one powerful word toward the heavens. "Amen," Pearl cried out, hoping that her prayer did not fall on forsaking ears. Despite the holy quotes that hung on her walls and the half dozen bibles scattered around her house, Pearl was far from religious. For most of her adult life, Pearl had refused to join a church. She believed churches were only good for weddings and funerals. She even blasted her friends, who would invite her to church events in hopes of converting her.

But, a few years back, Pearl's life had taken a drastic turn. When a pair of street thugs had invaded her home, she had found herself teetering on the razor's edge of life and death. What had began as a random robbery had stretched into two days of terror. The ruthless men had inflicted unspeakable pain on her family. Pearl had barely escaped alive, but her adopted son, Lamar, hadn't been so lucky. He'd been brutally murdered in cold blood, at just twenty-eight-years-old.

The hopeless feeling of losing Lamar had sent Pearl's faith into a tailspin. It had been hard to cope most days. Everything around Pearl had reminded her of her dead son. She'd desperately needed to find guidance and peace. There had been only one place she could turn—God. Pearl had picked up her bible, and didn't ever put it down. She studied the Word of God every chance she could, even watching a number of pastors on television in an effort to realign herself.

Her ultimate desire had been to move toward the salvation her soul craved. But there had been only one problem, which still remained. Pearl was burdened by past demons. The many lives she'd negatively touched began to haunt Pearl's conscious, and she'd begun to blame herself for Lamar's death. The guilt she'd possessed in her heart still burned inside. And she could barely make it through a single day without reflecting on the dark skeletons she harbored. No biblical passage or spiritual quote could ease her mind. Even today, as the pastor tried his best to speak to her through the television, Pearl's soul reeked of shame.

She grabbed the remote control, then turned off the television. The conflicting thoughts in her mind rattled, pushing her to drop her head. A sob slipped out uncontrollably. She was overwhelmed with sadness, and couldn't help but dwell on the mistakes she'd made as a younger woman.

The loud ringing of the house phone sounded off from the other room. Pearl ignored the call, though the shrill continued. She turned her attention to a precious pendant she wore around her neck, wiping away warm tears from her eyes, then removed the necklace. Carefully, she opened the locket and exposed a nearly thirty-year-old photo. The faded image made her heart flutter in anguish and more tears fall. The picture reminded Pearl of her dreadful secrets. It would take a lot more than cascading tears to baptize the soul of the woman Pearl used to be.

A few miles away, a cherry red Cadillac Escalade cruised down the wet streets of Newark. Tycen drove. Heidi sat quietly in the passenger seat with her cellphone glued to her ear. She waited impatiently as the phone continued to ring. She twisted her face, then disconnected the call.

"Where the hell is my mother?" Heidi whispered.

"She's not picking up?" Tycen asked.

"Not at all," Heidi said and looked down at her phone again.

"I just called her a couple of times, and she's not answering. She never does that."

"Damn," Tycen uttered. "Maybe she stepped out."

"And went where?" Heidi thought for a moment. "She doesn't have a damn car. And she knows we are coming to pick her up. I hope she didn't forget."

The vehicle fell silent as Heidi thought about her mother. Tycen reached over and grabbed his fiancée by the hand. He held on tight as the SUV continued down the road.

Heidi tried her mother's phone again, but there was no answer. She cursed out loud and disconnected the call. "I don't know what is going on with my mother lately. But she's been acting weird."

"Is she okay?" Tycen asked.

"I don't know." Heidi shook her head.

"You think she's not feeling well?"

"I don't think it's nothing like that," Heidi answered. "It's like she's been depressed or something. Ever since she moved back to the east coast my mother hasn't been doing a lot. All she does is stay cooped up in that damn house all day. I don't know. Maybe I'm just making a big deal out of nothing. But she's definitely making me nervous."

Tycen didn't know what to say. Heidi continued to stress over her mother, and all he could do was listen. He knew today was going to be a rough day for his fiancée. Today was her brother Lamar's birthday, and Heidi wanted to take her mother to visit his gravesite. Tycen never got a chance to meet Lamar. Heidi always told him stories of how Lamar cared for her. She confided that she and Lamar were actually first cousins, but her mom had taken Lamar in at an early age. After his parents died, Lamar and Heidi had become just as tight as flesh and blood relatives. They played like siblings. They fought like brother and sister. And protected each other like they'd been born to the same mother. Up until the day he died, Lamar had always put Heidi first. Heidi had beamed when she'd expressed that Lamar would've done anything to protect her and the family.

Heidi looked out the window, missing Lamar. He had been the person she would turn to for advice. He was always there to help her when things got extremely rough. Even today, as she sat in the truck, Heidi's thoughts were fixed on her brother. She would give the world just to get a chance to speak to Lamar one last time.

Tycen slowly pulled up to her mother's house and parked the truck. "We're here."

Heidi glanced at her cellphone again and dialed her mom. "Dammit," Heidi snapped. There was still no answer.

"She still not picking up?" Tycen asked.

"Hell no," Heidi responded and grabbed her bag. "I'm going in. I got to make sure she's fine."

"Okay, I'll go with you." Tycen nodded and turned off the SUV.

The couple got out of the Escalade, then rushed to the front of the house. Heidi pulled out her keys. She wasn't going to bother with knocking on the door. She quickly unlocked the deadbolts, and then rushed inside.

"Mom!" Heidi yelled and looked around. She waited for a second, listing for a noise. The house was silent. Heidi instantly became worried. She screamed for her mother again. She rushed into the living room, and then stopped dead in her tracks. Her mother was sitting on the couch staring into the face of a gold locket, crying. Heidi didn't know what to think as she watched her mother weeping uncontrollably. "Mom?" Heidi whispered. "What's wrong?"

Pearl noticed her daughter standing a few feet away from her, then scrambled to hide the locket. She frantically wiped away the tears from her face, trying to regain her composure.

"Oh my goodness, child. I didn't hear you come in," Pearl stammered. Her voice cracked with every word.

"Mom, what's the matter?" Heidi whispered again and began to get emotional. Seeing her mother crying froze her. "Are you okay? What happened, Mom?"

"Nothing, I was just watching something sad on TV." Pearl looked around the room and tried to act normal. She nervously hung the necklace back around her neck, and then stood to her feet. She walked over to her daughter and forced a crooked smile to come to her face. "I'm sorry. Was that you calling me on the phone?"

Heidi kept a sharp eye on Pearl as she hugged her. She released her, then looked at the locket around her mom's neck. Heidi dropped her eyebrows. She had never before seen her mother wearing the gold necklace. Heidi wanted to ask her mother about the locket, but Pearl had turned her attention to Tycen.

"Why didn't you tell me you were bringing your husband over?" Pearl tried her best to smile. She walked over to Tycen and gave him a hug. "I'm sorry y'all. I would have cooked something."

"I told you Mom, we are not married yet." Heidi turned around and surveyed the house again. She could tell something was bothering her mother, and she hated that Pearl tried to hide it.

"So when are you gonna marry my daughter, Mister Man?" Pearl sweetly joked, trying to lighten the mood.

"I was born ready to marry your daughter. I'm just waiting on Heidi, ma'am." Tycen smiled at Pearl. "I have my white tuxedo and my bowtie ready."

"See, I knew there was something I liked about you." Pearl smiled. "He is such a charmer."

"Yes he is," Heidi quickly blurted, and then tried to dismiss the statement. "You sure you okay, Mom? I called you like a hundred times and you didn't pick up."

"I'm fine, child," Pearl responded with an uneven smile. "I told you I was watching television. You know how I get when I get deep into those reality shows."

Heidi decided not to push her mother. She watched as Pearl headed to the kitchen and returned with a half dozen of white roses.

"I brought them for your brother," Pearl whispered and handed Heidi the flowers. "You know how much he loved white."

Heidi's jaw tightened as she stared at the roses. She looked at her mother, and could tell Pearl was holding back her tears. "You know we don't have to do this today if you don't want to, Mom." Heidi moved closer to her.

"No, I think we should." Pearl nodded. "I know we both miss him, and I think we should stop by and let him know we still think about him."

The house fell silent. Heidi gave her mother a warm expression and nodded her head. She handed Tycen the flowers, then helped Pearl gather her things and put on her jacket. Heidi nodded her head toward the door, letting Tycen know to follow, then left out with him on her heels. Pearl stayed behind and locked up her house. She took a deep breath, trying her best to keep calm. She slowly rubbed the gold locket draped around her neck, then turned around, preparing herself to once again say goodbye to her dead son, Lamar.

Chapter 8

Saturday, October 5
2:18pm
Newark, NJ

"Newark police and residents are reeling from the discovery of a teenage girl's body found in a recycling bin in the south ward of the city. The medical examiner has not yet identified the remains or the cause of death. Officials are, however, certain that the girl is not Lexi Hamilton, the young teen who went missing on her way to school, nearly five years ago. The blue recycling bin had been tipped over by last night's storm. A passerby noticed the mangled body and called police. Residents here are shocked by the discovery..."

Asad Banks turned off the news brief. Disgusted, he pressed a few buttons on his steering wheel. The story of the murdered girl turned in his stomach as he searched for another radio station. Relaxing calmly in the passenger seat was his best friend, Dante, who seemed to be unfazed by the story. Dante laid back coolly in the leather seat of the Maserati. He inhaled the rich white smoke from his cigarette and gazed out just beyond the car window.

"Man, what kind of sick animal would do something foul like that to a little girl?" Asad asked.

"Yea, that shit is crazy," Dante mumbled and took another hard pull on his cigarette.

"It's like people just don't give a fuck no more about nobody's life," Asad said angrily. "Who the fuck would do a little girl dirty like that?"

Dante remained silent and continued to look outside the window.

Asad glanced at the peculiar look on Dante's face. He noticed that Dante was barely listening to him. "That type of shit don't piss you off?" Asad asked.

"Man...I hate to sound heartless, but I really don't give a shit," Dante chuckled. "People been doing foul shit since the Bible days, man."

"I feel you, but that's what I'm saying," Asad uttered. "This ain't the fuckin' Bible days, and people still acting like they lost their fuckin minds."

"Damn, fam, don't catch a heart attack over that shit." Dante laughed again. "People always been fucked up."

"Nah dude, I don't know. It's never been this crazy." Asad thought for a moment and continued to speak. "People killin' each other like it ain't shit out here."

"Asad, where you been for the last million years?" Dante shook his head. He glanced over to Asad like a father looking at his naïve son. "People been killin' each other since forever."

"Yea, but putting little girls in trashcans?" Asad raised his voice.

"Huh? Fam, you must be high on something." Dante laughed out loud. "Do you remember Jeffery Dahmer? You remember the Ice Man? Or how about that crazy black dude in Cleveland that was killin' all those girls in his basement? Asad, don't tell me you got amnesia all of a sudden. There's some real killers out here doin' some fucked up shit."

"Damn," Asad whispered. His best friend's words started to ring true.

"Exactly," Dante said. "That's why I don't trust a lot of people. I don't care how cool and calm they act. Trust me, a lot of people would leave you bleeding and dyin' somewhere if they wasn't scared to get locked up."

Asad didn't respond. He thought about Dante's words and continued to drive.

"I remember I was watching this show about a high school

basketball coach that was on death row." Dante took another pull on his cigarette and continued his story. "Somebody killed his son, and the coach found the boys that did it and killed them all. I mean he didn't just kill them boys, he tortured them motherfuckers and made them suffer before he killed him. Everybody asked him why he did it, and he never said a word. They put this dude on death row, and he never spoke to the lawyers, the judges, the cops or nobody. Right before they executed him, they asked him to speak his last words. You know what the coach said?" Asad looked over to Dante. He shrugged his shoulders, and was clearly curious as Dante continued speaking. "This dude said everybody has a killer inside of them….just pray you never have to ask that killer to do you a favor."

"Oh shit." Asad nervously chuckled.

"Tell me about it," Dante said. "I never forgot that. I think everybody is just one crazy situation away from killing a motherfucker. You feel me? I know that sounds ill, but who knows how that little girl ended up in that trashcan. It's a lot of crazy shit going on out here. So nothing surprises me anymore."

Asad turned his focus back to the road. Dante's cold words caught him by surprise. His friend's twisted logic was harsh, but Asad started to understand where he was coming from. Before they could continue the morbid conversation, Asad's cellphone started ringing. He picked up the phone and noticed it was his older brother, Gary Banks, on the line. Asad turned off the radio and answered the call. "Mr. Mayor how can I help you?" Asad answered in a professional tone.

"Cut the bullshit, Asad," Gary sharply responded though the phone. "Where the hell are you? You were supposed to be here twenty minutes ago. I told you my schedule was tight today."

"Totally my fault," Asad changed his tone as he spoke. "I had to pick up Dante. We are on our way now."

"Who?" the Mayor barked.

"Dante," Asad repeated.

"Dante Harper?" Gary Banks sounded irritated. "Why, is he with you?"

"Remember I told you I was bringing him by today so I could let you talk to him," Asad uttered. "He wants to join the security team."

"Whatever, Asad," Gary snapped again. "Just hurry up. I have a lot of work to take care of today."

"We're five minutes away," Asad uttered.

"Okay. We'll talk when you get here." Gary disconnected the call.

Asad dropped the phone back into his lap. He pressed his foot harder on the gas and sped up the Maserati.

"Damn, man. That didn't sound like a good conversation," Dante nervously said.

"Nah, it's cool," Asad responded. "He's just acting pyscho because of this whole re-election thing."

"Oh okay." Dante took another pull on his cigarette.

"When we get in here just don't talk too much." Asad looked over to his friend. "Just nod your head and let me do the talking."

"That sounds good to me," Dante said. "Thanks for hooking me up with this job, fam. You don't know how bad I need this gig."

"It's cool." Asad nodded and continued to speed down the street. He pushed the Maserati over the speed limit and made his way to the Mayor's home.

A few miles away, Mayor Gary Banks sat at his desk in his home office and continued to look over a pile of paperwork. His mind was ruffled by the news of yet another young girl found dead in his city. The press continued to flood his voicemail, requesting an immediate statement about the murder. Gary decided to delay his public appearances until more information became available. After four years of being the Mayor of the largest city in the state, Gary learned the importance of staying away from the media while they were on a feeding frenzy. Today, Gary wanted to keep his focus on his upcoming neighborhood rally. He was reading over a few notes when he heard a soft knock on his door.

"Come in. It's open," Gary yelled out.

He slowly leaned back in his chair as a casually dressed woman walked through his door. Gary smiled when he glanced at her pretty face. Although Gary had seen this woman hundreds of times, he was still amazed at how attractive she was. Her name was Deanna Dickson, but she was affectionately known to Gary as Didi.

As the Mayor's Chief of Staff and closest colleague, Didi found herself working hard at Gary's home quite often. Because the election was less than a year away, Gary, Didi and the rest of his team down at City Hall were working around the clock to stay two steps ahead of all issues that plagued the city. As Didi walked through his door today with more stacks of papers, Gary could only imagine what was next on their long list of assignments to tackle.

"Sorry to bug you, Gary," Didi softly said and placed the folders on his desk. "So I just got off the phone with the chief of Newark PD. Not only did they find that poor girl's body in the trashcan today, but the chief also mentioned he has received reports that somebody jumped off the roof at Beth Israel hospital this afternoon."

"What?" Gary blurted. "Suicide?"

"That's what the preliminary reports point to," Didi responded.

"Goddamit." Gary let out a harsh gasp. He sank deeper into his chair and closed his eyes. "There's way too much blood on these goddamn streets." Gary shook his head and mumbled. "Where the hell did we go wrong?"

Didi closed her mouth and felt the passion in Gary's words. She could sense the heavy burden he was taking on, and she felt compelled to ease his pain. Didi moved closer to his desk and whispered his name. "Gary, don't do this to yourself today,"

Didi calmly said. "You are only one man, and you're doing everything you can. I know how hard you work and what you believe in. You can't solely blame yourself for everything that happens in this city."

Gary opened his eyes and looked over at Didi. Her worried expression made him sit up in his chair and gather his composure. He nodded toward Didi and acknowledged her advice. "You're right," Gary said. "Sometimes this shit just seems so senseless to me."

"Same here. I know how you feel," Didi stated. "I just have to keep reminding myself that we are truly doing everything we humanly can. Sometimes these people out here need to meet us halfway."

"I agree." Gary nodded his head and looked down at the folders on his desk again.

Didi sensed his tension and walked around to the back of his leather chair. She slowly grabbed the mayor by his shoulders and forced him away from his desk. "Sit back for a second, Mr. Mayor," Didi sweetly whispered.

Gary obeyed the request as Didi firmly gripped his shoulder blades. She started to slowly massage his back and neck. Gary felt a warm rush flow through his body.

A crooked smile came to Didi's face as she felt his tight muscles becoming more relaxed with every squeeze. "Do you need me to do anything for you, sir?" Didi whispered. Hearing her own words out loud made her heart flutter like she was a teenager.

Gary didn't say a word. The flirtatious tone in her voice made him chuckle. The atmosphere in the large office grew warmer. Didi's hands moved from Gray's neck down to his chest. Her boldness didn't surprise Gary at all. The two had grown closer than just political associates over the years. The undeniable chemistry the two shared only enhanced their situation. Today, Didi's hands were working their magic, and Gary felt himself becoming lost in the moment.

"Now, I'm only going to ask you this one more time, sir,"

Didi whispered smoothly. She moved her lips closer to Gary's ear. "Is there anything else you want me to do right now? And keep in mind...I do mean anything."

Gary's thoughts shifted away from his work and onto Didi's voice. Her warm breath caused the hair on his neck to stand up. The smell of her perfume relaxed him even more. All of a sudden nothing else mattered to Gary but the feeling he was experiencing. Gary closed his eyes as he felt Didi's hands moving toward his stomach and closer to his waist.

Didi noticed a throbbing bulge coming from the mayor's pants. She felt an adrenaline rush, and her heart started racing even faster. She smiled and gently kissed Gary on the neck.

"I'm going to take that as a yes, Mr. Mayor," Didi sweetly whispered and continued to seduce her boss.

Just outside the mayor's home, Asad pulled his Maserati up the driveway and shut off the engine. He looked at his watch and prepared himself to hear his brother's complaints about his lateness. Asad gathered his things while Dante gazed at the immaculate home for a moment.

Dante couldn't believe a house so beautiful was located within the city limits of Newark.

"So this is the mayor's mansion?" Dante gawked at the home.

"I wouldn't call it a mansion," Asad said and grabbed his jacket. "You should see the other crib. Trust me, that shit makes this one look like a goddamn doll house." Asad jumped out the car, and Dante followed suit. They both headed to the front door.

Dante continued to size up the property. "Damn this is crazy," Dante stated as they walked onto the porch and approached the front door. "And your brother is still single?"

"Yup and no kids," Asad added. "That's crazy right? So you know his ass-game is off the charts."

Dante started laughing and nodded his head. "Hell yes," Dante chuckled. "All you Banks brothers are just alike. Scared to death of commitment."

"Nope. Just not dumb enough to do it," Asad joked and gave his friend a slick expression.

"Whatever," Dante uttered and tried to shake off the subtle insult.

Asad rang the doorbell and checked his watch again. He looked around the quiet neighborhood, and then turned his attention to Dante. "Just remember to say as little as possible," Asad lowered his voice. "I just don't want him overthinking this decision."

"That's cool," Dante said.

Asad rang the doorbell again and looked around the front of the house. He peeked through a few windows and started to knock on the door. "What the hell is taking him so long?" Asad asked. "I know he's here. I just talked to him." Asad started knocking on the front door even harder, then pulled out his cellphone. He was just about to call his brother when the front door swung open.

A disheveled Gary looked at the men and invited them in. Asad gave his brother a strange look and entered the home. Dante followed close behind. Gary quickly buttoned up his shirt, and Asad watched him closely as he tried to put himself back together. Gary walked to the living room and pointed to the sofa. Asad and Dante took a seat as Gary handed each of the men a drink.

"Damn bro, what took you so long?" Asad asked, as he got comfortable on the sofa.

Gary fixed himself a Vodka and Coke and sat down across from the men. "That's my fault. I couldn't hear the bell. I was in the other room fucking my Chief of Staff," Gary bluntly confessed.

Dante exploded into an uncomfortable laughter and shook his head. After a few seconds he noticed that he was the only one laughing in the room.

"You think that's funny?" Gary asked and gave Dante a cold stare.

"Ummm…no sir. I'm sorry. I thought you were making a joke," Dante stumbled on his own words.

Gary looked over to Asad and shook his head.

Didi emerged from Gary's office and walked into the living room. She smiled when she saw Asad and walked over to him. "Hey, Asad. How are you sweetie?" Didi asked.

"Hey Didi, I'm good." Asad returned the smile and stood to his feet.

Didi embraced him and gave him a quick kiss on his cheek. "I see your brother already fixed you a drink."

"Yes ma'am," Asad uttered.

"Don't you 'ma'am' me." Didi waved her finger at Asad and smiled. "I'm old enough to be your…mature, yet sexy girlfriend, young man." Asad and Didi shared a quick laugh as she walked over and grabbed a glass of wine.

Gary looked over to Dante and continued to give him a hard expression. "There's one thing you need to know about us," Gary said and kept his eyes fixed on Dante. "We don't keep secrets here. You understand that?"

"Yes sir," Dante uttered and lowered his voice.

"If you're going to be on my personal security team, you need to know some information about us that many people don't know." Gary's expression was serious and deliberate. Dante sat quietly on the sofa as the mayor continued to speak. "We don't keep secrets amongst ourselves. Lies can hurt somebody…but secrets…can get somebody killed. You understand that?"

"Yes." Dante nodded his head. He barely moved as the mayor's words froze him.

"So do you have any secrets we should know about?" Gary asked coldly.

"No," Dante nervously replied.

"Are you sure?" Gary pushed and stared Dante directly in the eyes.

"I'm sure, sir," Dante responded.

"Okay good," Gary uttered. "If my brother says you're

good then I have to trust his judgment. We'll have to do a background check. Deanna will have our investigators call you. If they clear you, you're good to go. But, believe me, if there is anything you're not telling us, trust and believe, they will find out and they will let us know. Do you understand that?"

"Yes, sir," Dante quickly answered.

"And you," Gary blurted and turned his attention to his brother. "Are you ready for this rally?"

"Of course," Asad confidently responded. "I have been preparing alternate routes and working closely with the parks and recreation department for staging arrangements. They have assured me that there is more than enough room to keep you safe."

"Okay." Gary nodded his head, and then took a sip of his drink. "I don't know how many people we can expect, but the climate is a bit sketchy these days. People are on edge. Everyone's looking to place a lot of blame on this office for all of this goddamn violence that's going on. For now, we're going to keep the rally for next Sunday. That way we can minimize the traffic on the streets."

"That sounds good to me," Asad said.

"Okay. Is there anything else that we need to go over?" Gary asked firmly.

"No I don't think so," Asad responded. "I'll make a few more stops over to the park and make sure everything is set up properly before the rally."

"Okay good." Gary stood to his feet and motioned for the men to stand up. "So y'all can get the fuck out of my house and let me and Didi get back to business."

Asad chuckled and put down his drink. He knew exactly what kind of business Gary was referring to. He and Dante stood up, and Gary walked the men to the front door.

"Welcome to the team," Gary said and gave Dante a strong handshake.

"Thank you, sir." Dante humbly nodded his head.

"Okay bro, hit me on my cell if you need me," Asad said and gave his brother a quick hug.

"Okay. Not a problem," Gary responded. He watched from the front door as the men headed back to Asad's car. His brother fired up the engine of the Maserati and quickly pulled out of the driveway. The mayor thought about the conversation and closed the door. He turned around and looked at Didi. She moved from the dining room and sat down on the sofa. An enticing smirk grew on her face. Gary recognized the expression and smiled. He walked over to the sofa and sat down next to her. "So what do you think about, Mr. Dante?" Gary asked.

"I think he's perfect," Didi whispered as a sly expression grew on her face.

"You think?" Gary dropped his eyebrows. His tone was slightly malicious.

"Believe me. He will work out fine," Didi responded and returned the devilish look.

She pulled Gary closer and started pecking on his neck, clearly done with discussing business for the day. She moved up to his face and gave the mayor another passionate kiss. She ran her hands across his broad shoulders, and then forced her tongue deep into his mouth. Gary responded by grabbing a handful of Didi's breast. "Oooo," Didi groaned from the feeling.

She calmly backed away from Gary and gave him a sensual look. She wanted him badly, and Gary could see it in her eyes. Didi pulled her shirt over her head and tossed it to the floor. She exposed her naked breasts to the mayor and smiled. She dropped her head backwards when she felt Gary's tongue engulf her perky nipples.

"Yes, baby. Do it slow," Didi groaned. "Don't rush." Didi loved the feeling of Gary pleasing her body. Every smooth lick from his tongue sent a sensual chill over her. She grabbed the back of his head and forced him closer to her. Gary sucked and teased her nipples like a piece of soft candy. With a manly aggression, he ran his hands over her back. "Damn..." Didi sighed and licked her lips. She squeezed her thighs together and let out a guttural feminine moan.

Gary seemed to know every spot to touch. He was a professional at heating up her body but, today, Gary was setting her on fire. She couldn't take it anymore. She kicked off her shoes, ready to get completely naked for her boss. She rose to her feet and kept her eyes locked on Gary. She stood in front of him and unbuckled her belt. He watched her as she dropped her pants to the floor, then found himself eye level with her silk panties. The sweet aroma of her yearning pussy turned him on. He grabbed her by the hips and began to kiss on her thighs.

Didi caressed herself. "Baby!" she blurted as she felt his tongue run up the middle of her legs.

Gary didn't waste another minute. He knew exactly what his friend wanted. He gripped her panties and pulled them down past Didi's knees, but never got her underwear completely off.

With her panties still wrapped around her ankle, Didi lifted her left leg and cocked it over Gary's right shoulder. "Lick it, baby!" she moaned. She moved her hips closer to Gary's face and grabbed the back of his head.

The command was music to Gary's ears. He loved it when she took control. Her dominating tone made him feel submissive, and the role reversal was an exciting change of pace for a man who spent most of his life being in charge. Gary forced his face deep into Didi's crotch. She screamed with pleasure when Gary's tongue penetrated her walls and he began to gently suck on her pearl. He let loose a hard moan, and his deep voice made her pussy vibrate.

"Oh shit...baby....do that again," Didi desperately whined.

Gary readily obeyed the command. He was far from shy when it came to oral sex. He drove his tongue even deeper, moaning with every lick. The taste of her wetness sent chills up his spine. Watching her body react to his sexy technique only made him work harder. He wanted to push her to that ultimate pleasure.

Didi yelled out again as her excitement grew. She started bouncing her juicy pussy back and forth. Gary caught up to her rhythm and started to rock with her. Didi grabbed his head with both hands as her naked body started to gyrate. Her legs grew weak. She was inching closer to a huge climax. Gary reached around her waist and gripped her voluptuous ass.

"Yes, baby...yes. Please don't stop. . ." Didi screamed out as Gary made her body cream like never before. Just the sight of the most powerful man in the city pleasing her was driving her wild. She arched her back as a mini-orgasm hit her body like an electrical shock.

Gary knew she was close. He cuffed her ass tighter and pushed his tongue deeper.

"Oh God!" Didi yelled. She screamed Gary's name and moaned out loud. The sound of his soft lips banging against her moist pussy thrilled her. A loud silence fell over the room as Didi stopped screaming. She knew the climax she was longing for was only moments away. She braced her body and held on tight. "Oh, my God...I'm coming, Gary...GODDDAMMN!" Didi screamed like she was dying. The potent orgasm rocked her body. Didi shouted Gary's name again. She almost collapsed from the amazing sensation.

Gary never stopped licking as Didi continued to climax all over his mouth. A devilish smile came to his face. He'd tasted all of her and had loved every second of it. Gary gave Didi a quick who's-your-daddy smack on her ass, then looked up to her. "You like that?" he whispered.

"I love it!" Didi sweetly responded.

She swung her leg off of Gary's shoulder and stepped back. She helped Gary up from the sofa and grabbed him by the face. Didi gave him a deep kiss on his lips. She moaned as she tasted his tongue and grew more excited. She was ready for more. "You know what I want, baby?" she whispered and rubbed his shoulders.

"What you want, baby?" Gary playfully responded.

"I want a million dollar orgasm." Didi smiled and moved her hands down below his waist.

"That's what you want?" Gary asked.

"Hell yes!" Didi nodded. "Can I have one?"

Gary felt her hands caressing him and dropped his eyes. He took another long look at her naked body and licked his lips. "Yes, baby," Gary smiled. "Let's do it."

Didi gave Gary a wide smile. He grabbed his friend by the hand and they headed up to his bedroom. Didi was ready for all of Gary and she grew anxious with every step. She loved making love to the mayor, and she couldn't wait to get Gary up to his bedroom so they could finish what they started.

Chapter 9

Saturday, October 5
2:43pm
St. Mary's Cemetery
Newark, NJ

Tycen's Escalade slowly cruised up to the top of a quiet hill in St. Mary's Cemetery. The mood in the SUV was a somber one, and no one wanted to be the first to break the silence. Tycen slowly pulled over near a huge oak tree and shut off the engine.

Pearl was already in tears as she gazed at what seemed to be an endless sea of eroding headstones in the cemetery. The sight of the falling rain broke her heart as she thought of her deceased son. "It seems like every time I come out here, it's raining," Pearl whispered.

The emotion in her voice caused Heidi to turn around and look at her mother. Heidi watched Pearl closely as she wiped away her tears and shook her head. "Mom, you know we don't have to do this if you're not up to it," Heidi said quietly from the front seat.

"No, baby. I need to do this. I need to let Lamar know that we still think about him," Pearl said.

"Okay," Heidi whispered and reached for her umbrella.

"I'm going to stay here in the truck and give you guys some privacy," Tycen said and gave his fiancée a quick kiss.

"I think that would be best." Heidi nodded her head. "We'll be right back." Heidi got out of the truck and opened the back door. She helped her mother out of the large SUV as the rain started to pick up again. Pearl grabbed the flowers from the backseat and wrapped up tight next to her daughter.

Tycen watched them as they carefully made their way through the wet grass and headed to Lamar's plot. Tycen kept a protective eye on Heidi until she disappeared in the rain. He checked his watch. He knew he only had a few minutes to conduct some quick business before they returned. He reached for his phone and made a call.

"Legal department," a confident voice blurted from the other line.

"This is Tycen, I need to speak to Lawrence." he spoke quickly.

"Sure thing Mr. Wakefield," the voice responded.

Tycen heard the line click as he was placed on hold. He patiently waited for Lawrence Cohen, the most important man in his circle, to pick up the phone. Lawrence was Tycen's trusted campaign manager. As a former lawyer and one of the sharpest legal minds in the country, Lawrence spent most of his earlier years representing large corporations and fighting to change the public's perception of big business. When Tycen made the decision to run for Mayor of Newark he knew that Lawrence would be the perfect person to help him win over the public's favor and organize a strong campaign. Everything was moving along as planned and today Tycen was calling to check in with his senior advisor.

"Tycen, thank God you called," Lawrence huffed from the other line. "Where are you?"

"Hello, Lawrence," Tycen said. "I'm out with Heidi. I'm kind of in the middle of a personal matter right now. Is everything alright?"

"Actually, we are scrambling over here." Lawrence took a deep breath.

"Scrambling?" Tycen asked. "What's going on?"

"It's a lot going on, Mr. Wakefield," Lawrence sounded excited. "We started running the first campaign commercials today. We decided to run the thirty-second spots on all of the local channels in Newark and throughout Essex County."

"Great." Tycen smiled. "How does it look?"

"Fantastic," Lawrence replied. "The networks have been getting great feedback on the commercials from the public. They especially love the tagline and the imagery. I think we hit a homerun with this one."

"Excellent news." Tycen was thrilled. "So what else is going on?"

"Well, we just found out that Mayor Gary Banks called for an emergency rally next week in Military Park," Lawrence continued. "They are expecting thousands of residents to come out for this. It's being hyped as a Stop The Violence event."

"Oh okay. That doesn't sound like much." Tycen relaxed back into his car seat. "A lot of Mayors do that. Seems like he's getting desperate."

"You don't understand, Tycen," Lawrence raised his voice. "He is holding the rally on the fifth anniversary of the disappearance of Lexi Hamilton. The media frenzy is going to be massive. Believe me."

"Damn," Tycen whispered.

"That's right. Gary is no rookie," Lawrence said. "He knows how to work the press to his advantage."

"Okay, so what do we need to do?" Tycen asked.

"That's what we are trying to figure out," Lawrence responded. "I don't believe we have to hold our own rally. That is out of the question. But I do think we need to hold a large press conference and make a big announcement. Something big enough to take some of the spotlight away from him."

"Okay that sounds good. What's the announcement?" Tycen asked.

"Right now, I don't know. That's what we are working on," Lawrence's tone grew calmer. "A lot of media personnel will be in town all week, so I'll reach out and see how many outlets we can book for the press conference."

"Okay, Lawrence. I trust your judgment. So whatever you think is best," Tycen said.

"Thank you, Mr. Wakefield," Lawrence said. "But I do

have one more concern, sir."

"Okay what's that?" Tycen responded.

"Heidi," Lawrence stated.

"What do you mean? What about Heidi?" Tycen asked sharply. Just hearing Heidi's name come from Lawrence's mouth made his mood change. Tycen readjusted himself in the seat.

"Now, Tycen I don't want this to sound the wrong way." Lawrence was sure to be careful with his words. "I know you told me not to do a background check on your fiancée—"

"And I hope you respected my wishes," Tycen cut Lawrence short.

"Now Mr. Wakefield, don't get mad," Lawrence responded. He knew he was walking on thin ice when it came to discussing Tycen's personal life. "Believe me sir, everything we are doing is for the benefit of the campaign."

"What does that mean, Lawrence?" Tycen was edgy. "Did you do a background check on my fiancée without my permission?"

"Sir, all we did was some light research," Lawrence responded.

"What?" Tycen snapped.

"Mr. Wakefield...listen...the last thing I want to do is agitate you today. That's not my goal," Lawrence tried to sound as confident as possible. "Just understand, as your campaign manager I'm looking out for your best interest. I want to put you in the best position to win this election. The other side is going to pay a heavy price to get every bit of information about you and your fiancée, once this campaign kicks into high gear. I just want to prepare you for the inevitable."

There was a silence on the phone. Tycen thought about his campaign manager's words and sat back for a moment. He was torn between his love and respect for Heidi and his passion to become mayor of the city. He realized Lawrence was out of line for doing the background check, but he knew the research was necessary. It was just a matter of time before

Gary Banks and his team of investigators began to dig for any dirt that would give Gary a leg up in the election.

"So what did you find out?" Tycen quietly asked.

"Did Heidi ever tell you about a man named Jayson Carter?" Lawrence asked.

"Yes," Tycen answered. "She told me that he was her ex-fiancé. She said he died before they got married."

"Okay. But did she ever tell you how he died?" Lawrence asked.

"Actually, she didn't," Tycen answered. The pit of his stomach started to turn.

Lawrence continued, careful of his word choice, "Now, Tycen remember this is just preliminary research we are doing. It is not official."

"Goddamnit, Lawrence…just say what's on your mind," Tycen barked. "What's going on?"

"Well, we haven't found out all the details, but a lot of our sources believe that she was somehow involved," Lawrence said.

"What?" Tycen gasped.

"Again…sir…this is unofficial," Lawrence continued. "It happened so long ago, and the details are a bit unclear. But you have to get in front of this, sir."

"Shit," Tycen dropped his voice.

"Maybe it's not as bad as you think," Lawrence said. "But if we could find out more details we could get a clearer picture of what happened."

"So what are you proposing?" Tycen asked.

"I know you don't want us to conduct an official background check on Heidi without her consent," Lawrence continued. "But is there any way you can speak to her about it? Just ask her to work with us. I'm sure she's not hiding anything major, but we have to be prepared to do damage control if anything explosive comes to the surface."

"I understand," Tycen conceded. He realized that he didn't have any other choice but to take his manager's concerns serious. "I'll speak to her this weekend and get back to you by Monday. Just don't make a move without me knowing about it first."

"We won't, Tycen. Believe me," Lawrence said. "I just wanted to bring that to your attention. We will wait for your plan of action on this."

"Sounds good. I'll reach out to you first thing Monday morning," Tycen said. "Don't forget what I told you. Don't make another move without my okay."

"Sure thing, sir," Lawrence responded. "I will await your instructions."

Tycen disconnected the call. He gently tapped the phone on his leg and contemplated his dilemma. He had always been curious about Heidi's past. Lawrence's discovery just put things in a very shaded perspective. Tycen knew there was something hidden behind Heidi's beautiful eyes, but he always elected to respect her privacy. After the reality check from his campaign manager, Tycen knew he needed to have a much-needed conversation with his fiancée. He prayed that whatever was locked in her past would never rear its ugly head and destroy their future.

Meanwhile, down near the bottom of the hill, Pearl carefully placed the white roses near Lamar's gravestone. She had been crying since the moment she had laid eyes on her son's plot. Although, it had been a few years since Lamar's death, the pain of his absence felt fresh in her heart. She placed her head in her hands, and then wiped away the tears that flooded her face. She never anticipated that her grief would consume every inch of her soul. Pearl broke down again as she gazed at Lamar's name chiseled deep into the granite headstone.

"I'm sorry, Mom," Heidi whispered as she wept alongside Pearl. Heidi missed Lamar dearly, and could only imagine what her mother was going through. Memories of Lamar's life replayed in Heidi's mind. She tried her best to concentrate on the good times. She reminisced about his warm smile and his selflessness. She harbored the memories of their childhood and all the good times she had shared with her only brother. She never dwelled on the fact that, in reality, they were only cousins. The life that they had shared together was as tightly connected as blood siblings.

Today, Heidi felt a deep sorrow when she thought about Lamar. She wished she could spend one more day with her brother. She had so much to tell him, so many secrets to share. And, of course, Heidi wanted badly for him to meet Tycen.

Pearl was experiencing a different type of sorrow as she thought about Lamar. A harsh feeling of guilt and remorse caused her to drop her head in shame. She couldn't help but feel responsible for Lamar's death. The bloody memories of his murder flashed into her mind causing more tears to fall from her eyes. "I'm so sorry, Lamar," Pearl whispered, forcing the words out of her mouth. The deep emotions made her voice crack in pain. Pearl rubbed on the gold locket around her neck and continued to speak. "I pray you can forgive me, Lamar. Wherever you are, I pray to God that you're safe. I just want you to know that there's not a day that goes by that I don't think about you. You probably know so much more now, and I hope you can forgive me for everything that I've done. I miss you, son. And know that I will always love you forever."

A cold chill ran through Heidi's body as she listened to her mother's heartfelt words. Another rush of tears fell from Heidi's eyes and she pulled her mother closer. Pearl couldn't speak again. She was now sobbing uncontrollably, and Heidi sensed that it was time to get her mother out of the rain. Heidi looked at her brother's headstone one last time and forced a small smile to come to her face. "Happy Birthday, Lamar," Heidi whispered. "We love you."

Heidi held on to her mother and turned around. The rain started to fall harder, and the women made their way back to the SUV.

Pearl looked at her daughter and gave her a broken expression. "I hope he forgives me," Pearl sadly uttered.

"It's okay, Mom," Heidi whispered. "It's not your fault. Believe me. Lamar knows that."

Heidi felt bad that her mother was placing so much blame on herself. Her brother's murder was tragic. The men who had killed Lamar were now dead and gone. There was nothing more the women could do but keep the memory of Lamar's life alive. Heidi comforted her mother as they reached the SUV.

Tycen jumped out of the truck and helped Pearl into the back seat. Heidi wiped away more tears and Tycen gave her a hug. "Are you okay?" he asked.

"I will be," Heidi softly responded.

The couple got into the truck, and Tycen fired up the engine. Pearl tried her best to shake the feeling of guilt as she laid back and closed her eyes. Everyone in the SUV stayed silent as Tycen navigated though the winding road and made his way out of the cemetery.

Chapter 10

Saturday, October 5
5:40 pm
Beth Israel Hospital
Newark, NJ

The sun began to set over the chilly streets of Newark. Detective Bell coolly leaned up against the side of the building as the police scene in the back of the hospital grew larger by the minute. The calm expression on her face was a stark contrast to the chaotic war that was taking place in her mind. Detective Bell had just murdered a man in cold blood. She had managed to convince the investigators that Dent was a suspect and had fallen off the roof trying to flee her. She had downplayed the incident to her supervisors as they continued to gather evidence and take notes from the scene. But deep inside, she was praying that her body language wouldn't betray her.

Detective Bell reached into her pocket and pulled out her fourth cigarette of the hour. She quickly blazed the tip and looked around at all the police activity in the rear of the hospital. She inhaled the smoke and started to feel at ease. Ironically, the harsh taste of the tobacco calmed her nerves. She thought about Dent for a moment and shook her head. She was still upset that he managed to botch her bulletproof plan. Now that Kimi had escaped, Detective Bell needed to hunt her down before things became worse.

Before she could dwell on Kimi any longer, her cellphone started buzzing in her pocket. Detective Bell grabbed the phone and looked at the screen. She twisted her face when she noticed the call was coming from a blocked phone number. She plucked the cigarette to the ground and reluctantly answered the call. "This is Detective Bell," she sternly said.

"What the fuck happened down there?" an angry man snapped from the other line.

A rush of fear instantly came over the detective. She recognized the voice. She dipped off from the police scene and walked away. "I have it all under control," Detective Bell tried to remain calm.

"You got it under control? I don't fuckin' think so," the man barked through the phone. "The hospital is all over the goddamn television right now."

Detective Bell scanned the area and noticed a few media vans on the scene. She didn't realize the details of the incident had been leaked to the news networks. She turned her attention back to the phone call. "Don't worry. Like I said...I have it under control," she repeated.

"Where's Dent?" the man questioned Detective Bell. "Did you get the girl?"

"Not exactly," she replied nervously. "The plan got fucked up, and now I have to move to my plan B."

"Listen, you fuckin' dike!" the man yelled. "Fuck your plan B! This is gettin' all screwed up. My father won't stop callin' my phone. He's bitchin' hard about this situation. You need to get down here now."

"What?" Detective Bell couldn't believe her ears. "I can't do that. The crime scene is still live."

"I don't give a fuck," the man continued to yell. "Get your fuckin' ass down here like yesterday. We got to find another way to make this happen. Before we make another move my dad wants to talk to you. He's getting' worried. And you know what happens when my dad gets worried...people start dying."

Detective Bell's face tightened as she processed the threat. She knew the man's words were serious. She balled up her fist and continued to speak. "Where do you want to meet?" Detective Bell grunted and cautiously looked around. She was pissed off.

"Meet me at The Body Shop," the man ordered. "I'll be here for another few hours. Don't keep me waiting."

Before she could say another word, the call disconnected. The urgency and fury in the man's voice put the detective on notice. She slid the phone back into her pocket. Detective Bell thought about the man's dangerous words. She walked away from the police scene and headed back to her vehicle. She had no time to worry about who was watching her leave. After the phone call, Detective Bell realized she was now facing a life or death situation. She jumped in her unmarked car and started up the engine. She sped away from the hospital and prepared herself for what was waiting for her down at the The Body Shop.

A few miles away, Kimi Moore abruptly opened her eyes and took a deep breath. She clutched onto a thick pillow as she awakened from a midday-nightmare. Kimi's eyes quickly glanced around the room. She didn't realize she had been sleeping for so long. A few hours earlier, she had wisely checked herself into a hotel room under a fake name. She needed to lay low and get her thoughts together. The frightening dream was nothing compared to the real life drama she had been experiencing over the past twenty-four hours. Niko's face entered into her mind, and she tried to imagine what her boyfriend was going through. She prayed that he was somewhere alive and safe. A thousand questions swirled. Could The Marquez Crew really have kidnapped Niko? Why was Detective Bell involved with all of this? Who can I really trust to help me find Niko?

A throbbing headache started to nag Kimi. She pushed her mind to figure out what to do next. Kimi knew she needed to find Niko before it was too late. The dangerous Marquez crew was known for destroying a lot of lives in Newark, and Kimi refused to allow her boyfriend to become another victim. A grim emotion fell over Kimi as she sat up on the edge of the bed. She turned on the television to try to drown out her gloomy thoughts. She was worried. A harsh reality started to set in as Kimi's mind continued to race. Kimi had never experienced anything like this in her life, and she felt alone and scared. She didn't have any friends to call on to help her, and most of her family had moved away some years ago. Niko was her closest friend and her only companion. With Niko now missing, Kimi realized she was on her own.

"My name is Tycen Wakefield and I am running for Mayor of Newark, New Jersey!" a loud campaign commercial blared from the other side of the room. The familiar name made Kimi turn around and stare at the television. She unconsciously tilted her head as she watched the political ad.

"With violent crimes back on the rise and our educational system in shambles, Newark is in need of new leadership. As a public servant for over twelve years and the head of The Call and Response Program, I know what it's like to lead by example and make the tough decisions to get this city back on track. So it's time to send a message to City Hall. This election vote for me, Tycen Wakefield. Together, we can make Newark great again!"

Kimi's mouth fell open as the name struck another familiar cord in her mind. Niko had spoken about Tycen Wakefield on a number of occasions. As an active lawyer in Newark, Niko had volunteered at the Call and Response Program for the past five years. Niko and Tycen were business associates and longtime friends. Kimi realized Tycen was probably the only person in the city she could trust to help her find her boyfriend. Kimi relaxed on the bed and stared at the ceiling. She started to devise a plan to get next to Tycen Wakefield.

An hour later, Detective Bell's vehicle turned onto a small street located deep in The Ironbound section of the city. The dimly lit strip was lined with old warehouses and abandoned office buildings. It was the perfect area for anyone looking to conceal their shady activities after dark. The veteran detective always felt uneasy when she came to this part of town. Most of the huge structures appeared eerily desolate. But Detective Bell was wise enough to know better. Some of the city's worse criminals were conducting heavy business behind those walls. As her unmarked cruiser pulled over near the center of the block, Detective Bell braced herself to come face to face with one of those hardened criminals.

The detective turned off the engine and got out of her vehicle. She located the building she was looking for and took a deep breath. The cool air couldn't calm her as she headed toward the entrance. She looked at a corroded sign dangling just above the door. "The Body Shop," she whispered with contempt, then entered the building through a glass door. She looked around. The detective was approached by two security guards.

"Wait a minute! Who are you here to see? Do you have an appointment?" one of the men quickly snapped.

Detective Bell never opened her mouth. She showed the men her badge, and they parted like the Red Sea.

One of the guards finally recognized the detective and nodded toward her. "You remember where his office is, right?" the guard asked.

"That's right," the detective answered and scoffed at him.

The men stepped aside as Detective Bell walked by. She had been to the building a number of times, and she knew exactly where she needed to go. An anxious feeling came over the detective as she headed up the few flights of stairs. She kept her eyes and ears wide opened as she reached the top floor and entered a long corridor. The strip reminded her of a hallway inside of a high school with dozens of classrooms on each side. But there were no chalkboards, desks or chairs to be seen. Instead, every room was equipped with a bed, a television and burning-candles. Prostitutes of all ages, colors and sizes were entertaining men in each room. Loud screams of passion and masculine moans could be heard coming from the makeshift sex dens. The shadows of naked women bouncing up and down could be seen against the smoked out windows.

The Body Shop was an infamous brothel that catered to professional men and politicians. Because of the high security and the high price for membership, only a selected crowd was privileged to ever step foot into the extravagant building. The retro style whorehouse belonged to the most dangerous gangster in Newark, Leon Marquez.

For over ten years, Leon and The Marquez Crew ruled the gangland of Newark with a black hand. Marquez was not only a ruthless killer, but he was well educated. He used his business skills to keep the corporate money flowing to his foot soldiers. His dream was to rule Newark from the streets to the boardrooms. But after a long run, Leon Marquez started to grow greedy and reckless. He soon found himself arrested and facing a mountain of charges. He was now sitting in a county jail, waiting on yet another bail hearing. His son, Rojo Marquez, took over the businesses. The young hothead was now running the show. And tonight, Detective Bell had the tough task of convincing Rojo to give her another shot at finding Kimi.

Another feeling of uneasiness came over the detective as she continued down the long hall. She reached the office near the back of the building and knocked on the door.

"It's open!" a voice yelled out.

Detective Bell walked inside the large room and instinctively surveyed her surroundings. To her surprise, Rojo Marquez was calmly sitting behind his desk. A heavy cloud of smoke nearly covered his face as he pulled on a half-drawn cigar.

Rojo noticed the detective heading toward him. He tried to stop himself, but he couldn't help but turn his head and look over to the other side of the room at a brown-skinned woman, who was relaxing on the leather sofa. The curvaceous vixen sat quietly with her legs crossed. Her eyes were low from her own cigarette smoke. Her half naked body was smooth as caramel. Her piercing eyes cut to the detective. The girl's scowl was a direct contrast to her flowing hair and flawless make-up. Her name was Shayla Johnson, but she was known in the streets as Skittles.

Detective Bell looked over toward Skittles and sized up the situation. Two younger women sat on opposite sides of Skittles, caressing the sexy woman like she was a man. The frisky women were giggling and teasing each other as they drank back-to-back shots of liquor. The detective felt uncomfortable, as something seemed dangerously out of place.

Rojo gave Detective Bell a hard stare and motioned for her to come closer. "Have a seat," Rojo ordered and pointed to a chair directly in front of his desk. "Don't worry 'bout them bitches back there. They just waitin' for more clients to show up."

Detective Bell ignored her better judgment and turned her attention away from the women. She took a seat in front of Rojo's desk. His immaculate office was breathtaking. From the plush carpet to his large teak wood desk, Rojo was clearly a man of expensive taste. The large window behind him gave way to a distant view of New York City. Detective Bell was almost lost in the view when Rojo's voice snapped her back to reality.

"So what happened with Kimi?" Rojo abruptly asked.

"She got away," Detective Bell quietly answered.

"You told me that," Rojo fired back. "But what happened?"

"Rojo, listen...I sent Dent upstairs to go get Kimi...and... he said she ran from him. I don't know what exactly happened after that," The detective tried her best to remain calm.

"So how the fuck did Dent end up on the sidewalk with his head split the fuck open?" Rojo raised his voice.

Skittles and the women on the couch stop giggling as the mood in the office suddenly became uncomfortable.

"Rojo, with all due respect, you wasn't there. That shit got out of hand real quick in that hospital." Detective Bell adjusted herself in the chair. "Dent was talking all crazy and actin' way out of line so I had to make a quick decision."

"So you tossed my fuckin' worker off the roof?" Rojo

sharply asked and dropped his eyebrows. His glare was cold enough to freeze a furnace. The detective closed her mouth and gave Rojo a crooked look. No man had ever put fear in her heart like Rojo did. His hot temper was legendary, and Detective Bell refused to become a victim of his rage. She stayed silent as Rojo continued to chastise her. "Oh what? You didn't think I would find out what you did down there? So... not only did you violate my crew...you let Kimi get away."

"Actually, you let Kimi get away," the detective uttered under her breath.

"What the fuck is that supposed to mean?" Rojo yelled.

"I don't understand how the hell y'all gonna grab Niko and forget to grab his girl," Detective Bell slightly raised her voice. She was clearly growing agitated in the office. "I can't keep cleaning up your dirty work, Rojo. This shit is getting out of hand. Y'all might have to find somebody else to do this. I'm done."

"What?" Rojo twisted his mouth.

"I'm done," the detective repeated. "I can't keep puttin' myself out there, and y'all keep doin' this sloppy shit."

The women on the sofa watched on as the exchange grew more intense.

"You callin' us sloppy?" Rojo tightened his face.

"Hell yea," Detective Bell bravely fired back. "Look at the shit y'all doin."

"I'm tellin you right now, don't say somethin' you can't take back." Rojo pointed at the detective like he was scolding a toddler.

"Listen Rojo. The only reason I'm doing this is because your father thinks I owe him some shit." Detective Bell stared directly at Rojo. She was clearly tired of working for The Marquez Crew. The anger from years of mistreatment was coming to the surface. Detective Bell was clearly upset as she continued to speak. "Now, I don't know if he bumped his head or something...but...I did enough shit for y'all to pay him back five times. So I'm sorry, but this is a wrap. I can't do this shit no more. I'm done with y'all."

Rojo sat back in his chair. He glanced at the women on the couch and quickly turned his attention back to the detective. The room fell silent and Rojo took a hard pull on his cigar. The smoke seemed to linger extremely long as Rojo thought about the detective's rant. He was beyond angry but he never lost his cool. "I told you not to say somethin' you would regret," Rojo said. Detective Bell watched Rojo as he slowing reached on his desk. He grabbed his cellphone and turned it over. It didn't take long for the detective to realize there was a call connected on Rojo's phone. "Pop, did you just hear that shit?" Rojo shouted out. "I told you we can't trust her."

"You disappointed me, detective," a coarse voice calmly echoed from the phone.

Detective Bell's heart dropped to her stomach. The familiar voice scared her like a whisper from a ghost. It was Leon Marquez. Detective Bell nervously covered her mouth and sat up in her chair. "Marquez...believe me...I didn't mean no disrespect," Detective Bell nervously said. She sounded desperate. "I'm just sayin—"

"Shut the fuck up!" Marquez barked from the phone. "I'm fuckin' sittin' in this cage...dyin' every minute that I'm not on those street...and you got some fuckin' nerve to ask my son if I bumped my fuckin' head."

"I'm sorry Marquez—" Detective Bell tried to get a word out, but she was cut short again.

"Didn't I say shut the fuck up!" Marquez yelled through the cellphone. "See, this is what happens when people forget who the fuck is responsible for every breath they take. Right, son?"

"Right, pop!" Rojo quickly said as his face grew more serious.

"But you're right about one thing, Detective," Marquez's voice was laced with anger. "You're officially done with us. I can fuckin' guarantee you that."

On Marquez's last words, his son Rojo looked over to the women on the couch once more. The detective was too shaken to notice what was transpiring behind her.

She nervously adjusted herself in her chair and looked over to Rojo. "I think y'all blowing this way out of proportion," The detective stammered again.

"It's too late detective. I tried to warn you," Rojo whispered. He shook his head and gave the detective a pitiful look. "I always love working with women. You want to know why?" Rojo's question stumped the detective. She couldn't recognize the expression on his face as he continued to speak. "I love workin' with women because people always underestimate just how fuckin' sneaky and downright conniving y'all can be."

Detective Bell opened her mouth to speak, but she never got out another word. A hot flash of adrenaline burned her veins when she felt a thick electrical cord suddenly fly around her neck. A fist came out of nowhere and struck her on the side of her temple. The stunned detective realized she was being attacked by Skittles and the women who were sitting behind her. She felt the cord tightened around her throat as Skittles tried to strangle her. Detective Bell sprang into action and swiftly stood to her feet. She reached for her weapon, but another woman quickly kicked the pistol out of her grip. A huge brawl ensued as the women jumped on the detective like a pack of lethal hyenas. She tried to fight back, but the women punched and kicked the detective mercilessly.

Rojo gritted his teeth as he watched the bloody fight. "Teach that bitch a lesson!" he yelled out.

Skittles and the women turned up the heat on Detective Bell and continued to beat her. She screamed out in pain as one of the women slammed her head against the hardwood desk.

"Hell yeah!" Rojo yelled out like he was watching a sporting event.

Blood leaked uncontrollably from Detective Bell's face. She teetered on the brink of consciousness as the cord continued to cut off her air. The women continued to punish her with brutal kicks and punches. The beating was too much to handle for the detective. She crumbled to the carpet in pain. The cord around her neck became even tighter. She was too weak and battered to fight any longer. The detective cried as she realized this could very well be the end of her life. Skittles cocked her leg back and kicked the detective in the face until she was knocked unconscious. Rojo jumped to his feet and stared at her like a savage. All of the women grabbed the electrical cord and pulled it tighter until the detective took her last breath.

Rojo coldly looked on as an unnerving silence fell over the room. He slowly exhaled when he realized Detective Bell was no longer breathing. He picked up the phone and walked around his desk. "Pop, it's done."

"Are you sure?" Marquez barked through the cellphone.

"I'm positive," Rojo fired back. "She's dead." The chilling words echoed through the office. Skittles and the women stood over the detective's body and waited from their next instructions. They looked over to their boss as he continued to speak to his father. "What do you want me to do with her?" Rojo asked.

"I don't care. Just make sure it don't come back to us," Marquez coldly responded.

"It won't," Rojo uttered.

"Now get back to Niko and find out who this fuckin' witness is," Marquez raised his voice. "I can't risk another trial. I don't care what you got to do. But make this motherfucker tell us somethin'."

"True. I'll make him talk, Pop," Rojo said. "What about Kimi?" There was a silence on the phone. Rojo knew his father was thinking about the question, and he waited for an answer. Rojo took another pull of his cigar and slowly blew out the smoke.

"Find her.....and kill her!" Marquez said.

"Say no more," Rojo responded. He disconnected the call and tossed the cellphone to his desk. He exhaled a thick cloud of smoke as he thought about his father's orders. Rojo knew Niko was the last key to getting his father out of jail and back on the street. Finding Kimi in the process wouldn't be easy, but he knew she couldn't get far. Rojo looked out into the night sky and over the buildings in Newark. He wondered where in the big bad city Kimi could be hiding.

Chapter 11

Sunday, October 13
10:35 am
Newark, NJ

ONE WEEK LATER

"Regardless if we like it or not, God is the grand architect of this entire universe. He designed every nature of our being. The good and the bad. The holy and the unholy. A lot of people wonder why some of us can be like angels...and yet some of us can be like animals. The difference in all of us lies in the power to choose. Situations come and go in our lives that test us. They tell us who we are. When that moment arrives...will you ascend to the level of an angel or will you descend into the devil's trap and become an animal? God can't choose for you...your family and your friends can't choose for you...your spouse can't choose for you...the choice is yours!"

The congregation cheered from the words of the animated pastor. The large church became electrified. Seated alone in the back row was Heidi Kachina. She never lifted her head. Her focus was on the cellphone in her lap. As the preacher delivered his compelling message, Heidi tapped on her phone and ignored the sermon. Her body was physically in the Lord's house, but her mind was in another place.

A few hours earlier, Heidi used the Sunday Service as an excuse to get away from Tycen. She had a lot on her mind, and had become consumed with the memory of Aaron Smith.

Her strange nightmares continued to haunt her, and she wanted to know why. With each passing day, her thirst for answers intensified. Heidi was ready to confront the demons from her past. She had arranged a secret meeting today with an old friend, and had used the church as the perfect cover.

Heidi's phone started buzzing in her lap. She clicked on the screen and read the text message.

I'm in the lobby.

The words made Heidi's heart jump. A rush of anxiety burned her veins. Heidi didn't know if she was emotionally prepared for this meeting, but she had come too far to turn back now. She looked around the sanctuary, eased from the pew, then carefully slipped out the back door into the quiet atrium of the church. She set her eyes on a stout woman, who stood calmly near the door to the building. The woman's face was hard as stone, and her cold stare could freeze a volcano. Heidi instantly recognized her scowl. The woman had aged harshly over the past few years. But even at sixty years young, Heidi knew this ruthless lady was still blood thirsty and more powerful as ever. Her name was Bethany Stanford, but she was notoriously known in the streets as Dirty Betty.

"Thanks for meeting me," Heidi said nervously, walking toward the door.

"Only your crazy ass can get me to step foot into a damn church," Dirty Betty responded. Her coarse voice echoed in the lobby.

"This was the only way I could meet you," Heidi responded. "I gotta be careful these days. My fiancé is so paranoid about me sabotaging his campaign."

"That's right...look at you. All grown up," Dirty Betty teased. "I see you got yourself a big time politician now. I'm not mad at you, girl. I saw him on the news the other night. He's gorgeous. I bet he can fuck like a Kentucky stallion."

Heidi put her finger up and looked around. She was shocked at Betty's vulgar language. Heidi tried her best to laugh off the statement. "Yea, he does fine," she whispered with a hint of embarrassment.

"Whatever." Betty quickly shook her head. "So what's so goddamn important? You said you got some money for me. What's going on?"

"Yes, Betty. I do got some money for you," Heidi dropped her voice and walked with Betty to the other side of the atrium. She handed Betty a yellow envelope and looked at her. "I need you to find two people for me."

"You know that's what I do," Betty coldly responded, and then cracked the envelope. She took one look at the thick stack of cash and smiled. "Nice…they must be some important people."

"Yes they are…well…at least. . .he is," Heidi stated.

"He?" Betty twisted her face. "Don't tell me that the politician's girl is looking for something on the side."

"No, Betty," Heidi snapped, giving her a stiff glare. "This is serious. I've been trying to find these people for a couple of years now. The first one is a girl named Judith Smith. I have no clue where she is. She used to work up here in Newark for a company called Datakorp."

Betty looked at the black and white photo of Judith Smith and nodded her head. "Okay," she said.

"Now the guy…his name is Aaron Smith," Heidi said.

"Any relation to Judith?" Betty quickly asked.

"No…I don't think so. I checked that out already," Heidi responded. "The address I had for him is no good. So I don't have a clue where you can start."

Betty looked at Heidi's eyes. She didn't recognize the icy expression. Heidi was dead serious and Betty wanted to know more. "So who is this guy?" Betty asked. "And why are you looking for him?"

"Damn, Betty. You need to know all of that?" Heidi shook her head. "You just can't find these people for me?"

"Listen smart ass!" Betty moved closer to Heidi. "I need to know what I'm getting my people into. Now…if you looking for a high school sweetheart so you can give him one last blowjob, then that's one thing. But if you need me to find this dude so you can cut his balls off...now that's something else. Get it?" Heidi nodded her head. "So which one is it?" Betty asked.

"I just need you to find him...that's it," Heidi responded. "And it's not for no damn blowjob."

"Is he dangerous?" Betty asked.

"Without a question," Heidi replied quickly, reminiscing about the last time she seen Aaron.

"So what do you want me to do when we find these motherfuckers?" Betty took another look at the money.

"Just let me know where they are. I just need a good address on them. Especially Aaron. I can take it from there." Heidi said, looking around quickly. She put her focus back on Dirty Betty. "I put everything in the envelope. That's everything that I could remember about them. And believe me. . .they are some hard people to track down."

"We'll find them," Betty grunted with confidence. She looked at the grainy pictures of Aaron and Judith in the envelope. "You just make sure you got the other half of my money ready when we get 'em."

"Trust me, that won't be a problem." Heidi tightened her jaw.

"Okay. So you sure you want to do this?" Betty asked and looked up to Heidi.

"Yes," Heidi responded and paused to think about the strange question. "Why you ask me that?"

"Once I get my people out there...I can't turn this off." Betty gave Heidi a serious expression. "I hope you really want to find them. They're not gonna stop until they track 'em down. No matter what. You understand?"

Heidi picked up on Betty's vibe. Dirty Betty had been a notorious gangster in Newark for many years. Despite her advancing age, she was still a dangerous woman in the city, and was connected to some of the most ruthless people throughout the state. Heidi was all too familiar with her tactics.

"I understand. Do what you gotta do." Heidi nodded. "I need to find them, and I really need to find Aaron."

"And how much do I get if we deliver them to you on a silver platter?" Betty asked coldly.

"What you mean?" Heidi responded.

"We can find them and bring them to you, if that's what you want." A devious expression grew on Betty's face.

Heidi felt nervous as she thought about the proposition. "I'll give you another fifteen thousand if you can make that happen," she said.

"Fifteen thousand each, right?" Betty cut her eyes to Heidi.

"Each!" Heidi nodded her head.

Betty's eyes lit up when she heard the number. She nodded her head and looked around.

"Consider it done. I'm on it." Betty looked at her watch. "Is that it? Are we done?"

"Yes. That's it." Heidi nodded. "Thanks for doing this for me."

"No need to thank me, this is business," Betty responded. She tucked the thick envelope under her arm and headed out the church.

Heidi looked down to her cellphone and took a deep breath. She was relieved that the meeting had been quick and painless. She knew Betty was the perfect person for the job of finding Aaron. Heidi checked the time, then decided to leave the church. She only had an hour to get changed and meet up with her fiancé Tycen.

Chapter 12

Sunday, October 13
11:07 am
Newark, NJ

"If you are heading downtown this afternoon, be prepared for a lot of stop-and-go traffic. Today is the big gathering at Military Park, organized by city hall and Mayor Gary Banks. Traffic will be diverted to Route 21 as officials brace for what should be a crowded event on this mild Sunday. The demonstration comes on the fifth anniversary of the alleged abduction of Lexi Hamilton. The mayor has managed to use Lexi's mysterious disappearance as a rallying point for the city. For more information about today's events. . ."

Asad reached for the remote control and turned off the television in the hotel room. He stood to his feet and continued to get dressed. A tense emotion came over him as he walked to the mirror on the far side of the room. He put on his suit jacket and gazed at his reflection. Today was the big rally in the park. Everyone was expecting a huge crowd. Asad knew his security team needed to be at their best this afternoon. He didn't like the idea of holding the rally while things in the city were volatile. The mayor had agreed that the event was risky, but he had insisted on standing strong in the face of danger. Asad had no choice but to accept his brother's decision and support him. Even today, as he doubled checked his weapon, he tucked away his fear and focused on the goal of keeping his brother safe.

A loud knock on the door suddenly shook Asad out of his thoughts. He was clearly on edge. He almost laughed at himself as he walked toward the door. "Who's there?" he yelled out.

"It's me, man. Open up!"

Asad smiled at the familiar voice. He swung the door open and nodded toward his best friend, Dante. "Almost that time, huh?" Dante said and walked into the hotel room.

"Yessir, I'm locked and loaded," Asad confidently responded and gently tapped on his gun holster.

Dante shook Asad's hand while they stood in the middle of the room. Asad checked out Dante's Versini black suit, then gave Dante a thumbs-up. Asad looked at his friend's face and could tell that he was slightly nervous. Today was Dante's first day on the job. Asad knew the pressure would be high, but he was confident Dante was going to make a great addition to his security team.

"So, how you? You ready for this madness today?" Asad asked and gathered the rest of his things.

"Without a doubt." Dante smirked. "I'm just happy you put me on the team."

"No problem." Asad nodded his head. "I told you I got you."

"True," Dante said. "But man, you know I was so tempted to bring my piece with me."

"Your piece?" Asad quickly asked. "What? Your gun?"

"Yeah, man. You know I feel naked without it." Dante shook his head.

"Shit, I know that feeling," Asad agreed. "But that's all Gary right there. You know if it was up to me I would let you have two guns out there today. But Gary don't want you strapped up until he can fully trust you. You know he's extra paranoid 'cause of his position."

"Oh yea, I get it," Dante said with an uneven expression. "And let me tell you...they went hard on that background check, too."

"Why you say that?" Asad asked.

"Man, they grilled me all week." Dante made a whistling sound and chuckled. "They asked me everything about my jobs, where I went to school, my girlfriends, my family... shit, everything. I thought they was about to ask me if I was a still a virgin, damn." Asad started laughing as Dante continued to rant about his experience. "I'm serious, Asad. You think it's funny. It was crazy. They even asked me for blood."

"Huh? Blood?" Asad was shocked.

"Yea, dude." Dante chuckled again. "Your brother don't play. I had to give up two blood samples."

"Goddamn. That must be something new." Asad twisted his face and grabbed his keys. "Yea, Gary is growing more paranoid by the day. I'll ask him about that blood thing. That's kinda crazy right there."

"It's all good. So, what do you need me to do today?" Dante asked as the men walked out of the hotel room.

"I'm going to keep you close to me," Asad responded as they continued down the hallway. "I have two security teams working today, and I need you on the stage with me."

"That's cool." Dante nodded his head.

"It's gonna be a lot of people out there," Asad said. "I need all eyes on the crowd."

Dante made a mental note of the instructions as the men headed to the lobby of the hotel. Dante felt a nervous rumble in his stomach. He thought about the gravity of the day. He was now a member of the exclusive security team for the mayor of Newark. A feeling of pride came over him as they entered the lobby.

A group of ten security men approached Asad and he introduced them all to Dante.

"Fellas, this is Dante Harper." Asad nodded toward his best friend. "This is his first day, so keep an eye on him, and let's keep things tight today."

"Sure thing, chief!" one of the men yelled out from the small huddle.

Asad grew serious and confident, sensing his team was ready for the big event. He raised his voice as he continued to bark out his instructions in the lobby. "This is not a typical assignment today, fellas," Asad shouted. "City hall has been getting a lot of threats lately, and people are really hyped in the city. So don't take this rally lightly. Stay on top of your game. And trust your instincts out there. Is everybody ready?"

"Yes, Sir!" the men shouted out.

"Good!" Asad nodded. "Let's keep Mr. Banks safe today. And let me hear it…!"

All of the members of the security team yelled in unison. "ALL EYES ON THE CROWD…..ALL WEAPONS OFF SAFTEY….AND TOTAL FOCUS ON THE MAYOR!"

"Boom!" Asad shouted. "Let's go."

Dante's heart started racing as the motivating chant echoed in his mind. The security team mobilized and headed out of the glass doors of the hotel. Dante followed close behind Asad. Another rush of adrenaline hit Dante when he laid eyes on a row of four black SUVs. The security team rushed over to the trucks and got inside.

Asad warily looked around and opened the doors to the last vehicle. "We're riding in this one." Asad motioned for his best friend.

Dante got inside the front of the SUV and noticed Gary Banks was already comfortably seated in the back. Dante tightened up his demeanor as the mayor gave him a hard stare. "Good afternoon, sir," Dante stuttered, clearly nervous.

Asad got in the back of the SUV and sat next to his brother. The vehicle's driver waited for Asad's command, and then the trucks pulled away from the hotel. The convoy sped down the main streets, headed downtown. Gary took one last look at his notes, then gave Dante another strange glare from the back seat. Asad looked over to Gary and ignored his suspicious expression. He needed to keep his focus on today's assignment. The rally was going to be a huge challenge. Asad tried to prepare himself for the unpredictable event. He thought about his best friend in the front seat, and hoped Dante was ready to prove to the mayor that he was worthy of the job. Asad looked out the window as the vehicle made its way to Military Park.

Chapter 13

Sunday, October 13
12:02 pm
Newark, NJ

A few miles away in a buzzing news studio, Tycen paced back and forth and rehearsed his talking points in the green room. He was just minutes away from being interviewed by a national news network to discuss the mayoral campaign. His bid for the highest office in the city was catching steam. The rising call for change in Newark was becoming louder with each passing day, and Tycen was poised to challenge the current administration. Tycen was well aware of the large rally that was being held by Mayor Gary Banks just a few miles away. But that didn't stop Tycen and his team. They wanted to use today's interview as an opportunity to outline Tycen's budget plan for the city.

Watching him closely was his campaign manager, Lawrence Cohen. Despite standing at only five feet and three inches, Lawrence's presence was twice as large as his stature. The sharply dressed man was no stranger to these pressure packed situations. Most of his clients were high profile businessmen, so Lawrence knew exactly what Tycen was going through today. The campaign was heating up, and Lawrence knew Tycen was pushing himself to make all the right moves. "You'll do fine," Lawrence called out and interrupted the nervous silence in the room.

"I hope so," Tycen anxiously responded. "I have a feeling this is going to be intense."

"Oh, it will be." Lawrence smiled. "It's going to be very intense. But that's a good thing. People are very curious about you and how you plan to turn this city around."

"That's what I'm afraid of," Tycen admitted. "What if the people don't agree with the plan?"

"That doesn't matter," Lawrence quickly replied, then checked his phone.

"What do you mean…it doesn't matter?" Tycen asked and continued to pace back and forth.

"Tycen, if they do agree with you… great!" Lawrence responded. "If they don't agree with you…then that's still fine. At least we'll know they were listening. The goal is to get the debate started and to challenge what the current mayor has to offer. Believe me, you will do fine."

Tycen stopped pacing and looked over to his campaign manager. Hearing a different twist on today's strategy made him feel less nervous. "Okay Lawrence." Tycen nodded. "That makes sense. I guess that's why you make the big money around here."

Lawrence laughed at the quick joke and looked up from his phone. He was relieved to see his client was taking some of the pressure off of himself. Tycen looked at the clock and rehearsed a few more talking points. A loud thump startled the men, and they quickly turned around.

"I'm so sorry…am I too late?" Heidi said as she quickly rushed through the door with a worried look on her face.

"Oh no, sweetie, you are right on time." Tycen smiled and walked over to his fiancée.

"Good. The traffic was murder out there." Heidi tried to catch her breath.

Tycen gave her a quick kiss. "I'm glad you could make it." He hugged her.

"You know I had to come down to support you, baby." Heidi smiled and tightly squeezed her man. "I'm so proud of you."

"Thank you."

"Are you nervous?"

"Of course not," Tycen chuckled.

"Liar…!" Heidi playfully teased her fiancé. "It's okay, baby. They are going to love you out there."

Tycen's entire mood changed once Heidi stepped into the room. Seeing her gorgeous face calmed his nerves. Just having her at the news studio made him feel like he could accomplish anything.

Lawrence walked over toward the couple and reached out his hand. "How are you, Heidi? Glad you could make it," Lawrence greeted.

"Thanks." Heidi smiled and shook his hand. "It's good to see you." She felt uncomfortable when she looked into Lawrence's eyes. There was something odd about his demeanor. His facial expression became uneven, and his smile didn't match his shady handshake. Heidi quickly looked away from him and turned her attention back to Tycen.

"I made dinner reservations for us tonight." She reached for Tycen's necktie. She tightened up his suit, then brushed lint off of his shoulders.

"Where are we going tonight?" Tycen asked.

"It's a surprise." Heidi smiled again. "I think you'll like it."

Before the couple could continue the conversation a female intern gently knocked on the door to the green room. "Mr. Wakefield?" the young intern politely called out. "They are ready for you."

"Great." Lawrence squeezed his hands together. "This is it."

"Seems so." Tycen nervously cleared his throat and nodded his head. He tried to shake off the last second jitters. He kissed his Heidi on the lips again, then looked over to Lawrence.

"Just remember to be yourself and speak slowly and

clearly," Lawrence advised. "The goal today is to introduce your plan to the voters. We will win them over later."

"Got it." Tycen gave his campaign manager thumbs up. He headed toward the door, then turned back to Heidi. "Love you, babe."

"Love you back." Heidi smiled and gave him a confident look. She watched as Tycen walked out the door, headed to the main studio. She was extremely proud of Tycen, and knew he was going to do well in the interview. Heidi walked to the opposite side of the room and sat down on a small sofa.

Lawrence cut his eyes at Heidi and decided to take a seat directly across from her. He played with his phone for a few seconds, then placed it on the table. The room fell silent. They eagerly waited for Tycen to appear on the television monitor in the green room. "This is exciting, right?" Lawrence blurted in an attempt to make small talk.

"It sure is," Heidi quietly answered.

"So where are you from?" Lawrence asked.

Heidi dropped her eyes and turned to the campaign manager. She was baffled by the question. "Where am I from?" she asked. She wanted to make sure she had heard him correctly.

"Yes. Are you from Newark?" Lawrence asked and gave her a direct expression.

"Born and raised," Heidi quickly answered with a slight attitude.

"Oh okay," Lawrence said. "I don't know why I thought you were from Philadelphia."

"My mother is from Philadelphia," Heidi said.

"Got it." Lawrence took a mental note. "So all of this political talk about Newark doesn't seem to faze you."

"Not at all," Heidi responded and twisted in her seat. "Tycen is my fiancé, and I'm going to support him in everything he does."

"That's wonderful," Lawrence said in a bland tone. "You guys make a beautiful couple."

"Thank you," Heidi whispered and forced a fake smile to

come to her face.

The room fell silent again but Lawrence was determined to keep their conversation going.

"So are you ready for all of this?" he asked.

"Yes," Heidi responded, trying her best not to look agitated. She dropped her eyebrows and glared at the campaign manager for a brief moment.

"That's good." Lawrence sat up in his chair and rubbed his chin. "You know politics is a dirty game. You have to have very thick skin to be in this business."

"I understand that." Heidi nodded. "Me and Tycen talk about this all the time, and he knows I'm ready for this. Like I said, I will do anything to support him, and I'm going to be right by his side. I love him."

"There's no doubt about that," Lawrence whispered. "But you know what they say about being in love."

"No…I don't know what they say," Heidi mumbled with a tight face.

"They say it's very easy to deceive and manipulate the person who loves you the most," Lawrence coldly whispered.

"What the hell is that supposed to mean?" Heidi quickly fired off. She felt offended by the statement.

"Come on now, Heidi. Cut the shit," Lawrence boldly fired back. "Tycen might be blinded by that pretty face you got, but I can see right through your bullshit."

"What?" Heidi raised her voice. "What is your problem? Are you on medication or something?"

"Listen, Heidi. I didn't work my ass off to make it this far and come up short." Lawrence grew serious as the mood in the room quickly turned sour. "Tycen has a real shot at being the mayor, and I don't think he realizes how quickly you can screw this all up."

"Listen Lawrence…" Heidi also sat up in her seat. "I don't know what the hell crawled up ya ass today, but you need to calm the hell down and watch the way you speak to me. I'm not screwing nothing up over here."

"Is that right?" Lawrence started to raise his voice. "Who is Jayson Carter?"

"What?" Heidi blurted.

"Come on now, Heidi. You heard me," Lawrence continued to push. "Who the hell is Jayson Carter?"

"He was my fiancé," Heidi responded with confusion.

"And he died right?" Lawrence snapped.

"Right!" Heidi lowered her voice.

"Hear me clearly, Heidi." Lawrence unconsciously looked around the room and continued to speak. "I don't think we ever had a chance to talk like this before, but let me tell you what I do for a living. I protect my clients from looking bad and being embarrassed out there. I need to protect them from their enemies. I also need to protect them from their family and friends...and...from their lovers. I've been trying to figure out your angle and what's your game. And you better believe that I don't like what I'm seeing."

Heidi gave Lawrence an icy stare, and she didn't know how to respond. His words had caught her off guard.

"Now I'm going to ask you a question, and I don't give a shit how you take this," Lawrence raised his voice even louder. He was in rare form. "I know Jayson Carter died, but the question is how did he die?"

"Are you fuckin' serious?" Heidi snapped. The question brought back a rush of emotions that she had been trying to keep hidden. The night her ex-fiancé died flashed into her mind.

"Answer the question, Heidi," Lawrence yelled over the table. "Unless you got something to hide."

"Listen, asshole. I don't know what you think you know about me, but you're dead wrong," Heidi shouted. "You don't know a damn thing about my life or what I've been through. Jayson died in a fire. Tycen knows that."

"Of course Tycen knows about the fire," Lawrence said and gave Heidi a slick expression. "But tell me something about that night that Tycen doesn't know. I read the investigation report. You were in that same fire, and it's funny that you made it out alive but your ex-fiancé died. You don't find that's a bit odd?"

Heidi felt a boiling rush of anger in the pit of her stomach. She didn't like the feeling of being questioned by Lawrence, and decided it was time to end this conversation. "I don't need this shit from you today, Lawrence." She waved him off. "If you read the report, then you know it's nothing more to the story. It was a fuckin' tragedy. I don't appreciate you questioning me like this. I'm trying to move on with my life. It's no crime in that." Heidi stood to her feet and gathered herself. She was angry. "Tell Tycen I will see him later. I don't need to stick around here and listen to your bullshit."

A crooked smile came to Lawrence's face as he watched Heidi struggle to gather her composure. The room fell silent again as Heidi slowly made her way to the door. Lawrence grabbed his phone from the table and stood to his feet. He waited until Heidi reached the door and yelled out to her. "I know about Aaron!" he blurted. Heidi froze in her tracks. The name sent a bitter chill down her back. Heidi's freezing told Lawrence he'd struck a sensitive cord.

"I know everything, Heidi," Lawrence lowered his voice. "It took me a while, but I found out everything. I know you are still looking for Aaron to this day. I know about Datakorp and the robberies. Believe me, Heidi, I'm very close to piecing it all together."

"Why are you doing this?" Heidi whispered as she slowly turned around and looked at the campaign manager.

"I told you, Heidi," Lawrence said. "I came too far to let you fuck up this opportunity. When were you going to tell Tycen the truth about Aaron?"

Heidi thought about the question and closed her mouth. The shocking revelation of her past stunned her. Lawrence was holding a lot of ammunition, and Heidi realized it was best to come clean with him. "First of all…there is nothing major to tell," she softly responded. "I was waiting for the right time."

"The right time?" Lawrence snapped. "Heidi, your fiancé is running for mayor. Do you understand the gravity of that statement? There is no time to waste. Why are you still searching for Aaron anyway? What exactly happened between you and him?"

Heidi paused for a moment and let the question swirl around in her mind. Aaron's face invaded her thoughts. Heidi felt herself being thrust into the dark shadows of her past. Her emotions were running high. She looked over to Lawrence. Something deep inside of Heidi caused her mouth to slowly open. She decided to make a shocking admission. "It's true that I knew Aaron…or at least I thought I knew him." Heidi's words had to fight through the heavy emotion in her voice. "I met Aaron after Jayson died, and he helped me through a very rough patch in my life. But, for some reason, everything started to fall apart after I met him."

"Everything like what?" Lawrence's tone grew more forceful. "Talk to me, Heidi. What do you mean 'everything started to fall apart'?"

"I don't know how to explain it," Heidi strained her voice. She felt compelled to continue. "A lot of shit just started spinning out of control. People started dyin' around me. It was crazy. And Aaron turned out to be nothing like the person I thought he was."

"So why are you still searching for him?" Lawrence shouted at Heidi.

"I'm not searching for him anymore," Heidi raised her voice again. "That part of my life is over. I've moved on."

"Don't lie to me, Heidi," Lawrence yelled. "We know you are looking for him."

"I don't know where you're gettin' your information from, but they are wrong," Heidi said. "I've moved on."

"Heidi, I don't know if you realize it or not, but you're not in a position to be stubborn right now," Lawrence said.

"What?" she asked.

"Heidi, you walk around here all high and mighty. Acting

like your ass is squeaky clean when you got all of this dirt on you. We did a number of background checks on you, and what we found was downright damaging. Your name was connected to a million-dollar scam. Don't you realize that?" Lawrence continued to stare at Heidi as he spoke. "You were being investigated for years, and now we find out that you are chasing down this Aaron guy? What is with you? After Tycen's interview today everyone is going to know the name of Tycen Wakefield. Now I can't have anything coming up that's going to blow this chance for us. So you got until the end of the day to tell Tycen everything."

"Are you serious?" Heidi shook her head.

"Yes, Heidi! I'm dead fucking serious," Lawrence snapped at her. "You need to tell Tycen everything today or I will do it myself!"

Heidi had heard enough of Lawrence's threats. She turned around and stormed out of the green room. A defeated feeling came over her as she thought about her past. She felt her demons starting to resurface. Hearing Aaron's name had put her emotions in a state of turmoil. She felt angered by Lawrence's interrogation, but she realized she needed to brace herself for the worst. How would Tycen react if he knew the truth about Aaron? A million questions swirled around her mind. She left the news studio and decided to head home. She wanted to be alone. She needed to get her thoughts together and come up with the best way to come clean with Tycen.

Chapter 14

Sunday, October 13
12:36pm
Military Park
Newark, NJ

"As most of you in this audience already know, I was born and raised in this beautiful city of Newark. So it makes me sick to my stomach to witness all of the violence and mayhem that has crippled our city for these past few years. Although many of us don't want to admit it, believe me, there are downright ugly people in this city who would love to tear us down, piece by piece. They don't care that you and I wake up every morning with the sole purpose of making this a better place to live, work and raise our children. That's why I wanted to call this emergency rally today to send a clear message to these hoodlums and hooligans. I want them to know that we will not be moved and we will fight to the bitter end to save our city!"

A thunderous roar resounded from the frustrated crowd in Military Park. The emotional tone of the speech seemed to energize the audience like a Sunday morning sermon. The enormous crowd of nearly one thousand strong gathered to hear the much-needed message about the harsh conditions that plagued the city of Newark.

The Honorable Mayor Gary Banks stood at the podium and briefly took a moment to let the words of his well-prepared speech connect with the crowd. For the past four years, Gary Banks had tried to govern Newark with a fair yet forceful policy. Despite his best efforts, the city of Newark was constantly rocked by an explosion of violent crimes and poverty levels, which were never before seen in the city's colorful history. Residents were losing their homes in record numbers. Violent gang members were terrorizing school-aged children, and the local government's mounting corruption continued to hinder any hopes of moving the city forward. With the election coming up, Gary wanted to the opportunity to speak to the people of Newark. He needed to reassure them of his commitment to bring prosperity back to the city.

The poised mayor calmly readjusted his tie and looked out into the vast sea of worried faces that seemed to be searching for answers in unison. The fall weather was cool and breezy, but that didn't stop the fire from burning in Gary Banks's mind. He knew if he had any chance of re-igniting the voter's confidence in his policies, he had to deliver a powerful message today.

"You know, when I was younger, the people of this city used to call Newark the Brick City," Gary Banks continued to speak in a forceful tone. "I think a lot of people believed it was because of the cobblestone that was used to pave some of the North Ward streets. Other people believed that we were nicknamed the Brick City because of all the housing projects that sprung up back in the day, like the young kids would say. But I have another theory." Gary Banks took a short pause and glanced into the audience again. "If you know anything about the people of Newark, you know that we are strong and resilient like concrete. We don't succumb to the pressures of those forces that try to knock us down. We stand strong in the face of adversity, and our unbreakable bond is what keeps us united in solidarity. I ask you to stand with me today strong as bricks and without fear as we vow to take back our city together! Are you with me?"

The crowd erupted once again in response to the mayor's powerful words. The loud roar could be heard for blocks as the fired-up residents cheered in triumph. Among those moved by the speech was Gary's younger brother, Asad. He had heard a number of Gary's speeches, but none more commanding than today's. As he did for the past four years, Asad stood watchfully behind his older brother and scanned the faces in the crowd for any threats of danger. Asad knew that the city was in an unpredictable state and everyone could feel a massive tension building around town. As Asad looked over the crowd, he realized that it was filled with all types of people. It was difficult for him to recognize anything out of place. Asad turned around and looked at his best friend. Dante was watching the crowd carefully. He gave Asad a confident nod to let him know he was being vigilant.

Asad turned his focus back to the crowd. He took notice of a church-group of seniors and made a mental check. He also turned his attention to a group of high school students and made another mental check. A buzzing noise forced Asad to turn his attention to the rear of the stage, but he noticed it was just a couple of city workers that were blowing leaves and maintaining the park grounds during the rally. The mayor began to speak again, and Asad turned his attention away from the leaf blowers and back to the crowd.

"What we must do is work together, and work together diligently to return our city back to greatness," Gary Banks yelled into the microphones. "As residents and law abiding citizens we all must do our part. If you see something illegal happening in your neighborhood, you have to say something to somebody. It is our responsibility to take care of the places we live first. That is how we win."

People began cheering again, and Asad continued to keep a watchful eye. He noticed a group of four young men gathering together, just a few yards away from the front of the stage. He took a mental note. At first glance, the men looked to be harmless, but Asad's intuition reminded him to never trust appearances. He warily surveyed the young men as Gary Banks continued to address the audience.

"Last month alone, we seized nearly two hundred illegal firearms in this city. That is ridiculous," Gary yelled. "Some of these people are our family members and friends. We know they are doing wrong, and we refuse to speak up. Yet, these illegal weapons are used to tear down our city every single day."

"That's a bunch of bullshit!" an angry man yelled from the center of the crowd. "You are a fuckin' liar, Gary Banks!"

The audience gasped at the outburst.

"Show some respect!" an older woman quickly screamed at the man.

Asad's eyes widened as he zeroed in on the heated exchange brewing from the audience.

"No, fuck that!" the man screamed again. "The mayor is up there lying, and you expect me to be quiet?"

"Wait one minute," Gary Banks calmly responded. "Sir, if you want to dispute something you've heard today, I have no problem with that. But you must watch your language. We have children in the audience."

"Well, with all due respect, Mr. Banks...you are a fuckin' hypocrite and you know it!" the man continued to yell to the top of his lungs. The entire audience seemed to turn their focus away from the stage and toward to the angry man as he continued to yell at the mayor. "How can you say that our family members and friends are criminals, when you are the biggest fuckin' criminal there is in Newark!"

A few groans and moans could be heard emerging from the crowd. A few residents started to agree with the angry man, but most wanted him to remain silent.

"Sir, you may not agree with my politics, but falsely labeling me as a criminal is not going to help us rebuild this city," Gary Banks coolly responded to the man's hostile words.

"Rebuild this city?" the angry man shouted again. "How in the hell can you talk about rebuilding something that you and your cronies are helping to tear down? All of that shady shit you do in the dark is going to come to the light, Mr. Banks.

You betta believe that."

"Sir, you are so disrespectful!" a young woman yelled from the rear of the audience.

"No, let him speak!" another man shouted from the right section of the crowd. "At least he's keeping it real!"

"If you don't want to hear what Mayor Banks has to say, why don't you go home?" an older gentleman raised his voice.

"Fuck all y'all!" the angry man screamed. He was clearing growing more aggravated by the second. "And I tell you what...y'all better shut the fuck up before I show you just how disrespectful I can get!"

On his last words a small scuffle broke out. People started shoving the angry man, trying to get him to leave the rally. Asad noticed that the gathering was beginning to unravel and decided it was time to cut things short. He slowly walked up behind Gary and put his arm around his shoulder. "I'm sorry, big brother, but this is getting out of hand," Asad cautiously whispered. "I don't like where this is going."

Gary slowly nodded in agreement as he looked out into the crowd. The minor fracas seemed to escalate into an all-out brawl in a matter of seconds. People in the audience started shoving each other, and the shoving quickly turned into swinging. A small platoon of Newark Police Officers rushed into the middle of the crowd and tried to maintain order.

"Wait, people! There is no need for this type of behavior," Gary pleaded to everyone to try to defuse the tension.

A few terrified women screamed and grabbed their children. The crowd erupted again into a violent melee, and more police officers rushed in to make sure the feud didn't explode into a full riot.

Asad turned his focus to the young men who were gathering in front of the stage. An eerie feeling came over him. He noticed that despite all the fighting that was going on in the center of the crowd, these young men kept their eyes on Gary. Asad sprang into action and stepped in front of his brother. He quickly motioned for his security detail to secure the mayor while he secured the front of the stage.

"Team Bravo…!" Asad yelled out. "Make a path and escort Mayor Banks to the secondary vehicle. Team Alpha stay here and secure the stage. Dante, I need you to shadow the mayor. Stay close to him and make sure he gets to the vehicle safely."

"I got you…!" Dante shouted out. Dante grabbed Gary by the shoulders and rushed him off the back of the stage.

Asad reached for his weapon as four other security members joined him. With his gun and his security force by his side, Asad stared down the young men in front of the stage who seemed to be contemplating what to do next. Asad's intuition was correct again. The young men were there to do harm to the mayor, and, for the moment, it seemed as if Asad had foiled the plot. The tallest man in the group stood off to the side, sizing up the security team. When they made eye contact, a rush of adrenaline attacked the pit of Asad's stomach. A crooked smirk came to the tall man's face. Asad realized something was wrong.

A drumroll of gunshots rang out from the back of the stage. Asad ducked for cover in a panic and raised his gun. He quickly spun around as more bullets ferociously flew through the air, sending everyone in the park running for their lives. Asad managed to take cover near a pile of steel chairs. He got a good look at the gunmen behind the stage and noticed that his second security team was under heavy fire.

"Shit!" Asad yelled out. He took a closer look and realized that the maintenance men with the leaf blowers were not city workers after all. They were two thugs in fake uniforms, and the leaf blowers were used to conceal their assault rifles.

His second security team tried to fight them off, but they were outmatched by the combat-ready firepower. The thugs moved in relentlessly.

Dante tried to get the mayor to safety, but the chaotic scene was spiraling out of control. Gary stumbled and fell to the turf. Dante tried to act fast and picked up Mayor Banks. Another round of gunshots rang out. Three bullets tore through Dante's back and neck, and Dante dropped to the ground. He never knew what hit him. He died instantly.

"Oh GOD!" Asad screamed as he watched his best friend get cut down by the thugs.

A loud bang rocked the crowd, and it seemed like a war was erupting. Asad realized he had to act fast. He looked around and noticed that most of the Newark Officers were trying to maintain the chaos in the crowd. The officers had no idea the true threat was behind the stage. Realizing that they were running out of time, Asad called out the orders to his first unit.

"Team Alpha!" Asad shouted. "On my signal, I need heavy cover-fire to back down those leaf blowers. I'll grab Gary, but y'all better cover my ass!"

"What's the signal, chief?" one of the security members yelled out.

Without answering the question, Asad bravely stood to his feet and zeroed in on the group of men near the front of the stage. He couldn't tell if the men were armed, but he refused to take any chances. Asad singled out the tall man who suspiciously smiled at him, and then let off two gunshots toward him. One bullet painfully struck the man in the arm, and another one caught him on the side of his chest. The other young men scattered like wild horses, fearing they would be next to fall victim to Asad's rage. The second security team picked up on the signal and began to fire bullets toward the leaf blowers behind the stage.

Powerful gunshots and automatic fire transformed Military Park into a battle zone. The violent exchange between the thugs and the security team gave Asad a small window of opportunity to save his brother's life. Despite the deadly consequences, Asad jumped off the back of the stage to find the mayor crawling on his knees, searching for cover. Bullets skipped and ricocheted around the men, but Asad seemed unfazed. He snatched his brother up by the shoulder, and then rushed him off toward the black SUV that was parked a few hundred feet away.

"Keep moving!" Asad yelled out.

Gary frantically rushed toward the truck and Asad followed close behind, protecting his brother with a storm of gunfire. The plan worked to perfection as the leaf blowers scrambled for cover. Gary reached the SUV first, fearfully jumping into the back seat. Asad realized his brother was safe, and then secured in the vehicle. He turned around to check on his security team.

Three of his men were down, and two others were badly wounded. Asad looked over at Dante's lifeless body on the ground. He couldn't believe his eyes. A heavy feeling of grief flooded his chest. Asad was tempted to run to Dante. Another loud bang brought Asad back to reality. He didn't have much time to get his brother away from the park and back to a secured location. He reluctantly jumped in the front seat of the truck and fired up the engine.

"Gary, are you good back there?" Asad shouted toward the backseat. "Are you hit?"

"No…!" Gary yelled. His voice cracked with fear. "No… .I'm good!"

Asad punched the gas and sped away from the park. "I fuckin' can't believe this shit!" Asad shouted and furiously banged his fist on the steering wheel.

The heated gun battle boiled his blood and filled his mind with revenge. He knew the mayor had a lot of enemies, but had no clue of who would be bold enough to make a move on Gary in a public arena. "Whoever did this shit is fuckin dead!" Asad yelled again, pushing the SUV through the Newark streets. He knew he had a short amount of time to find out who was behind the assassination attempt, but his first job was to get Gary to safety. He looked in the rearview mirror to check on his brother. "Don't worry, big bro. You're safe now," Asad reassured.

Gary dropped his head in his hands and tried to calm himself. He was almost in tears from the rush of fear that overcame him. He couldn't believe how fast things had spiraled out of control, but he was beyond grateful that his brother, Asad, was there to protect him. He looked out the window as the SUV sped down the street. The mayor couldn't help but reflect on how close he had come to meeting his own demise.

Chapter 15

Sunday, October 13
4:38 pm
Newark, NJ

A few hours later, Heidi nervously twisted her engagement ring as she drove through downtown Newark. She was extremely jittery after she'd heard about the drama in Military Park. The news of an assassination attempt rocked the city of Newark. People everywhere were stunned by the brazen shooting.

Despite the violent history of the city, nothing so wicked had ever happened to an elected official before today's incident. No one could believe that Mayor Gary Banks was almost gunned down in broad daylight. Everyone was on edge including Tycen Wakefield.

Tycen called his fiancée an hour earlier, requesting that she come down to his office. She heard the distress in his voice and didn't hesitate to follow his instructions. As she made her way back downtown, she didn't know what to expect. Heidi punched the gas, rushing to be by Tycen's side.

A few minutes later, her phone started buzzing in her lap. Heidi felt relieved when she read the name on the display. "Hey Mom," Heidi answered, forcing a smile to come to her face.

"Child, what in the world is going on down there?" Pearl

gasped through the phone.

"I know, right?" Heidi responded. "This is crazy."

"I've been watching it on the news all afternoon. It's everywhere," Pearl said. "Is the mayor okay? Was he shot?"

"I really don't know, Mom," Heidi responded. "I'm heading down now to see Tycen, so I'll find out everything in a few. Are you okay, Mom? How are you feeling?"

"I'm okay," Pearl uttered. "I'm still having this nagging pain on my side, but I'll be fine."

"Mom, I keep telling you to get that checked out," Heidi raised her voice. "Is the pain getting worse?"

"Wait a minute. Now…I keep forgetting. Did I carry you for nine months or did you carry me?" Pearl snapped.

"Huh?" Heidi quickly responded.

"I keep forgetting….I need you to refresh my memory. It sounded like you was my mother for a minute. You talk to me like you raised me," Pearl joked.

"Whatever, Mom. I'm being serious. Don't take that type of stuff lightly," Heidi sounded concerned. "You have to get that pain checked out soon."

"I will." Pearl dismissed her daughter's statement.

Heidi noticed her mother becoming defensive, so she decided not to push the issue. She turned her vehicle onto a busy street and slowed. Tycen's office was just ahead. "Okay Mom, I have to call you back," Heidi said. "I need to make sure my baby is good."

"Okay, Heidi," Pearl said. "Please be careful. And don't forget to call me later."

"I won't, Mom," Heidi whispered. "Goodbye."

Heidi hung up the phone and pulled up to the front of Tycen's building. She felt her stomach turning as she parked her vehicle. She started to become more nervous, and she didn't know why. She parked the car and grabbed her bag. Another tense emotion came over her as she quickly rushed into the building.

Tycen's campaign headquarters was louder than Times

Square on New Year's Eve. Telephones, computer screens, tablets and televisions were buzzing with bulletins surrounding Mayor Gary Banks. Everyone in the office scrambled to find out more information behind the drama at the rally. Heidi walked into the main area and couldn't believe the scene. She was approached by a young intern with a stack of folders in his hands.

"Hello, Ms. Kachina." The young man smiled at Heidi. "Mr. Wakefield wanted me to bring you straight to his office once you arrived."

"Okay." Heidi nodded her head. She followed close behind the young man as they walked through the busy headquarters. The intern walked straight to Tycen's office and gently knocked on the door.

"It's open," Tycen yelled out.

The young man opened the door and looked at Tycen. "Sorry to bother you, Mr. Wakefield. Your fiancée is here," the intern announced.

"Okay…please let her in," Tycen said.

"By the way, sir," the intern continued. "The people from CNN just called back. They informed me that they are sending a car for you. They want you to do the live interview today."

"Okay," Tycen said. "Let me know when they arrive."

The intern nodded toward Tycen, and then stepped aside.

Heidi walked by the young man and entered. She smiled when she laid eyes on her handsome fiancé. Tycen was standing behind his large desk, reading over a few sheets of paper. Heidi noticed he was clearly on edge and walked over to him. "Hey, sweetie. How are you?" Heidi sang and gave him a comforting hug.

"Hey babe," Tycen spoke softly. He kissed his fiancée and looked at her.

"I hope I'm not too late," Heidi whispered as the couple made eye contact. "I tried to get down here as soon as I could."

"No sweetie, you're not too late." Tycen looked at Heidi. His eyes were distant, and Heidi could tell something was heavy on his mind. "This shouldn't take too long. I spoke to Lawrence about an hour ago, and he said he wanted to meet with us…together. He said it was important."

Heidi's face grew stiff once she heard Lawrence's name. Her bitter conversation with the campaign manager flashed into her mind. Heidi finally realized why she was feeling uneasy.

Tycen notice her mood changing and looked at her. "Is that okay with you, babe?" he softly asked.

"Oh yes. I don't mind," Heidi stuttered as she snapped back to reality. "What does he want to meet about?"

Before Tycen could answer the question, the door to his office swung open. Heidi stared at the short man walking through the door. It was Lawrence.

"Hey guys…great…both of you are here," Lawrence said. He sounded out of breath. "Can we do the meeting now?"

"Of course," Tycen responded and grabbed his fiancée by the hand. He walked her over to the middle of the office, and they took a seat at a small round table.

Lawrence sat down across from the couple and pulled out a small notebook. "Wild news about Gary Banks, huh?" Lawrence looked over to Tycen, trying his best to break the ice.

"Very wild news," Tycen mumbled.

"Just to let you know, I have made a lot of calls to my sources out there. I'm still trying to get some hard data on the condition of the mayor," Lawrence gasped. "I forgot to ask you Tycen, how did the rest of the interview go earlier?"

"It was solid." Tycen nodded. "I think we accomplished a lot with that one."

"I'm sorry I had to leave the news studio so abruptly." Lawrence glanced over to Heidi. "I needed to gather some very important information."

Heidi's facial expression never changed. She picked up on the double-talk coming from Lawrence.

"No problem at all," Tycen said. "So what's the game plan

for this Gary Banks situation?"

"Well, first we need to release a statement," Lawrence said. "I have one of the interns drafting a standard one now. The statement will have the basic jargon in it. You know...we're sorry about the news, justice will prevail...blah blah blah."

"Okay," Tycen nodded his head.

"Now, I did hire a separate security team to come in for extra protection." Lawrence started to look over his notes.

"Protection from what?" Tycen asked and glared at his campaign manager.

"We have to take all precautions, Tycen," Lawrence continued. "It's better to be safe than sorry. There are real shooters out there now."

Tycen nodded his head, and then grabbed Heidi by the hand. She looked over to him and noticed he was slightly growing nervous. "Okay, I guess the extra security sounds good." Tycen took a deep breath. "I can't believe this craziness. Who would do something so ruthless like this?"

"You...!" Lawrence stated in a low tone.

"Excuse me?" Tycen twisted his face.

"That's what your enemies are going to say out there." Lawrence looked up from his paperwork and glanced at Tycen. "In a few hours, everyone is going to start placing blame and pointing fingers."

"And why the hell would they even think about mentioning me?" Tycen asked.

"Because you're running against Gary Banks," Lawrence responded. "Of course the accusations are not going to hold water, but believe me, every conspiracy theorist and nut job is going to crawl from under their rock and put a story out there. That's why we have to do damage control before the damage even begins."

Tycen didn't say a word.

"So I know this is going to be a tough conversation, but we need to do it now." Lawrence grabbed a pen from his jacket pocket and prepared himself to take notes. "Tycen, I need to know...is there any possible way...you can be linked to the shooting today?"

"What? Seriously?" Tycen gasped and almost chuckled at the ridiculous question.

"I know this sounds crazy, but we have to do this." Lawrence grew serious. "And if you can't be connected...is there anyone you know that can be connected to the shooting?"

"Absolutely not," Tycen quickly responded and tightened his face. "Hell no."

"Okay good." Lawrence jotted down a few notes. "And what about you, Heidi?"

The question seemed to snatch all the air out of the office. Lawrence looked up to Heidi and gave her a serious stare. She was jolted by the question. "What about me?" Heidi grunted.

"Is there any way that you or somebody that you know can be connected to the shooting today?" Lawrence's tone was rigid.

"Why are you asking me that?" Heidi gave Lawrence a heavy attitude. Tycen squeezed her hand and tried to calm her.

"I'm asking you this because you're connected to this campaign," Lawrence dropped his voice. "I'm going to repeat the question for you. Is there any way you or somebody—"

"Hell no!" Heidi fired back, cutting Lawrence off before he could ask the question again.

"Are you sure?" Lawrence gave her an uncomfortable expression.

"Are you deaf?" Heidi grew angry. "I just said no."

"Heidi, this is serious." Lawrence sat back in his chair and stared. "I need you to be honest with me. Are you going to sit over there and tell me that you don't know anybody who could have been involved with this? There are no shady characters that you know or, better yet, there are no shady characters that you knew who could have pulled this off?"

"Are you serious with this bullshit right now?" Heidi raised her voice.

Tycen sensed Lawrence was going too far with his questions

and decided to interject.

"Wait a minute, Lawrence. Where are you going with this?" Tycen calmly raised his palm.

"Tycen, understand that I'm your campaign manager and I'm only protecting your best interest here," Lawrence continued. "Now, Heidi is not being totally honest with us here today. I'm not saying that the people she knew were involved in the shooting, but Heidi definitely knows a few shady characters. Ain't that right, Heidi? Go ahead and tell us the truth."

Heidi closed her mouth. She gave Lawrence a stare that was hard enough to cut through him. Tycen felt her hand slightly trembling in his grip.

"What is he talking about, baby?" Tycen looked over to his fiancée.

"I don't know," Heidi whispered. "But we can talk about this later."

Lawrence looked over to the couple and grew annoyed. He decided to push the issue. He reached for his cellphone. "So you don't know what I'm talking about, Heidi?" Lawrence snapped. "Maybe this will help you remember." Lawrence started pushing a few buttons on his phone. Tycen's face grew concerned as he watched his campaign manager place the phone on the desk. An audio clip started playing from the device. Tycen recognized the voice. It belonged to Heidi.

"'It's true that I knew Aaron...or at least I thought I knew him. I met Aaron after Jayson died and he helped me through a very rough patch in my life. But, for some reason, everything started to fall apart after I met him. I don't know how to explain it. A lot of shit just started spinning out of control. People started dyin' around me. It was crazy. And Aaron turned out to be nothing like the person I thought he was.'"

Heidi's mouth fell wide open. Lawrence reached for the cellphone and stopped the clip. Heidi couldn't believe Lawrence taped their conversation from earlier. A rush of anger hit her hard like a stiff punch to the stomach. Heidi stood to her feet. "You son of a bitch!" she yelled out. "I should fuckin' slap the shit out of you."

The angry words from Heidi's tongue made Tycen jump up from his seat. He had never seen this side of his fiancée. Tycen was shocked. He grabbed Heidi by the arm and tried to calm her down.

"Who the fuck do you think you are?" Heidi yelled at Lawrence. Her face was flushed with fury. "I don't know who you think you're dealin' with, but you got me fucked up for real."

Tycen stood in front of Heidi and tried to make eye contact with her. She was close to losing control in the office. Heidi started pointing at the campaign manager and continued to yell in his direction.

"Heidi, you can get angry with me all you want," Lawrence yelled at her and stood up. "The bottom line is that you're not being straight with me. I know you're hiding something. You still haven't told us about this Aaron person. Who is he?"

"I don't have to tell you shit," Heidi barked.

"Wait....Heidi, please calm down," Tycen said.

"Don't tell me to calm down. Tell him to calm down." Heidi bobbed her head in frustration.

Tycen grabbed Heidi firmly by the shoulders. He had never seen her acting so wildly. She seemed to turn into a totally different person in the office. "Wait guys, seriously... everybody just calm the hell down," Tycen yelled out, trying to restore order in the office. He put a tighter grip on Heidi's shoulder and gave her an intense look. "Babe, why are you so angry?" Tycen whispered and looked at his fiancée. "Lawrence is actually right. This is serious business right here. He just needs to know who this Aaron guy is."

Heidi gave her fiancé a crooked look. She tried to read Tycen, but she was too angry to think clearly. "I told you about Aaron before," Heidi said. "You don't remember when I mentioned him, Tycen?"

"Yes, I do remember." Tycen looked at her. The skeptical expression on his face alarmed Heidi as he continued speaking. "I remember you bringing up his name, but you never told me anything about him. Who is this guy anyway?"

"He's nobody," Heidi quickly responded. "Aaron was somebody I knew a while ago. But that part of my life is over. Like I said. He's nobody."

"Heidi…that tape doesn't sound like he's nobody." Tycen shook his head. "Baby, you can talk to me. Who is he?"

Heidi closed her mouth for a moment. She looked into Tycen's eyes. She nearly buckled from the soft expression on his face. She wanted badly to tell her fiancé about her past. Heidi wanted to give Tycen all the details about her and Aaron, but she was afraid to unleash the skeletons in her closet. Heidi had spent the past few years running from her memories of Aaron. She knew that if she told Tycen the entire story things would never be the same between them. Heidi looked away from Tycen. There was a dead silence in the office. Tycen looked at his fiancée and waited for her to respond.

"This is a waste of time," Lawrence blurted. "I told you she wasn't going to tell us anything."

Tycen looked over to Lawrence and twisted his face at the ill-advised statement. Heidi frowned like she smelled something foul in the room. Her mind started racing and she looked over to the campaign manager.

"What the hell is that supposed to mean, Lawrence?" Heidi raised her voice. Nobody said a word. The office went silent again. "Answer my question, you asshole. What is that supposed to mean?" Heidi shouted toward Lawrence and her rage caused him to blink in fear. The anger in her eyes unexpectedly made him nervous.

"Don't look at me. I'm just following orders," Lawrence nervously dropped his voice.

"What?" Heidi shouted and looked at her fiancé.

Tycen closed his eyes and was visibly upset with Lawrence.

Heidi looked at both of the men. "What the hell is going on here, Tycen? What does he mean he's following orders?" Heidi questioned.

Tycen gritted his teeth and shook his head at Lawrence. Heidi's mind started racing as she tried to figure out why the men were suddenly speechless. Tycen tried to remain calm.

Heidi sensed his guilt. "Did you put him up to this, Tycen?" Heidi raised her voice, and then backed away from him. "Did you tell this asshole to tape me today?"

"Now wait, Heidi...before you get upset let me explain this," Tycen stuttered. His words sent his fiancée into a rage.

"What the fuck is wrong with you, Tycen?" Heidi yelled. Her voice shook the office. "Why would you do that to me?"

"Babe...wait...let me tell you what happened." Tycen moved closer to her.

"Get away from me, Tycen. I'm leaving," Heidi yelled.

Tycen didn't realize what a big mistake he made by deceiving his fiancée. Heidi felt embarrassed and upset as she made a move to leave the office.

"No...hold up...don't leave." Tycen grabbed his fiancée by the arm.

"Get the hell off of me!" Heidi screamed. She was livid. Heidi hated the feeling of being manipulated. Old feelings of distrust started to consume her.

"Heidi, don't leave! I want to talk to you," Tycen yelled out again and grabbed Heidi with both hands. "Lawrence, can you please excuse us!"

Lawrence didn't say a word. He noticed things were becoming explosive and grabbed his folders. He quickly bolted out of the office and closed the door. Tycen turned back to Heidi as she continued to pull away from him.

"Why would you set me up like that, Tycen?" Heidi yelled at him. The feeling of betrayal made her angrier.

"Wait a minute...will you calm down." Tycen grew serious and squeezed her harder. "What else do you expect me to do? You won't tell me anything about you. Every time I ask you about something, you clam up. You keep leaving me to guess everything."

"So this is how you try to find out shit?" Heidi shouted. "By getting somebody to tape me like I'm some goddamn criminal? That's low, Tycen. What the fuck is wrong with you?"

Tycen glared at his fiancée. For a moment he felt like he couldn't recognize her. Tycen was taken aback by the fire in her voice. He had never seen Heidi so upset, and the sight began to turn him off. Tycen found himself growing less patient with Heidi as she continued to yell at him.

"I'm so angry with you right now, Tycen," Heidi yelled even louder. "I'm your fiancée, and you're treating me like I'm the enemy here—"

"You know what, Heidi, you're right," Tycen cut her off. "You are my fiancée, and that's why we're having this conversation. Don't you understand that? How else am I supposed to feel if you won't tell me about this Aaron person? Who is he? And why won't you tell me how you know him? For all I know, you could be fuckin' this guy right under my nose."

"Is that what you think?" Heidi shouted. Tycen's words cut deep.

"I don't know what to think anymore, Heidi," Tycen fired back. "That's the problem. How can I trust you when you won't tell me shit!"

"He's nobody!" Heidi shouted again. "Please stop bringing him up. Seriously, Tycen. He is nobody. I told you that part of my life is over. I don't want to talk about that."

"Then...you know what, Heidi...either you're fucking him or you're protecting him." Tycen pointed at her in anger. "Either way, I can't do this no more."

"What does that mean?" Heidi calmed down for a brief moment. Tycen's words stopped her.

"You heard me, Heidi," Tycen shouted. "You either tell me what's going on or I don't see the point in doing this no more."

Heidi froze as she thought about the ultimatum. Tycen's face was serious. Heidi couldn't believe how fast things had escalated in the office. "Tycen, why are you doing this?" Heidi asked. "I've never been disloyal to you. Why can't you believe me on this Aaron thing? We can talk about this some other time. I'm just not ready now."

"You don't understand, Heidi." Tycen shook his head. "There is no later. I need to know that I can trust you."

"You got some real nerve trying to lecture me about trust," Heidi's voice quivered with emotion. "Are you taping this conversation right now?"

The room fell silent as Tycen refused to respond to the subtle jab from Heidi. The heated argument had taken a lot out of him. He closed his eyes and slowly rubbed on his forehead.

"So you're not going to tell me who this Aaron person is?" Tycen asked.

"I told you...he's nobody," Heidi calmly responded.

Tycen took another moment to think, then looked Heidi in her eyes. His face grew concerned. He knew what he had to do. He chose his next words carefully. "Heidi, I'm sorry," Tycen apologized. "I really feel like I can't trust you. And right now, I'm not in a position to feel that way. Heidi...if I can't trust you, then I don't see the point of all of this."

"What are you saying?" Heidi whispered.

"I think we should take a break from each other to figure this out," Tycen responded. The statement was cold-blooded.

The words from Tycen's mouth shocked Heidi. Never in a million years would she have imagined Tycen would take it this far. Her entire world crumbled in a matter of seconds, and Heidi didn't know how to respond. She looked into Tycen's eyes and saw he was serious. Her emotions started rising, and she was tempted to reach out for Tycen, but her pride held her back. Her eyes became flooded. Tycen's heart started breaking when Heidi's tears started falling. He was hoping she would tell him everything, but she remained silent. The mood in the room sunk into sadness.

"Don't do this, Tycen," Heidi groaned as more tears started to build in her eyes.

"Take your own advice, Heidi," Tycen's voice trembled with emotion. "You can turn this all around right now, but you have to tell me what's going on."

"I can't," Heidi said and dropped her head. "Not right now." A single tear bubbled from her eye and slowly fell to the floor. The sight was an ironic reminder of how Heidi's beautiful world was in an unexpected freefall. Tycen had backed her into a corner, and Heidi hated him for making her feel trapped. His distrust for her brought back a sea of buried emotions.

Tycen looked down to Heidi, praying she would reconsider, but she never said a word. A gentle knock on the door broke up the tension in the office. Tycen turned around and watched as his young intern poked his head back into the room.

"I'm sorry to bother you again, sir," the intern nervously said. "The people from CNN are here, and the car is waiting for you out front."

"Okay, thank you. I'll be out in a second." Tycen nodded.

The young man closed the door and left the couple alone. Heidi wiped away her tears and gathered her composure. The young intern had inadvertently reminded Heidi of a harsh reality; she was slowing Tycen down and it was time to let him go.

Heidi took a deep breath and walked to the other side of the room. She grabbed Tycen's suit jacket from the coat rack. Tycen watched her as she headed back over to him. Heidi turned him around and helped him put on his jacket. She dusted off his back and shoulders, making sure he looked good for his interview. She slowly turned him around and looked into his eyes. She tried to hold back her tears but she was clearly hurting. "Good luck today." Heidi forced a smile to break through her pain. She gave Tycen a quick kiss on his cheek, then headed to the door. "I'm leaving."

Tycen went against his better judgment and never said a word. He watched Heidi leave the office and felt hollow inside. Before Tycen could dwell on his feelings any longer, Lawrence walked through the door.

"Are you all set to go?" Lawrence asked. "The car is out front."

"Yes," Tycen said. He looked around the room and slowly gathered his things. Everything started to feel surreal. Tycen couldn't believe the empty feeling that had come over him. He never opened his mouth again as he and Lawrence left the office, and then headed outside the building. Lawrence opened the car door for Tycen, and the men got inside the backseat of a black town car.

Tycen relaxed in his seat as the vehicle pulled off. He thought about Heidi. Already, he was starting to miss her. He looked down at his notes, trying to shake the feeling. He pushed the argument with her to the back of his mind, then turned his focus to the CNN interview. Today was going to be a big step for him, and Tycen knew he needed to be prepared. He cleared his mind. He decided to write down a few key notes for the interview. Tycen reached in his jacket pocket for a pen, but he found something more startling. His heart skipped a beat. A feeling of regret came over him as he stared at the object. It was Heidi's engagement ring. She had slid the ring in his pocket when she grabbed his jacket from the coat rack. She had sent Tycen a message that things between them would never be the same.

Chapter 16

Sunday, October 13
7:38 pm
Newark, NJ

Two miles away down at The Body Shop, Rojo Marquez struck a match and a large flame sparked in front of his face. He lit his cigar and relaxed deep into the sofa in his office. Tonight Rojo felt like a true boss. Loud music blared from his entertainment system, but Rojo was unfazed by the deafening tunes. His attention was on the incredibly sexy scene in front of him.

When things were slow at The Body Shop, Rojo had the tendency to bring his female workers to his office. He wanted them to brush up on their seduction skills. Tonight the lesson was fellatio and the lucky employee was Skittles.

A crooked smile came to Rojo's mouth as he looked at Skittles' pretty face. She was his best worker and now she was becoming his best soldier. Skittles was a true ride-or-die girl. A few years ago, she'd been one of the best con-women in Newark. Skittles utilized her seductive talents of sex and deception to lure dozens of men into her well laid traps, and then would rob them of their money. She was a brave girl, who never seemed phased by the dangerous life. After a few close calls of being on her own, Skittles had decided it was time to look for steady money. That led her to Rojo and The Marquez Crew. She loved working at The Body Shop, and never hesitated to do the dirty work that Rojo asked of her. Even tonight, when she had been invited to Rojo's office for a sexual favor, Skittles obliged without hesitation. Rojo sat back and relaxed as Skittles showed off her skills.

The young vixen had her face buried deep in Rojo's lap. She bobbed her head to her own sexy rhythm, trying to give her boss the best blowjob he ever had. Rojo was far from a sex fiend. The only thing that seemed to hold his attention these days was making money and concentrating on his father's legal problems. But tonight he wanted to forget about his stress. He challenged Skittles to make him climax with just her mouth, and she accepted the test with a smile. As Rojo sat comfortably on the sofa, Skittles performed like a star. She teased his dick like a seasoned professional. Rojo's body trembled from the sensation, prompting Skittles to go even harder. She loved the feeling of controlling a powerful man with just her mouth. She squeezed his thighs and took his swollen cock further into her mouth. Rojo moaned like a bull. He pulled on his cigar again, and then blew the thick smoke directly toward her pretty face. Skittles coughed and gagged on his cock. Rojo took pleasure in watching her struggle. He was sick like that.

Skittles slowed down her rhythm, composing herself. She firmly grabbed his dick again, then looked up to Rojo's calm face and smiled like a willing servant. She puckered her lips and started teasing him.

"You want me to check under the hood for you, baby?" Skittles playfully asked. She stared her boss directly in the eyes.

"What?" Rojo twisted his face. "Check under the hood?"

Before Rojo could ask another question, Skittles cracked his legs apart. She held his cock to the side and lifted up his nuts. Her tongue stretched out of her mouth, and she started licking deep between his manly crevice.

"Oh shit!" Rojo grunted with approval.

A deep chill shot from the small of his back as Rojo submerged in the feeling. He grabbed Skittles by the back of her neck as she continued to please him. She smiled, knowing

Rojo was loving every moment. She jerked his dick wildly, knowing she could make him climax within minutes. The deep groans from Rojo became louder, and Skittles felt her own body heating up. His dick grew harder with every firm stroke and gentle twist. She knew Rojo was close to popping, but before she could finish her job something unexpected happened. Rojo's phone started ringing.

"Fuck!" He yelled. Skittles stopped. The ringing of the phone became louder, making Rojo yell in frustration. "I gotta get that call," he grunted. He was pissed off.

Skittles backed off of Rojo when he stood. He put back on his jeans, then walked over to his desk. When he noticed who was calling, his entire demeanor shifted. He quickly turned off the music and answered the phone. "Yea, this is Rojo. Don't say nothing yet," Rojo quickly blurted. He turned his attention to Skittles, who was still on her knees near the sofa. He covered the phone. "This is my pops…don't say shit!"

His rude tone caused the vibe in the room to instantly change. Rojo watched Skittles as she got off of her knees, and then quietly sat on the sofa. Rojo waited for a few seconds, then turned his attention back to the call. He took a seat behind his desk and activated the speakerphone.

"Yea Dad. . . I'm here," Rojo called out. "How you holdin' up?"

"Shit. I'm just maintaining, if that's what you wanna call it. I fuckin' need to be home," Marquez responded from the other line. "We need to talk."

"Okay Pop, that's cool. What's up?" Rojo asked.

"I gotta get the fuck outta here," Marquez's voice sounded desperate. "I'm not built for this concrete hotel."

"Stop talkin' like that, Pop. We're built for anything!" Rojo barked.

"Fuck that!" Marquez raised his voice in anger. "Then you come down here and do this time for me."

Rojo didn't respond. His father's angry voice gave him pause. "What's the deal with this Niko situation?" Marquez continued. "Is this motherfucker talkin' yet?"

"Hell yea, he's talkin'. . .but we not speakin' the same language," Rojo responded. "He keeps saying he doesn't know who the witness is. And trust me, we've tried everything except cutting his tongue out."

"Goddamit. . . Is he still alive?" Marquez asked.

"Let me check," Rojo replied, then grabbed a remote control off his desk. He turned on three security monitors near his entertainment system. Rojo rubbed his chin, looking at the live surveillance footage of the sub-basement that was just a few floors below. Rojo took a good look at the overhead view of a beaten man tied to a metal chair. Blood leaked from the man's head and mouth. It appeared as if he had been beaten within an inch of his life. The man was Niko Stanton. "Yea that motherfucker is still alive," Rojo yelled out.

"Good, don't kill him yet," Marquez coldly ordered. "We need to find Kimi first. Trust me. . .if you put that bitch under pressure in front of him. . .I bet that asshole will tell us everything."

"Okay, Pop. I'm on it," Rojo responded.

"Don't give me that shit!" Marquez yelled. "I'm dead serious. Get out there in those streets and find that bitch. I need to get outta here. I'm telling you. . . I'm not gonna last much longer."

Rojo nodded his head and gritted his teeth. He hated being yelled at by his father, but he knew Marquez was not himself after being incarcerated for so long. He lowered his tone and continued the conversation. "I'm on it, Pop." Rojo was serious. "As we speak, I got a bunch of soldiers lookin' for her. They're posted at her old house. They're at her banks, and I even got some people at Niko's old job. Trust me, if she pokes her head out even for a second, we gonna find that bitch. And I'll hit the streets hard too."

"Good!" Marquez uttered. "And another thing: have you been puttin' that Body Shop money to the side?"

"I'm trying to," Rojo explained. He prepared himself for

another round of verbal abuse. "It's slow around here."

"What the fuck, Rojo! What the hell you mean, it's slow?" Marquez yelled even louder. "The pussy game is never slow. Come on, Rojo. You're really fuckin' up now. I told you we need that fuckin' money."

"I know, Pop. Im tryin'." Rojo shook his head.

"How much you got saved?" Marquez sharply asked.

"Close to three hundred and fifty thousand," Rojo said.

"Fuck. Man, that's not enough!" Marquez shouted. "We still need a lot more. I hope you got a plan to get the rest."

"I'm working on it." Rojo rubbed his forehead in frustration.

"There you go with that bullshit again," Marquez continued to yell at his son. "Get your fuckin' head out of your ass and get crackin', Rojo. This shit is coming down to the wire. People need to get paid off. These motherfuckers are serious. You hear me?"

"Loud and clear, Pop," Rojo said.

"I hope so," Marquez grunted. "Don't let me call this phone again, and you don't have Kimi. Stick to the plan, Rojo. Find this bitch and work on gettin' the rest of that fuckin' money!"

Rojo heard the line click and realized his father hung up on him. His temper kicked in and he became enraged. He picked up the phone and slammed it to the floor. Skittles shook in her seat as she watched Rojo grow angrier by the second.

"This motherfucker!" Rojo shouted and waved his hand.

Skittles looked over and felt bad for Rojo. She stood to her feet, and then walked over to his desk. "Are you okay?" Skittles mumbled.

"Fuck no!" Rojo snapped.

"Is there anything I can do?" Skittles asked.

"You got three hundred thousand dollars?" Rojo's expression hardened.

"No, I don't," Skittles whispered.

"Then no. There's nothin' you can fuckin' do," Rojo fired back.

Skittles didn't take offense to Rojo's rude statement. She

knew he was upset and clearly under pressure. She gave him a sympathetic expression and nodded her head.

Rojo stood to his feet and looked around his desk. An idea came to his mind and he picked up his phone. "You know what? There is something you can do." Rojo scrolled through his cellphone. "I got a few people looking for this bitch named Kimi Moore. I'm going to text you a picture of her, and I want you to keep an eye out for her when you leave here. Can you do that?"

"Hell yes." Skittles nodded. "You know I would do anything for you."

"If you hear about anything out there, just call me." Rojo reached under the desk. "I need to get out here and get this fuckin' money."

Skittles watched him as he pulled out a .357 SIG-Sauer handgun. He checked the firearm, then tightly tucked it in his waistline. "I will," Skittles assured. She could tell that Rojo was dead set on his objective, and she wanted him to know she had his back.

Rojo's demeanor grew dangerous as his father's instructions echoed in his mind. He headed to leave the office like a man on a mission. His immediate objective was to find Kimi and finish off their big plan for her and Niko.

Chapter 17

Monday, October 14
7:30 am
Newark, NJ

"It's been nearly twenty-four hours since a brash shooting stunned the city of Newark. Authorities remain baffled as no arrest have been made in connection with the apparent assassination attempt of Mayor Gary Banks. The family of Lexi Hamilton has spoken out against the incident as the shooting fell on the anniversary of Lexi's disappearance. Investigators are urging anyone with information to contact them."

Heidi reached over and slammed her hand on the clock radio. She turned off the alarm, then twisted her body on the uncomfortable sofa. Heidi slowly opened her eyes and realized she was staring at a ceiling she hadn't seen in years. Instead of waking up against Tycen's warm body, she found herself on her mother's old couch. She was tired and confused. After the unexpected separation from her fiancé, she didn't know where to go. She knew Pearl would never refuse her, so she decided to stay with her mother until she got her mind back in order.

"Good morning, sunshine," Pearl sang as she dawdled through the living room, headed to the kitchen.

"Damn, Mom...why are you up so early?" Heidi

grumbled and buried her face in the pillows.

"Now girl, I told you about cursing in my house." Pearl ignored Heidi's question. "Do you want some breakfast? I'm about to cook something."

Heidi turned and tossed the pillows to the floor. She knew she didn't stand a chance to fall back asleep with her mother banging around in the kitchen. Heidi slowly sat up on the sofa and stretched out her exhausted arms. "I don't want anything to eat, but I'll take some coffee," Heidi groaned and manage to stand. She waved toward her mother and headed to the bathroom.

She hadn't gotten much sleep the night before. Her tears of anger and regret had flooded the sofa cushions for most of the night as she tried to make sense of the breakup with Tycen. She had battled with her conscious all evening. There was no question that she loved Tycen enough to marry him, but their argument made her realize she didn't totally trust him. Despite his full court press to find out about her past, she couldn't bring herself to open up to him.

Heidi entered the bathroom with Tycen still on her mind. She moved to the mirror and stared at her own reflection. She was emotionally tired. The pain she'd harbored for years was hidden deep behind her eyes. She didn't know anyone else who had ever been introduced to the torment she had, and hers was simmering deep within.

Heidi took a handful of cold water and drowned her face. "Damn," she whispered and took a deep breath. She moved her hands slowly down past her neck and started to massage the welts on her chest, then pulled down her t-shirt and exposed her old bullet wounds. She could no longer feel the scorching hot slugs beneath her skin, but she felt vengeful every time she glared at the ugly scars.

In the back of her mind, she could still hear a gunshot ring out. Heidi flinched as she recalled the bullets ripping into her torso. The cold expression on her attacker's face incensed her. A cloud of betrayal engulfed her as she thought about Aaron's soulless eyes. Heidi found herself renewing her secret promise. The man responsible for trying to murder her had to pay. No amount of time could make her forget. Forgiving him was out of the question. Aaron's actions had cut her deeper than any scar on her body could reveal. Heidi tried her best to move on with her life, but the hunger for revenge became stronger with just the slightest mention of Aaron's name. The argument in Tycen's office awakened a dark side in Heidi that yearned to settle the score.

Heidi hadn't seen Aaron since the night he shot her and left her clinging for her life. There were so many questions left unanswered. Aaron had seduced Heidi with his charm and empathy. Things between them had never escalated beyond a passionate kiss, but their brief relationship had a major impact on Heidi's heart. Something about Aaron had felt familiar and magnetizing. She never imagined that he would transform into a killer before her very eyes. He had directed his inner rage toward her, and she wanted to know why. Surviving the deadly episode was not enough for her. She wanted to make sure Aaron paid for deceiving her. As Heidi gazed at her own reflection this morning, she realized that her thirst for revenge was too strong to ignore any longer.

Back in the kitchen, Pearl fired up the stove and began to prepare breakfast. Having her daughter at home made Pearl happy, despite the circumstances that brought her there. Since the death of her son, Lamar, Pearl's house had become different. It was always quiet, and Pearl didn't leave much. Most of her conversations were with bill collectors, neighbors and the mailwoman. She felt delighted to finally have a live body in the house with her.

"How do you want your coffee?" Pearl asked as her daughter walked into the kitchen.

"Black as hell," Heidi answered and sat down at the table.

"There you go with that mouth." Pearl shook her head. She poured her daughter a cup of coffee, and then sat down across from her. She watched as Heidi filled her cup with sugar, then aggressively stirred.

"I forgot how hot it gets in this house," Heidi gasped. "Why do you keep it so hot in here?"

"Don't blame me. It's those old radiators," Pearl said. "They burn really hot. I tried to turn down the thermostat, but those radiators blow steam like you wouldn't believe."

Heidi nodded and slowly wiped a bead of sweat from her forehead. Pearl sipped on her tea and gave her daughter a blank expression.

"So what exactly happened last night? Do you want to talk about it?" Pearl asked.

"No...not really," Heidi responded and stared into her cup.

"You looked so pissed off when you showed up on my porch last night." Pearl shook her head. "You scared me for a minute. You had that look...like somebody died."

"Nah, nobody died...not yet," Heidi harshly mumbled.

"What did you and Tycen fight about?" Pearl asked and took another sip of her tea. "Was it that bad?"

"I don't want to talk about it, Mom," Heidi whispered.

"Don't act like that, Heidi. I'm your mother," Pearl snapped. "I hate when you make me feel like you can't talk to me."

"It's not that... It's just..." Heidi cut herself short and gave her mother a familiar glance.

"What is it?" Pearl twisted her mouth.

"It's just stupid when you think about it. It's nothing." Heidi shook her head.

"Nothing?" Pearl took another sip. "Child...trust and believe...I been on this earth too long to believe it was nothing. It had to be something serious that made you walk away from a man that fine."

Heidi chuckled at her mother's statement. Pearl had an uncanny knack for pressing her daughter for answers. Pearl knew that something was troubling Heidi and she wanted to help in any way she could. She kept her eyes fixed on her daughter across the table, watching as Heidi continued to stare into her coffee.

"Mom, let me ask you a question," Heidi whispered.

"Sure," Pearl responded.

"Why you never got remarried after Dad died?" Heidi looked up to her mother.

The question caused Pearl to close her mouth. She contemplated her response and unconsciously fiddled with the gold locket around her neck. Heidi rarely discussed her father, and Pearl was thrown off by the question. "Your father was a good man," Pearl whispered as if she was the only one in the room. "He was a damn good man."

Heidi didn't say a word. She watched her mother and realized Pearl was thinking about her father. The kitchen fell silent for a moment. Pearl almost seemed hurt by her memories.

"We definitely had our problems….me and your father did," Pearl lowered her voice. "But I guess nobody ever came around that could come close to the man your father was."

"Mom, you ever felt like you didn't deserve to be with anybody else after Dad died?" Heidi asked.

"What do you mean?" Pearl raised her head.

"I don't know…ever since Jayson died it just seems like I keep sabotaging myself. I mean, I think I want to be with somebody, but I can never get it right." The words from Heidi's mouth lingered for a moment.

"So…wait… You think you don't deserve Tycen?" Pearl asked.

"I really don't know," Heidi confessed.

"Do you love him?" Pearl stared at her daughter.

"Without a question." Heidi nodded. "I love him a lot. But I just don't trust him."

"Why not?" Pearl continued to push. "Is there another woman or something?"

"No. Oh no. Nothing like that." Heidi shook her head. "Tycen's a good person. He never tried to hurt me on purpose or nothing crazy. I just thought I would be able to open up to him by now, but I can't. I don't know why. Is it normal to feel like you don't deserve to be with somebody?"

Pearl didn't answer the question. She felt for her daughter. She could see the emotional anguish in Heidi's expression just as she could hear the confusion in her voice. Pearl took another sip of her tea. She knew a thing or two about feeling guilty and undeserving of having a man in her life. She empathized with her daughter. Her conscious started to get the best of her and she slowly rubbed her forehead. Pearl knew she had to give her daughter some much-needed advice. "Baby, I want to tell you something that I've never told a single soul," Pearl dropped her voice and pushed her cup to the side.

"Okay." The edginess in her mother's tone made Heidi take notice. She watched as Pearl's facial expression started to sink into a look of contrition.

"I can't believe I'm about to tell you this." Pearl looked up to the ceiling and nervously chuckled. "I hope you don't judge your mom too harshly for what I'm about to tell you."

"Of course not, Mom," Heidi replied and twisted her own expression. "What's on your mind?"

"You were too young to remember this, but right around the time you were born, me and your father use to fight a lot." Pearl took a deep breath. "We were a couple of young and stupid kids just floating through life and trying to get by. God. . .we were so young." Pearl dropped her head and thought back to her past. Her voice became emotional. "Now. . .I loved your father. From the first day I met that man…I loved him more than life itself. But he had his ways. It was just a different time back then. We would fight a lot, and sometimes things got physical. Not violent…he wasn't that type of man. He would just get physical, and it scared me. Your father didn't know it at the time, but he started to push me away from him. And I felt it." Pearl got lost in her own story. She slowly rocked as the memories of Heidi's father began to consume her. Pearl continued to speak and pushed her words past the lump in her throat. "After a while. . .I started to get more restless and confused about things." Pearl shook her head. "We were crazy back then. I was so stupid and lost. And don't ask me how it all started, but me and your father kept having problems. The next thing I knew, I was waking up in another man's bed." Pearl put her hand on her chin. She looked down at the kitchen table. She was clearly ashamed of her last statement. "I cheated on your father, Heidi. I can't believe I'm telling you this. But it's true. I cheated on him."

"Mom. . ." Heidi gasped at the shocking revelation.

"Let me finish, baby. You need to know this." Pearl wiped her eyes. She was now beyond the point of no return. Her confession brought her to tears. Heidi felt conflicted as her mother continued to speak. "Your father found out about my affair, and it almost destroyed us. The short time I spent with that other man brought hell to our family." Pearl continued to twiddle with the locket around her neck. More tears slid down her face. "But I can say this about your father. . .he forgave me. That's why I will always say he was a good man. When it was all said and done, your father was right by my side. I know it wasn't easy for him, but he was right there the whole time."

"Damn, Mom. I don't know what to say," Heidi whispered.

"And then there was you." Pearl looked at her daughter.

"What about me?" Heidi questioned.

"You were only like two-years-old when all of this was going on," Pearl said. "But when your father found out I was cheating on him. . .you changed."

"Me?" Heidi asked and touched her chest.

"Yup. . ." Pearl nodded her head. "Heidi, you never looked at me the same. I know you was only a child when this all happened, but you would stare at me with those big eyes and not say a word. You was one of those kids that just knew when something wasn't right. It's like you knew what I did. You knew I cheated on your father. You knew how bad I hurt him and what I did to this family. Every time I looked at you. . .I saw you judging me with those eyes. Sometimes I had to just look away from you. And even as you got older, I could see the same look in your eyes. You never forgave me."

"How could I forgive you for something I don't remember?"

Heidi asked.

"I don't blame you for not forgiving me," Pearl mumbled. She ignored her daughter's question. "I did some ugly things in my life, and I guess that's why I never remarried. And the truth is...I don't think I ever forgave myself for what I did." A rush of tears fell from Pearl's eyes. She became overwhelmed by the memory of her indiscretions.

Heidi felt for her mother, and got up and walked to the other side of the table. She sat down next to Pearl and grabbed her hand. "Mom, are you okay?" Heidi asked. "I'm sorry I asked you about Dad."

"It's okay, baby." Pearl wiped her tears. "I needed to tell you that for a long time. I've been wanting to get that off of my chest." Pearl tapped on her daughter's hand and looked into her eyes. "Heidi, I don't know if I'm the reason you don't trust nobody. Well, I hope I'm not the reason, but I want to tell you this. We all do bad things. That's part of being who we are. God made us all with this free will to sin and act the fool. But deep down inside, I believe that we are all good people by nature. When we do ugly things in this life, I think we all die inside. And when somebody forgives us, it gives us a chance to live again. Even after we're dead and gone. Forgiveness gives us all a chance to live again."

Heidi closed her mouth and glanced at her mother. The wisdom of her words gripped Heidi's heart. She felt moved by Pearl's voice.

"Now...I don't know what's going on in your life right now...and honestly I don't want to know, baby. That is your business and I understand that." Pearl forced a pleasant expression to emerge on her face. "Heidi, I know you better than you know yourself. You always held grudges too tight, and it's always been hard for you to move on. Even when you was a little child. That's the Kachina in you." Pearl smiled. "But don't be like me, baby. You have to start to forgive people. And the biggest thing you need to do is forgive yourself too. What's done is done, and you can't change the past. But you can lift that heavy burden off of your shoulders, sweetie. Give yourself a chance to live again."

Heidi dropped her head. The words from Pearl's mouth spoke directly to Heidi's conscious. The kitchen fell silent. Pearl cleared the tears from her face, then stood. The morning conversation had changed her mood. Pearl went and turned off the stove, then made her way back to Heidi. She leaned over and kissed her daughter on the forehead.

"I think I need to lay back down, and then try this breakfast thing in a few hours," Pearl uttered. "Just remember what we talked about, Heidi. I know forgiveness is a curse word for you, but it's a small thing that can make a big difference." Pearl walked out of the kitchen and left Heidi alone with her thoughts.

The unexpected conversation was a lot for Heidi to take in. She hadn't been home for a full day, and Pearl had already dropped a bombshell on her. She reached to the other end of the table, grabbing her coffee. She swallowed the last of it, then took a deep breath. The troubles in her life flashed in her mind. Pearl had given her a lot to think about. Her mother seemed to speak directly to Heidi's soul. Aaron's face flashed into her mind. Maybe it was time for her to forgive him. Maybe it was time to keep the past in the past. She needed to move on with her life. Heidi had a loving man waiting for her to come clean. It was up to her to decide to keep harboring her feelings of vengeance for Aaron or try to reconcile things with Tycen. Heidi sat alone at the kitchen table and quietly debated the dilemma.

Chapter 18

Monday, October 14
10:15 am
Newark, NJ

Kimi Moore wrung her hands tightly together as she stood in the lobby of the Hilton Hotel. She couldn't remember the last time she'd felt so afraid to be in public. She carefully glared at the faces of everyone who passed her as she waited for her taxi. After a week of hiding out in the hotel, Kimi had finally mustered up the courage to seek out the one person who could help her find Niko. Kimi missed Niko, and found herself praying for him every night. Something inside of her told her that he was still in Newark. And still alive. After learning that Niko had been kidnapped by The Marquez Crew, she knew she had to be careful as she moved through the dangerous city. She needed to be on point.

Kimi looked at her watch, and then glanced out of the hotel's glass doors. Her eyes grew wide when she saw a yellow taxicab pulling up to the front. She surveyed the lobby one last time, then headed outside. The chilly air caused Kimi to tighten up as she walked to the driver's side window. "Excuse me, sir." Kimi tapped on the roof of the cab. "Can you drop your window?"

The cab driver rolled his window down and gave Kimi an odd look. "Did you call for a taxi?" the driver asked.

"Yes, I did," Kimi responded, suspicious. She studied the driver's face, trying her best to read him. "Do you have some identification, sir?"

The driver hesitated for a moment. "Are you a cop?" he snapped.

"No, I just need to know you're a real cab driver. I know this is not normal, but it's a lot of bullshit going on out here," Kimi replied and stared at the man.

He paused for a brief moment, and then pulled out his wallet. He showed Kimi his license, and she crosschecked it against the certification on the dashboard. She couldn't be careful enough. She needed to treat everyone as a potential threat.

"Okay, sir. Thanks," Kimi slowly nodded. "One last thing. Can you show me your arms?"

"What lady?" the cab driver gasped. "You need a ride or not?"

"I do. But you gotta work with me too. I'll pay you five hundred dollars to make two stops and bring me right back here to the hotel." Kimi was serious. "Are you okay with that? I just need to know that I can trust you. I just need you to show me your arms. That's it."

The cab driver shook his head in disbelief. The strange request almost caused him to pull off and leave Kimi standing in front of the hotel. He looked up to Kimi and decided to see where the conversation would lead. The easy money intrigued him. He rolled up the sleeves on his jacket, then thrust his arms out the window. Kimi inspected the cab driver for any tattoos that would link him to The Marquez Crew. There were none. She felt relieved as she surveyed his bare arms. Kimi took a deep breath and got into the backseat of the taxi.

"Where are you headed to?" the driver asked, looking into the rearview mirror.

"First, I need to make a stop at First National Bank on Market Street," Kimi said. She carefully looked around the back of the cab as the driver left the hotel. Today, she needed to trust her intuition. She had to if she was going to find her boyfriend Niko and make it back safely.

Just a few miles away on the south side of the city, Rojo Marquez struggled to keep his eyes open as his vehicle cruised through the streets. He'd spent the entire evening making runs and collecting money from various illegal businesses he ran in the city. In between his stops, he had also searched for Niko's girlfriend, Kimi, but he continuously came up empty. Rojo was pressed to find her. The sound of his father's desperate voice continued to wreck his brain. But locating Kimi was only the beginning of his problems. He was also under an extreme amount of pressure to raise the money to help his father beat his charges. Leon Marquez was ready to be freed from jail, and Rojo knew he was the last hope to make it happen. As he parked his car in front of a small sneaker store, the stress of his situation was written all over his face. Rojo was ready to take on an army to raise the money he needed.

"This motherfucker betta be in here," Rojo groaned as he got out of his car. His phone started ringing in his pocket, but he ignored it. He was ready to get down to business and collect more money. His face became hard as a statue as he walked into the empty sneaker store. "What the fuck?" Rojo whispered as he headed straight for the counter.

A large man emerged from the back of the store. Despite being twice his size, the man became nervous the moment he recognized Rojo. "Uh..."

"Now this is what I don't understand," Rojo blurted and pointed directly at the man. "Why I gotta come down here like a fuckin' bill collector to pick up the money you know you owe us!" Rojo gave the man a menacing glare and put his hands in front of himself like an Italian mobster. Rojo had a serious reputation in the city for getting violent over the smallest issues.

The large man didn't want any trouble from his visitor and decided to defuse the situation before things escalated. "Come on Rojo...you know it's not even like that." The man nervously smiled. "I was gonna come see you, but the girl I had working here quit. It's hard to get down to your office when I'm by myself running the store. You feel me?"

"Whatever. . .you got the money for this month?" Rojo rudely cut the man short. He had no time for small talk.

"Yeah, I got the money," the man said and walked over toward the register. He reached under the counter and pulled out a blue sneaker box, then handed the box to Rojo. "You can count it if you want, but the money is all there," the man said with a confident nod.

Rojo took the sneaker box and flipped the lid open. He looked at the scattered c-notes and nodded. "Shit, I'm a Marquez," Rojo announced. "We always count our money."

"Okay. . .that's cool. . .knock yourself out." The man gestured toward the box and took a seat while Rojo counted the cash. "Speaking of being a Marquez, did you hear about the mayor?" the man asked.

"Yeah…I heard somebody tried to take his head off yesterday," Rojo responded.

"Yeah, that's crazy," the man continued speaking. "A lot of people are sayin' The Marquez Crew did it."

"What?" Rojo mumbled as he kept his focus on the box.

"Yeah…that's what people are saying," the man continued. "People are saying that y'all tried to do us all a favor and get rid of his ass."

"Is that what they're sayin' out there?" Rojo calmly asked and continued counting.

"Yea, you know the neighborhood is always talkin', right?" The man laughed.

"Yeah, people always talkin' 'bout shit they know nothing about." Rojo finished counting the money and closed the box. "It's all here. Good doing business with you. Don't make me come down here next month…alright?"

"I won't, Rojo," the man replied and picked up on the subtle warning.

"And about that bullshit with the mayor, don't believe everything you hear," Rojo yelled out as he headed for the door. "Trust me, if The Marquez Crew was involved with that shit. . .the mayor would be dead. My shooters don't miss." Rojo left the store and headed back to his car. His phone started ringing again, and Rojo took a deep breath. He recognized the number. Skittles. Rojo waited until he sat down in the driver seat before he answered the call. "This is Rojo. . .make it quick," he answered harshly.

"Oh my God, Rojo where have you been? I've been tryin' to reach you," Skittles shouted from the other line.

"Okay. . .you got me now. . .what's up?" Rojo bitterly responded.

"Guess who I just saw walking out the bank?" Skittles screamed with excitement.

"Who?" Rojo sat up in his seat.

"Kimi fuckin' Moore!" Skittles shouted.

"Oh shit!" Rojo said. "Are you sure it's her?"

"What? You goddamn right, I'm sure!" the woman shouted again. "She just left the bank downtown and got into a yellow cab. I don't know where she's going, but I'm going to follow her."

"Hell yes! You do that." Rojo fired up his engine. "The minute Kimi gets out of that cab, I want you to text me the address. I don't care where it is. You got that?"

"Yup. . .I'll text you," the female replied. "You sure you don't want me to handle this for you? You know I will snatch her ass up."

"Hell no...Don't do shit but follow her," Rojo shouted through the phone. "Just don't lose her. Stay on your job and follow her. See where she's goin'."

"Okay," Skittles quickly responded.

Rojo disconnected the call and closed his car door. He sped away from the sneaker store and headed downtown. The news from Skittles made his adrenaline rush. Rojo couldn't wait to finally get his hands on Kimi.

A few minutes later, the loud ringing of a telephone startled Tycen Wakefield. Despite a few televisions blaring from the lobby, the campaign office was relatively quiet this morning. Tycen was reading over another draft of his budget proposal when the phone call shook him out of his zone. "Wakefield Headquarters, how can I help you?" Tycen politely answered the phone.

"Tycen, it's me," a familiar voice responded.

"Lawrence! How's it going this morning?" Tycen asked.

"It's going fantastic," Lawrence responded. "Same fight... different round!"

"I'm right there with you," Tycen replied.

"So, I hope you're sitting down," Lawrence said. "I have some exciting news."

"Exciting news? That's always a good thing. . .lay it on me." Tycen braced himself.

"So...I'm not sure whose ass you kissed over there, but you impressed somebody over at CNN," Lawrence continued. "You did such a good job last night that they want you back."

"No shit!" Tycen stated.

"Hell yes, Tycen! They're doing a thirty-minute segment on violence in America, and they want to discuss the shooting this past weekend. Of course, they'll give you a few minutes to discuss your agenda and strategy to change things. And you'll be one of the featured panelists."

"Damn. . .that's amazing." Tycen felt slightly nervous. He sensed his campaign was speeding up.

"You bet your ass this is amazing," Lawrence raised his voice with elation. "This segment with CNN will be worth more than any campaign commercial we can put out there. This is our big opportunity to introduce you on an international level."

"Wow. . .this is great" Tycen was speechless. The unexpected news humbled him. Tycen smiled. "So what do we do next? I'm definitely interested."

"I'm just waiting for them to confirm everything, but, as of now, you are in," Lawrence said. "You should definitely feel proud of yourself. This is just the first big step of many more to come."

"Thanks, Lawrence," Tycen dropped his tone. "Very good job on your end. Please keep me posted and let me know how we need to proceed."

"I sure will," Lawrence responded. "I'll call you back later."

"Sounds good," Tycen stated. "Goodbye."

Tycen hung up the phone and relaxed back in his chair. Learning of the second CNN interview made him feel excited, but nervous. That made him think of Heidi. He thought about how strong she made him feel whenever he began to second-guess himself. Despite the argument they'd had yesterday, he wanted to hear her voice and share the good news. He picked up his cellphone and dialed her number, then sat back and waited for the call to connect. With each unanswered ring, he started to regret his decision of pressuring her about her past. Tycen held the phone to his ear for a few seconds more, and then disconnected the call. "Damn," he whispered. He looked at the phone and decided to try Heidi again. He was about to redial her number when his office phone started ringing.

"Wakefield Headquarters, how can I help you?" Tycen answered.

"Yes, Mr. Wakefield. This is the front desk," a voice announced from the other line. "You have a young woman here to see you. She said it's very important."

"Oh okay. . .no problem at all. . .please let her in." Tycen smiled and stood to his feet. He was excited and assumed that Heidi had come down to the office to surprise him. He quickly made himself presentable. Even though he had just seen her yesterday, Tycen missed Heidi.

A gentle knock on his door made Tycen even more excited. He looked down at himself and made sure he looked his best this morning. "Come in. . .it's open," Tycen called out.

The door swung open and made way for a stunning young woman. It wasn't Heidi. The worried expression on the woman's face caused Tycen to move from behind his desk. "Tycen Wakefield?" the woman calmly asked.

"Yes. . .and you are?" Tycen asked and approached the woman. He was thrown off.

"My name is Kimi Moore," she replied. "I'm not sure if... he ever mentioned my name to you...but I'm Niko Stanton's girlfriend."

The statement froze him. Niko and Tycen had been business associates for a long time. Tycen had heard about Kimi, but he never had the pleasure of meeting her. Kimi's beautiful face was breathtaking, and Tycen could see why his friend, Niko, was infatuated with her. "Hello Kimi. It's nice to meet you," Tycen politely said and pulled out a seat for her.

"Thank you Mr. Wakefield," Kimi responded and sat down.

"No, please call me Tycen." He smiled at her and walked behind his desk. "So how can I help you, Kimi? How is Niko? Did he ever get a chance to leave New Jersey?"

Kimi's smile hardened as she thought about the questions. Niko's handsome face flashed into her mind, and Kimi's heart jumped. Tycen noticed her uneven expression and grew concerned.

"Is everything okay?" Tycen asked.

"I need your help," Kimi whispered with emotion. She almost appeared to be ashamed of her statement. "I didn't know who else to turn to. I could really use your help right now."

"Sure," Tycen uttered and sat down. "What's going on?"

"Niko...was...umm..." Kimi stuttered. She tried to force the words to come to her mouth. Her eyes began to water as she continued to speak. "We got carjacked about a week ago. I think they was following us or something. I don't know. But somebody kidnapped Niko."

"What!?" Tycen gasped. "Please tell me this is a joke."

"No." A few tears fell from Kimi's eyes. Tycen realized she was serious as she continued stuttering. "Somebody...umm... took Niko...I don't know where he is."

"Oh shit..." Tycen covered his mouth. "Did you go to the police?"

"I can't," Kimi whispered.

"Huh?" Tycen grunted. "I don't understand."

"The night we got carjacked they put me in the hospital." Kimi shook her head. "When I woke up...this detective was in my room. She told me that The Marquez Crew was involved with the kidnapping. And the next thing I know...somebody else came to see me posing as a detective and tried to kidnap me. So, right now...I don't know who to trust. I'm not going to the police."

Tycen was speechless. The insane story caught him off guard. Tycen leaned back in his chair. Kimi wiped away her tears and looked down to the floor. Tycen tried to remember the last conversation he had with his friend, Niko. "I can't believe this," Tycen whispered. "I just seen him last week."

"I know," Kimi looked up to Tycen. "We were leaving here the night we got carjacked," she said.

Tycen twisted his face. He thought about the night Niko had been in his office. Tycen remembered his friend saying he was leaving New Jersey after getting into trouble with his law firm. He didn't realize Niko was caught up in the mix with the notorious Marquez Crew.

"So how can I help?" Tycen asked.

"Did Niko ever mentioned anything to you about the clients he was dealing with?" Kimi asked. "Niko only talked to me a few times about his business. He never gave me specific details about these Marquez people."

"Yeah, that's the thing about Niko," Tycen responded. "He always kept a lot of secrets. He never mentioned anything to me about his cases... I'm sorry."

"Damn." Kimi shook her head. "What about that night he came to see you? Did he say anything that made sense? Anything that could let me know why he would get kidnapped?"

"The only thing he mentioned to me was that he was leaving New Jersey. I know he was under investigation for his law firm, but he didn't say why. Niko said he would call me once he got situated. That was really it." Tycen thought back and tried to remember every detail about Niko's visit. "But you know what?" Tycen's face lit up as he thought back. "I do remember Niko giving me a DVD. He said there was something important on it, but I never watched it."

"Oh okay," Kimi whispered in disappointment. "I told him to give you that DVD."

"What's on it?" Tycen asked and dropped his eyebrows.

"I'm not sure." Kimi took a deep breath and shook her head. "Somebody gave the DVD to me, and Niko suggested I give it to you."

Tycen looked around his office and nodded his head. "I think I still have it here. Let me check." Tycen stood up and walked over to his file cabinet. He rummaged through a few folders and retrieved the DVD from a pile of papers. There was no writing on the white disc. A strange emotion came over Tycen when he looked at the DVD. He thought back to when Niko handed him the disc, then walked over to Kimi. "You know what? I'm not sure what's on this, but you can have it back." Tycen handed Kimi the DVD. "Maybe it can help you more than it can help me." Tycen thought about his campaign and the upcoming CNN interview. Tycen realized he needed to be careful and play things safe. He didn't know why Niko was kidnapped. He felt bad about Kimi's situation, but he didn't know how else he could help her. Tycen realized he needed to get far away from the scandal and protect his bid to be mayor of the city. "I'm sorry I can't assist you with more information, Kimi," Tycen dropped his tone. "I know you don't want to contact the police, but at this point...I think they are the only ones that can help you find him."

Kimi reluctantly took the DVD back and put it in her jacket pocket. She gave Tycen a hard glare and stood to her feet. She realized she wasted her time coming to see Tycen, and the disappointment was written all over her face.

"If you want, I can call some people I know down at the police department," Tycen offered. "Maybe they can help out."

"No... please don't do that," Kimi quickly responded and

wiped the few remaining tears from her face. "I just need to think about this. I want to figure out what I'm going to do. I'm sorry to bother you today, Mr. Wakefield."

"No problem," Tycen quickly responded. "It was definitely no bother—"

Before Tycen could finish his statement, Kimi was out the door. She was furious that she'd wasted her time coming to Tycen's office. She thought about her boyfriend, Niko, as she walked out of the building. Kimi felt alone again. She realized she was no closer to finding her boyfriend. Kimi felt herself becoming emotional, so she tried to hold back her tears, but was unsuccessful. Kimi wiped her eyes as she got into the backseat of the yellow cab. She could barely see straight. Her head was in another world. Kimi started to feel like she would never see Niko again. "Please take me back to the hotel," Kimi yelled out to the cab driver.

She never picked up her head as the cab sped away from the campaign headquarters. Kimi put her face in her hands. Niko's image entered her mind again. She could only imagine what her life would be without him now. The cab continued to speed down the street. Kimi felt the vehicle swerving and finally lifted her head. She wiped away her tears and focused her eyes outside the window. She noticed the cab was traveling at a high rate of speed. "Excuse me...you can slow down a bit," Kimi raised her voice from the backseat. "I'm not in a rush... Damn!" On Kimi's last words the cab screeched to a violent stop. Kimi tried to brace herself, but she was relentlessly thrown forward. "What the fuck?" she screamed.

The cab driver turned around and reached for her from the front seat. Kimi screamed in a panic. She couldn't believe her eyes. The driver wasn't the same person she had been traveling with for the past hour. It was Rojo Marquez.

"Oh my God!" Kimi screamed and reached for the back door.

Rojo's face turned demonic as he grabbed Kimi by the neck and punched her twice in the face. Kimi tried to fight him off, but she was trapped in the back of the taxicab. She shouted out for help, but no one could hear her desperate screams. Rojo continued to punish Kimi. She made one final attempt to open the back door, but Rojo grabbed her head and thumped it against the back window. Kimi was knocked out cold. Rojo looked around the street and wiped his mouth. He stared at Kimi's face to make sure she was unconscious. He felt no remorse for her. He reached for his cellphone and quickly made a call. He placed the phone to his ear and threw the taxicab back into gear. The vehicle swiftly moved down the street. A devilish smile came to Rojo's face as the call connected.

"I just got her," Rojo announced. "Meet me back at The Body Shop. We got some serious work to do."

Chapter 19

Monday, October 14
11:24 am
Newark, NJ

Asad Banks woke up from a frightening nightmare. His body was drenched with sweat, and he shivered like he was freezing cold. Asad released a defiant yell and swung a few punches at a phantom foe before he realized he had just awakened from a horrifying dream. "Shit," Asad groaned as a sharp pain pulsated on the side of his head. Asad grabbed his face and howled like a wounded animal. He looked around the hotel room and tried to focus his eyes. His memory of last night was hazy at best. Empty vodka bottles were littered across the floor. Asad had never drunk so much liquor in his life. After witnessing his best friend Dante being murdered, Asad nearly suffered a nervous breakdown. The violent incident replayed in his mind like a graphic movie scene. Asad couldn't believe it. His best friend was dead. To make matters worse, his older brother, Gary, almost suffered the same fate. Who would have the balls to pull off such heinous acts?

Asad slowly rose to his feet and cleared the cobwebs from his eyes. His hotel room was in shambles. Broken mirrors, turned over furniture and scattered trash were all evidence of a night Asad wanted to forget. His phone started ringing from under the bed. Asad dropped to the floor and quickly reached for his phone. It was Gary. Asad connected the call. "Gary, where are you?" Asad asked.

"No...the question is...where the hell are you?" Gary yelled from the other line.

"Huh?" Asad grabbed his head.

"I told you to be down here by eleven o'clock, Asad," Gary yelled again.

"Damn...be where?" Asad stuttered and glanced at the clock. His headache became worse. "I can't remember a damn thing, bro. What did I miss?"

"I'm not surprised, Asad," Gary sounded angry from the other line. "I told you I needed to do an emergency press conference this morning. We're all in the lobby of the hotel. I'm just waiting on you."

"Damn..." Asad mumbled and tapped his forehead. "Okay, I'll be down in five minutes."

Asad hung up the phone and grabbed his clothes. He kicked his way through the trash and snatched up his shoes. Despite the pounding headache, Asad was fully dressed in record time. He grabbed his pistol and bolted out the door. He knew he needed to be by his brother's side when he addressed the media about yesterday's shooting.

Downstairs in the lobby, Gary Banks sat in a secluded section of the hotel. A wall of police officers protected the mayor from the reporters and photographers, who clamored to get a glimpse of him. The news of the assassination attempt was still buzzing throughout the city. The topic was on everyone's tongue. No arrests had been made in connection to the crime. Despite their best efforts, the investigators had no clue who was responsible. The residents of Newark were still in an uproar, and people demanded answers.

Gary seemed to be unfazed by the ballyhoo around him. He calmly sat with his legs crossed and played with his phone. Sitting next to Gary was his Chief-of-Staff, Didi. She reviewed a few stacks of paper, and prepared herself for what was sure to be an eventful day. She looked over to her boss and smiled at him.

"How are you feeling, Mr. Mayor?" Didi leaned over and whispered to him.

"I'll be a lot better once we get this press conference over with," Gary responded. "I don't know what these people expect me to say."

"The usual." Didi shrugged her shoulders. "You are their fearless leader. They're going to look at you now like a super hero. You survived a crazy shooting. Talk about being bulletproof." Didi giggled and leaned in closer to Gary. She spoke softly so only his ears could hear her words. "Personally, I think it's sexy."

Gary laughed and tried to keep himself composed in front of their nosey audience. He gave Didi a familiar expression, and they shared an intimate moment of connection. "Damn Didi...how long have we known each other?" Gary asked and smiled at her.

"Eight years, Gary," Didi lowered her voice. "And like I told you when I first met you, I'm not going no damn where. You hear me?"

Gary nodded his head, and they shared another laugh. Gary was glad Didi agreed to be with him today. He knew it was going to be a tough day filled with press conferences and police interviews. The spotlight was now on Gary for all the wrong reasons, but he was strong enough to handle the pressure. Gary knew he was built for this moment. As a bright-eyed and fresh-faced politician, Gary had spent most of his twenties dreaming of changing things in New Jersey. Even back then, he realized the road to success would be tough and he would have to fight hard to climb the political ladder. Despite all the odds that were stacked against him, Gary never backed down. He fought through every obstacle that was in his path. He didn't stop until he clawed his way to the most powerful position in the city, and the job seemed to be waiting for him his entire life.

Being a young, handsome and single mayor had its advantages. Soon after becoming mayor, the money, the power and the fame flooded into Gary's life in a rush. The everyday rollercoaster ride of flashing cameras, high profile meetings and nationwide attention kept Gary's mind in a state of euphoria. But the unnatural high only made him fiend for a stronger hit. Like a drug addict craving more medication to numb the pain of reality, Gary sought out more reckless ways to keep his buzz for the fast life going strong. It didn't take long for the ugly demons of his past to catch up to the mayor. His addiction to unlimited power, fast cash and faster women started to change his life for the worse. So-called friends, who smiled in his face, transformed into enemies who lurked in the shadows. Local reporters investigated him constantly and disrespected him in the newspapers. Even some of the most loyal residents of his beloved city eventually turned their backs on him and prayed for the mayor's downfall. But, despite his convoluted lifestyle, Gary refused to buckle under the pressure. He never showed the public his wild ways, and he always seemed poised, even in the face of danger. As he sat in the lobby today, Gary almost relished in the fact that no one had a clue of the secrets he kept buried deep in the chambers of his twisted mind.

"Your brother is finally here," Didi announced and gently nudged the mayor on the arm.

Gary snapped back to reality and looked around. The sight of his younger brother made Gary tighten his face. Asad looked raggedy. He could barely keep his balance as he slowly made his way over to Gary and Didi. "What the hell, Asad?" Gary stood up and approached his brother.

"I'm sorry I'm late. I slept through those goddamn alarms," Asad slurred his words. The stench of liquor escaped from his rancid mouth.

"Asad, you really don't look like you're ready for this today," Gary uttered and held his nose.

"No…no…no…I'm ready." Asad shook his head. He gave Gary a hard stare. "I'm ready. You can bet your ass on that. Whoever did this…won't get another chance at my brother…I promise you that. I'm ready."

Asad patted his hip and Gary picked up on the gesture. He knew Asad was referring to his weapon. Asad's demeanor made Gary nervous. He could tell Asad was having a rough time coping with yesterday's attack.

"Let me talk to you real quick before we leave, Gary," Asad said and looked around.

"What is it?" Gary twisted his face again.

Asad put his arm around his brother's shoulder and walked him away from the police. Asad stopped just behind Didi's chair and looked at Gary. "I fucked up yesterday." Asad grew serious.

"It's not your fault—"

"No…let me finish!" Asad quickly cut his brother off. "I did…I fucked up. I should'a been more on point."

"We got ambushed yesterday, little brother." Gary shook his head. "It's not your fault."

"Yes it is!" Asad raised his voice. Didi looked up to the men as Asad continued to speak. He was clearly growing more stressed. "You know I'm never slippin', and I fucked up. I thought about that shit all night, and I can't believe I didn't see that bullshit coming."

"What are you talking about?" Gary snapped.

"First of all, Dante should'a never been on that detail," Asad's voice cracked. "He wasn't ready, and…I pushed for him to be out there."

Didi heard Dante's name and looked up to Gary. They both exchanged an awkward moment, and Gary quickly turned away from her. He focused back on Asad as he continued to speak.

"Let me ask you this, what day did we have the rally on?" Asad asked.

"What is wrong with you, Asad?" Gary tilted his head at his

brother. "The rally was yesterday."

"I know that, Gary." Asad emphatically started to shake his head. "What day was yesterday?"

"It was Sunday!" Gary closed his mouth.

"Exactly!" Asad pointed at his brother. "It was Sunday. And when was the last time you seen a bunch of city workers doing work on a Sunday? Those sons of bitches were acting like they were leaf blowers and working in the park. I saw them and didn't realize they were watching us the whole time. I fucked up. I really should'a been more on point."

"It's okay, Asad," Gary assured.

"It's not okay, big bro," Asad fired back. "I know I was dead wrong, but they can't get that shit off again. We need to find out who was behind this and deal with these assholes. They fucked with the wrong family. I want to make them pay. We got to find these motherfuckers."

Didi heard the venom in Asad's words and became edgy. She looked at Gary as he tried to calm his younger brother. Their loud voices began to echo throughout the lobby, and the reporters started to take notice.

"Asad I know you're pissed off about your friend." Gary put his hands up. "But you really have to calm down right now."

"Nah, fuck that." Asad shook his head. "I don't know why we can't hunt these bastards down and kill 'em like the dogs they are."

"Because that's not what we do," Gary tried to reason with his brother.

"So let me do it then." Asad sharply stared at the mayor. "I'm ready to put a motherfucker deeper than six feet."

Gary put up his fingers to his neck and made a slicing gesture. Asad's mouth was spewing very incriminating words, and Gary had to put an end to it. "Asad, seriously. . .you need to simmer down. Right now." Gary grabbed his brother and made him take a seat. Gary pulled another chair over and sat next to Asad. Gary looked around the lobby and dropped his voice. "Every branch of law enforcement is in this hotel right now, and every asshole with a microphone is waiting to interview me about that bullshit yesterday. Asad, you can't talk like that in here. Seriously...every little move is being watched. Especially today."

Asad balled up his lips as he looked over to Gary. He took a quick glance at Didi and shook his head. "What's with you?" Asad dropped his voice and gave his brother a suspicious glance.

"What do you mean?" Gary asked.

"Yesterday, somebody tried to bury a box of bullets in you, and now today y'all acting like everything is normal." Asad raised the corner of his mouth with disgust. He looked at Gary like he was a stranger. "What's up with you?"

"What's up with me?" Gary scowled. "What's up with me is that I'm the mayor of this goddamn city. I can't afford to look weak or look bloodthirsty right now. There's ways of dealing with things, and what you're talking about is not the way."

"This is bullshit." Asad was angry.

Didi looked over and squeezed her lips together. She wanted desperately to try and convince Asad to calm down, but she didn't want to speak out of turn. Gary dropped his head and thought for a moment. His brother was clearly angry, and Gary knew exactly what was on his mind.

"I think it's time for you to take a break." Gary looked directly at his brother.

"What!" Asad blurted. "I don't need no damn break."

"I'm not asking you, little brother," Gary said. "I'm telling you. You need a break. You don't realize it, but you're grieving bad. I don't want you out here doing something crazy. We can't make this situation worse. You need a week off. Trust me, you just need to relax right now."

"Why you doing this to me?" Asad whispered and tried to read his older brother.

"Doing what?" Gary asked.

"Why are you kicking me off your detail?" Asad shook his

head.

"I'm not kicking you off the detail. I'm just giving you a week off." Gary tried his best not to anger Asad. "We got some good people working on the investigation. They'll find out what happened in that park yesterday. You just need to go somewhere and unwind. Get your mind in a better place. This is for your own good, little brother. Believe me. You need to get away from all of this."

Asad gave his brother a blank stare. Something didn't seem right in Gary's voice. Asad cut his eye over to Didi, who looked away from Asad.

"It's only for a week." Gary put his hands on his brother's shoulder.

"You know what, get the fuck off of me," Asad snapped and stood up. "I don't know what the hell is going on over here, but I don't like it. If this shit happened five years ago, you would'a been begging me to take care of this shit. Now you want me to take a break?"

"Asad, this is different." Gary looked up to his angry brother.

"Nah, this ain't different. You're different," Asad shouted. "People out there playing dirty, and you think we can stop it with a fuckin' press conference. Fuck that. I can't sit here while these assholes are out there getting' ready to try to hit us again. Nobody else is dying from my team…I promise you that! I'm out of here!"

Gary tried to reach out for his brother. Asad pulled away from him. Gary watched his brother as he stormed past the small crowd of police and reporters, and then left the hotel. "Shit." Gary mumbled, then sat down in frustration. He wanted to chase after his brother, but he realized the commotion would turn the lobby into a media circus.

Didi looked over to her boss. "You think he's going to be okay?" she whispered.

"I hope so," Gary quietly responded. "I just don't want him to do nothing stupid to make this situation worse."

Didi gave the mayor an uneasy expression. Asad's anger was unpredictable. Didi knew that he could spin things out of control if he wasn't careful. She sat back in her chair and thought for a moment. "Do you want me to try and reach out to him?" she asked.

"No…" Gary shook his head. "Asad is a grown ass man. He's not a kid anymore. He'll be okay. We just need to stay with the plan and let this play out."

Gary's calmness settled Didi. She slowly nodded her head and showed Gary she was behind his decision. Gary sat back in his chair and checked the time. His press conference was in a few minutes, and he realized he needed to get back on his game. He pulled out his phone and doubled checked his talking points. His goal today was to restore order in his city. He wanted to put everyone on notice, including the shooters in the park.

Gary was a tough cookie to crack. He was not going to break under any circumstances. He wanted to show his city that he was standing strong and it was back to business as usual. As he went over his notes, Gary couldn't help but think about Asad. He prayed that his younger brother would heed his warning and lay low for the upcoming week.

Chapter 20

Monday, October 14
4:11 pm
Philadelphia, PA

A few hours later, Dirty Betty calmly cracked the window of her parked SUV. She took a long pull of her cigarette, then blew the smoke out into the cool air. The parking lot of the Sugar House Casino was packed with vehicles. Tourist and gamblers flooded the casino like it was a Saturday night. Betty laughed at the parade of losers as they strolled by her truck. She could see the delusional look in their eyes. Most of them were hoping they could turn their fortunes around before they left with broken dreams and broken pockets.

Betty was far from a gambler. She was a gangster down to the bone, loved what she did, and she was good at it. She never seemed to be fazed by the dangerous life. Most criminals never lived to celebrate their twentieth year in the game, and Betty was close to doubling that number. She had seen a lot of so-called thugs come and go, but none of them had lasted as long as Betty. She considered herself one of the smart ones. She never did anything too risky, and she was wise enough to take the right chances.

Today Betty was placing her money on a different kind of bet. She had called every dirty cop and gangster she knew from New York to Chicago, and put a bounty on Aaron's head. She wanted to find him quickly. It didn't take long for her sources to come back with information on Aaron's location. He was believed to be in the Philadelphia area. As Betty waited in the parking lot of the casino, she knew she was one step closer to hitting the jackpot.

Betty's phone started ringing. She flicked the cigarette out the window and answered the call. "Talk to me."

"Hey, it's Heidi. Thank God you answered your phone."

"Your ears must be burning, girl." Betty sat back in her seat. "I was just thinking about that money you gonna owe me."

"Listen Betty, I might've jumped the gun on this whole Aaron and Judith situation." Heidi's voice sounded child-like on the other line. "I thought about it, and maybe I need to let this shit go and move on."

"Heidi, get off my phone with that bullshit," Betty snapped. "I told you that once the wheels started moving on this thing, there's was no stopping it."

"I know, Betty," Heidi quickly responded. "I know…this shit is crazy but—"

"But nothing!" Betty cut her off. "Listen, I'm down here in Philly now, and I think we found out where Aaron is."

"What? Already?" Heidi gasped. "You found him?"

"I think so," Betty quickly responded. "We found out that Judith is dead."

"What?" Heidi yelled through the phone. "Dead? How?"

"I guess she was living in Atlanta for a while. She got robbed down there, and somebody killed her," Betty coldly gave Heidi the news.

"Oh my, God." Heidi couldn't believe her ears.

"Yea, I guess karma is really a bitch," Betty muttered.

"And what about Aaron?" Heidi asked. "How in the world did you find Aaron?"

"Girl, there's a billion cameras in this world. Even if he was a goddamn ghost, that motherfucker couldn't hide for long." Betty let out a weird chuckle. "One of my old partners put me on to him. He said they might've found a match on a facial recognition camera at their casino. Seems like your boyfriend has a real bad gambling problem. He comes to this casino a lot."

"Oh shit," Heidi whispered.

"I told you I'd find him," Betty said. "It's amazing what happens when you wave some money around. People will do all types of shit for you."

"Damn. I can't believe you found him. Are you sure it's him?" Heidi asked.

"I'm not a hundred percent sure yet," Betty responded. "But that's why I came down here myself. I'm at the casino now."

"So wait… Is Aaron at the casino?" Heidi asked.

"No, he's not here now," Betty quickly responded. "I'm waiting to meet with my contact down here. He'll let me know if that's really Aaron on the surveillance footage."

Heidi was silent on the other line. The thought of finally being able to confront Aaron scared her. Hearing that Betty was so close to finding him was the last thing she expected to hear. "Shit, Betty. I don't know what to say," Heidi whispered.

"You don't have to say a damn thing, girl," Betty quickly responded. "Just have my money ready when I get back." Betty looked out the window of her vehicle and raised her voice. "Listen, my guy is coming to the car now. I need to talk to him really quick and find out everything. I'll call you back when I'm done."

"Okay, Betty."

Before Heidi could say another word, Betty disconnected the call. She turned her focus to a tall man as he walked toward her SUV. The man appeared to be a member of the security team for the casino. The scars on his face, along with the tattoos on his hands and neck, didn't match his well-pressed uniform. Betty took one look at the security guard and recognized him from the old neighborhood in Newark. His name was Kevin Nottingham, but he was known in the streets as Knotts. Betty waved for Knotts to go to the passenger side of the vehicle.

She watched him closely as he opened the door and got inside the SUV. "Now come on Knotts…you know I gotta clown you about that costume you wearing." Betty laughed at the man. "I can't believe somebody gave you a job out here. There's no way you're using your real name. Dude…you are a bona fide gangster, and you wearing a cop uniform out this bitch."

"Come on Betty, don't even start. It's not a cop uniform, it's a security uniform. Big difference." Knotts shook his head and tried to laugh off the joke. "I got bills to pay, you feel me? Fuck that, I gotta get this money however I can get it."

"I hear that." Betty nodded. "Speaking of money, let me see what you got."

Knotts handed Betty a white envelope. She quickly grabbed it from his hand and pulled out the contents. A crooked smile came to her face when she looked at a grainy picture of Aaron cashing out his chips at the casino window.

"That's that motherfucker right there." Betty nodded. Dollar signs came to her eyes as she looked at more pictures of Aaron. "Damn, you were right on point. This motherfucker comes to the casino a lot."

"It gets even better." Knotts gave Betty another folder. "This guy won twenty grand one night, and we had to scan his driver's license for him to get paid. So we got his address and a phone number for him."

"Oh shit." Betty smiled. "This will definitely work." Betty continued to look over the pictures. Knotts glanced at his watch and put out his hand to Betty. "What?" Betty snapped.

"Where's my money?" Knotts asked. "You owe me fifteen hundred for the pictures. I told you I had some good information."

Betty didn't say a word. She reached into her jacket, and then counted off fifteen c-notes from her bankroll. She handed the money to Knotts and watched him count the bills. "Knotts, you wanna make two thousand more?" Betty asked and gritted her teeth.

"Depends on what I gotta do," Knotts responded and tucked

the money away in his pocket.

"I need to snatch this motherfucker up today, but I didn't bring my team down with me." Betty looked at the grainy photos as she spoke. "I'm not going to this dude's house... That's fuckin' suicide."

"Okay...so what you wanna do?" Knotts quickly asked.

"This is how I see it, you should call him and make up some bogus shit to get him down here to the casino." Betty twisted her face. "If we can get him to come down here we can snatch him right out of the parking lot."

"We?" Knotts nervously asked.

"Yea. We!" Betty snapped. "You said you got bills right? Well, it don't get no easier than this. Just help me snatch this motherfucker up and put him in the back. I'll drive him back to Jersey myself. I just need a little bit of muscle to make that happen. Don't tell me you on some scared shit right now."

"Stop it, Betty! I'm never scared." Knotts turned up his lip. "Don't let this uniform fool you. They don't call me Knotts for nothing."

"Okay, so let's do this fuckin' thing." Betty tossed the photos in the back seat and stared at Knotts.

"That's cool. Two thousand right?" Knotts raised two fingers up. "In cash right?"

"Two thousand in cash." Betty nodded. "It's easy work."

"I'll try to see what I can make happen," Knotts said. "Give me a couple of hours, and stay by your phone. I need to get back to work."

"Sound good." Betty watched as Knotts got out of the SUV. As he walked back to the casino, Betty couldn't help but think how close she was coming to scoring big with just one day's work.

Back in Newark, Heidi's stomach was still turning from the news she got from Betty. Aaron's face flashed in and out of her mind and made her heart race. Heidi was feeling conflicted. She felt nervous and excited about the news. She realized that she might finally get a chance to confront Aaron. Before Heidi could think any longer her phone started ringing. She assumed it was Betty calling her back. "Hello," Heidi answered.

"Hey beautiful," a man responded from the other line.

Heidi's heart fluttered the second she heard the familiar voice. Tycen. "Hey," Heidi whispered.

"I've been trying to reach you for the past few hours," Tycen tried his best to sound sincere.

"Oh…it's been a long day," Heidi admitted. "I got a lot on my mind."

"Oh okay," Tycen said. There was a silence on the phone. Tycen didn't know what to say now that he heard Heidi's voice.

Heidi looked at her cellphone and twisted her expression. "So is that what you called me for?" she blurted. "To tell me that you've been trying to reach me all day?"

"No…" Tycen nervously laughed. "I called because I wanted to talk to you."

"Okay…talk," Heidi quickly responded. She was still upset with Tycen and she wanted to keep their conversation short.

"I actually wanted to talk to you in person."

"I don't think that's a good idea right now," Heidi quietly responded. "I really need to get my mind together."

"I understand that, but I just want to apologize to you, Heidi," Tycen lowered his voice. "I want to say I'm sorry, and I would rather do that in person. It won't take long."

Heidi thought for a moment as the phone went silent again. She thought about the conversation she'd had with her mother earlier, and then decided to let down her guard. "When do you want to talk?" Heidi took a deep breath.

"I have one more meeting in an hour, but I will be done by six o'clock," Tycen said.

"Okay, but I'm not coming to that office," Heidi snapped.

"I understand," Tycen responded. "I can come to you."

"That's fine," Heidi mumbled. "Meet me at my mother's house. We can talk when you get here."

"Thanks Heidi," Tycen uttered. "I'll see you in a few."

Heidi disconnected the call and took another deep breath. It had only been one day since her argument with Tycen, but she clearly missed him. She forced her mind to switch gears, and decided to call Betty back. Heidi dialed her a few times, but there was no answer. "Shit!" She tried Betty one last time. The phone continued to ring without an answer. Heidi disconnected the call and waited by her phone. She couldn't help but wonder if Betty really located the man that had eluded her for so long. Aaron's face flashed in her mind. Heidi started to become overwhelmed by that familiar cloud of vengeance all over again.

Chapter 21

Monday, October 14
5:22 pm
Newark, NJ

Rojo Marquez impatiently paced back and forth on the front steps of The Body Shop. The temperature in the city was dropping quickly, but Rojo seemed to be unfazed by the cold air. He had been outside for nearly twenty minutes with his cellphone glued to his ear. He had tried to reach his father all day. He was anxious to give Leon Marquez the news about Kimi. With each passing minute, Rojo became more concerned. Where the hell is my dad?

Rojo's father was the most popular detainee at the Essex County Jail. His influence around the facility was just as strong as it was on the streets. Leon Marquez had only been incarcerated for a few months, but he was a master of manipulation. He sought after the greedy guards at the jail and added them to his payroll. They all tried to make life easy for Marquez while he awaited his big trial. The guards smuggled in magazines, drugs and even a cellphone for Marquez. But despite the perks of being a celebrity gangster, Leon Marquez needed desperately to get back on the street. He felt himself dying slowly inside the jail. The concrete walls were crushing him from within. Leon knew he wasn't going to make it much longer.

Rojo didn't like the way his father sounded during their

last conversation. As he continued to try his father's phone, Rojo could only imagine what Leon was going through. He continued to pace outside the building, and then called his father one last time. "Dammit!" Rojo yelled as the phone went straight to his father's voicemail. He didn't have any other choice but to leave a message. "Pop, it's me. I hope nobody confiscated that phone from you. I just wanted to let you know that we found the girl today. I'm going to handle everything tonight. Call me back!" Rojo disconnected the call. He was angry. He turned around and headed back into The Body Shop. Skittles was walking down the stairs and bumped into Rojo. "Where are you going?" Rojo quickly asked.

"I'm late for a client." Skittles looked at her watch.

Rojo noticed her sexy outfit and nodded in approval. She looked good enough to eat.

"Cool," Rojo said. "So…is this a house call?"

"Yup…it's only for a few hours. I'll be back later tonight," Skittles said.

"Don't worry about coming back. Take the rest of the night off after your client," Rojo said. "Things are about to get crazy around here, and I'm shutting down the shop for the night."

Skittles looked at Rojo. She tried to read his demeanor. There was something disturbing in his tone, and Skittles was afraid to find out what was behind his eyes. She kissed him on the cheek and proceeded to leave the building. She didn't want to keep her next client waiting.

Rojo turned around and continued up the stairs. He thought about the fact that he finally had Kimi in his custody. It was time to get down to business. Rojo walked up the stairs and approached three large security guards. "Listen fellas." Rojo gave the men a hard stare. "This shit is about to get real in here, so I don't want nobody around. Send all the girls home, and then make sure this place is empty from top to bottom. I need two people on the front door, and don't let nobody in this building. If any customers come by…just tell them motherfuckers that we're closed for the night. Y'all got that?"

All of the men nodded in unison.

"I need one person downstairs with Niko," Rojo said. "I need somebody to keep an eye on that son-a-bitch until I'm ready for him."

One of the men turned around and headed downstairs into the sub-basement. The other two men continued to listen to Rojo's orders.

"Don't forget what I said, fellas," Rojo barked. "Get everybody out of this fuckin' building right now and keep an eye on that front door. I don't need no goddamn witnesses."

On Rojo's last words, the two men turned around and proceeded to clear out every room in the building. They yelled at the working girls and their customers until the hallway was filled with people. They forced everyone to file out of the building without an explanation or refund.

Rojo headed to his office while his team turned The Body Shop into a ghost town. Rojo needed to handle some very important business, and he didn't want to take any chances. Tonight was his final opportunity to get the information he needed that could help with his father's trial. Rojo walked into his office and slowly closed the door. His entire mood changed as he looked around. Large white sheets were draped over his office furniture. A large plastic drop cloth was spread across the entire carpet. The room looked like a construction site. Rojo walked to the rear of his office and sat down behind the desk.

"It smells like fear in here" Rojo coldly announced. "Are you afraid?"

Rojo slowly lifted his eyes and stared across his desk. Seated strapped to a chair in the middle of the room was Kimi Moore. Her wrists were bleeding from the wire hangers that bounded her hands. Her lips and cheeks were swollen from the quick beating she took from Rojo earlier. Kimi's terrified face was flushed with tears. She was petrified. Rojo stared at her. Kimi didn't know what to make of his blank expression. She looked into his distant eyes and began sobbing. She couldn't believe she was in this situation.

"What do you want?" Kimi cried out. "Why am I here?"

"That's funny you asked that question… I was sittin' here thinkin' the same thing." Rojo leaned back in his chair. "Why are you here? What are you doing fucking around with a worthless scab like Niko Stanton?"

Kimi froze when she heard her boyfriend's name.

"Niko is a piece of shit," Rojo barked. "He fucks over everybody he does business with. He's a shitty person. But I think you already know that. . .right?"

Kimi didn't say a word. She looked around the office and continued shaking.

"Please let me go," she pleaded.

"I can't do that." Rojo shook his head. "Niko got my father locked up. He snitched on him. That motherfucker gotta answer for that. He tried to bury my dad. I can't have that. I won't let him bite the hand that feeds his sorry ass."

Kimi continued trembling in the chair. More blood dripped from her wrists.

"There's only one way you're getting outta here tonight, Kimi." Rojo reached into his drawer and pulled out a knife. He placed it on the desk in full view of Kimi's horrified eyes. "Niko knows some information and he's not talking right now. But if it's one thing I know about cowards like that…they will tell you everything you want to know if you give them the right motivation." Rojo slowly spun the knife around on his desk. He frowned at Kimi. "Now…how bad I hurt you…is going to depend on how much your boyfriend loves you." Rojo chuckled like a demon. He stood to his feet and grabbed the knife. Kimi started breathing heavily as Rojo moved around his desk. He slowly walked over to her.

"Please don't…" Kimi cried out. She didn't know what to expect.

"Don't what?" Rojo yelled. "You can save all that cryin' bullshit for later. I'm not goin' to touch you yet…that'll spoil all the fun." Rojo stood directly in front of Kimi and pointed the sharp knife at her face. "I want you to listen to me carefully. When I bring Niko in here you better convince him to tell me everything he knows...or...this...is goin' to turn out bad for you. You understand?"

Kimi stared at the knife and continued sobbing. She looked at the tattoo on Rojo's wrist and realized this was the same man that carjacked her and kidnapped Niko. Kimi had seen Rojo in action and knew exactly how dangerous he could be. She nodded her head and closed her mouth as the tears continued flowing. All Kimi could do was pray that she would make it out of The Body Shop alive.

Chapter 22

Monday, October 14
6:01 pm
Newark, NJ

"News 12 New Jersey has just learned that city officials are still working overtime to investigate what went terribly wrong at a rally headed by Mayor Gary Banks yesterday in Newark. What started out as an impromptu gathering called by the mayor, quickly turned into something out of a gangster movie as shots were fired leaving three people dead and almost two dozen people wounded. Investigators have yet to confirm the exact cause of the violence in Military Park, but some sources are identifying the mayor as the target of the shooting. A fifteen thousand dollar reward has been announced by the Newark PD for any information leading to the arrest of the suspects responsible for the violence."

Asad Banks slowly pulled his exhausted eyes up from his drink and turned his attention toward the television. Despite the music and the loud chatter that engulfed the Brick City Tavern, Asad managed to hear the newscast blaring from the television just above the bar. He took another long sip of his drink and listened closely as the reporter announced more details about the shooting that shook up the city.

Asad rubbed his chin in frustration. Yesterday's drama was weighing heavy on his mind, and no drink in the world was strong enough to ease his pain. His best friend, Dante, was dead and the anguish was evident in Asad's demeanor. He had spent most of the day searching for leads to get closer to the men who were responsible for the murder, but he continued to come up empty. The Newark Police department was also clueless. The normal snitches and street informants all seemed to clam up and were all too eager to protect the culprits. Asad sensed there was something more to this vicious shooting, and couldn't help but feel like something ugly was brewing just beneath the surface.

Gary Banks had many enemies in the City of Newark, and Asad was well aware of his growing list of usual suspects. The mayor constantly received death threats from bankrupted business owners, evicted tenants and disgruntle inmates. Gary even received video threats on the Internet from masked gang bangers on a weekly basis. But there was something unnerving about the men Asad and his security team encountered in the park. These men were professional gunmen and were well equipped. The clever diversion and timely assault reminded Asad of a police exercise. Men like this had to be tracked down and eliminated quickly in order to protect his brother. With each passing minute, Asad knew that the trail would grow colder and the men would undoubtedly return to make another attempt on the mayor's life. Asad refused to take that chance.

"Bartender!" Asad yelled out. "Can you please turn that television up a bit?"

A female bartender heard the yelling across the bar and grabbed the remote from her station. She turned up the television and glanced over toward Asad. The attractive bartender winsomely bounced over toward him. Asad was so wrapped up into the bulletin that he never noticed the bartender's flirtatious swaying.

"Can I get you another drink?" the bartender softly asked.

Asad unconsciously nodded his head and pushed forward his glass. She poured his drink and slightly twisted her face at him. She waited for the news report to end and gently tapped him on the wrist. "Asad…" The bartender frowned. "Why do you insist on calling me bartender today? I have a name you know."

Asad dropped his eyebrows and looked over to the woman. He was shocked when he heard his name spill from her lips. Before he could respond to her question, the bartender cut him short.

"Don't give me that guilty face, honey," the bartender playfully chastised him. "I know who you are. Everybody knows who you are, Asad. You can't be the mayor's brother, and not expect everyone in the city to recognize your face."

"Yea, I guess that's my gift…and my curse. Being the mayor's brother," Asad slurred his words and downed the drink. The hard liquor burned his chest, and Asad gritted his teeth. He looked up to the bartender. His bloodshot eyes scared her.

She tapped his hand again. "Maybe you should slow down tonight, honey," the bartender calmly warned.

"Slow down for what?" Asad snapped. He looked at the empty glass. "We all gotta die someday right?"

"Are you okay, Asad? You don't look well at all." The bartender looked concerned.

Asad pointed at the television screen and pushed his glass forward. He wanted another drink, but the bartender purposely ignored his request.

She glanced at the news story and shook her head. "Very sad about that shooting. So many folks got hurt down there. I don't know what's wrong with people these days," the bartender huffed.

"Those were not people that did that yesterday," Asad dropped his voice. "Those were animals."

There was something sinister about Asad's statement. The bartender picked up on his gloomy remark and looked at him. "So do they know who did it?" the bartender asked.

"Not a damn clue." Asad shook his head.

"Everybody's been talking about it all day in here," the bartender added.

"Is that right?" Asad looked up. "I wish I knew who the fuck did this," Asad slurred his words again.

"What about The Marquez Crew?" the bartender asked.

"What about them?" Asad snapped.

"Have the police questioned them?" the bartender asked. "A lot of people in here mentioned their name. I don't know if it's just people talking, but, for whatever reason, I keep hearing about The Marquez Crew."

Asad closed his mouth and thought for a moment. He kicked himself for not thinking of the most dangerous family in the city of Newark. Asad was very familiar with Leon Marquez and the ruthless ways of his crime organization. His, brother, Gary spent tons of money and time trying to clean up the streets of Newark, and The Marquez Crew was slowly becoming the biggest threat to his efforts.

Asad looked at the bartender and gave her a strange expression. He reached deep in his pocket and peeled off a fifty-dollar bill from his bankroll.

"Thanks," Asad uttered and placed the money on the bar. "The rest is for you." Asad stood up from the stool and stumbled through the tavern. He reached in his pocket and grabbed his phone. Asad could barely see straight as he headed outside to his car. He had been drinking a lot today, and Asad found himself struggling to keep his balance. He dialed his brother's phone and waited for him to answer the call. "Gary, where are you?" Asad blurted as the mayor picked up the other line.

"I'm heading to my house right now," Gary responded. "I'm meeting with Didi tonight. Where are you?"

"Just leaving the bar," Asad slurred again. "Let me ask you a question...did the police grab anybody from The Marquez

Crew?" There was a silence on the phone. Gary didn't respond. Asad got angry. "Gary, did you hear me?" Asad yelled. "Do you have the police going after The Marquez Crew?"

"Asad, what are you doing?" Gary barked at his younger brother. "I thought I told you to take a break. The investigation is under way."

"So are they going after The Marquez Crew or not?" Asad pressed.

"For what?" Gary snapped.

"Goddammit Gary! For murdering my best friend yesterday?" Asad yelled.

"What the hell, Asad…no…they are not going after them… they're not on the short list," Gary tried to plead with his brother. "There's nothing that they found that's pointing in that direction. But like I said…the investigation is underway—"

"Don't give me that bullshit, Gary!" Asad was screaming now. "You know those motherfuckers will do anything to get rid of you. Why are we even having this discussion? Somebody should be putting a boot to their fuckin' heads right now."

"Asad…listen to yourself. You're drunk and you're angry," Gary sternly said. "You need to pull yourself together and let the process work. The investigators are all over this thing."

"So you're telling me that The Marquez Crew had nothing to do with this?" Asad yelled.

"I don't know," Gary fired back. "But if the investigation points in that direction…believe me…they will bring somebody in for questioning."

"You know what Gary…you're right. I might be drunk and pissed off…but…I'm not stupid," Asad dropped his voice. "If nobody got the balls to find out the truth…then I'll step up and do the dirty work."

"Wait…Asad…what are you talking about?" Gary quickly asked.

"I'll do my own questioning!" Asad yelled and ignored his brother. "Fuck that—"

Asad disconnected the call and turned off the phone. He

was angry with Gary. Asad awkwardly opened his car door and plopped down into his seat. He released a frustrated yell and started the engine. Asad's temper was getting the best of him. All he could see in his mind was Dante's lifeless body in Military Park. A strong thirst for street justice came over him. Asad wasn't thinking straight, but that didn't stop him from speeding out of the parking lot. The only thing on his mind was seeking out his best friend's killers. One way or another... somebody has to pay!

A few miles away Gary Banks held the phone tightly in his hand. Gary's vehicle coasted down the dark Newark streets as he made his way home. He tried to reach his brother a few more times before he realized that Asad refused to pick up the phone for him. The fire in his brother's voice scared Gary. He prayed that Asad would calm himself and curb his hunger to retaliate. Gary knew that the Marquez family was not involved with the shooting. Going after such a high profile figure in broad daylight didn't match the style of the notorious family. The mayor and his team were eyeing a separate batch of suspects, and Gary was hoping Asad's anger would not botch their investigation. As Gary continued to make his way home, his phone started buzzing in his hand. "Asad...don't do nothing stupid...!" Gary yelled into the phone.

"Hello...Gary...It's me...Didi," A female voice stammered from the other line.

"Shit...I'm sorry, Didi. I thought you was my brother," Gary uttered.

"Is everything okay?" Didi asked.

"Yes..." Gary let out a frustrated sound. "Asad called me a few minutes ago...he was drunk as shit. He sounded like he was on a damn rampage. I just got off the phone with him, and I thought he was calling back."

"Where is he?" Didi sounded worried.

"I don't know," Gary responded. "He brought up The Marquez Crew."

"What?" Didi gasped.

"Yup. I don't know why he just won't get away from this thing." Gary shook his head. "Dammit…I hope he doesn't do nothing stupid tonight."

"Wow Gary…I'm sorry," Didi whispered. "This is getting really complicated."

"I know," Gary quietly replied. "But we just need to hold on and let all of this play out. We'll be fine."

"I hope so, Gary," Didi mumbled.

"We will be…I promise," Gary confidently responded.

"So do you want to cancel for tonight?" Didi asked.

"Oh no…I'm on my way home now," Gary quickly answered. "I'm only about twenty minutes away."

"Good…I'm already at your house. I hope you don't mind that I let myself in already," Didi's voice started to become less professional and more flirtatious with every word. "Everything is set."

"Okay…Didi…good." Gary smiled. "I will see you when I get there."

"Hurry up, Mr. Mayor," Didi let out a slight moan with her words. "We got work to do."

Chapter 23

Monday, October 14
6:28 pm
Newark, NJ

Twenty minutes later, Gary Banks pulled up to the front of his luxurious home and parked in the driveway. The last two days were taking a toll on his body. The tired mayor was long overdue for some rest and relaxation. As Gary headed to the front door, he noticed a few lights were on in the house. He smiled, knowing Didi was already inside. He pushed his problems to the back of his mind and headed inside the home.

The living room was empty and there was no sign of his Chief-of-Staff. There were a half dozen candles lit around the house, and the intoxicating aroma of blonde wood calmed Gary's nerves. He slowly took off his jacket and walked into the dining room. There was a chilled glass of wine on the table next to a small note. Gary smiled and slowly shook his head. Didi was always full of surprises.

Gary took a sip of the smooth red wine. A subtle thump came from the second floor, and Gary twisted his face. He turned his attention back to the note on the table. He read it.

Good evening, Mr. Mayor. You've had a very busy day and I know you deserve a break. I decided to move our meeting to the second floor. I hope you don't mind. Meet me in your bedroom, I have a gift for you. When you get upstairs, do me a favor and knock first. *smiles* —Didi.

A crooked smile came to Gary's face. His imagination started to run wild, and he could only imagine what Didi was up to. He downed the rest of the wine and headed to the second floor. With each careful step Gary was growing more anxious to see exactly what was going on in his bedroom. He thought about the note, and an even wider smile came to his face. Gary gently tapped on the door and announced that he was home.

"One second, Gary," Didi sang from behind the door.

A few moments later, Didi playfully poked her head out of the bedroom. Gary smiled when he glanced at her pretty face. Looking at her gorgeous grin made Gary think about their very complex relationship. By day, Didi and Gary worked very closely together in the channels of city hall. As the mayor's Chief of Staff, Didi helped him build an unstoppable team that managed the rigorous duties of running the city of Newark. But, by night, the two constantly engaged in steamy bouts of passion and lovemaking. The two grew very close as time passed. They agreed to keep their love affair a total secret.

Didi and Gary were perfect for each other. The mayor was the biggest sex fanatic she had ever known, and behind Didi's professional exterior was a raging freak ready and willing to do anything to please him. Didi and Gary only had two rules for their arrangement. Rule number one: always keep bedroom business in the bedroom. And rule number two: no fantasy was off limits. For Gary and Didi it was a dream situation. And when it came time to sexually explore each other, they pushed their encounters to the max. Not a soul down at city hall had a clue what Didi and Gary were up to behind closed doors. The mysterious nature of their arrangement only made their wild sexcapades more exhilarating.

Tonight Didi had a treat for her powerful friend. A fantasy had been brewing in her mind, and she was ready to take her sex game to another level. As she seductively stood in the doorway to Gary's bedroom she gave him an all too familiar smile that drove Gary crazy. He looked her up and down. Didi was now delightfully donned in a jet-black leather bra and panty set. Fitted snugly around her neck was a black leather choker with diamond studs. Gary's eyes nearly popped out of his head as he followed four small metal chains that draped around her stomach and ran smoothly down and around her curvy hips and thighs. Gary felt a warm rush of adrenaline flow through his body. He instantly became horny when he took one look at her high black leather boots. Didi reminded him of a sexy dominatrix. The leather outfit was just the beginning of her wild fantasy.

"You like what you see, baby?" Didi whispered.

"Hell yes." Gary smiled.

"You know I got a surprise for you, right?" Didi softly asked.

"I'm already surprised just from looking at you," Gary joked as he gave his sexy friend another onceover.

"Baby...you are goin' to love this surprise." Didi's face became seductively serious as she reached out her hand to Gary. "Close your eyes, baby."

Gary smiled and obeyed the command. He shut his eyes as Didi slowly placed a leather blindfold around his head. She wanted to make sure he couldn't see a thing. She softly grabbed him by the wrist and led him all the way into the bedroom. He walked slowly behind Didi as she guided him to his king sized bed. She sat him down on the edge of the mattress and whispered in his ear.

"Promise me. No peeking," Didi softly said.

"I promise," Gary responded.

Didi stepped back and began to undress the mayor. She started up top and softly kissed him on the lips as she tossed his shirt to the floor. Didi ran her soft palms across Gary's smooth chest and smiled when she saw his nipples hardening from the sensation. She continued to rub him gently and moved her hands down to his pants. "Oh my, somebody is ready for some attention," Didi giggled as she exposed Gary's rock solid dick.

It had been a while since Gary and Didi were together, and

his pulsating manhood was proof of that. Didi felt compelled to put her longing lips on him, but she resisted the temptation. She had an even sweeter treat for Gary, and she didn't want to ruin the surprise. She calmly pulled off his pants and stepped back away from Gary. "Now remember, you promised…no peeking. And one more rule, baby," Didi softly continued. "You can't use your hands until I say so."

"Okay," Gary responded in a boyish tone. "As you wish." He smiled as he heard the slight jingling of the chains draped around Didi's body. He could only imagine what she had planned as he let his imagination run wild. He placed his palms on the bed and got more comfortable on the edge of the mattress.

Gary nearly jumped when he felt her warm fingers crawl from his feet and slowly up his legs. Her wet lips softly pecked between his thighs, and Gary's dick began to grow even larger from the tease. He heard the dangling of her chains once again as she moved further up his thighs and placed her face directly between his legs. She grabbed hold of his hard dick and started to stroke him. Something felt different about her grip, but Gary was too wrapped up in the pleasure to protest. Her wet tongue started to dance around his shaft, and Gary quietly moaned from the feeling. He could tell she was growing more excited by the second. She quickly moved to the top of his dick and started to lick him wildly. The slurping sound of her wet tongue thrilled Gary even more, and his head fell back in bliss. She opened up her mouth wide and forced him deep inside like a chocolate lollipop. Gary moaned louder when he felt the head of his dick touch the back of her throat. Her wet mouth felt very different tonight, and all Gary could do was enjoy the ride.

"Damn, baby!" Gary grunted in amazement. Didi had never inhaled him like this before. Gary was stunned by how much of his dick she swallowed. He almost broke the second rule by grabbing the back of her head, but he forced himself to keep his hands still. The chains started dangling even louder as she bounced her head up and down on his throbbing dick. Gary picked up on her smooth rhythm and started to eagerly hump her face. He felt a cool chill rush up his spine and realized a huge orgasm was building up. He started breathing heavily. He didn't know what felt better, her warm hands stroking the base of his cock or her piping hot mouth sucking tightly on his head. Didi was trying some new tricks tonight, and the sensation was heavenly.

Gary tightened his eyes as he got closer to climaxing. He didn't want the episode to end this early, so he decided to hold back. He tried to ignore the sound of her wet tongue but she was slurping uncontrollably now. She was never this loud before, and Gary loved it. She sensed he was getting closer and started to stroke him faster. The sound of the chains echoed off the walls in his bedroom. Gary let out a louder moan as another chill flushed through his body.

"Goddamn girl, you gotta slow down," Gary groaned. He struggled to get the words out.

"Okay daddy. I'll slow down," a voice responded.

What the hell? Gary's mind froze for a moment. His heart almost skipped a beat when he heard the unfamiliar voice. Gary knew he had one glass of wine tonight but there was no way the alcohol was affecting his hearing. He reached up to the blindfold and ripped it off. His heart started pumping faster. Didi was known to pull off some amazing tricks, but tonight it seemed she had truly outdone herself. When Gary opened his eyes, he was surprised to see a total stranger with her head in his lap. Didi was standing a few feet away from the strange woman, smiling at Gary's flushed expression.

"Surprise baby," Didi whispered.

Gary looked down at the girl's face again but he didn't recognize her. She was a young girl in her early twenties. Her deep bronze skin was smooth as butter, and her attractive face complimented her young tight body. Gary gazed into her sexy protruding eyes, trying to figure out who she was.

"I hope you're not mad at me, baby," Didi said and moved

closer to Gary.

"No, I'm not mad…I'm just…shocked," Gary quietly replied. "I didn't know we were going to have company tonight."

"Yes…I wanted to surprise you so I brought her along." Didi smiled.

Gary looked over to his friend and gave her a playful angry face. Didi could be very sneaky when she wanted to. "Who is she?" Gary asked and looked down at the girl's sexy body again.

"She's a new friend of mine." Didi smiled. "I asked her to do me this favor, and I rented her for the evening."

Gary chuckled at her response. He realized Didi had hired a working girl to join their party tonight. He started to grow more excited as he realized he now had two sexy women in his bedroom. "What's her name?" Gary asked.

"Skittles," Didi quickly responded.

"Huh…?" Gary chuckled again. "Skittles?"

Didi laughed and looked at the young girl. "Show him, honey," Didi whispered.

Skittle rose to her feet and stood in front of the mayor. A sly smile emerged on Gary's face. He looked at the girl and became more aroused when he noticed a tattoo of a rainbow on her stomach. "Yes, baby. My name is Skittles," the young girl whispered to Gary and gave him a seductive glare. "Taste the rainbow, baby."

Gary's dick responded to the sound of Skittles' frisky voice. He was beyond excited. The young vixen wore the exact leather outfit that Didi was wearing. The choker around her neck gave the girl a submissive vibe that awakened a dominant side in Gary. He watched Skittles closely as Didi walked over and connected a metal leash to the back of the girl's leather bra. Didi stood over her like a master to a slave.

Gary reached out and rubbed the young girl's soft skin. He moved his hand down to her soft thighs and smiled. He quietly groaned and couldn't believe her skin was so tight and ripe.

"I like Skittles," Gary softly whispered.

"You want to kiss her?" Didi smiled.

Gary nodded his head like a little boy answering his mother.

Didi slightly tugged on the leash and got the young girl's attention. "Kiss him, Skittles," Didi commanded.

Skittles moved closer to Gary. She calmly grabbed him by the face and put her luscious lips on his. Gary's body reacted to the wet kiss. He reached out his hands and started to caress her perky breast. Her nipples were rock solid, and she started to moan as Gary played with them.

Didi noticed Gary's dick rising even higher and smiled knowing he was getting horny again. "You want to fuck her don't you?" Didi whispered to Gary. The words started to turn her on as well.

Gary nodded his head and moved his lips down to Skittles' neck. He pulled back the cups on her leather bra and licked his lips as he exposed her brown breast. He opened his mouth and started to run his tongue back and forth between her sultry titties. Skittles grabbed the back of Gary's head and let out a girlish whine. He pulled her closer and flicked his tongue against her nipples. Skittles moaned again from the feeling, and Didi felt her own pussy getting wetter just watching the action. Gary moved up to Skittles' face and started to kiss her passionately. He felt like a teenager again from all of the excitement. An idea came to his head, and he slowly pulled his face away from Skittles.

"You ever had a million dollar orgasm?" Gary quietly asked as a devilish smile came to his face.

"Um....no. I don't think so?" Skittles dropped her eyebrows and gave Gary a strange look.

Didi shook her head and smiled. She knew exactly what Gary was referring to.

"Are you sure, baby? You never had a million dollar orgasm before?" Gary asked again.

"No, I don't think so," Skittles responded. "What's that?"

"Didi knows what that is...and she loves it," Gary whispered and another crooked smile came to his face. "Ain't that right, Didi?"

"Oh yes," Didi exclaimed. "I love a million dollar orgasm. I think she'll love it to."

A nervous smile came to Skittles' face as she tried to uncover the big mystery of what a million dollar orgasm could be. She had never heard the term before, and became curious.

"Okay let's do it," Gary said.

Didi slightly tugged on the metal leash again and looked over to the young girl. "Come stand by me, Skittles," Didi commanded. "You're going to love this."

Skittles turned around and walked over to Didi, who wore a sexy grin on her face. Gary looked at the both of them and was astounded by the gorgeous scene. They watched Gary closely as he walked his naked body to the far side of the bedroom. He turned his attention to a large oil painting on the wall. Gary reached up and removed the framed canvas, revealing a two hundred pound steel safe that was housed firmly in the wall. He turned back to Didi and Skittles and gave them a suspicious glance. Didi chuckled and grabbed Skittles by the shoulder. She knew Gary would never allow them to watch him as he entered his secret combination. Gary's expression never changed as Didi turned Skittles around, then slowly followed suit. He quickly spun the combination dial a few times and unlocked the safe.

"Okay," Gary announced.

Didi and Skittles turned back around just in time to see Gary pull out an enormous stack of one hundred dollar bills from the huge safe. He dumped the large pile on the king sized bed, and then walked back to grab another stack. Skittles' eyes lit up. She had never seen so much money in her young life. Gary pulled out more cash and dumped it on his bed. He smiled at Skittles' expression, and knew she was impressed by all the money he was spreading on the mattress.

"You ready?" Gary whispered to Skittles as he tossed out one more pile of c-notes.

"She's ready," Didi answered for the young girl and walked her over to the bed. "Take off your panties," Didi commanded.

Skittles obeyed and slowly dropped her leather underwear to the floor.

Gary smiled when he took a close look at her shaven pussy. "Pretty," Gary said. He couldn't help himself.

"Baby, how do you want her?" Didi asked and looked over to Gary.

"You sure you have to ask me that question?" Gary chuckled.

Didi smiled at the mayor. She knew him long enough to know exactly how to please him and how he enjoyed his sex. Gary was an ass-man and always wanted to see his women face down. Didi nodded her head and glanced over to Skittles. "Turn around and get on your knees," Didi ordered.

Skittles obeyed the command and turned around on the bed. She got on all fours and spread her thighs apart. Didi was far from a lesbian, but Skittles' sweet pussy was very hard to go unnoticed. Gary climbed onto the bed and began to rub on Skittles' back again. He kissed her body softly and savored the moment. Didi kept a tight grip on the metal leash and stood next to the bed. She watched closely as Gary kissed the back of the young girl's neck and started to run his tongue down her back.

Skittles started shaking from the feeling of his warm tongue on her body. She looked down at all the money on the bed, becoming mesmerized by the view. She felt Gary get behind her and grab her by the hips. He was clearly ready to feel her.

Gary didn't give her another moment to brace for him. Gary forced his thick dick inside of her tight pussy in a rush. Skittles screamed in pain as the penetration caught her off guard.

"I think she likes it," Didi giggled and tugged on the metal leash.

Skittles screamed again as Gary forced his dick deep inside. She tried to keep up with him but Skittles was not use to a man of Gary's size. He grabbed her tighter by the hips and started ramming her hard like a pinball machine. His huge dick relentlessly spread her lips wide open, and her pussy became uncontrollably wet.

Didi moaned as she looked on. She raised one of her legs to the edge of the bed. She wanted badly to get in on the action, but tonight belonged to Skittles. Didi dropped her hands between her thighs and started to play with her burning clit. “Yes baby, fuck her good,” Didi moaned as she masturbated.

Skittles’ ass bounced back and forth as Gary started to grow more excited. He stroked Skittles’ pussy like he had known her for years. He grunted heavily and felt his orgasm building again. Skittles cried out as every inch of Gary’s head touch something deep inside her. The pain quickly turned into pleasure, and Skittles started moaning and screaming loudly. She looked down at the bed full of money, and the marvelous spectacle seemed surreal. She laid her face flat on the mattress and arched her back for Gary. She welcomed him to go deeper. He started stroking her faster, and Skittles screamed his name. “Yes, Gary please fuck me harder!” Skittles cried out.

Didi moaned as her pussy got even wetter. She smacked Skittles on the ass and yelled at her. “Bounce that shit on him, girl!” Didi shouted with excitement.

Gary loved it. “Yea!”

Skittles’ pussy was getting creamier with every stroke, and he could tell she was close to a climax. Skittles reached out to the edge of the bed and held on tight. Gary was hitting her spot over and over again, and she let out a harsh grunt. Gary’s forceful fucking was unlike anything she had ever felt. “Oh my God!. . .Gary…wait—” Skittles couldn’t finish her statement as an enormous orgasm rushed from the corners of her pussy. Her thighs started shaking fiercely as a second orgasm quickly followed, engulfing Gary’s dick.

“Goddamn…” the mayor groaned. He felt the walls of Skittles’ pussy tightly contracting.

She was having multiple orgasms, and Didi smiled at her quaking body. Gary couldn’t take it anymore. Skittles’ tight pussy had finally got the best of him, and Gary had to pull out.

Didi noticed Gary was climaxing, and then quickly reached down and grabbed his soaking dick. She jerked him wildly until he ejaculated all over the crisp one-hundred dollar bills. He moaned in pleasure and called out Didi's name.

"Oh my goodness, y'all are nasty," Didi giggled. She laughed at Gary and Skittles as they both collapsed onto the bed full of money. The scene was a huge turn on for Didi. She couldn't wait to get her turn. She smiled knowing her sexy surprise for Gary was an enjoyable one. Didi unhooked the metal leash from Skittles' bra and dropped it to the floor. She walked over to where Gary was laying and climb onto the bed. She snuggled up behind the mayor and grabbed him tightly. Didi could still feel his warm body slightly trembling. She could only imagine how good he was feeling. She kissed him on the back of his neck and whispered in his ear. "You got thirty minutes, Mr. Mayor," Didi softly said and kissed him again. "And then I want my million dollar orgasm."

"That sounds real good to me," Gary whispered.

"And Skittles...baby...this time you get to watch me." Didi looked over to the young girl and smiled.

Skittles let out another pleasing moan and nodded toward Didi.

Gary closed his eyes. He couldn't erase the smirk off of his face. He felt good knowing he was in for a long and sexy evening with two beautiful women. The bedroom fell silent. Gary, Didi and Skittles relaxed on the mattress covered with money. They marinated in a state of ecstasy.

Chapter 24

Monday, October 14
7:18 pm
Newark, NJ

Heidi Kachina calmly stood over the sink in her mother's kitchen. The clanging of the dishes was the only sound that could be heard throughout the quiet home. A restless feeling came over Heidi as she carefully washed the pots and pans from tonight's dinner. She wiped a bead of sweat from her forehead and took a look at the metal radiator in the kitchen. It was unusually hot in her mother's house. She looked at the old radiator and cursed out loud.

"Damn, I wish my mom gets rid of those things," Heidi whispered. "It's hot as hell in here."

Heidi shook her head. She tried to keep herself busy. She needed to take her mind off the conversation she had had with Dirty Betty earlier in the day. Learning of Aaron's whereabouts had changed her entire mood. Heidi hated feeling consumed by her thoughts of Aaron. She had never come this close to tracking him down. The news from Betty had revived Heidi's fire. It had been three hours since her last update, and Heidi prayed that Betty would call her phone any minute now.

Heidi looked down at her soaking hands in the dishwater. She turned her focus to the circular tan line on her left ring finger. The ironic sight reminded her that there was something missing in her life. She didn't feel complete. The turmoil that occurred in her past boiled over into her present situation. Although Heidi was far removed from the physical pain of being betrayed, the emotional scars were still punishing her. Heidi was not ready to move on until she closed Aaron's chapter in her life once and for all.

Pearl slowly walked into the kitchen. She headed to the refrigerator and noticed her daughter standing motionless near the sink. "I don't think it's going to get no cleaner than that," Pearl called out.

"Huh....what?" Heidi asked from the other side of the kitchen.

"That pot," Pearl responded. "You have been scrubbing that same pot for about ten minutes now. I think it's clean."

"Oh. . .dammit," Heidi blurted and snapped out of her daydream.

Pearl poured herself a drink of water and looked over to Heidi. "You okay?" Pearl asked.

"I'm fine, Mom," Heidi assured.

Pearl continued to look over to her daughter. Heidi never turned around. Pearl sensed something was bothering her and wanted to make sure her daughter was okay. "You don't seem fine." Pearl took a seat at the kitchen table. "You been quiet as a mouse all day."

"I'm fine," Heidi repeated. "I just been thinking about a lot today."

"Really? That makes two of us," Pearl uttered.

Heidi turned around and looked at her mother. There was something different in Pearl's tone that caught Heidi's attention. "Thinking about what?"

"Moving," Pearl answered and took another drink of water.

"Moving?" Heidi dried her hands and walked over to the table. "Mom, you just came back."

"I know...but I think that was a mistake." Pearl shook her head. "I thought I was homesick when I was living with your aunt. But now that I'm back in Newark...I'm ready to leave again."

"Wow." Heidi took a seat.

"It just feels like I shouldn't be here...you know." Pearl

put down her glass and started twisting the locket around her neck. "I don't know. I'm just starting to get bad feelings about this city."

"Wow, Mom. I didn't know you were thinking about moving." Heidi looked at her mother. "Did you talk to Aunt Valerie about this?"

"Not yet," Pearl responded. "But I'll call her soon. Like I said…I'm just thinking about it. But I do feel like I need to leave." Before Pearl could continue, Heidi's cellphone started ringing in the next room.

"Bout time!" Heidi mumbled and quickly stood up. She bolted out the kitchen and rushed to her phone. Her expression changed when she noticed it wasn't the call she had been expecting.

"Hello, Tycen," Heidi quietly answered the phone.

"Hey, babe. I just pulled up to your mother's house," Tycen said.

Heidi peeled the curtains back and noticed Tycen's SUV out front. "Okay. . .I'm coming outside now." Heidi disconnected the call and grabbed her jacket. She walked to the kitchen and looked at Pearl. "I'm sorry, Mom. Tycen's outside. We just need to talk really quick." Heidi nodded toward her mother.

"That's fine." Pearl smiled at her daughter. "Tell that handsome devil I said hello."

"I'll do that." Heidi shook her head. Heidi turned around and headed for the door.

Pearl watched her daughter as she walked out the house. Pearl continued to twist her locket. She thought about the possibility of finally leaving Newark behind for good.

Back in Philadelphia, Dirty Betty stood just outside of her parked SUV. She was pulling on a lit cigarette and holding her phone tightly in her hand. It had been nearly three hours since Betty had last spoken to Knotts. She was angry. The cool air whipped though the parking lot. Betty slightly shivered from the dropping temperature. She looked down at her phone once more, and then decided to call Knotts again. The call went straight to voicemail. Betty cursed at the phone. She looked up and noticed Knotts was walking toward her SUV. "What the fuck?" Betty yelled as Knotts approached her.

"I'm sorry, Betty." Knotts shook his head. "It was crazy trying to get out of there. But I do have some good news for you."

"You better!" Betty raised her voice. "I'm freezing my tits off out here. What's the word?"

"Let's talk in the truck." Knotts looked around as he spoke.

Betty tossed the cigarette and got back inside the SUV. Knotts swung around to the other side and got in.

"So what happened?" Betty quickly asked. She was anxious to find out what took him so long to return.

"You are goin' to love me after I tell you this." Knotts peered out the front window. "I had my supervisor call Aaron…right. Check this out, he told Aaron that he won ten thousand dollars in free chips, but he needed to claim the prize today."

"And he believed that bullshit?" Betty questioned.

"Hell yes. He's on his way down here now."

"Get the fuck out of here. Are you serious?" Betty gasped.

"No bullshit," Knotts responded. "Trust me…he's heading down here right now. We told his greedy ass to be down here at nine to pick up the prize and sign the paperwork."

"Oh shit." Betty sat back in the chair and thought about the story. She hesitated to believe Knotts and gave him a skeptical glare. "So how do we get him?"

"Check it…they tell all the winners to go to the service entrance to pick up their prizes." Knotts pointed around the back of the building. "We can basically wait for Aaron to show up. Wait for him to get back into his car and follow him until we find a good place to snatch him up."

"Are you serious?" Betty cut her eyes at Knotts.

"Yea..I think it can work," Knotts stated.

"That has got to be…the dumbest fuckin' plan I ever heard," Betty yelled. "What kind of mickey mouse shit is that?"

"What…?" Knotts twisted his face. "It can work."

"That sounds like a bunch of bullshit." Betty waved at Knotts.

"Come on Betty…work with me. It's the best thing I could think of," Knotts said. "We can't snatch him up at the casino. It's too many cameras out here. You got a better plan that I don't know about?"

"Shit," Betty mumbled under her breath. She shook her head and looked out into the parking lot. Betty wasn't convinced of the shaky plan. Betty thought about the money again and decided to go with it. She made a hissing sound and looked over to Knotts. "And you sayin' that Aaron is gonna be out here by nine?"

"Absolutely." Knotts gave her a confident look.

Betty went against her intuition and decided to follow Knott's plan. Heidi's promise of a cash payout was clouding Betty's judgment. The gluttonous voice in Betty's head convinced her that the money was worth the risk. Betty looked at her watch and got comfortable in her seat. Betty and Knotts waited patiently in the vehicle for Aaron to arrive at the casino.

Back in Newark, Heidi and Tycen sat in his quiet SUV in front of Pearl's house. Tycen tried his best to make small talk, but Heidi continued to give him the cold shoulder. "How's your mother doing?" Tycen quietly asked.

"She's good," Heidi responded and continued to look out the window. "She wanted me to tell you hello."

"Cool. Tell her I said hello back," Tycen replied. Heidi nodded her head. The SUV turned silent again. Tycen couldn't take the suspense and decided to break the ice. "Listen, Heidi. I really want to apologize about yesterday," Tycen blurted.

"I thought we went over this already, Tycen." Heidi turned and looked at him. "I told you that you don't have to apologize."

"I really want to say I'm sorry," Tycen continued speaking as if he didn't hear Heidi's words. "I can't believe I let Lawrence talk me into taping you the way he did. That was so foul of me, and I know I violated. It's just that this election is coming up so fast and, I guess, I'm getting paranoid. I really want this job."

"I know," Heidi quickly said. "You're an ambitious man, and I have to respect that. You don't have to apologize for what you want."

"I know. But I really wanted to see your face…and let you know that I'm sorry." Tycen stared at Heidi. "Do you accept my apology?"

"Of course I accept it," Heidi responded quickly. "But that doesn't mean that I'm still not mad at you."

"I understand that. And I don't blame you," Tycen spoke softly in the vehicle. "It was wrong for me to allow that to happen. I promise that I won't let this campaign get to me again."

"Don't do that, Tycen." Heidi roughly shook her head.

"Do what?" Tycen asked.

"You're blaming the campaign for what you did. See… this is why I don't like apologies," Heidi sounded angry. "You don't even understand why I'm mad at you."

"Of course I do," Tycen fired back. "You're mad at me because I taped you—"

"No, Tycen!" Heidi raised her voice. "I'm mad at you because of the way you made me feel."

Tycen gave Heidi a blank expression. He didn't know how to respond.

"Why did you accuse me of fuckin' Aaron yesterday?" Heidi asked. "You accused me of fuckin' somebody I haven't seen in years. Of all the things you could've accused me of… you decided to put me in the category of some goddamn whore or something."

"Come on…stop it, Heidi." Tycen put his hand up. "You're being dramatic. Now I didn't say that."

"You didn't have to say those exact words, but I could see it in your face." Heidi turned away from Tycen. "You reminded me of somebody when you did that shit."

The car fell silent. Tycen's jaw tightened as he thought about Heidi's last words. "What does that mean?" Tycen sounded stern. "What do you mean I reminded you of somebody?"

"The night Jayson died…we had a big fight," Heidi dropped her voice. "Actually, I can't even call it a fight. Jayson beat me senseless that night. He almost killed me in that house. Till this day I still can't believe that I made it out of there alive." Heidi rubbed her face and continued speaking. "Of all the bizarre things that happened that night in that house…I could never understand why Jayson was accusing me of fucking somebody else." Heidi paused for a second.

"Jayson kept saying he knew about us and everything we did," Heidi continued. "But that was impossible. I never fucked around on Jayson. Ever. But he was sure I was cheating on him. He believed it. I could see it in his eyes. I know that look. It's terrifying. It was the same look you gave me yesterday."

"I was just upset," Tycen whispered.

"You know I made a lot of mistakes in my life when it comes to men." Heidi dropped her head. "When I first met you that day in your office I was going through a lot. I don't know if you could tell. But the minute I saw you…something changed in me and I knew I had to have you. Sometimes…when I look at you, I feel like I don't deserve you. Who knows…maybe I don't. But what I do know…is that I love you, Tycen. Without a shadow of a doubt."

"I love you, too." Tycen nodded.

"Please let me finish," Heidi whispered. "I don't want you to love me just because I love you, and I don't want you to apologize just because I'm mad at you. And the same goes for me too. It's true that I still need closure from the bullshit that happened to me in the past. And that's not fair to you. I gave you back the ring yesterday because I realized that I'm hiding behind you. You make me feel safe, and I don't need that right now. I need to face my issues."

Tycen didn't respond. He continued to stare in Heidi's direction.

"We both have stuff to deal with right now. You got this big campaign...and believe me...I will support you the whole way. But I think we need to take this break and really try to figure out what we really want. If it makes sense down the road...we will make it happen. I believe that. Nothing will stop it from happening if it's meant to be."

There was a thick silence in the SUV. Heidi's words were surprisingly poignant. Tycen forced his lips together and didn't say a word. He resisted the urge to try and make Heidi reconsider her thoughts. Their separation was inevitable. Between Heidi's baggage and Tycen's campaign, the two were headed down a slippery slope. Tycen decided not to fight it any longer. Heidi and Tycen shared a quiet moment of reflection.

"I have to go back inside the house now," Heidi whispered. "Me and my mother were talking, and I need to make sure that she is okay."

"I understand," Tycen whispered. He was hurt.

Heidi reached over and gave him a kiss on his cheek. She squeezed his hand one last time and got out of the SUV. Heidi stood just outside the truck and looked at Tycen. "You remember that dream I told you about? The one about me... and all of these other people...running away from this big monster?" Heidi's face was serious.

"Yes...I remember the dream," Tycen responded.

"I had the same dream last night," Heidi said. "When I woke up this morning it got me thinking. What if all of those people in my dream are actually running from me? What if I'm the monster?" Heidi paused and thought about her last statement again. "Maybe that's why I can't get away in my dream. I can't run from myself, right?" Heidi looked down for a minute. Her face was flushed with emotion. She looked up to Tycen and shook her head. "Just a thought."

Heidi turned around and walked toward her mother's house.

Tycen didn't know what to say about the awkward moment of clarity from Heidi. He watched her closely as she opened the front door and disappeared into the dark home.

Chapter 25

Monday, October 14
8:38 pm
Newark, NJ

"Who is the witness? We know you know. We been at this for almost a week now. Who are you protectin'? Tell us who the witness is...or this is it for you. You won't make it out of here alive tonight ...I promise you that. This is the last night we are doing this. Tell us!" Rojo's angry voice bounced off the concrete walls in the sub-basement of The Body Shop. He stood in front of a bloody man, who hung helplessly from the ceiling by his arms. The chains around his wrists were tight enough to cut off his circulation. The man's battered face was nearly un-recognizable. He could barely open his swollen eyes. After a week of constant beatings and interrogations, the man was edging closer to death with each passing second. Rojo grabbed the man by the neck and looked closer at him. His name was Niko Stanton.

"I ... I swear I don't .... I don't know shit," Niko whispered. Spit and blood leaked from his mouth. Niko was in bad shape, but Rojo showed him no mercy. Rojo continued to punch and smack Niko until he spoke again. "Please...stop...!" Niko cried out. Those were the only words he could muster.

"Why the fuck are you makin' me do this shit again?" Rojo yelled. "Niko...you're makin' it really bad for yourself right now."

Niko didn't respond. He was too weak. His body continued to swing from the ceiling and Niko dropped his head in defeat. He was barely conscious. The brutal punishment was taking a toll on him.

Rojo noticed Niko fading away, and then turned his attention to the other man that was in the basement with them. The tall security guard watched on as Rojo contemplated what to do next. "Jake....I need you to do me a favor," Rojo yelled toward the security guard. "Wake this motherfucker up for me!" Rojo pointed at Niko's legs.

Jake nodded his head and walked to the other side of the room. He unplugged a dry iron from the wall and made his way to the now unconscious Niko. Jake pulled up Niko's pants leg and pressed the scorching hot iron up against his exposed skin.

"Oh God....No....PLEASE....STOP!" Niko's eyes flashed open and he yelled out in pain. The sizzling iron burned the flesh off of him, and Jake seemed to relish in the torture. "Please...please....please...I don't know a damn thing. I don't know!"

Rojo looked at Jake and nodded his head. Jake pulled the scorching iron off of Niko and tossed it to the ground. Niko sobbed in agony. The excruciating pain made tears come to his bloody eyes.

"Maybe he's tellin' the truth," Jake offered and looked over to his boss.

"Shut the fuck up!" Rojo yelled out. "Did I ask you for your opinion?"

Rojo's cold stare caused Jake to back down. Rojo shook his head and grabbed Niko by the face again. "You want to die tonight? Is that it?" Rojo yelled.

"No..." Niko painfully gasped.

"Then tell me what I want to know," Rojo shouted out again.

"I don't know nothing." Niko dropped his head. "I swear...I don't know."

Rojo punched Niko in the face out of frustration. He walked away from Niko's limp body and shook his head. He tried to come up with another brilliant idea, but it was time for Rojo to turn things up. Rojo glanced over to Jake. "Get him down from there," Rojo ordered.

Jake walked closer to Niko and pulled the chains from the ceiling. Niko's body crashed to the floor as the chains came loose.

"Bring his stupid ass upstairs to my office," Rojo shouted as he spoke. "I'm through playin' games with this motherfucker." Rojo headed out of the basement and squeezed his hands together. He was fresh out of patience. He was ready to get the information he needed from Niko, and he had the perfect weapon in Kimi to make that happen.

Just a few blocks away, the sound of a speeding Maserati echoed off the concrete streets. The calm expression on Asad Banks' face didn't match the intense fire that was burning throughout his body. As he wildly sped through the city, Asad was still boiling over the revealing conversation he had with his brother Gary. The shooting in Military Park gripped Asad's conscious. He was devastated that his best friend, Dante, was murdered yesterday. Asad decided it was time to do some investigating of his own. Asad knew that The Marquez Crew had a hand in most criminal activities in the city. The chances they were involved in the shooting were high. Asad disregarded the fact that he was slightly intoxicated and kept pushing toward his destination.

The engine of his black Maserati screamed in defiance as it tore down the back streets of Newark. Asad was clearly in a rush to pay a visit to one of the most powerful and dangerous gangsters in the city. He needed answers to the pressing question of who was involved in the shooting this past weekend that left members of his security team dead and the mayor on edge. After hanging up with Gary, Asad regained his focus. He made up his mind that he would not get another minute of rest until the shooters were found and dealt with.

Asad thought back to the conversation with his brother and realized he overlooked a major clue that could help him find the shooters. Because the killers were well equipped and they appeared to be heavily financed, Asad realized that he would have to squeeze the bosses at the top to flush out the foot soldiers at the bottom. The list of powerful thugs who controlled the underbelly of Newark was a short one. But Asad knew exactly where to start.

Asad sped to his destination and looked at his watch. It was getting late in the city but the streets were wide awake and buzzing with life. His adrenaline started pumping faster as he zipped through the back blocks. Asad finally made a quick turn onto a dark street that was lined with abandoned buildings and vacant warehouses. He cautiously slowed down the sports car and looked around the eerie street. The desolate area seemed to be in another world. A few dope-fiends and dusty prostitutes peered into the vehicle as Asad slowly cruised down the block. The expression on the faces of the abandoned souls reminded Asad of just how far the city had fallen from greatness. Asad shook his head in disgust and continued to push forward. His eyes widened when he noticed his target building. Asad had heard about the illegal establishment and its ruthless owner for years now, but no one downtown had the courage to shut the place down. He knew he was taking a very big gamble doing this alone, but now was not the time for fear and caution. Asad parked his car directly across the street from the building. The place was dark, but Asad noticed a few cars parked off to the side. He read the sign above the door and knew he was at the right place.

"The Body Shop," Asad whispered, then reached under his seat and grabbed his weapon. He checked the clip and made sure he was locked and loaded. A rush of fear made him hesitate for a moment as he thought about the consequences of going renegade tonight. Asad slowly nodded as a voice in his head reassured him that now was the time to act.

Back inside The Body Shop, Rojo angrily marched up the stairs and headed to his office. Jake was trailing not too far behind with Niko draped around his shoulder. Niko could barely keep up as Jake dragged his limp legs across the floor. Fresh blood leaked from Niko's head and left a messy trail in the hallway. Rojo walked into his office and noticed Kimi was still strapped to the chair. She was unconscious.

Jake carried Niko into the office and slammed him to the floor. Rojo walked to his desk and made sure everything was in order. Jake closed the office door and grabbed another chair. He made Niko sit down and strapped him in tightly. Niko was too weak to resist. Jake made sure he couldn't move. Rojo's face hardened as he looked on. He knew it was time to get down to business.

"Wake this bitch up," Rojo ordered and pointed at Kimi.

Jake walked over to Kimi and smacked her hard in the face. Kimi screamed when she came to. She tried to shield her head from a second slap, but her hands were still bounded behind her.

"Wake the fuck up," Jake yelled at her and threatened to hit her again.

"That's enough," Rojo yelled out.

Jake walked away from Kimi and stood near the door. Rojo looked at her terrified face and smirked.

"Now ain't this cute...we have ourselves a little reunion here," Rojo laughed at his own joke.

Kimi twisted her face for a moment. She followed Rojo's eyes and looked across the room. Her face exploded into tears when she took one look at Niko. She could barely recognize him. His face was badly swollen and his clothes were nearly ripped to shreds. Niko was shoeless. His legs were bleeding uncontrollably. Kimi cried out for him.

Niko heard her voice and looked over to her. He was clearly in pain and could barely keep his eyes open. The sound of her voice was the sweetest thing he heard in a week. "Kimi... baby....is that you?" Niko asked through his swollen jaw.

"Niko...! Yes...yes...I'm here," Kimi cried. "It's me, baby."

"I'm sorry—" Niko stuttered. He dropped his head in shame. He couldn't believe The Marquez Crew had his girlfriend at The Body Shop. Niko became afraid for their grave situation. "I can't believe this is happening," Niko's voice trembled.

"Baby...what the fuck did they do to you?" Kimi was heartbroken at the sight of her bludgeoned boyfriend. She became angry and looked over to Rojo. "What the fuck is wrong with y'all?"

Rojo's face turned wicked. His patience was wearing thin, and he was ready to get the information he needed for his father. Rojo suddenly reach on his desk and grabbed for his large knife. "Niko...! I hope you watchin' motherfucker," Rojo yelled out and moved closer to Kimi. "Now...I want you to watch this shit. You gonna tell me what I want to know... or your girlfriend...is gonna fuckin' die...right now!"

Rojo's grim threat got Niko's attention. He forced his eyes open just in time to see Rojo grab Kimi by the hair.

"Get the fuck off of me," Kimi boldly yelled.

Rojo swung behind the chair and got a good grip on Kimi's scalp. He put the knife dangerously close against her throat.

Kimi froze. Her body shivered in fear. She felt the cold blade up against her jugular.

"Rojo...please don't do that!" Niko screamed.

"Tell...me...who...the fuck...is...the witness!" Rojo yelled and pressed the knife closer to Kimi's neck. "You better tell me now...or it's over for your fuckin' girlfriend."

Jake looked on as the mood in the room quickly turned murderous.

"I swear to you...I don't know," Niko started talking fast. He stared at Kimi's petrified eyes. For a moment, Niko thought he could see deep inside her soul. He sensed that Kimi knew this was the end.

"Tell me what the fuck I want to know," Rojo yelled again. "Who's the fuckin' witness? Tell me...!" Rojo's overpowering voice sent a shockwave through the room.

"Please, Rojo...I don't know who the witness is," Niko cried out again. "Don't do that to Kimi. Please don't. If you want to punish somebody...please...punish me...she has nothing to do with this."

Rojo gritted his teeth on Niko's last statement. Rojo realized that Niko was not going to give him the information he wanted. Rojo became enraged. He put a tighter grip on the knife. The blade made contact with Kimi's throat and she screamed. Niko got a burst of energy and tried to break free from the chair, but he was strapped in tight. He helplessly watched as Rojo pressed the blade against the right side of Kimi's neck. Rojo's eyes were cold blooded as he mercilessly sliced across Kimi's neck and tossed her head forward.

"OH MY FUCKIN' GOD....NO!" Niko screamed to the top of his lungs.

Kimi coughed and gagged. She just knew she was good as dead. Niko screamed her named and rumbled in his chair trying to break free. Rojo threw the knife down in frustration and cursed out loud. Niko quickly looked at the knife and noticed something was out of place. There was no blood on the blade. Rojo kicked his desk and was obviously infuriated. Niko looked over to Kimi. She was still coughing. She was still alive. In all the commotion Niko never noticed that Rojo had the knife turned around the whole time. He had sliced Kimi's neck with the flat part of the blade, never puncturing her skin. Rojo was bluffing.

"Kimi...are you alright?" Niko yelled out as the tears continued flowing down his face.

"Baby..." Kimi struggled to speak.

"Look at me, Kimi! You are going...to be alright," Niko tried his best to console his girlfriend. "You're not bleeding Kimi. You're going to be okay."

Jake looked over to Kimi and was surprised by what just occurred. He turned his focus to his boss and finally realized that Rojo's plan to get the information didn't work. "I told you…he might be telling the truth," Jake offered. "Maybe… he don't know shit."

Rojo turned around and looked at Jake with rage in his eyes. Rojo stormed back over toward Kimi. He cocked his arm far back. He let out a primal grunt and punched Kimi square on the side of her head out of frustration. The force of the swift blow threw her body backwards, and her chair toppled over. Kimi crashed down in a rush. She screamed out in pain as her face hit the floor. Rojo stood over her. He was about to strike Kimi again when he noticed something on the floor. A square envelope fell out of Kimi's jacket pocket and caught his attention. Rojo stepped over Kimi's body.

"What the fuck?" Rojo asked and grabbed the white envelope. His expression changed when he noticed it was a DVD in the envelope. There was no writing on the all-white disc. Rojo twisted his expression and focused on the DVD. "What the fuck is this?" Rojo yelled at Kimi.

She never responded. Kimi could barely see straight after the vicious punch to the face. Rojo turned around and showed Niko the disc. "What's on this DVD?" Rojo harshly asked.

Niko's eyes widened when he saw the envelope in Rojo's hands. "I don't know," Niko stuttered.

"Don't fuckin' lie to me," Rojo yelled out.

"I swear I don't know," Niko repeated.

Rojo gave Niko a suspicious look. He turned his focus back to the DVD. Rojo looked down to Kimi as she twisted in pain. Rojo didn't trust Niko or Kimi. He became increasingly curious about the disc. "Keep your fuckin' eyes on them," Rojo yelled at Jake. Rojo inspected the white envelope again. He slowly walked over to his entertainment system. He turned on the large flat screen television and the DVD player. He didn't waste another minute as he put the disc in the player. He was curious to see what was on the DVD. A loud scream blared from the television as the video automatically started playing. Rojo stepped away from the television to get a better look at the home movie. "Holy shit…!" Rojo gasped.

The disturbing images quickly flashed on the television. The desperate screams and moans became louder and the shaky images began to come into focus. All eyes in the room were fixed on the video. Rojo couldn't believe what he was watching. He was tempted to turn off the DVD, but something in his twisted mind wanted to see more. Rojo scanned the faces on the video, and then he put his fist up against his mouth.

"Oh…fuck…do you see this shit?" Rojo turned around and looked at Jake. "That's Mayor Gary Banks!"

Meanwhile, just outside The Body Shop, Asad Banks was preparing himself to enter the building. He had finally mustered up the courage to make his move. Asad reached in his middle console, removed a small black box, then placed it in his jacket pocket. He turned his attention to his weapon. He checked his gun one last time and took a deep breath. He was ready to question the current boss of The Marquez Crew and find out who was responsible for killing his friend, Dante.

Asad awkwardly rose out of his Maserati. The cool breeze sobered him up just enough to focus his eyes across the street. The front of The Body Shop was eerily quiet. Asad started to get a funny feeling as he cautiously approached the front door. Before he could check the lock, he was approached by two security men.

"We're closed…!" the larger security guard yelled out as he exited the building. "You gotta come back tomorrow to get your rocks off. Everybody's gone for the night."

Asad twisted his face and realized the security guard had mistaken him for a late-night customer. Asad kept his hands in his pockets, trying his best to look non-confrontational. "I'm not a customer," Asad coolly responded. "I need to speak to Ronald Marquez."

"You gotta be fuckin' kidding me?" The huge guard laughed. "There's no way you getting into this fucking building." The security guard twisted his face and looked back to his partner. The smaller guard laughed and waved his hand at Asad.

"Listen fellas. Just let me in," Asad slightly raised his voice. "I just need to see Ronald Marquez for a few minutes, that's it."

The larger guard stiffened his face and moved closer to Asad. "Fam...are you hard of hearing or something?" the guard barked. "You not gettin' in this building tonight."

"I hear you big man, but you're not listening to me," Asad added some bass to his voice realizing things were growing serious in the front of The Body Shop. "My name is Asad Banks, and I'm here on behalf of the mayor. I just need to talk—"

"Yo, I know who the fuck you are?" the guard cut Asad short and moved even closer to him. "You still not gettin' in this fucking place. I don't know why you throwin' the mayor's name around. He don't call no fuckin' shots on this side. So why don't you get the hell out of here before you get seriously fucked up."

A shot of anger rushed through Asad's body as the guard's threat cut through his ears.

"Whoa. . ." Asad shook his head. "If somebody is getting fucked up out here, believe me, it's going to be you. I promise you that."

The guard had heard enough of Asad. He rushed him like a bull. The guard reached out his arms and tried to grab Asad, but Asad was too quick and avoided his grasp. The smaller guard backed away as he realized a brawl was brewing. The larger guard attempted to rush Asad again, and Asad quickly took his hands out of his pockets. When the guard got close enough, Asad punched him square in the chest with what appeared to be his cellphone. The smaller guard groaned and reacted to the huge hit. The larger guard was clearly stunned by the punch and dropped to the ground in a heap. The smaller guard was shocked when he noticed his partner shaking uncontrollably on the ground.

"What the fuck?" the smaller guard yelled out.

He looked up to Asad, who was wearing a look of fury on

his face. He watched as Asad threw the cellphone on top of the guard. It was then that he realized the black box was a hand-held stun gun. Asad had just pumped two hundred volts of crippling electricity into the larger guard's body, which had rendered him temporarily paralyzed. The smaller guard hesitated to approach Asad. Before he could think of what to do, Asad quickly reached in his waist and pulled out his 9mm pistol.

"Open the fucking door!" Asad shouted. He spun the guard around and placed the gun barrel tightly on his back. "Now take me to Ronald, or I'm going to blow your fucking spleen all over the place."

"Okay…chill out fam. It's not that serious," the guard stuttered.

Asad kept the gun on his back as the guard led him through the empty building. They headed up the stairs, and Asad looked down at the floor. He saw a trail of blood leading down the hallway and became alarmed. "What the fuck is going on in here?" Asad mumbled.

"Rojo's office is right down there," the guard nervously pointed as they proceeded to walk down the dimly lit hallway.

Asad didn't hesitate to make his next move. Before the guard could take another step, Asad smashed him flush on the side of his face with the heavy stainless steel. The guard collapsed to the floor, clearly out cold. Not wanting any surprises, Asad smartly pulled the laces out of the guard's boots and tied his hands and feet together.

Asad's heart nearly jumped out of his chest when he heard a loud scream come from just beyond the door at the end of the hallway. Asad quickly jumped to his feet and raised his gun. He hesitated for a brief moment as another violent scream echoed from the room. It sounded like a female's voice, but Asad wasn't sure. His mind raced to figure out what to do next.

"Please God! Please don't do this! No!" the voice screamed again from the room.

Asad cautiously approached the office. He tried his best

to control his heavy breathing. He smothered the panic in his heart and became fearless.

Come on Asad...you can do this. He pointed his gun at the door and calmly aimed at the deadbolts. He could only imagine what was occurring on the other side of the door.

Just a few feet away, inside the office, Rojo was still watching the gruesome video. The loud screams were disturbing, and Rojo had seen enough. He flicked off the DVD and turned his focus back to Kimi.

"What the fuck are you doing with that video?" Rojo asked with confusion. The crazy images on the disc swirled around in his mind. Rojo looked at Kimi again and yelled at her. "What are you doing with that video?" Rojo repeated. Kimi grimaced in pain, but she didn't answer him. Rojo moved over to Kimi and picked her chair up off the floor.

Niko yelled toward Rojo and started jerking wildly in his chair.

"Answer me!" Rojo yelled and grabbed Kimi by the neck. His rage was out of control and Kimi saw the evil in his eyes.

"Get the fuck off of me," Kimi yelled out.

Rojo made a move as if he was attempting to strike Kimi again. Two loud gunshots suddenly rang out. The heavy blasts blew the door open and somebody rushed into the office like a one-man SWAT Team. Rojo fell backwards. He looked at the man's face and recognized him. It was Asad Banks.

"Nobody fuckin' move!" Asad shouted. He quickly scanned the office.

Rojo froze and looked toward the door. He couldn't believe his eyes.

Asad raised his weapon toward Rojo and continued to look around. He noticed Kimi and Niko tied up in the middle of the room. It didn't take long for Asad to realize that he'd stumbled into a precarious situation. Rojo was perplexed. He tried to read Asad's eyes. The room fell silent.

"Back up," Asad ordered as he slowly walked into the

office.

"What do you want?" Rojo asked as he slowly backed away from Kimi.

"What's goin' on in here?" Asad barked.

"It's obviously none of your fuckin' business," Rojo shouted out and gave Asad a cold stare.

"Please untie me—" Niko pleaded to Asad.

"Shut the fuck up!" Rojo shouted.

The verbal exchange made Asad realize he'd just walked into the middle of a kidnapping. Asad contemplated what to do next. What should have been a simple investigation had turned into something more volatile.

"Listen...this shit right here...doesn't concern you." Rojo cut his eyes to Asad. "Why don't you just turn around...and get the fuck out of here."

Asad looked over to Kimi. Her battered face and frightened eyes silently begged for his help. Asad couldn't walk away and allow this to continue. He stared at Rojo again and raised his weapon higher. "Back the fuck up," Asad ordered again.

"Listen, asshole." Rojo pointed at Asad. "I don't know what you think you doin' here. I'm goin' to give you one more chance to leave out of here with your life."

Asad didn't budge. He squeezed his weapon tighter and motioned for Rojo to back up again.

"Hard-headed motherfucker," Rojo said. He knew it was time to show Asad that he meant business. Rojo looked just beyond Asad and quickly nodded his head. "Jake...!"

Before Asad could turn around he was clobbered over the head with a heavy fist. Jake pounced on Asad and tried to wrestle the gun away from him as they crashed into the adjacent wall. A huge fight broke out in the office. Rojo rushed around his desk and scrambled to find his own gun. Niko and Kimi yelled out in horror. Jake grabbed Asad's wrist and a few gunshots rang out. Rojo ducked down. He grabbed his weapon from the bottom drawer. Kimi and Niko continued screaming. Asad summoned all the strength he could and punched Jake with a series of heavy blows. Jake stumbled backwards when Asad caught him with a lucky shot square on the nose. Rojo stood to his feet and started shooting toward Asad.

"Oh God…!" Kimi yelled out. She tipped her chair over to avoid the gunfire.

Asad discharged his weapon and sent a bullet square into Jake's body. Asad and Jake both fell to the floor, but Jake wasn't breathing any more. Rojo moved from around his desk and frantically fired toward Asad. Rojo was too nervous to aim straight, and the missed shots gave Asad an opportunity to fire back.

"I'm goin' to fuckin' kill you…!" Rojo yelled out and continued shooting.

Asad fired off six rounds and manage to squirm against the wall. Rojo screamed in pain as one of the bullets struck him on the top of his shoulder. The two men continued the reckless gun battle

Click. Click.

Rojo glanced at his gun and realized he was out of bullets. Asad stared at Rojo and kept his weapon on him. Rojo knew he didn't have a fighting chance anymore and bolted out the office. He never realized that Asad's clip was also empty.

Asad looked down and inspected his shaking body. It was a miracle that he wasn't hit. His heart pounded as the adrenaline set his body on fire. He stood to his feet and looked at Kimi. She was scared out of her mind. Asad sprang into action realizing he only had seconds to get her and Niko safely out of the office. He pulled up the chair and quickly unscrewed the wire hangers from her hands and feet. Kimi screamed in agony as her limbs were finally set free. "You okay?" Asad asked and looked at Kimi. Asad twisted his face at her blank expression. She stared behind him, and Asad grew concerned. "Hello, ma'am. Can you hear me?" Asad examined her closely.

"My God…..Niko…?" Kimi quietly whispered.

Asad turned around and looked at the man strapped in the chair. All the blood left Asad's face when he looked at Niko's wounded body. His chest was riddled with bullets. Niko had been murdered in the crossfire at the hands of Rojo.

Kimi rushed to her dead boyfriend and grabbed him by the face. "Baby…nooo…Niko. Wake up, baby," Kimi cried out. "Please! Wake up!"

Asad looked on as Kimi wept for Niko. The scene was heartbreaking, but Asad knew they had to move fast if they wanted to survive.

"Niko don't leave me…wake up," Kimi cried.

Asad reached out and grabbed Kimi by the shoulders. He looked at the front door and feared that Rojo could return at any given moment. "We got to get out of her ma'am," Asad warned. "We need to get to safety."

"Niko…baby…please," Kimi whimpered and ignored Asad. She didn't care if she had to die next to her boyfriend. "Baby…don't leave me."

Asad knelt down and became face to face with Kimi. "Ma'am…look at me," Asad's voice was even. "We have to get out of here now. That maniac Ronald will come right back in here…and I don't have another gun. We have to go now."

Kimi looked at Asad, then turned her focus back to her boyfriend's lifeless face. She didn't want to leave him, but she knew what the consequences would be if she didn't make a move. She reached up and kissed Niko on the lips. "I'm sorry Niko," Kimi whispered.

Asad picked Kimi up and draped her arm around his shoulders. He helped her out of the office and rushed her down the hallway. There was no sign of Rojo. Asad's eyes were vigilant as they made their way out the building and to his vehicle. Asad didn't waste as second as he placed Kimi in the car and jumped into the driver seat. He fired up the engine. The screeching tires echoed off the abandoned buildings on the block as Asad sped away from the murder scene at The Body Shop.

Chapter 26

Monday, October 14
8:56 pm
Philadelphia, PA

Dirty Betty calmly squeezed her hands together and took a deep breath. She caught a glimpse of her watch, and felt more tired with each passing second. The long day of tracking down Aaron was taking a toll on her aging body. Betty looked over to Knotts. He was relaxing in the fully reclined passenger seat. "Wake your ass up," Betty barked.

"What...huh...I'm not sleep," Knotts stammered as he awakened from a quick nap. He quickly sat up and looked at his own watch. "Is it go time?"

"Almost," Betty said. "This motherfucker better show up."

"He will," Knotts said with confidence.

Betty glared at Knotts. She still felt funny about his plan. She ignored her suspicions once again and reached in the back seat. She grabbed a small handbag and pulled out a chrome .45 caliber handgun. She handed the gun to Knotts and gave him a hard stare. "We only got one shot to grab this motherfucker. I'm not coming back down here to do this shit all over again." Betty squeezed her hands together. "Let's just keep this simple as shit. We grab him. Knock his ass out and tie him up. One, two, three...easy breezy. Understand?"

"Without a doubt." Knotts put the gun under his seat. "We'll get him."

A red Corvette zipped through the parking lot like the Indy 500 speedway. The roaring of the loud engine caught Betty's attention. She glared at the shining car as it headed to the service entrance.

Knotts locked his eyes on the vehicle and got excited. "That's him." Knotts pointed at the Corvette.

"How do you know?" Betty asked.

"Believe me...I know," Knotts raised his voice.

Betty gave Knotts another suspicious glance. She fired up the SUV and turned off the lights. She proceeded around the back of the casino. Betty kept a safe distance behind the red Corvette, and then parked in the shadows.

Knotts watched her as Betty reached in her handbag and pulled out another handgun. He looked at Betty's weapon and realized things were about to escalate. "Let's stick to the plan, Betty," Knotts calmly said. "Let's wait until he comes back out and follow him."

Betty ignored Knotts' statement. She kept a close eye on the car. A tall man coolly stepped out of the red Corvette. His demeanor was smooth as silk. His extravagant taste was evident from his sparkling diamond studs down to the two thousand dollar shoes on his feet. The man took a final pull on a thick cigar, and then tossed it to the ground. He calmly surveyed his surroundings before entering the back of the building.

Betty got a good look at his face and smiled. That's him. The man's name was Aaron Smith. "That's my money right there," Betty whispered. She watched as Aaron walked into the Sugar House Casino. She started to feel antsy. Aaron was alone. Betty realized that her job had just become easier. She looked over to Knotts. "Are you ready to do this?" Betty asked.

"Fuckin' right," Knotts replied.

Betty looked down at Knotts' hand. His false bravado didn't match his trembling fingers. He was clearly nervous. Knott's tried his best to man-up in front of Betty. He kept an eye on the red car and rehearsed the plan in his mind.

A few minutes later, Aaron Smith stormed out of the back

entrance. His angry face was hard as stone. Aaron looked around the rear parking lot and jumped into the Corvette. He sped away from the entrance, and Dirty Betty slammed the SUV into gear. She punched the gas and started following the red Corvette. Betty felt her adrenaline rushing as the vehicles turned onto the main street. Betty stayed two car lengths behind Aaron as he weaved in and out of the heavy traffic. Betty stayed on him. Knotts braced himself as both vehicles started to gain speed. Aaron turned onto a dark street, and his sports car suddenly accelerated like a rocket.

"Oh shit," Betty yelled and punched the gas.

"I think he saw us," Knotts yelled out.

The engine of the red Corvette roared in defiance. Aaron sped down the tight street. It was hard for Betty's SUV to keep up. She pushed the gas pedal to the floor. Knotts grunted as the large truck bounced violently. Betty put a tighter grip on the steering wheel and sped up closer to the red Corvette. Aaron quickly zipped through the maze of streets. Betty noticed they were entering a rough part of Philadelphia. She was determined not to lose him. Betty stayed hot on his trail as he turned down one dark street after another.

"Don't lose him," Knotts shouted out.

"Shut the fuck up...!" Betty yelled.

Aaron tried to get away from Betty, but she refused to let him out of her sight. She didn't come this far to let her money slip out of her hands this easily. She continued to push the SUV to the limit and stayed close to the sports car. Aaron made a violent left and turned onto a dead end road. There were no street lamps and the strip was pitch black. It seemed as if the vehicles were in the middle of nowhere. Betty's heart jumped out of her chest when she saw the brake lights flicker on the red Corvette. Aaron got to the end of the street and slammed to a violent halt. Betty stomped her brake pedal with two feet. She frantically stopped the large SUV from crashing into the back of the Corvette.

"What the fuck!" Betty screamed. The sound of the

screeching tires scared her. The truck fell silent. Betty looked around the dark street and grew nervous. There was no movement in the red Corvette in front of them. Betty could see Aaron's head through the back window of his car. He sat motionless in the front seat. Betty realized it was time to make her move. She took a deep breath and reached for her gun.

"Don't you fuckin' move!" Knotts yelled out.

Betty turned to him. She huffed at the sight of Knotts pointing his gun directly at her. Betty twisted her face. "What the fuck are you doing?" Betty shouted.

"Don't reach for that gun, Betty. I would hate to put a bullet in you," Knotts coldly threatened.

Betty froze. She looked at Knotts and tried to read his eyes. She didn't know what was going on. Knotts put a tighter grip on his gun and leaned over toward Betty. He reached for the steering wheel and beeped the horn twice. Betty's mouth fell open. Aaron heard the signal and slowly emerged from the Corvette. Betty's stomach turned with fear. She looked at Knotts again. He raised his gun higher and pointed it at Betty's face. Her heart started pounding and her mind started racing. Betty realized she was on the wrong side of a deadly set up. She had unknowingly sped into a trap. Knotts had used her greed against her and played her like one of the suckers she mocked at the casino.

Aaron smoothly walked toward the SUV. He held a chrome gun tightly in his hand. The heavy metal flickered in the bright headlights, and Betty realized she was in trouble. Aaron strolled to the driver side door and tapped on the glass with the gun.

"Betty…put the fuckin' window down," Knotts ordered.

"Why you doin' this shit, Knotts? I thought we had a deal," Betty's rough voice echoed in the vehicle.

"You right…we had a deal…but Aaron's deal was better," Knotts responded.

"You set me up?" Betty asked.

"I wouldn't call it that," Knotts said. "When I called Aaron,

I had to tell him what was going on. He offered me more money, so I had to take it. I told you Betty…I got bills to pay."

Betty hated hearing the words from his mouth. She knew she had been double-crossed, and there was nothing she could do now but cooperate. Betty slowly reached for the door and pressed the button. The window slowly retracted. A rush of cold air flooded the truck, but couldn't cool down the boiling tension inside her.

Aaron stood a few inches from the door and looked at Betty. "Who are you?" he asked and raised his gun.

"None of your fuckin' business," Betty harshly responded. Betty had been eye to eye with a lot of guns in her lifetime, and tonight Betty decided she was not going down without a good fight.

"Oh…you're a feisty old bitch," Aaron coldly snapped.

"Fuck you," Betty snarled.

"I told you…she's no joke, Aaron," Knotts shouted out behind Betty. "So I brought her to you, like you said. I hope you got my money on you."

Betty heard Knotts' words and shook her head. She looked at Aaron, who was becoming angrier by the second. He looked past Betty and gave Knotts a hard stare.

"You know I hate snakes." Aaron gritted his teeth. "The only thing worse than a snake is a greedy one."

In an unexpected move, Aaron shifted the gun away from Betty's face and pointed it directly at Knotts'. Before Knotts could react, Aaron let off two bullets into the SUV. The deafening blast from the gunshots blew Betty back against the seat. She screamed as the bullets tore into Knotts' face. He died instantly in the passenger seat.

"Holy…fuck!" Betty cried out. The scene was gruesome. Blood was everywhere.

Aaron quickly opened the door and grabbed Betty by the neck. He dragged her out of the SUV and slammed her to the cold asphalt.

"Listen, you old bitch…who the fuck are you?" Aaron

yelled and pointed the gun to her.

"Betty…!" She responded.

Aaron smashed her in the face with the gun. The heavy metal dazed her. Aaron became enraged and hit her again. "Why the fuck are you chasing me?" Aaron yelled. "What do you want?"

"Fuck you," Betty yelled again. Blood flew from her quivering lips.

Aaron went into attack mode. He slammed the gun against her cheek like a sledgehammer. Betty tried to endure the pain, but she cried out in agony. Aaron hit her again and yelled at her. "Why the fuck are you chasing me," Aaron screamed out. "What the fuck do you want? Answer the fucking question?"

Betty tried to hold her ground, but she was taking too much punishment. Aaron continued to strike her mercilessly and Betty found herself giving in. "Okay. . ."

"I'm going to ask you one more time, bitch. I will fuckin' kill you if you don't answer me." Aaron stared at her. "Why the fuck are you chasing me?"

"Somebody….somebody is lookin' for you," Betty forced the words out of her mouth. She was hurting bad.

Aaron stood over her like a fierce lion ready to pounce. "Who's lookin' for me?" Aaron yelled. "Somebody from the casino?"

"No," Betty groaned. Her face was badly bruised and she could barely speak.

"Then…who?" Aaron yelled. "Tell me."

"Heidi…!" Betty called out in pain. "Heidi Kachina is looking for you."

Aaron heard the name and stopped like a freeze frame. His face turned white as a ghost. He froze for a moment and thought about a woman he hadn't seen in years. He looked down at Betty. His mouth fell open. He couldn't believe it. Betty could see the trepidation in his eyes.

"Heidi…?" Aaron whispered in shock. "Heidi's alive?"

Back in Newark, Heidi Kachina was sleeping on her

mother's sofa. The flickering light from the television danced on her troubled face. Heidi was in the middle of having another bad nightmare. Her body slightly jerked on the sofa as she dreamed about running from her old house again. Her legs were heavy as bricks in her dream. Too heavy to run fast. Heidi screamed to the top of her lungs. She tried to run to safety. People bolted away from her and didn't bother to help. Heidi knew something large was pursuing her. She was too afraid to challenge the monster. Heidi cried uncontrollably in her dream. The tears flowed heavy like a river. More people ran from her as Heidi screamed for help. She felt a deep buzzing on her leg and a harsh ringing in her ear. Heidi suddenly awakened from her nightmare and realized her cellphone was ringing loudly from her lap.

"Shit...!" Heidi groaned and wiped her face. Her heart was still racing from the dream, and she realized her eyes were drenched from the tears. She caught her breath and tried to calm herself. She looked down at the ringing phone and jumped to her feet. She saw Betty's name on the display and became nervous. Finally. This was the call Heidi had been waiting for all day. Heidi took a deep breath and answered the phone. "Hello," she whispered nervously. There was no answer. Heidi twisted her face and spoke again. "Hello!" she raised her voice. Still no answer. Heidi looked at the phone. She wanted to make sure the call was still connected. Heidi put the phone back to her ear and tried one last time. "Hello... Betty? Can you hear me?" Heidi blurted.

"I can't believe it. Heidi? Is this you?" Someone answered on the other line, but it wasn't Betty.

Heidi recognized the man's voice and froze. Aaron Smith. All of the blood from Heidi's head rushed to her stomach. She felt like her body was thrust back into a wicked place when she heard the familiar voice. She covered her mouth. She didn't know how to react. For years she wondered how she would respond if she had a chance to confront the man who tried to end her life. Just the sound of Aaron's voice put the fear of

God in her.

"Heidi is that you?" Aaron repeated.

"Yes..." Heidi nervously mumbled.

"So you sent somebody to find me?" Aaron coldly asked from the other line.

"Where's...Betty?" Heidi's voice trembled.

"Oh...Betty? She's right here," Aaron sounded sadistic. "Betty is in no shape to talk though. I got a gun pointed directly at her face. I don't think she has much to say right now."

"Don't hurt her," Heidi's voice cracked again.

"I can't believe you're alive," Aaron said. He ignored Heidi's last statement. "I thought we said goodbye forever." Aaron taunted Heidi. "How the fuck did you walk away from that?" Aaron became louder. "I thought I ended you."

Heidi didn't respond. Aaron's voice started to anger her. Heidi heard the treachery in his tone, and the familiar feeling of betrayal consumed her. She calmed herself and took another deep breath.

"So what's this about?" Aaron raised his voice again. "You sent somebody to hunt me down like I'm a fuckin' animal or somethin'?"

"You are an animal motherfucker!" Heidi fired back. Her heart became brave.

"You have no idea, Heidi," Aaron lowered his voice.

"You better pray we don't see each other again motherfucker," Heidi tried her best to sound menacing.

"Don't try to threaten me princess," Aaron warned. "You have no idea who you fuckin' with."

"I'm not afraid of you," Heidi snapped.

"You should be," Aaron calmly responded. "You got lucky twice, bitch. There won't be a third time."

Heidi's lips fell open. Her mind started racing. She slowly walked to the other side of her mother's living room. "Twice..." The word unconsciously fell out of her mouth.

"Oh....that's right," Aaron grunted with a twisted grin. "You don't remember."

"Remember what?" Heidi whispered.

"I'm not gonna bore you with the details. But let's just say. . .it was a fuckin' waste you didn't die in that fire with Jayson," Aaron coldly confessed. "I had a fuckin' perfect set up, and, somehow, you walked away from that. You were supposed to die with your piece of shit fiancé that night. I tried to kill two birds with one stone. . .get it?" Aaron cleared his throat and almost chuckled at his own twisted joke.

Heidi was confused. She tried to piece together Aaron's last statement. She thought back to the night Jayson died. Images of the deadly house fire raced across her mind. "Oh my…God!" Heidi shouted into the phone. She finally figured out what Aaron was saying to her. Heidi continued screaming. "Oh my. . .God. . .you killed Jayson?" Heidi felt sick. A rush of tears came to her eyes. "You heartless motherfucker."

"Watch your fuckin mouth, Heidi!" Aaron yelled back. "You haven't seen heartless yet."

"I can't believe you. . .killed. . .Jayson," Heidi cried out and grabbed her chest. She wept for her dead fiancé. A pleasant memory of Jayson came to her mind. The shocking revelation was hard for Heidi to handle. More tears flooded her face. She realized she was dealing with a soulless creature on the other line. "I swear, Aaron. I'm gonna find you. And I'm gonna fuckin' kill you."

"Is that right?" Aaron felt the direct threat through the phone. "Don't you fuckin' threaten me!"

"It's not a threat," Heidi shouted and tried to hold back another rush of tears. "I'm gonna find you motherfucker. And when I do. . .I'm gonna kill you."

"Okay. . .since you want to play it that way," Aaron dropped his voice to a cold whisper. "Are you listening right now?"

Heidi didn't respond. Aaron stopped speaking and Heidi could hear a commotion through the phone.

"What are you doing?" Betty screamed in the background. "Get the fuck off of me. . ."

Heidi's heart buckled when she heard Betty's terrified

screams. Another loud scuffle broke out. Heidi yelled into the phone, but there was nothing she could do. A thunderous gunshot rang out. The loud bang almost blew Heidi's eardrum. Betty's screams stopped.

"Oh my God. . ." Heidi yelled into the phone. She prayed that her imagination was betraying her. Another gunshot rang out. There was more stark silence. Heidi yelled into the phone for Betty. There was no response. Aaron's rage had claimed another victim. Heidi grabbed her forehead. She couldn't believe the madness.

"Heidi, you really have no clue what's going on here," Aaron returned to the phone and spoke as if nothing happened. His murderous tone scared Heidi again. "This is bigger than you."

Heidi froze with the phone to her ear. Her heart ached through her chest.

"You don't even have to waste your time trying to find me, bitch," Aaron coldly continued to speak. "I'm coming to you. And believe me. . .this time. . .Heidi…you won't make it out alive. I promise."

Chapter 27

Tuesday, October 29
9:35 am
Newark, NJ

TWO WEEKS LATER

"News 12 New Jersey has just received a breaking development in the Lexi Hamilton abduction case. Authorities have announced that the body of sixteen-year-old Lexi Hamilton has been recovered and identified. In a shocking twist, Dante Harper, a member of the mayor's security detail, has been linked to what police have ruled a homicide of Lexi Hamilton. Investigators have reason to believe that Mayor Gary Banks was not the intended target of the deadly shooting in Military Park two weeks ago. Instead, Dante Harper, one of the killed security men, was the target in an apparent retaliation by the unknown gunmen who remain at large. Police have used physical evidence, including DNA, to link Harper to Hamilton's death. Mayor Gary Banks is expected to hold a press conference later today to offer more details on the case. Please stay tuned to News 12 for further details on this and other shocking developments."

Tycen Wakefield sat behind his desk in campaign headquarters. He quietly relaxed and twisted the engagement ring on his finger. Despite the bulletin blasting from his television, he was too deep in thought to pay attention to the riveting news story. His mind was on Heidi. It had been a long time since he'd laid eyes on Heidi. Tycen missed her. His mayoral campaign was in full swing. The momentum was steamrolling on. Things looked very positive for his bid. Tycen tried to stay focus on his lifelong goal, but the past few days proved to be difficult for him. Heidi had chosen the wrong time to go missing on him. She'd refused to answer his calls. Even his unannounced visits to Pearl's house were fruitless. Heidi and her mother had fallen off the radar and Tycen didn't know why. Heidi's request for space echoed in his mind, but he sensed something deeper was going on. Before he could think any further, his campaign manager interrupted him.

"Mr. Wakefield, you got a minute?" Lawrence inquired as he poked his head into the office.

"Sure," Tycen quickly responded and readjusted himself in his seat. "What's up?"

"I just wanted to go over some poll numbers with you, sir." Lawrence smiled and dropped a stack of papers on Tycen's desk. "We're still trailing Gary Banks, but his margin is diminishing. You're doing very well among the unions and the young people. Believe me, this is wonderful news."

Tycen reviewed the polling records and nodded his head. He quietly flipped through the sheets and barely reacted to the positive results.

"What do you think?" Lawrence asked with anticipation.

"I think it is good news," Tycen calmly responded.

"What are you talking about, Tycen? This is great!" Lawrence raised his voice. "Hello....earth to Tycen. Where's the excitement? Where's the joy?" Lawrence smiled. "Geez... if you respond with this much enthusiasm if we actually win the election...I may have to check your pulse to see if you're still alive."

Tycen chuckled and shook his head. He placed the results back on his desk. "I know. I'm sorry," Tycen said. "I'm just a bit out of it today. Just a lot on my mind."

"I can understand that, but you need to pull it together." Lawrence started nodding with a wide smile. "Tonight is the big night!"

"I know," Tycen mumbled.

"Debate time..." Lawrence started to get hyped. "Mono e mono." Lawrence put his fists up as if he was a heavyweight prizefighter. "Gary Banks versus Tycen Wakefield. The first debate of the campaign. The old versus the new. The biggest debate of the season. This is where the men are separated from the boys. This will separate the wolves from the sheep...the nuts from the breasts—"

"Okay I get it." Tycen started laughing at his campaign manager.

"Yes...now there's that million dollar smile." Lawrence nodded. "That's the spirit. I need you amped for tonight, Tycen. We can do this. You ready?"

"I guess I am," Tycen dropped his voice again. Heidi was still on his mind.

"You guess?" Lawrence snapped. "You can't guess right now, Tycen. You got to know it! Those people out there smell fear. They know when you're not ready for the moment. They want a leader. Somebody who's braver than them. No guessing right now!"

Tycen didn't respond. He thought about Lawrence's words and stared off for a brief moment.

Lawrence recognized the uncertainty in Tycen's demeanor. Lawrence clapped his hands together to wake him up. "Let me ask you a question, Tycen." Lawrence stepped away from his desk and pointed outside into the campaign headquarters. "If we started running out the building right now, what do you think those people out there would do?"

"They would probably start running too," Tycen responded.

"Right! But why?" Lawrence quickly asked.

"Shit...because they would probably be scared as hell." Tycen nervously smiled.

"Wrong!" Lawrence yelled. "It's not just fear that motivates everyone, Tycen. Those people would start running because they would believe that we know something that they don't know. They would trust us and run right with us. You want to know why? Because deep inside all of us there's a need to be led. Most people go through life needing a leader. They're like sheep. All they do is graze and roam in the direction of the other sheep. Never looking up for another direction or another option. All they do is stare at the asshole in front of them... literally...and just wait around to be led. Even if they're walking toward death. Sheep to a slaughter."

Tycen leaned back in his chair and listen closely to his campaign manager. Lawrence's words echoed in the office.

"That's why the power is with the person who moves first," Lawrence continued. "Even if you don't know the answers, all you have to do is act like you know. People will always relinquish their power to a believable leader."

"Damn," Tycen said and thought about Lawrence's words.

"So don't worry about a thing. You're going to do fine." Lawrence reached on the desk and grabbed the poll results. "We can win this election, Tycen. You just need to show the people you can lead them better than Gary Banks. You don't have to be the best leader in the world. You just have to be better than Gary."

"Got it." Tycen nodded.

"Okay good." Lawrence gave his client a thumbs-up, and then showed Tycen his fist. "I'm going to give your ears a rest for now and get back to work. We got a debate prep later, so I will give you the details in a few."

"Okay... sounds good to me," Tycen said. He watched as Lawrence left the office. Tycen spun his chair around and tried to focus on the debate. His mind switched back to Heidi's face. Tycen grabbed his phone again and dialed her number. He grew frustrated when her voicemail came on. He waited for a few seconds and decided to leave her a message. "Heidi... baby...it's me," Tycen whispered. "I hope everything is fine over there. Where are you? I've been trying to reach you. The big debate is tonight, and I would love for you to be there. Please call me back. I miss you."

Chapter 28

Tuesday, October 29
9:51 am
West Milford, NJ

"It pains me to confirm that a former member of my security team has been linked to the kidnapping and murder of Lexi Hamilton. Our investigators, along with the aid of the FBI, have confirmed this information to my office late last week. We delayed this press conference out of respect for the Hamilton family. But please note…the public can rest easy knowing that the man responsible for Lexi Hamilton's murder has been identified. As many of you already know, Dante Harper was killed during what is believed to be a retaliation effort by those sympathetic of Hamilton and her family. We ask that the residents of Newark stay vigilant and patient as we continue to search for those parties involved in the shooting in Military Park. Thank you."

The strained voice of Gary Banks echoed from the television screen in the hotel suite. Pearl Kachina sat quietly on the sofa and barely paid attention to the mayor's press conference. She was aggravated. Pearl choked the remote control and started flipping through the channels. She needed to entertain herself. Pearl was all alone in the beautiful top floor suite of the Marriot Hotel, located nearly an hour away from her house. Despite the luxury accommodations, for the past few weeks, Pearl felt like a prisoner. She missed her home.

Two weeks ago, without warning, Heidi packed up their things and forced her mother to relocate out of her house. Pearl and Heidi had been living out of their suitcases in the hotel. Pearl hated feeling like a gypsy. Heidi refused to give her mother a real explanation as to why she couldn't return to her home. Pearl trusted her daughter, but lately Heidi had been acting strange and unreasonably paranoid.

A loud rumble startled Pearl, making her sit up on the sofa. She felt relieved when she noticed her daughter Heidi stumbling through the door with two suitcases in her arms.

"Okay, Mom, this is the last of it," Heidi blurted as she slammed the bags down near the door. "I'm not going back to that house for nothing else."

Pearl walked over to the door and greeted her daughter. "Are you okay?" Pearl asked and looked down at the luggage.

"I'm fine." Heidi shook her head in frustration.

Pearl looked at her daughter's face and knew she was not being straight with her. Heidi's body language was awkward. She seemed worried and disheveled. Pearl was about to reach out for her, but Heidi continued walking toward the kitchen area.

Heidi fumbled through her purse and grabbed her phone. Her face tightened when she noticed she had nearly a dozen missed calls. Before she could scroll through the numbers, her phone started buzzing. Another call came through. The phone number was restricted. "Hello!" Heidi spoke loudly. There was no answer. Heidi could hear someone breathing through the phone. "Who is this?" Heidi yelled. The breathing continued to get louder. Heidi got nervous and disconnected the call.

"Who was that?" Pearl looked over to her daughter.

Heidi never answered. She continued to search through her bag, and then pulled out a small notepad. Heidi looked at her mother and walked over to her. "Mom, I need you to listen to me," she whispered and handed her mother the notebook.

Pearl became alarmed when she looked at her daughter's face. "Baby...what's wrong with you?" Pearl asked. "You don't look good."

"Listen, Mom. I got you a plane ticket," Heidi uttered. "Here's the flight information."

"Flight information?" Pearl huffed. "Child, what in the hell has gotten into you? What are you talking about?"

"I need you to stay with Aunt Valerie for a while." Heidi pointed to the notes. "Mom, seriously, you just need to trust me right now."

"Heidi, I do trust you," Pearl tried her best to remain calm. "First, you force me out of my own house, and now you putting me on a flight. Heidi, you got to meet me half way on this. What in the world is going on? Talk to me."

"I am talking to you Mom. This is me talking to you. I gotta take care of something here," Heidi raised her voice. "I really don't need you around for this. It could be dangerous."

Heidi's phone started ringing again. She gritted her teeth and answered the call with an attitude.

"Stop calling my phone!" Heidi shouted. There was still no answer on the other line. Heidi had a good idea of who the phantom caller was. "This is ridiculous," Heidi shouted. "If you're not gonna say nothin'...don't bother callin' my phone." Heidi disconnected the call and tossed the phone to the sofa.

"Heidi...okay...what is going on? Really." Pearl pointed toward Heidi's cellphone. "What was that about?"

"Mom, you wouldn't believe me if I told you." Heidi shook her head. "I don't know if you can take all of your things on the flight, this time around. So only take two or three bags. Okay?"

"What is with you and this flight stuff?" Pearl started to grow annoyed. "I'm not getting on no flight today."

"Mom...you have too. You don't understand. You have to!" Heidi repeated. She gave her mother a strong glance. "I can't risk anything happening to you right now. It's too dangerous to be around me."

"What..." Pearl whispered.

"I know this sounds crazy. But you have to trust me, Mom...

please?" Heidi closed her mouth and looked at her mother.

There was something in Heidi's tone that caused Pearl to think for a moment. She looked down at the flight information and shook her head. Pearl had no clue what was going on with Heidi, but she knew she needed to trust her daughter. "How long is this for?" Pearl asked.

"I don't know. A week...two weeks...maybe a month." Heidi put her hands up. "I just need to know you're safe, Mom."

Pearl forced her lips together and nodded her head. She looked down at her luggage.

"What time is the flight?" Pearl asked.

"It's not until seven o'clock tonight," Heidi responded. "I just need you to lay low here for a couple of more hours. That's it."

Before Pearl could speak again, Heidi's phone started buzzing from the sofa. Heidi rushed to the phone and answered it. "Listen motherfucker. . ." Heidi yelled. "This is the last time I'm goin' to tell you to stop callin' my phone."

Pearl was shocked by Heidi's language.

A male voice gasped on the other line. "Heidi...is everything okay...it's Tycen!"

"Jesus Christ...Tycen...I thought...dammit...I thought you was somebody else." Heidi put her hand on her head.

"Well damn...I hope so," Tycen said. "Is everything okay?"

"No....yes...well...hell no..." Heidi stuttered. "Where are you, Tycen? What's goin' on?"

"Did you get my messages?" Tycen asked.

"No....it's been a very long few days," Heidi huffed. "I've been dealing with something serious over here."

"Do you want to talk about it?" Tycen asked.

"No, I can take care of it," Heidi quickly responded. "So what did the message say?"

"I was calling to remind you about the big debate tonight." Tycen cleared his throat. "I wanted to know if you could make it. It would be nice if you were there."

"I doubt if I can make it, Tycen." Heidi looked over to her mother. Pearl was shifting through the luggage and taking out the items she didn't need for her unplanned trip. Heidi shook her head and turned her attention back to the phone call. "I'm sorry, Tycen. I have to take my mother to the airport tonight. I don't think I can make the debate."

"Damn." Tycen sounded disappointed.

"I know…I am so…sorry," Heidi said. "It's just a really crazy time for me right now."

"Well…what are you doing in about an hour?" Tycen asked.

"Just helping my mother with her things," Heidi responded. "Why?"

"Can I at lease see you for a few minutes?" Tycen lowered his voice.

"I don't know, Tycen. I really don't want to be in public right now." Heidi thought about her situation. Having Aaron on the hunt for her kept Heidi on edge. The last thing she wanted to do was wander the streets of Newark.

"That's fine. Just come to my house," Tycen said. "It would be just for a few. I haven't seen you in weeks, Heidi. I miss you."

The words sent a warm chill through Heidi's body. She hadn't spoken to Tycen in a while. Hearing the words come from his mouth reminded her of the reason why she was so attracted to him. She looked at Pearl again. Heidi knew she had a few more hours to kill before the flight left. "Tycen… listen to me," Heidi said. "If I meet you at the house…it can only be for a few minutes. I have a lot to do today."

"That's fine, Heidi. Me too," Tycen responded. Heidi felt him smiling through the phone. "I will see you in a few, Heidi."

"Okay, Tycen. Goodbye." Heidi disconnected the call and walked over toward her mother. She noticed that Pearl's face was tight. "What's wrong, Mom?" Heidi asked.

"My jewelry." Pearl shook her head. "It's not in the bag either."

"Huh?" Heidi looked down.

"The locket!" Pearl shouted. "The locket is not in this bag."

"Damn, Mom. Are you sure you didn't bring it with you the first time we left?" Heidi asked.

"No, child! Dammit." Pearl was upset. "Heidi, you rushed me out the house so fast that I didn't even think about it. I thought the locket was in this hotel room, but it's not. I have looked everywhere."

Heidi didn't know what to say. Pearl was beyond upset that she was unable to find her gold locket. Heidi tried to think of where it could be. "I can check through my things again." Heidi nodded.

"No, I know it's not there," Pearl snapped. "It's back at the house. I know it."

"Well...we're not going back there, Mom. We can't," Heidi tried to sound forceful and respectful.

"We have to. You don't know how much that locket means to me." Pearl stared at her daughter. "I have to take it with me."

Heidi closed her eyes and cursed. Pearl was putting her in a tight bind with the missing locket. Heidi looked up to her mother. "Mom—" Heidi began.

"Child, listen to me," Pearl dropped her voice. "I don't want to get on this plane later without that locket. Now I trust you...I know you're sending me away for a good reason. But I'm not catching this flight without that locket. I'm serious, Heidi." Pearl didn't blink as she gave her daughter the ultimatum.

Heidi huffed at her mother. She had no choice but to respect her request. "Okay, Mom." Heidi nodded. "When I get back... we can go to the house together. I will only be gone for an hour. We can go then."

Pearl felt relieved and walked away from the luggage. Heidi looked at her watch and grabbed her purse. She headed for the door and looked back at her mother. "Mom, don't forget...if anybody calls the room—"

"I know...don't pick up the phone." Pearl waved at her daughter. "I got it."

Heidi closed her mouth and didn't say a word. She hated to keep her mother in the dark, but she needed to be cautious now. Heidi waved at her mother and left the hotel room to pay a much-needed visit to Tycen.

Chapter 29

Tuesday, October 29
10:08 am
Newark, NJ

Rojo Marquez grimaced in pain as he slowly made his way down the hallway of The Body Shop. It had been two weeks since the huge shootout that left him wounded. The hard expression on his face shielded his anger. He pushed the broken door open and walked into his office. Five members of his security force were lounging around waiting for his arrival. Rojo looked at the men with disgust.

One of the security guards stood up and watched as Rojo walk over to his desk. "You need anything boss?" the man nervously asked.

"Yes. I do need somethin'," Rojo coolly responded and sat down slowly. He nursed his ailing shoulder. "I need you to grab your shit and get the fuck out of here. As a matter of fact...everybody...get the fuck out. Everybody's fired!"

The small group of men looked on in shock. They all turned to Rojo and tried to read his demeanor. He was clearly serious.

"Am I speaking fuckin' Chinese?" Rojo yelled out. "Everybody....is fuc...king....fired! Let's go! Get the fuck out!"

"Wait boss...don't overreact," the first man tried to plead

with Rojo.

"What? I'm not overreacting." Rojo shook his head. "This is overreacting!" Rojo reached in his waist and pulled out his gun. He placed the chrome weapon on his desk for all to see. "Everybody get the fuck out before I cover my eyes and start squeezing off in this bitch! Let's go!"

A few of the men realized Rojo meant business. They quickly exited his office before things escalated.

"And tell all those bitches to go home too," Rojo yelled at the last man out. "The Body Shop is officially closed for business. Everybody is fucking fired," Rojo repeated. "If you see Skittles out there, tell her to come to my office. I want to see her. But everybody else gotta go! Get the fuck out!"

Rojo's office cleared out in record time. He rubbed his forehead in frustration. The past two weeks of recovery had given him too much time to think. He needed to make a major move, and he couldn't wait to get back to his office. He grabbed the remote control off his desk and turned on the television. The white DVD was still in his player, and Rojo turned on the video. The graphic images caused his wheels to begin turning. Rojo snatched up his phone and called his father. "Please pick up, dad," Rojo whispered under his breath as he waited for the phone to connect.

"Where the fuck you been?" Leon Marquez angrily yelled from the other line.

"I'm sorry, Pop," Rojo responded. "We had a situation here and I got shot. They just released me from the hospital today."

"Shot? What the hell happened?" Marquez's voice was loud.

"Pop....you won't believe this shit," Rojo sounded confused. "The mayor's brother showed up. And Kimi got away. Niko's dead. Trust me, Pop...it was a fuckin' mess down here."

"What the...fuck?" Marquez stated. "Niko's dead?"

"Yeah I know. I'm sorry." Rojo leaned back in his chair. "Shit just went haywire. This motherfucker came in here like he had an army with him."

"So did somebody tip him off about Niko and Kimi?" Marquez asked.

"I don't know," Rojo responded.

"Goddamit, Ronald. This shit is all fucked up," Marquez shouted through the phone. "So the case is done? Shit...I have no shot of winning now."

"Nah, Pop...it's not over yet." Rojo coolly looked at the video. "I actually got a DVD off of Kimi."

"A DVD?" Marquez sarcastically asked.

"Yup...it got the mayor on it," Rojo added.

"Okay. So what the hell does that have to do with me?" Marquez was confused.

"Follow me for a second, Pop." Rojo nodded as he took another peek at the repulsive images on the television screen. "The mayor is on here doing some real foul shit. And let's just say...I know he'll pay a serious amount of money to make sure this video doesn't get out."

"Oh shit. Like that?" Marquez asked.

"Like that, Pop. Believe me," Rojo replied. His voice sounded confident.

There was a gentle knock at the door. Skittles peered into the room and Rojo motioned for her to come inside. He continued to speak to his father on the phone as Skittles walked over to his desk.

"Let me work this out on my end. I think we can take advantage of this." Rojo sat up in his seat. "I think we can handle the money issue...and...handle the case with this. I'll call you back later today."

"Okay, Ronald," Marquez lowered his voice. "Make sure you get on this. We're running out of time."

"I'm on it, Pop." Rojo disconnected the call and turned to Skittles. She was staring at the television screen, and Rojo motioned to get her attention. "I got to shut down The Body Shop for a while." Rojo looked up to Skittles.

"What?" she blurted. "What happened?"

"It's too much heat coming down on us right now, and too many people know where we are," Rojo exclaimed. "We need to move this place from around here. I know it's gonna take a few months to make this whole thing happen. But we gotta do it. I'm sending everybody home."

"You got to be kidding right?" Skittles dropped her eyes.

"I wish I was kiddin'," Rojo quickly responded. "This is serious. The mayor's brother showed up here, and that's too close for comfort. We need to go deeper underground so we can survive."

"Damn, Rojo. So what about me?" Skittles asked.

"I know you gonna be hurtin' so that's why I wanted to see you." Rojo gave her a confident gesture. "I'm going to take care of you until we open back up."

"I don't need no fuckin' handouts," Skittles raised her voice. "I need money."

"Okay...so what do you want me to do?" Rojo grew agitated.

"Put me on to something." Skittles put her hands on her sexy hips.

"I don't have nothing right now," Rojo responded. "I told you...I'm sending all of our customers home."

"What about this?" Skittles pointed to the television screen.

"What about it," Rojo uttered.

"Don't play with me, Rojo." Skittles smiled at him. "I heard you talkin' to your dad about this video. Put me on this. I can help you."

"Is that right?" Rojo almost laughed at her audacity. "You think you can help me with this?"

"I know her," Skittles blurted. "That's Didi on that video with the mayor. That's his Chief of Staff."

"I know that." Rojo twisted his face. "Any idiot that watches the news can see that."

"No, Rojo...you don't understand. I know her...know her." Skittles smiled. "She's one of my clients. I was just with them a few weeks ago."

"Bullshit…!" Rojo shouted out.

"Don't call bullshit unless you ready to put some money behind that, baby." Skittles smiled.

Rojo looked at Skittles' eyes. He knew she was a slick girl, and decided to call her bluff.

"Okay…if you can get me close to her…I'll give you five percent of what we get for this video." Rojo leaned back in his chair.

"Ten percent." Skittles gave Rojo a direct stare.

"Don't press your luck, bitch," Rojo snapped at her. "This is not a negotiation."

Skittles picked up on Rojo's dark tone and decided to back down. She was all too familiar with Rojo's violent side. The last thing Skittles wanted to do today was wake up the beast. "Okay…five percent is more than enough." Skittles forced a smile to come to her face. "Watch this." Skittles grabbed her phone from her tight jeans. She quickly scrolled to Didi's name and dialed her number. She put the phone on speaker so Rojo could hear every word of their conversation. He rubbed his chin and looked on as Skittles began to pace in the office. She waited for the phone call to connect.

"Skittles…hey…I can't talk right now," Didi answered on the other line. "Things are crazy down here."

"Oh…I think you might want to make time for this, Didi," Skittles sounded forceful on the phone.

"Huh? What's going on?" Didi picked up on her tone.

"I'm watching a video right now of you and Gary," Skittles chuckled. "And if I was you, I would not want the world to see this."

"What are you talking about, Skittles?" Didi dropped her voice. "What video?"

"It looks like an old DVD," Skittles responded. "But I bet it will pop like it's brand new once CNN gets a hold of it. Ropes…chains…bondage…this is really not a good look for the mayor right now."

"Jesus Christ…!" Didi uttered and didn't know what else

to say.

"Now...now... Didi. Let's leave JC out of this." Skittles laughed. "This is all about you and Gary."

"What do you want?" Didi quickly blurted.

"It depends on what you're willing to give," Skittles quickly responded. "I'm going to come down there to discuss this—"

"No...don't come down here," Didi interrupted her. "The media is going crazy down here."

"Okay...you better tell me something," Skittles raised her voice. "We need to handle this today."

"Shit..." Didi sounded frustrated on the other line. "Don't come down here, Skittles. I will talk to Gary in a few, and then call you right back. I'll tell you where we can meet."

Skittles disconnected the call and looked over to Rojo. He was clearly impressed with her. "So you believe me now?" Skittles smiled.

"Without a doubt." Rojo nodded. "This is going to be a lot easier than I thought."

"You goddamn right." Skittles gave Rojo a sassy gesture.

Rojo looked over to the television and shook his head at the images. For the first time, he felt confident that he could get the money up to save his father. Rojo was ready to help Leon Marquez get out of jail and get him back on the streets where he belonged.

Chapter 30

Tuesday, October 29
11:37 am
Hackensack, NJ

Asad Banks calmly walked down the second floor hallway of the Hackensack Medical Center. A small gift bag dangled from his right hand, and he balanced two large coffee cups in his left. Today was a bittersweet day for him. Learning of his best friend's involvement with Lexi Hamilton's murder was devastating. It had only been a few weeks since Dante's death, and the pain was heavy on Asad's conscious. He decided to ease his mind by paying a visit to a new friend who stumbled into his life just two weeks back. As he approached the hospital room, Asad's face started to brighten with each step.

"Good morning officers. Here you go…as promised." Asad nodded and handed over the freshly brewed coffee.

Two Hackensack police officers reached out and grabbed the coffee cups from Asad. They had been standing guard in front of the hospital room all morning and were looking forward to taking a break. Seeing Asad was a relief, and both officers showed their gratitude.

"How's everything this morning?" Asad asked.

"Relatively quiet," one officer calmly responded. "No visitors today, and nothing out of the ordinary."

"Okay…that's the good news I wanted to hear." Asad

grinned. "Thanks again for doing this for me, fellas. I think she'll be here a few more days, then that's it. I can't tell you guys how much I appreciate you doing this favor for us. I couldn't trust any of the hospitals in Newark."

"No problem at all." The second officer nodded. "We'll take a quick fifteen minute break, and then come right back."

"Sounds good." Asad nodded. The officers left their post. Asad turned around and gently tapped on the door.

"Come in," a voice called out.

Asad slowly walked into the hospital room. Kimi Moore was sitting on the edge of the bed, staring out the window. She turned around and noticed it was Asad coming through the door and gave him a smile.

"How are you holding up?" Asad asked and walked to the other side of the room.

"I'm doing a lot better," Kimi softly reported. Her face was healing tremendously, and Asad could tell she was getting healthier every day.

"You look good." Asad smiled at her.

"I'm sure I've looked a lot better than this…but thanks." Kimi pursed her lips together and shook her head. She knew she looked terrible in the hospital robe, but she appreciated Asad's attempt to be polite.

"I brought you somethin'." Asad handed Kimi the small gift bag, then took a seat across from her bed.

"Really?" Kimi twisted her face and looked in the bag. She pulled out a small bracelet made of onyx Shamballa beads. "Wow…." Kimi marveled at the bracelet. She was speechless.

"I know it's not platinum or nothing fancy…but…I thought about you when I seen it." Asad grew serious and almost embarrassed at his confession.

"It's nice." Kimi smiled at him. "I like it."

"It was handmade in India," Asad continued. "It means blissful protection. I figure you could use it after all that craziness you been through."

Kimi looked over to Asad and closed her mouth. His

handsome face was so fresh, and Kimi shook her head toward him. "How old are you?" Kimi quickly asked.

"I'm twenty six. Why?" Asad harshly responded. His mood instantly changed.

"No offense, Asad," Kimi lowered her tone. "I didn't mean it like that. You just seem so young and innocent. What are you doing playing with guns at your age?"

Asad started laughing. He looked at Kimi as if she was from another world. "Well, when your brother is Gary Banks...you tend to play with guns a lot." Asad continued laughing.

"Wait...you're the mayor's brother?" Kimi twisted her face.

"Yup. Asad Banks...that's me." He put his hand up.

"Oh shit," Kimi said. She thought for a moment. Asad looked at Kimi and expected her to continue her thought. Kimi decided not to say what was on her mind.

"Oh shit...what?" Asad quickly asked.

"Nothin'...I knew you looked familiar," Kimi quickly responded. She thought about the video she witnessed in Rojo's office. Kimi didn't want to discuss it and decided to change the subject. "So what were you doin' in that building the other night? What made you try to save us?"

"I would be lying if I told you I was there to save you and your boyfriend. I wasn't there for you," Asad confessed and shook his head. "I was there to question Rojo Marquez about something that happened with the mayor...and when I came in the office...y'all were there."

"Are you serious?" Kimi tilted her head and looked at him.

"Dead serious," Asad responded. "When I saw y'all tied up...there was no way I was going to leave you there like that. I had to do something. What are the chances right?"

"Wow." Kimi dropped her head.

The mood in the room started changing, and Asad sensed it. Kimi fiddled with the bracelet and seemed to fall into deep thought. "You okay?" Asad spoke softly.

"Uh huh." Kimi nodded and started to feel emotional.

"You sure?" Asad looked at her.

"You need to take this back." Kimi looked over to Asad and raised the bracelet toward him. "I don't deserve this. You really need to take this back."

"What?" Asad asked. "You do deserve it. What do you mean? It's yours."

"Look, Asad. You are really sweet." Kimi's face was breaking down. "I don't know why you're being nice to me. I don't know what type of person you think I am…but…you don't know me. Believe me. I'm not the person you want."

"What are you talking about, Kimi." Asad shook his head. "It's just a gift…and it's yours…I'm not taking it back. You act like I just asked you to marry me."

"I know it's just a gift." Kimi gave Asad a hard stare. "But you got that look in your eyes. I know what you're thinking."

"Is that right?" Asad closed his mouth.

"Yes…you're thinking you can give me this gift…and maybe…that can open the door for something more." Kimi shook her head. "It doesn't work like that. You can't come in here and save the day…and we just supposed to live happily ever after."

"Damn, Kimi. You are a trip. You got it all wrong." Asad shook his head.

"Do I really?" Kimi asked. "Do I really got it all wrong?"

"Hell yes!" Asad raised his voice in the room. "I was hoping we could at least do dinner first…and then…live happily ever after."

Kimi dropped her head and smiled. The offbeat joke lightened the mood in the hospital room.

"Stop it, Asad. This is not funny. You really don't know me," Kimi repeated. "I really did some bad things in my life."

"Join the club," Asad quickly responded. "Who hasn't?"

Kimi looked up to Asad's fresh face. He had no idea of the type of secrets that were weighing heavy on her conscious. She looked down at the bracelet and calmly put it on her wrist.

"Thank you for the gift, Asad," Kimi lowered her voice.

"I do appreciate you thinking of me. I'll keep the bracelet... but...I really need you to leave now."

"Seriously?" Asad's smile was quickly erased from his face.

"Yes...I'm tired. I need some rest and I really don't like where this is going." Kimi nervously wiped her forehead. "You really are a sweetheart, Asad. I can smell it all over you. You still have the best part of you left. You don't have to end up changing into a person like me."

"You need to stop saying that," Asad said.

"Seriously, Asad." Kimi's expression grew intense. "Just listen to me for a second." Asad noticed Kimi's eyes were turning red as she continued speaking. "The whole time that asshole had me tied up...I just knew that I was going to die in that room. There was no reason I should have made it out of there alive. I just knew I was going to lose my life sitting in that chair. And the crazy thing is...I knew I deserved it. I knew I was goin' to pay for that ugly shit I did to other people. I just didn't realize it was going to happen that fast." The hospital room fell silent. Kimi wiped her eyes as she reflected on the scary night back at The Body Shop. Asad listened closely as she continued speaking. "And then something strange happened." Kimi looked up to Asad. "Something in the back of my mind kept tellin' me that I wasn't going to die. It was like a voice tellin' me to stay alive. It was the oddest thing. And then... here you come rushing through the door. I thought it was the police...but...to find out that it was just you, and we still made it out alive...that is....damn. . .that is something."

"I know—" Asad mumbled.

"Wait...let me finish," Kimi politely cut him off. "Because you saved my life...I feel like I owe you this much, to be honest with you, Asad. You could've left me in there to die if you wanted to. But you didn't...that says a lot about the person you are. So whatever it is...that you got inside of you...don't lose it, Asad. Don't lose it." Kimi stood up and walked toward Asad. She leaned in front of him and grabbed him by the face.

Asad's eyes were fixed on her, and Kimi softly smiled. She reached down and kissed him gently on the cheek. "Thank you," Kimi whispered. "You're a good man." Kimi turned around and walked to the window. She stared out into the afternoon sky and closed her mouth.

The silence in the room became deafening. Asad knew she didn't have anything else to say. He didn't know how to react, so he gathered himself to leave. There was so much he wanted to know about Kimi, but he decided to respect her request for him to leave. Asad quietly walked out the hospital room and left Kimi alone. As he made his way down the long hallway, Asad couldn't help but wonder if he would ever see Kimi again.

Chapter 31

Tuesday, October 29
12:23 pm
Newark, NJ

"I'm only going to say this one more time...all the details were outlined in the press conference earlier. Dante Harper is the only link to the death of Lexi Hamilton. I'm sorry, I don't have any more details, but that is as much as you're going to get from this office. Please forward your questionnaire to our press department and they will process your media request. Thank you and have a good day." Didi rudely hung up the phone and let out a dull scream. The calls were coming in from every direction, and it was hard for Didi to catch a second to breathe. The media outlets and investigators were buzzing heavily over the announcement of Lexi Hamilton's killer. Reporters from all over the state clamored to get a statement from the mayor or anyone from his staff. Didi was beyond fed up with the calls, so she unplugged her phone. Her mind was tortured by a more pressing issue.

Her stomach turned when she thought about the conversation with Skittles. The very mention of the video, made Didi's hands tremble. She looked down at her phone as a text message came in. Skittles had obviously taken a still-frame photo from the video and sent it to Didi's phone. Didi couldn't believe her eyes. She knew her career and her life would be over if the video ever leaked to the press. She quickly left her office and sought out her boss. When she arrived at the mayor's door, she didn't bother knocking. She barged into the office.

"Damn....Didi...what the hell?" Gary stuttered as he looked up from his desk. He was going over his notes for the big debate tonight. He took one look at Didi's worried eyes and knew something was wrong. "Is everything okay?"

"Hell no," Didi gasped. "We need to talk, Gary. This is serious." Didi locked the door to the office, then walked around to the back of his desk.

"What's going on?" Gary's eyes widened as Didi moved closer to him.

"Take a look at this." Didi leaned over Gary and showed him the text message with the photo attached.

"What the fuck..." Gary covered his mouth. "Is that what I think it is?"

Didi almost cried from the fear that shot through her body. "How the fuck did she get this video, Gary?" Didi shouted.

"She? What do you mean?" Gary quickly responded.

"This is Skittles," Didi blurted. "Skittles just sent me this text message. She has the video."

"Skittles? The girl that came to the house? What the hell? Wait...she got the video?" Gary's face was in shock.

"Apparently so," Didi raised her voice again. "How the fuck did she get that DVD, Gary? I thought you took care of this."

"Shit...I don't know." Gary stood to his feet. "I have no fuckin' clue how she got that video. Fuck!" Gary put his hand on his head. He knew he was heading for political annihilation if he didn't do something soon. "What does she want?" Gary stammered.

"I don't know yet." Didi wiped her face. "But I'm sure that bitch is looking for money."

"How much?" the mayor desperately asked.

"Gary, I don't know," Didi quickly responded. "We didn't get that far. She wanted to come down here, but I stopped her.

We need to take care of this shit right now. What do you want to do?"

"Goddamnit...I need to think." Gary paced behind his desk for a second. He couldn't believe the video had resurfaced. With the election coming up, he knew this would be disastrous for him. A shot of adrenaline rushed through his body. He tried to think of how much cash he had on hand. "Okay...this is what we can do," Gary's voice shook with a slight hint of fear. "Call her back and tell her to meet us at the house. We can do the exchange there."

"You're actually going to pay her?" Didi asked.

"We have to." Gary shook his head. "We need to get this shit over and done with. Tell her to meet us there in an hour. We can take care of this shit right now."

"What about security? Should we bring some men with us?" Didi nervously asked.

"Hell no." Gary twisted his face. "If anybody sees that video...we are done. This ship will go down faster than the goddamn Titanic."

Didi thought about Gary's words. Her heart started racing as the consequences mounted in her mind. She nodded her head toward the mayor. "Okay. I will call her now," she uttered and walked out of Gary's office. Didi's mind raced with corrupt thoughts as she headed back down the hallway. She reminisced back to the night when the video was made, and then shook her head. She couldn't believe the DVD still existed. Gary's and Didi's one night of bad judgments was so close to ruining the rest of their lives. Didi let out a frustrated gesture, preparing herself to call Skittles. She was desperate to retrieve the video before this entire situation spun wildly out of control.

Back at The Body Shop, Rojo sat behind his desk and took a long pull of his cigarette. Skittles was comfortably sitting on the sofa when her phone started buzzing. She sat up and answered the call.

"Hello…talk to me," Skittles spoke loudly and activated the speakerphone.

"Skittles…it's me," Didi sounded like she was whispering.

"Okay…I'm listening. What's the plan?" Skittles sounded serious.

"The mayor has agreed to meet with you at his house in one hour," Didi said.

"Sounds good. I'll be there, and I'll bring the video." Skittles nodded her head. "And I'm coming alone, so don't try nothing slick," Skittles warned.

"We won't. Just be there in an hour," Didi raised her voice. "Gary will have the money."

Skittles disconnected the call and looked over to Rojo. "Why the hell did you tell her you was coming alone?" Rojo snapped.

"So they won't be expecting you," Skittles responded with a sly gesture. "We won't give them a chance to prepare for you."

Rojo huffed and smirked at Skittles. He was again impressed with her cunningness.

"So you ready?" Skittles smiled at him.

Rojo looked at his watch, then stood to his feet. He ejected the white DVD from the player and placed it in his jacket pocket. Skittles watched him closely as he retrieved his chrome gun from the top drawer. He checked the clip, then tucked the weapon in his waistband.

Rojo nodded toward Skittles. "Now…I'm ready."

A few minutes later, Didi was nervously tapping her feet in her office. She looked at her watch and waited for the mayor to buzz her phone. No matter how hard she tried, Didi could not calm herself. Nothing about the upcoming campaign could get her mind off of the seriousness of retrieving the DVD. She knew that everything she had strived for and the decades of hard work she'd put in could all go up in smoke in a matter of minutes if the video leaked. Didi looked down at her phone. The mayor's words replayed in her mind, but Didi felt compelled to make one more call. She didn't want to leave anything to chance. Didi quickly dialed the number and waited for the call to connect.

"Hello," a male voice answered on the other line.

"Asad.…it's Didi," she whispered.

"What's going on, Didi?" Asad quickly responded.

"I need you to listen to me closely," Didi continued to whisper. "Please don't call your brother on this. I need you to trust me."

"Okay, Didi," Asad's voice grew serious. "What the hell is going on?"

"Listen…we're about to have a meeting at Gary's house," Didi uttered. "Something crazy is happening right now…I have to explain later. But I need you to come by the house."

"Okay, but what's goin' on, Didi?" Asad's voice grew louder. "You making me hype over here."

"I know…I'm sorry. But I really can't explain it now," Didi continued. "Please don't park in front of the house. I don't need you to come inside. I just need you to watch out for us. I need to make sure nothing crazy is going on outside while we take care of this shit over here."

"Damn, Didi. Is everything alright?" Asad asked. "This sounds serious."

"It is. But we can handle this." Didi tried her best to mask her anxiety. "We just don't want no surprises outside."

"Okay, Didi," Asad said. "I am on my way."

"Good…" Didi responded, feeling a bit better. "I will call you back once we get there."

Didi hung up the phone and felt a titbit of relief. She didn't know what to expect once Skittles showed up at Gary's house with the video. She gathered her things and prepared herself to leave. Getting the DVD back and finally destroying the damming evidence was the only thing on her mind.

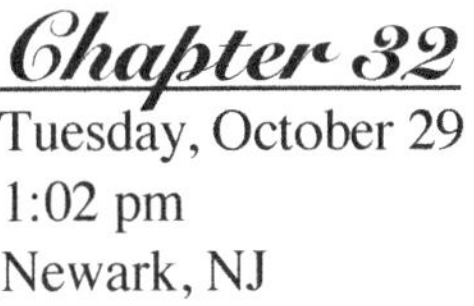

Chapter 32

Tuesday, October 29
1:02 pm
Newark, NJ

"Tune in tonight to News 12 New Jersey. Our network will be carrying the live debate between incumbent Mayor Gary Banks and rising star Tycen Wakefield. The race for the next leader of Newark is heating up, and the candidates have been hot on the campaign trail. Tune in tonight for full coverage of what is sure to be a feisty debate."

Tycen Wakefield took a nervous sip of his drink and stood in front of his kitchen television. The commercial for tonight's event got his blood to boiling. Tycen's life had been like a rollercoaster ride for the past few weeks. The clash between his personal and political life was a difficult challenge, but Tycen was strong enough to handle the pressure. He realized tonight's debate could be a big boost for his campaign. Tycen needed to be on his A-game, and there was one person that could help him regain his focus.

The loud doorbell startled Tycen. He put down his glass and felt a nervous tremor in his stomach. He walked to the front door and opened it. "Heidi..." Tycen's face lit up as he laid eyes on her.

"Hey," Heidi whispered and gave him a gentle smile.

Tycen reached out and embraced her like he hadn't seen her in months. It felt like years.

Heidi let out a soft groan when she squeezed Tycen's solid body. For the first time in days, Heidi felt safe.

"I'm glad you stopped by," Tycen said.

Heidi walked into the house. She took off her jacket and placed her purse on the sofa.

"You want something to drink?" Tycen asked.

"No, I can't stay long." Heidi slowly took a seat. Tycen sat next to her on the sofa. Heidi looked at him. "So…I heard the commercial for the debate. How are you feelin' about tonight? Are you nervous?"

"Honestly…I am," Tycen admitted. "Gary's a sharp guy."

"He is." Heidi nodded. "But people are ready for change. They're just tired of him and his bullshit…I think that's something that can play in your favor."

Tycen nodded toward Heidi. "I hope you're right," he said.

"You'll do fine, Tycen." Heidi touched his hand. "You've come too far to start doubting yourself now."

Heidi's warm touch woke up Tycen's body. He looked at her as his mood started to change. "You know I miss you right?" Tycen whispered and stared directly in her eyes.

"I miss you too, Tycen," Heidi quietly responded.

"So where you been?" Tycen asked. "Why haven't you returned my calls? I went by your mother's house and everything."

"We had to leave." Heidi shook her head. "It's too much to explain now. But we couldn't stay there."

"So what happened?" Tycen pressed. "You could've at least called me back."

Heidi felt Tycen's energy changing and she started to feel uncomfortable. "Tycen…we don't have to talk about this. We both know I got a lot goin' on right now." Heidi looked away from Tycen's face. "I hope that's not why you asked me to come see you."

"No, I really wanted to see you tonight at the debate." Tycen kept his eyes on her. "You know it would mean a lot to me if you were there."

"I told you, Tycen. I'm taking my mother to the airport," Heidi said.

"And then what?" Tycen snapped.

"'And then what?'" Heidi repeated. "And then, I have to take care of something."

Tycen tried to read Heidi. She was not giving him any straight answers, and Tycen was growing frustrated with her. He tried his best, but couldn't hold back his next question. "Does any of this shit have to do with Aaron?" Tycen blurted.

"What...Stop it!" Heidi snapped.

"Stop what?" Tycen fired back. "I'm just saying...ever since his name was brought up a couple of weeks ago...shit hasn't been the same with us."

"I have to go," Heidi said and stood to her feet.

"Wait...what...hold up...what do you mean?" Tycen stuttered.

"I don't want to get into this with you today, Tycen," Heidi raised her voice as Tycen jumped up from the sofa.

"See this is what I'm talking about." Tycen grabbed his head. "The minute I want to discuss this, you clam up. Heidi, you are killing me with this secretive shit."

Heidi had heard enough. She reached for her purse and her jacket. She stormed toward the front door and didn't say a word. Tycen quickly pursued her. Heidi grabbed the knob and pulled the door open. Tycen caught up to her, and then slammed it back shut. Heidi never turned around. Her face was inches from the door. Her adrenaline was flowing from the angry mood in the house.

"Don't leave me again," Tycen forcefully said. The sound of his deep voice froze Heidi. Tycen was breathing heavy from the quick sprint. He looked at Heidi from behind and moved closer to her. "Please don't leave me again, Heidi," Tycen repeated.

Heidi began to feel weak. Tycen moved even closer to her and pressed up against her body. "What are you doin'?" Heidi whispered.

Tycen never responded. He tapped his warm lips up against her neck. The smell of her skin made him groan. "I miss you," Tycen grumbled and let his tongue slip from his mouth. He tasted the back of Heidi's neck and shoulder.

"Tycen...," she cried out.

Tycen pinned her forcefully against the door. She felt his hips pressing up against her body and she closed her eyes. She smelled his passion for her and became lost in the moment. The brief argument vanished from Heidi's mind. The only thing that mattered now was his body up against hers. She missed Tycen.

Heidi's jacket and purse fell to the carpet. Tycen smoothly reached under her arms and cuffed her breasts. Heidi grabbed Tycen's hands and forced him to squeeze her harder.

"Damn..." Tycen said, savoring the feeling of her soft body.

Heidi turned her face to the side, and Tycen kissed her lips. She moaned his name when she tasted his wet tongue in her mouth. Her body started heating up. Tycen reached down and pulled her shirt up over her head. Her smooth skin turned him on. Tycen kissed the dip in her back, and then worked his way down to the top of her golden-brown ass. Heidi moaned his name again. Tycen got on his knees like he was worshipping a goddess. He unbuckled Heidi's jeans, stripping them off. He grew more excited when he watched Heidi's long legs step out of her panties. He put his mouth on her thighs and ran his tongue up and down her legs.

"Oh...shit...baby... yes..." Heidi's voice bounced off of the door.

Tycen's aggressiveness made her submissive to his strength. Heidi felt his hands all over her and grew excited. He reached up to Heidi's ass. He smacked her bottom like she'd done something wrong. She begged for another one. Tycen squeezed her again, then smacked her harder. She moaned loudly. Her whine excited Tycen. He forced her to bend over against the door. He spread her legs wide apart like he was about to search her. Tycen hummed again and glanced at her ready pussy.

"Shit! ooh..." Heidi cried out when she felt Tycen's stiff tongue enter her wetness from behind.

Tycen moaned with every lick as he pleased Heidi. He missed the taste of her smooth walls. The sound of him lapping her pussy drove Heidi crazy. She slowly bounced against his face as Tycen's tongue went deeper inside of her. She reached around and grabbed the back of his head. His mouth grazed her clit. Her legs buckled. Tycen felt her body tremble, and then started licking faster. Her sweet juices dripped from the side of his mouth, and Tycen knew she was close to climaxing. Without warning, Tycen stood to his feet. He dropped his pants to the floor. Heidi tried to turn around, but, before she knew it, she was up against the door again. Tycen kissed her neck and started grinding on her ass. Heidi put up her hands, grabbing his neck. She felt his naked skin against hers, and her mouth fell open. Tycen reached down low and grabbed himself. He kicked Heidi's legs apart, and she arched her back. She wanted him to know she was ready for him.

"Ooh," Heidi tilted back her head and moaned out loud as Tycen put his throbbing dick inside of her. Heidi exploded deep within from the first penetration. Tycen squeezed her tighter. Her creamy body felt like heaven to a born sinner. With every strong thrust, Heidi begged for more. Her titties bounced against the front door. Tycen deeply grunted as he showed Heidi how much he missed her.

Heidi didn't know it, but Tycen was fucking her with a jealous passion. He wanted to show Heidi that no man could please her like he could. Out of love and possession, he held on to her tightly. Heidi's loud moans made him go harder. She had never felt him so deep.

"Oh shit, baby....damn...please...don't stop." Heidi wrinkled her face from the beautiful mix of pain and pleasure.

Tycen grinded deeply, moaning her name. He bounced his hips against her ass. Heidi felt his dick growing stiffer. Tycen was close to exploding, and Heidi was not far behind. She screamed again. "Godammit....Tycen!"

Tycen fucked her like crazy. He panted and huffed with every extended stroke. Heidi started moving faster, and Tycen was right with her. Her body gyrated as the building orgasm consumed her. The hairs on her neck grew stiff. Tycen felt her walls squeezing around him. He forced his bulky dick into her tightening pussy, and Heidi had to let go.

"I'm coming!" she thought she heard herself say. Her body quaked with pleasure, and she sounded like she was speaking another language. Her wet pussy drowned Tycen's dick with a heavy orgasm. She felt him growing inside of her, and knew he was close. She reached around and grabbed his hips. Another orgasm rushed through her, and she gripped Tycen's skin. He felt so strong behind her.

Tycen's body shook. He grunted and moaned in her ear. "Shit ...Heidi...you 'bout to make me...cum!"

His words gave her the chills. Heidi gripped his waist. Tycen's hard body pinned her even closer against the door. Tycen exploded like a volcano. His seed shot deep inside her. Heidi felt his final relentless strokes. Another hard orgasm hit her. Heidi's body was lost in ecstasy.

"Oh my God, Tycen....that....was fuckin'....incredible..." Heidi panted and tried to catch her breath.

Tycen leaned against her and rested his sweating forehead on the back of her shoulder. He kissed her and tried to calm his breathing. Heidi felt his heart pounding. He had never felt more alive. Tycen made her body feel like an angel. She knew he missed her, but she didn't expect him to be so intense. She didn't want Tycen to move an inch. She kept her hands on him, pulling him nearer. Something deep within Heidi made her feel like she wanted to stay this close to Tycen forever.

Chapter 33

Tuesday, October 29
1:37 pm
Newark, NJ

Asad Banks watchfully peered through the front windshield of his Maserati. He was parked a few hundred feet away from Gary's house. The neighborhood was quiet. For the moment, there was nothing out of place. Asad tried to tap into his intuition to spot anyone lurking in the shadows. Didi's instructions had put him on edge. After the violent episode in Military Park, Asad felt compelled to be on point and protect his brother at all costs. He refused to let anything slip by him today.

A few minutes later, a jet-black SUV slowly coasted to a stop in front of the mayor's house. Asad ducked low in his seat. He gazed at the suspicious vehicle. The truck looked familiar, but he wasn't sure. His heart started racing. The headlights of the SUV flicked off. Asad tried to get a good look inside, but the windows were tinted.

"Shit..." Asad whispered. He didn't blink an eye as he continued to examine the vehicle. He knew he had to be ready for anything.

A few seconds later, a curvy female slowly stepped out of

the passenger side. She looked into the tinted windows, calmly grooming herself. Asad tried to get a good look at her face, but couldn't recognize her. She played with her hair until a large man stepped out of the vehicle. A shot of anger flowed through Asad's body. He couldn't believe his eyes. Rojo Marquez.

Meanwhile, inside Gary's house, Didi anxiously twisted her hair as she stood in the middle of the living room. She glanced at her watch. Time was moving faster than a bullet. She had given up on trying to calm herself. Her heart pounded like a bass drum. She had no clue what to expect today. She still couldn't believe the demons of her past were so close to destroying her. Before she could think any longer, there was a hard knock on the front door.

"I'll get it," Gary shouted, emerging from the kitchen. He looked over to Didi and saw she was scared out of her mind. He knew it was up to him to take the lead on the transaction. He needed to make sure everything went smooth. "Are you ready for this?" Gary nodded toward his Chief-of-Staff.

"I think so," Didi stuttered like she was on trial.

"That's good enough for me," Gary quickly responded. He carefully approached the door and took a deep breath. He put his game face on. It was time to put this daunting issue to bed. He opened the door and froze. His entire mood changed when he laid eyes on Skittles and her uninvited guest. "What the fuck is this?" Gary pointed at Rojo. The mayor stared at the man as if he could kill him.

"Let's us in, Gary!" Rojo barked and made direct eye contact with the mayor. "We don't have time for this bullshit."

Gary recognized Rojo's scowl from dozens of mug shots he'd accumulated over the years. He hesitated to let them in. Inviting the devil into his home had not been part of today's plan.

Skittles looked up to Gary and shook her head. "We gonna do this or not?" she asked, braking up the heavy tension. "I'm sure I can get top dollar for this video if you want me to go somewhere else."

Her statement brought Gary back to reality. He realized he was in no position to dictate the terms of the exchange. He stepped away from the front door and let them in. Rojo slowly followed Skittles inside and looked around the immaculate home.

"Look at this shit." Rojo surveyed the house and shook his head. "My Pops always told me that I was in the wrong business. He said if I wanted to be a heartless criminal and make the most money...I needed to go into politics. Looks like he was dead ass correct. Ain't that right, Mr. Banks?"

Gary kept his mouth shut. Skittles chuckled at her boss' joke. Didi looked at Skittles and gave her a disappointed look. Skittles seemed to be unfazed by her judging eyes.

"Okay...so how we gonna make this happen here?" Rojo clapped his hands together and looked at the mayor.

Gary closed the front door and headed to the kitchen. He was ready to get this nightmare over with. Rojo watched him like a hawk as he returned with a yellow envelope. Gary tossed the package to Rojo, and then went and stood by Didi.

"Where's the DVD?" Gary sharply asked.

Rojo didn't respond. He looked down at the envelope and cracked the seal. "What's this?" Rojo asked.

"That's twenty thousand dollars right there." Gary pointed toward the package. "Now where's the DVD?"

"Get the fuck out of here with this bullshit! What the fuck do I look like?" Rojo tossed the package to the floor and twisted his mouth. "Do I got the word idiot written all over my face? I wipe my ass with twenty gees every week. Where's the real money?"

"What are you talking about?" Gary shouted out. "Take the money and give us the DVD!"

"Or what?" Rojo's shouted. He stepped toward the mayor.

Gary didn't back down. He stood his ground and continued to stare toward Rojo. Didi started breathing heavy as the mood in the room grew more intense.

"Skittles told me everything...I know you got money motherfucker." Rojo pointed at Gary. "Don't play stupid now."

Gary looked over to Skittles. His regretted that Didi invited her inside his home.

"Come on, Gary," Skittles antagonized the mayor. "Don't make this more difficult than it has to be. We know you got more cash than that." Skittles pointed to the envelope on the carpet. "Remember...the million dollar orgasm?" Skittles let out a girlish snicker.

Gary curled his lip. He was mad enough to choke the life out of Skittles.

Rojo looked over to the mayor. "Come on, motherfucker. You're wasting time." Rojo glared at Gary and Didi. "Let's go get the money."

"I can't do that," Gary shouted.

"Oh no?" Rojo titled his head like a rock wilder dog. He quickly reached in his waistband and brandished his chrome gun. Rojo pointed the weapon directly at the mayor. "How 'bout I give you a little motivation then?"

Didi put her hands up and screamed. In one quick move, Rojo put everyone in the room on notice. Rojo was clearly ready to do anything today to get the money from Gary. "Now I'm not goin' to say this shit again," Rojo yelled. "Move your fuckin' ass! And unless you got bulletproof skin, I suggest we do this shit now!"

The ferocious look in Rojo's eyes made the mayor nervous. Didi looked over to her boss. She was petrified. Gary didn't want to take any more chances, so he decided to lead Rojo to his safe. He turned around and walked with Didi. Rojo followed closely behind as the mayor lead them up the stairs to the second floor.

"Nice and slow motherfucker," Rojo shouted and kept the gun on the mayor.

Gary made it to the master bedroom, and then slowly pushed open the door. Didi followed Gary inside and they stood near his walk-in closet.

Rojo rushed through the door and kept his gun on the mayor. "So where is it?" Rojo quickly looked back at Skittles.

"It's right over there." Skittles pointed to a large painting on the wall.

Gary shook his head. Skittles walked to the other side of the room. She pulled down the large painting and exposed the heavy-duty wall safe.

"Oh shit," Rojo said and laughed. He took one look at Gary's angry eyes and realized Skittles' information was correct. Gary was hiding a big secret in his bedroom. "So how much money you got up in there, Mr. Mayor?"

Gary didn't respond.

"Open it!" Skittles yelled at the mayor and pointed at the safe.

Gary made a move, but Rojo raised his gun to him.

"Wait!" Rojo ordered. "You stay right there, motherfucker. Just give Skittles the combination. I don't fuckin' trust you. You probably got a gun or somethin' inside that goddamn safe."

Skittles nodded toward Rojo and looked back to Gary. She appreciated the fact that Rojo was always thinking ahead. Gary gave Rojo a weird expression, and then stepped back closer to Didi.

Rojo kept his gun on Gary and looked him in the eyes. "What's the combination?" Rojo asked.

"You don't have to do this," Gary said. "There's more than enough money in that envelope downstairs—"

"What's the fucking combination?" Rojo yelled.

Gary tightened his jaw. He didn't have any other options left. He looked over to Skittles and gave her a strange look. "One..." Gary called out. "Spin it to the left first."

Skittles looked away from the mayor and turned her attention to the safe. She became eye level with the combination spindle, and then twisted the dial to the first number. "Okay," Skittles confirmed.

"Twenty-nine..." Gary called out again. "Spin it twice

around to the right, then go to the number twenty-nine."

Skittles calmly followed the directions. She spun the dial around twice and came to the second number. "Okay."

Gary paused for a moment. Rojo looked over to him.

"What's the last number, motherfucker?" Rojo yelled.

Gary seemed to hesitate. Skittles grew impatient and looked over to Rojo.

"Don't make me do something bad to you, Mr. Banks," Rojo warned and pulled the hammer back on his gun.

Gary gave them another odd look and proceeded. "Fifty-four…" Gary whispered. "Spin it once to the left again …and stop at fifty-four."

Skittles turned back to the wall safe. She spun the dial around and came to the last number. She heard a click from inside the safe. A devilish grin came to Rojo's face, and he knew they were close to the big payday.

"You have to pull the lever down to open the safe," Gary called out.

Rojo turned his attention to the large safe. He was ready to see how much money they were getting. Gary slowly reached down and grabbed Didi by the hand. Skittles took a deep breath. A feeling of excitement came over her as she imagined the stacks of cash.

Skittles reached out for the lever. It was heavy. She mustered all of the strength she could and pulled the lever straight down. A loud gunshot rang out. The heavy blast startled Rojo. He fell up against the wall.

The mayor squeezed Didi's hand. "Run!" Gary screamed, pulling on Didi's arm as Didi panicked and rushed behind Gary. They made a move for the bedroom door as Rojo fired three shots in their direction. Didi yelled in terror as the bullets barely missed them. Gary ran down the hallway to an adjacent bedroom. He pushed Didi inside and locked the door behind them.

Rojo turned to the safe and saw Skittles lying motionless on the floor. He rushed over to her body and his jaw dropped.

She was dead. A single bullet wound was in the center of her forehead. She never even had the chance to close her eyes. Rojo looked up to the safe and noticed it was rigged. The mayor had given her the wrong combination that triggered a countermeasure. The safe was still locked.

"Fuck..." Rojo screamed to the top of his lungs. He bolted out the bedroom and searched for Gary and Didi. A loud thump came from the first floor. He kept his gun raised and ran toward the steps. He heard another loud thump and assumed Gary and Didi were on the first level. Rojo rushed down the stairs with his gun high in the air. "Where the fuck are you?" Rojo frantically screamed out.

Before Rojo could turn around and continue the search, he felt a heavy piece of metal smash him on the back of his head. Rojo cursed loudly and spun around. Another hard crash knocked him to the floor. He felt a heavy boot kick the gun out of his hand, and Rojo tried to fight back. The attacker was on him like a rabid bear. Hard punches and heavy metal blows continued to batter Rojo's face until he was barely conscious. Blood flew from Rojo's mouth and nose as the hefty metal cracked against his head like a hammer. Rojo couldn't fight any longer. He knew he was only moments away from witnessing the end of his life. Rojo opened his eyes and finally saw his attacker leaning over him. A bloody grin came to Rojo's face. It was Asad Banks.

"What the fuck are you doing here?" Asad yelled out. He continued to thrash Rojo in the face. "Why the fuck are you here... at my brother's house? What the hell is going on?"

Asad was in full attack mode. Rojo could barely get a word out as the violence continued. Asad saw Rojo's mouth moving, so he held back his last punch. "What?" Asad yelled and held his fist in the air. "What the fuck are you trying to say?" Asad leaned over and listened closely to what were sure to be Rojo's last words.

Back upstairs, Gary Banks slowly approached the door to

his guest bedroom. Didi was standing nervously in the corner trying to calm down. Gary slowly cracked the door and peered down the hall. The second level was quiet. He crept outside and rushed back into his master bedroom. He reached under his mattress and grabbed a .357 Ruger revolver. His heart jumped when he heard a noise come from downstairs. Gary turned his attention to Skittles on the other side of the room. He rushed over to her body and knelt down beside her. Gary started to frisk her.

"Shit!" he barked when he knew she didn't have the DVD on her.

Gary quickly stood to his feet and raised his gun. He heard another noise come from the second level, and he assumed Rojo was still on the loose. He left the bedroom and carefully walked down the stairs. Gary twisted his face when he saw his brother, Asad, leaning over a battered and bruised Rojo. Asad was listening to Rojo's words, and Gary felt a rush of anger. He moved faster down the stairs, approaching Rojo. Without warning, Gary pushed Asad to the side and pumped three bullets into Rojo's chest.

"What…THE…FUCK!" Asad yelled, then looked at his brother like he was a mad man.

Gary ignored Asad. He put another bullet in Rojo and quickly leaned over him. Gary frisked Rojo's dead body for the DVD. "It's not here," Gary yelled. "Shit…where is it?"

"What the hell is wrong with you?" Asad shouted. He had a confused look on his face. The mayor scared him.

"The DVD….it's not here!" Gary desperately looked around the living room. He didn't see the video.

"What are you talking about, Gary?" Asad grabbed his brother by the arm and tried to calm him down.

"This asshole and Skittles were here to blackmail us," Gary shouted. "They was supposed to bring a DVD with them. It's not here." Gary scurried back to Rojo's body. He leaned over him and grabbed his car keys from his pocket.

"What are you doing?" Asad yelled.

"I'm going to check his vehicle for the DVD." Gary rushed out the door.

Asad looked at Rojo's body, then grabbed his temples in shock. Didi slowly walked down the stairs with both of her hands over her mouth. She was close to crying.

Asad rushed over to her. "What the hell happened in here, Didi?" he tried to comfort her. "Gary mentioned a video."

"Oh my God…I'm so sorry, Asad," Didi cried.

"Sorry for what?" Asad was confused.

"Please forgive us, Asad. I am…so…sorry," Didi frantically repeated.

Gary rushed back into the house with a look of fury. Asad turned and glanced at his brother. "It's not in there," Gary said, shaking his head. "What the fuck! The DVD is not in there."

"What?" Didi's face broke down into more tears. "Where is it…they don't have it?"

"Shit!" Gary yelled out and slammed his fist against the wall.

Didi closed her eyes and dropped her head. Her tears were flowing heavy now. Gary didn't know what to do next. He looked over to Asad.

"This doesn't look good, big bro," Asad warned. He glanced down at the dead body in the plush living room and shook his head. "You gotta get out of here, Gary. I can take care of this. But you gotta get out of here…now. When the police come… you can't be nowhere near this."

Gary stared at Asad and thought about his words. There was too much at stake for the mayor to be connected to the bodies in the house. He looked up to Asad again and they shared a moment of clarity.

"This one is all on me…I'll take this one head on for you, Gary." Asad nodded to his older brother. "Y'all need to get the fuck out of here now."

Gary walked over to Asad and handed him the gun. He grabbed Didi by the hand and tried to calm her. "So what are you going to do?" Gary asked as he approached the front door.

"I don't know yet. I'll figure out something," Asad huffed and tucked the gun away. "Y'all just get somewhere safe. You gotta act like this shit never happened today."

Gary nodded toward his brother. He grabbed Didi tightly and walked her outside. Asad moved toward the front door and watched as Gary and Didi got into his car. Gary fired up the engine and left the house like it was any normal day.

Asad turned around and looked into the living room that reeked of mayhem. He walked over to the television and turned on the power. He slowly lifted the white DVD out of his jacket pocket and placed it in the player. In his haste to kill Rojo, Gary never noticed that Rojo had given the DVD to Asad and warned him of its contents. Asad thought about Rojo's last words as he turned up the television. The video started playing. Asad took a look at the grainy video and covered his mouth. He couldn't believe the horrific images.

Chapter 34

Tuesday, October 29
3:15 pm
Newark, NJ

"Dammit...I can't believe it's after three o'clock!" Heidi frantically woke up from a quick nap. Her naked body was still sweating when she looked over to a snoozing Tycen. She frowned at her watch and shook her head. She couldn't believe how fast the clock was moving. Tycen and Heidi had made love multiple times and almost slept the day away. Heidi had no time to fantasize about the amazing sex. She hopped out of bed and started to get dressed. Tycen turned over and put the pillow over his head. "You need to wake up," Heidi uttered and pulled up her jeans. "Baby....it's quarter after three."

Tycen heard the hour and dropped the pillow to the floor. He looked up to Heidi as she rushed to put her shoes back on. "Damn... What time is it?" Tycen grunted.

"After three...I have to get the hell out of here," Heidi huffed and continued getting dressed.

"Whoa...!" Tycen forced his eyes open. He looked at Heidi's sensual body and chuckled. The episodes replayed in his mind, and Tycen couldn't help but bask in the memories. "I need to get up, too."

"What time do you need to be downtown?" Heidi asked.

"About five o'clock. I think Lawrence wants to do a debate prep with me." Tycen stretched out his arms and yawned. "As long as I'm there early. The debate doesn't start until eight."

"Okay…I need to get back to the hotel." Heidi grabbed her purse. "My mother is probably worried sick."

Heidi's last words made Tycen sit up on the edge of the bed. He looked at Heidi's troubled face and reached out for her. "Come here…baby," Tycen whispered.

"I can't, Tycen. I have to leave. You're really trying to start more trouble." Heidi shook her head.

"No, baby. I just want to hug you." Tycen's face was serious.

Heidi moved closer to Tycen. He reached out and gave her a warm hug. They shared a passionate kiss and Tycen looked at her. "Thank you for stoppin' by." Tycen's eyes were beaming with emotion.

"Thank you for making me stay." Heidi smiled. "Good luck with the debate. I really hope you do well."

"Call me tonight after you drop your mother off." Tycen squeezed her one last time. "Maybe we can do dinner later."

"Okay, Tycen. I will call you." Heidi gave him one last kiss on his lips. She grabbed the rest of her things and left Tycen alone in the bedroom. She glanced at her watch one last time and bolted out the door. The cold air brought Heidi back to reality. She rushed to her car and quickly got inside. She was running short on time. She needed to get back to the hotel to get her mother. Heidi's vehicle pulled off from in front of Tycen's house. She sped down the street and tried to make it back to Pearl as fast as she could.

A few miles away, a black Maserati tore down the busy streets of Newark. Asad Banks kept his red eyes on the road as he zipped through the congested blocks. Asad wiped the angry tears away from his face. He tried to focus. Asad's mind was still being tormented by the disturbing images he'd seen on the DVD. With two dead bodies back at his brother's house, Asad needed to know the truth behind Gary's sickening actions.

The engine of the Maserati rumbled as Asad punched the gas. He knew he only had a few hours left before the police got involved. Asad wanted a few answers before he made the call.

The black Maserati quickly turned onto a side street. Asad parked the car and peered out the window. He looked at the sign for Ruth's Soulfood Restaurant and saw he was in the right place. Asad didn't waste another minute. He shut off the engine, hopped out the car and rushed into the building.

The small restaurant was busy today. Busboys and waitresses buzzed through the small dining room. Asad looked for the owner and tightened his jaw when he spotted Ruth on the other side of the restaurant. Asad quickly rushed over to her. "I need to talk to you," Asad raised his voice and approached her.

"Okay…talk!" Ruth scoffed at the sight of Asad. "Make it quick…It's busy in here as you can see."

"Why did you fire Dante?" Asad gave her a direct expression.

Ruth tried to remain calm, but her body language changed when she heard Dante's name.

"Did you hear me?" Asad moved closer to her. "I asked you…why did you fire Dante?"

"I had to." Ruth twisted her face at Asad. "Things were slowing down here…and…I needed to get rid of him."

"Things slowed down?" Asad whispered and gave her a suspicious look. "You know when Dante told me that before it sounded like a bunch of bullshit. But now that I'm hearing it come directly from you, I know it's a goddamn lie."

"Why do I have to lie to you?" Ruth asked and moved to the other side of the restaurant.

"I don't know…you tell me." Asad stayed on her. "This place is never slow. And why did you just get rid of him? What did he do?"

"I just told you…" Ruth shook her head.

Asad grabbed her by the arm. The sudden moved scared

Ruth, and she looked up to his serious eyes. He gripped her tight and the expression on his face got her full attention.

"Listen to me…I know you're lying to me." Asad gave her another dangerous expression. "Dante is dead. You understand? My best friend is dead. I just need to know one simple thing… what's the real reason why you had to fire him?"

Ruth momentarily froze and thought about the question. She looked around her small restaurant and pointed to the door. "Not in here," Ruth whispered. "Let's talk outside."

Asad stepped out of her way. Ruth walked in front of him and they headed out into the cold air. Asad kept his eye on her as they moved to the edge of the parking lot.

"The only reason why I'm telling you this is because Dante was a good worker. I actually liked him." Ruth looked around the neighborhood. She tightened her collar around her neck to knock off the chill. Asad looked down to her as she began to speak again. "One night…a group of professional people came in here to eat. A big group. It was right before closing, and we served them anyway. I think they ordered over three hundred dollars' worth of food. So it was a good night. When they were getting up to leave…the woman that paid the check gave me a thick napkin. It was money in it."

Asad folded his arms and listened closely to her story.

"I didn't think anything of it. I just thought it was a big tip." Ruth looked around and continued speaking. "Turns out that it wasn't a tip. The lady had left me a note. It was a thousand dollars in the napkin. The note said that if I fired Dante within a week, she would be back to give me five thousand dollars more…in cash."

"Are you serious?" Asad asked.

"Yes…I needed the money…so I did it." Ruth felt slightly remorseful as she thought about her last statement. "I came up with some bullshit story…and…I had to let him go. I really didn't think he was going to flip out the way he did. I felt bad…but I needed the money."

"So did she pay you?" Asad sarcastically asked.

"Yes..." Ruth nodded her head. "The lady came back that next day...after I fired Dante...and paid me the money."

"Who was it?" Asad quickly asked. "Who was the lady that paid you the money?"

"I don't know her real name." Ruth raised her eyebrows. "But she told me to call her Didi."

Asad felt sick to his stomach. Ruth's words sucked all of the life out of him. Asad grabbed his head and cursed out loud. He didn't say another word to Ruth. Asad almost broke down as he stumbled back to his car. A heavy feeling of betrayal rushed through his body. Ruth yelled out for him, but Asad never turned around. He jumped into his Maserati and sped away from the restaurant. Asad knew exactly what he needed to do.

Chapter 35

Tuesday, October 29
4:25 pm
Newark, NJ

The steaming shower water slammed against Didi's naked skin like a million hot pellets. She covered her face in shame as the tears flowed from her eyes. Didi spent the last twenty minutes punishing herself with the scorching hot shower. No amount of water could cleanse her conscious of the heavy burden that was weighing on her mind. Images of Skittles' dying face haunted her. The loud gunshots rocked her memory, and she tightly closed her eyes and tried to erase the madness from her head. She slammed her fist up against the wall and yelled in the shower. She couldn't take it anymore. The violent episode replayed in her mind. Didi yelled again. Her heart raced out of control. The once buried secrets of Didi and Gary were now threatening to expose their wild lifestyle. The fear of the consequences caused Didi to cry uncontrollably. She had no clue of how to make things right.

"Is everything alright in here?" Gary Banks yelled out as he barged through the door. He noticed the thick steam coming from the top of the shower and pulled back the curtain. "Shit!" Gary blurted when he glanced at the scorching water bruising Didi's body. He frantically turned off the shower and pulled Didi out of the tub. She cried in his arms as he covered her with a large towel. "What are you doing?" Gary blurted. He carried Didi out of the shower and walked her to the bedroom. He laid her down on the mattress and glared at her. Didi was clearly distraught.

"Didi…you got to pull yourself together." Gary shook his head and sat next to her on the bed.

Didi squeezed herself tight and looked up to the mayor. Her eyes were emotionally drained. "What are we going to do?" she cried out.

"We're going to be fine." Gary nodded. He rubbed Didi's shoulder and never looked away from her. "We just need to let this play out. We'll be okay."

Didi turned away from Gary. She didn't believe him. For the past few hours, the two had been held up in Didi's house. They tried to figure out what to do next. "Did you hear from Asad yet?" she whispered.

"No…he's not picking up his phone," Gary responded. "I left him a message, but he hasn't called me back."

"You think the cops are at your house by now?" Didi quickly asked.

"I don't think so," Gary uttered.

"How can you be so sure?" Didi snapped.

"Because…my house is not all over the goddamn news." Gary looked at her.

The bedroom fell silent. Didi decided not to push the issue. She closed her eyes and wiped her face.

"Hey…Didi….relax," Gary tried to calm her nerves. "We will be fine. We can spin this…like it was a robbery. When the news breaks…all we have to do is keep pushing it like they broke into the house. Asad will look like a hero and we can move on."

"And what about the video, Gary?" Didi whispered. "How do we move on from that?"

Gary closed his mouth. Didi knew they were in big trouble and for the first time today, she knew that Gary didn't have an answer for her. She grabbed herself tighter and shook her head.

"We'll figure out something," Gary said. "But the last thing we should do now is panic."

Gary stood to his feet. He gathered himself and brushed off his clothes.

"What are you doing?" Didi looked over to him.

"I'm going to get myself ready for this debate in a few hours." Gary moved to the other side of the room.

"Wait...you're still going down there?" Didi gasped.

"We have to," Gary quickly responded. "Nothing can look out of place right now. I told you...we just need to let this thing play out. Everything has to continue as nothing happened. We have to keep our schedule."

Didi looked at the mayor's cold expression. She couldn't believe Gary was so detached from the horrific reality.

He prepared himself to leave. "I'm going to pick up a few things from my office, and I will be down to the arena by seven." Gary gave her a serious glare. "Please be there. And make sure the team is ready. We need to keep up appearances." Gary didn't say another word. He turned around and left Didi's bedroom.

She closed her eyes and took a deep breath. The violent scene at Gary's house replayed in her mind. Didi squeezed herself again and tried to shake the horrific thoughts.

A few miles away, Heidi quickly entered the Marriott Hotel. She glanced around at all of the faces in the huge lobby. She wanted to make sure nothing was out of place. Heidi's erotic visit with Tycen allowed her to escape for a few hours, but now Heidi felt herself growing paranoid again. All of the strange faces seemed suspicious to her, and Heidi felt funny. She picked up her pace and safely made it to the elevator. Heidi's phone started buzzing in her hand. She glanced at the screen and twisted her face. The call was coming in from a restricted number.

"Hello," she answered as she entered the elevator. There was no answer. Heidi thought she heard someone breathing through the phone, but she wasn't sure. She quickly disconnected the call as the elevator shot to the top floor. Heidi's phone buzzed again.

"Hello…who is this?" Heidi answered and yelled into the phone. There was still no response. Heidi disconnected the call and walked out the elevator. As she headed to her hotel room, the phone started ringing yet again. Heidi cursed out loud. She was beyond angry.

"Listen asshole…I know who this is!" Heidi screamed. "You are a coward….stop calling my phone!" Heidi didn't bother to wait for a response. She quickly disconnected the call again and stepped into the hotel room.

"Mom…I'm sorry it took me so long. I had to go see Tycen," Heidi called out as she walked into the hotel suite. She looked around for her mother. The suite was quiet.

"Mom…?" Heidi's face tightened. She moved to the bathroom. She started breathing heavily when she noticed it was empty. "Mom…where are you?" Heidi became worried. She quickly rushed into the bedroom, and there was no sign of Pearl. "Mom!" Heidi yelled out again. She checked all of the rooms once more, but Pearl was not there. Heidi rushed over to the phone and was just about to call the front desk when she saw Pearl had left her a note. "Goddammit…" Heidi yelled, picking up the small pad. Her heart dropped to her stomach when she read the note.

Heidi, you were taking too long to come back so I decided to catch a cab to the house. I need to go get my locket. I will be back soon. – Mom

Heidi shook her head and became angry with her mother. Her imagination was getting the best of her, and Heidi was ready to scream at Pearl for scaring her. She reached for her phone and called her mother's cellphone. There was no answer. Heidi paced through the suite and called the number again. Pearl still didn't pick up. Heidi became more fearful and called the house phone. The call was connected after just one ring.

"Mom...!" Heidi yelled out.

"I'm sorry...your mother can't come to the phone right now," a male voice grimly spoke from the other line.

A crippling fear came over Heidi the second she heard the voice. She couldn't believe it. Aaron Smith. His voice cut through her ears like a rusty blade. Heidi's mouth fell open, but there was nothing to say. Aaron had found her. Nothing could prepare her for this moment. Her emotions got the best of her, and Heidi's limbs trembled in fear.

"Talk to me, Heidi," Aaron whispered into the phone. "I don't feel the love."

"Don't you touch my mother, Aaron," Heidi mumbled. She said the first thing that came to her mind.

"Too late..." Aaron coldly responded. "She's a feisty bitch!"

"I'm gonna kill you motherfucker," Heidi shouted into the phone.

"There's no need for idle threats," Aaron's voice was heartless. "I told you once before...you have no idea who you fuckin' with."

Aaron's words sent a hard chill through Heidi's body. Something in his tone scared her like never before. She was about to respond, but Aaron cut her short. "Save it, bitch! You know where I'm at." Aaron slammed the phone down.

The line went dead and Heidi screamed. Heidi frantically dialed her mother's house again. There was no answer. Heidi cried. She tried Pearl's phone again, but no one picked up. Heidi sprang into action. She grabbed her bag and left the hotel suite. Heidi knew she was racing against time. She had to get to Aaron and save Pearl.

Meanwhile, at the Hackensack Medical Center, Asad Banks quickly rushed to the second floor of the hospital. He was pressed for time as he maneuvered through the busy herd of nurses and medics in the hallway. Asad needed to see Kimi Moore. He knew he was taking a chance coming back to see her, but he didn't know where else to turn. Asad reached her hospital room and nervously knocked on the door.

"Give me one minute," Kimi's shouted out from the room.

Asad took a deep breath and looked around the hallway. He was anxious to see Kimi.

"What are you doing here, Asad?" Kimi groaned as she opened the door.

"I'm sorry…I know this doesn't look right…but I needed to talk to you," Asad pleaded and gave Kimi a worried expression. "Just give me a few minutes to talk to you."

Kimi looked at Asad for a moment. His urgent demeanor put her on notice, and she let him inside. Asad quickly closed the door. "What happened to you?" Kimi looked at Asad's disheveled appearance. He looked as if he had been through a war.

"I need your help," Asad said.

"What kind of help?" Kimi gave Asad a suspicious look.

"I can't explain it all right now," Asad responded. "But I need you to trust me. There's something going on with my brother."

"The mayor?" Kimi asked.

"Yes." Asad nodded. "I need you to come with me to the debate."

"Asad…what are you talking about?" Kimi was confused. "Look around. . .I'm not really in the best condition to be your date tonight."

"Kimi…please…listen to me," Asad pleaded. "Something is going to happen tonight, and I need you there. I can't trust nobody down at city hall. There is somethin' ugly goin' on. And I have to end this tonight."

Kimi slowly shook her head toward Asad. His frantic voice scared her. Kimi gave him a long onceover. She noticed fresh blood under his fingernails, and then walked away from him.

"I can't go with you tonight," she nervously refused his request. "I don't know what you got goin' on…but I really don't want to be a part of it. I have my own problems right now."

Asad grew frustrated. He tried his best to hold back his emotions. "Kimi…I need you there," Asad repeated.

Kimi turned around and looked at him. The stress in Asad's voice made Kimi shake her head. "Asad…listen…I appreciate what you did for me," Kimi said. "I'm grateful for that."

"It's not about that," Asad quickly responded. "I'm not asking you to return a favor…or nothing like that. I really don't have anyone else I can trust right now. And I swear…I will protect you tonight. I just need you there."

The hospital room fell silent. Kimi didn't know what to say. She put her hand on her head and looked out the window.

"Look…Kimi…look at me," Asad whispered. Kimi turned around and stared at him. "Earlier you said that you didn't want me to be like you. I know you think you're not a good person…but I think you're wrong. I see something in you, too. I saw it that night when I looked at you…tied up in that office. That's why I risked my life for you." Asad's face was slightly emotional. "Kimi…I don't care what you did in the past. Maybe you did something…I don't know. Maybe you did something that made you feel like a piece of trash." Asad shook his head. "But that's all over with. The fact of the matter is…you're here right now. We both are. And now we have an opportunity…to make something right. I need to do this tonight. And I could really use you by my side. All I ask is that you trust me on this."

Kimi slowly raised her hands to her eyes. She wiped her face and thought for a moment. Asad's words hit her deep. It was like he was reading her like an open book. She had no clue what he wanted her to do, but something deep within told her not to refuse him. Kimi took a deep breath and looked into Asad's honest eyes. "Okay Asad," Kimi whispered. "I'm in."

Chapter 36

Tuesday, October 29
6:45 pm
Newark, NJ

The Prudential Center in downtown Newark was alive. News media, political heavyweights and anxious spectators all crammed into the extravagant arena to attend the first mayoral debate of the campaign season. People came from all over the tri-state area to witness the highly publicized debate between Gary Banks and Tycen Wakefield. Security was airtight. Helicopters circled the huge building. Thousands of people filed into the arena as the enormous event started to draw near.

Lawrence Cohen confidently strutted through the large crowd backstage. He was flanked by a half dozen interns and three press agents. Lawrence felt excited. His team was poised and ready for a good debate. Lawrence approached a small room near the backstage area. He smiled when he laid eyes on his client, Tycen Wakefield. "He hails...all the way from Newark, New Jersey!" Lawrence yelled as if he was introducing a NBA Player. "At six foot...three inches... it's the unstoppable ....unmovable ...unbreakable ....Tycen Wakefield...!"

The interns playfully cheered. Tycen laughed at the group.

Lawrence patted Tycen on the back and nodded to him. "So

are you ready to make history?" Lawrence asked with a huge smile.

"Heck Yes!" Tycen confidently nodded and stood to his feet.

"Just remember what we talked about, Tycen." Lawrence handed him a sheet of paper. "You don't have to be the leader of the free world tonight. Just be better than Gary."

"Got it." Tycen nodded in agreement.

Tycen took a deep breath. He was extremely nervous about the debate. He tried his best to conceal his fear. He could hear the large crowd just beyond the curtains. People were ready to watch the important issues of the city discussed. Tycen quietly went over his notes. His phone started buzzing in his pocket. Tycen pulled out his cellphone, and Lawrence snatched it out of his hand.

"No....Tycen!" Lawrence snapped like a high school teacher. He cuffed the phone in his fist. "Not tonight...you really need to be focused."

"I need my phone." Tycen's squeezed his jaw together.

"Tycen...tonight might be the most important night of your political career," Lawrence said. "Remember what we talked about. Those people out there can smell doubt and fear. You need to be one hundred percent focused on the task. This debate with Gary is the only thing that is going on right now. Everything...and everybody else can wait."

Tycen closed his mouth. He didn't agree with his campaign manager, but he knew Lawrence was correct in his decision. He nodded his head again and turned his focus back to his notes. Lawrence walked to the other side of the room and turned off Tycen's ringer. He didn't want any other distractions.

A loud commotion came from just outside the small room. Lawrence and Tycen turned around. They noticed a large entourage walking by their door. Tycen looked up as one of the men entered the small room. It was Mayor Gary Banks.

"Good evening Mr. Wakefield." Gary walked directly over to Tycen and shook his hand.

"Mr. Mayor." Tycen sternly nodded.

"I just wanted to come in here and offer my good luck wishes to you." Gary's face was hard as stone.

"I wish you the same." Tycen tried his best to look poised and confident.

"I'm honored to engage in this debate with you tonight." Gary gave Tycen a hard stare. "Sometimes it takes a big man to admit just how insignificant he really is."

Tycen closed his mouth and showed no reaction to the sardonic statement. Gary turned around and left the room.

Lawrence moved closer to Tycen. "What the hell was that about?" Lawrence asked.

"I have no idea," Tycen whispered. Gary's overconfident statement gave Tycen all the motivation he needed. He was now ready for the debate.

A few minutes later, Asad Banks cleared the security checkpoint at the entrance of the Prudential Center. Kimi was right by his side as they rushed through the bright concourse of the arena. Asad looked around. He couldn't believe the size of the crowd attending the debate. The wild energy was in the air. Media and residents alike were excited to watch the candidates spar over the right to run the biggest city in the state. Asad reached down and grabbed Kimi by the hand. They rushed through the thick droves of people. A loud announcement blared from the television monitors in the concourse. Asad stopped in his tracks and looked up to the screens.

"Please welcome the candidates as they come to the stage…I would like to remind the audience it is not necessary to cheer or applaud during the debate. Each candidate will be asked a series of questions, in which they will be given an opportunity to respond and debate the topic at the designated times. Good luck to both of you gentlemen. Please let us begin."

The moderator's voice echoed throughout the building. People scrambled inside to grab their seats.

"Dammit…" Asad yelled.

"What's wrong?" Kimi looked at him.

"We're too late. The debate is starting," Asad grimaced. He looked up to the television screen again. He watched as his brother, Gary Banks, and Tycen Wakefield stood behind the podiums on the stage. The moderator asked the first question, and the two began to engage in a heated discussion.

An idea came to Asad's mind. He rushed to the nearest concession stand and snatched a pen. Kimi watched him as he wrote something down on a napkin. He rushed back to Kimi and handed it to her.

"Listen to me closely." Asad reached into his pocket and pulled out the white DVD. "I need you to find the media room and give this to the manager." Asad gave her the DVD and pointed at the note. "Tell him that you're with Asad Banks and the mayor…tell him that it's very important that he follows the directions. Okay?"

"Okay…" Kimi said, then looked down at the DVD and the note. Asad's voice had been nearly frantic. Kimi nervously nodded her head.

"Thank you." Asad gave Kimi a soft expression. He wanted to say much more to her, but there wasn't enough time. He turned around and sprinted down the concourse. Kimi watched Asad as he disappeared into the thick crowd of people.

Didi nervously stood backstage. She got a good view of the debate from just beyond the side curtains. The heated discussions between Gary Banks and Tycen Wakefield raged on. Her boss was doing an excellent job, and she couldn't believe how composed Gary was after such an explosive day.

Tycen Wakefield held his own as he and Gary Banks exchanged great ideas for the future of the city. The audience was fully engaged as the debate grew more intense.

Didi wrung her hands together. She tried to stay focused, but her mind continued to wander with a larger issue brewing. She was thinking about her future when a small scuffle broke out just behind her.

"Get the hell off of me...!" Asad shouted out.

A few members of the mayor's security team tried to hold Asad back. Didi noticed the drama and rushed over. "Let him go," Didi harshly whispered.

Asad pulled his arms away from the security men.

"Asad..." Didi gasped and reached out for him. "What are you doing here?"

Asad gave her a cold expression and pulled away from her. He was clearly angry and never responded to her question.

"Asad...wait." Didi pulled on him as he moved quickly toward the curtains. "What happened at the house?" Didi looked around and pulled Asad away from everyone.

His eyes were dark red. Asad was furious. "How the fuck can you live with yourself?" Asad chastised her.

"Huh...Asad...What are you talking about?" Didi was taken aback by the harsh question.

"You're nothing to me right now. It's unbelievable what you did," Asad shouted in her face.

His words were like a harsh kick in the chest. Didi's mouth fell open. "Asad...please calm down. What are you talking about...calm down, please," Didi's voice cracked.

"Don't fuckin' tell me to calm down." Asad pushed her hands away. "I saw the video. You hear what I'm sayin'? I saw the goddamn video, Didi. It's over. All of this...is fuckin' over."

Didi stopped. She covered her mouth and tried to breathe. Didi felt like a trapdoor was suddenly opened under her feet. She wanted to explain herself, but her emotions got the best of her. Didi realized her dark secret was no longer hidden. The day she'd dreaded for so long had finally arrived.

Asad pushed her to the side like she was a total stranger. He turned his attention to the debate. He pulled the curtain back and looked at his brother, Gary, on the stage. Asad wasn't in his right mind. He unconsciously walked out into full view of everyone in the arena. A loud gasp emitted from the audience as Asad walked out onto the stage. No one knew what was happening. Gary turned around just in time to see his younger brother running over to him.

In a move that shocked the crowd, Asad lunged at his brother and punched him directly in the face. "You son of a bitch!" Asad violently yelled out and continued to swing at his brother.

Tycen was shocked as he looked on. A huge fight between the brothers exploded on the stage. Gary and Asad fell to the floor. Everyone in attendance stood to their feet.

"What the fuck are you doing?" Gary shouted as he wrestled with his irate brother. "Get the fuck off of me!"

Asad continued to assault the mayor. Everyone behind the curtain rushed out onto the stage. Didi yelled for the brothers to stop fighting. Tycen sprang into action and tried to break up the scuffle.

Lawrence darted out onto the stage. He grabbed Tycen and pulled him away from the brawl. "Don't get involved, Tycen," Lawrence yelled out and pulled his client to the other side of the stage.

Gary's security team rushed in and restrained Asad. They stood him up and tried to calm him down. Asad fought hard to get back at his brother. "You heartless son of a bitch!" Asad shouted again.

Gary picked himself up off the floor. Didi rushed to him. The security team quickly cleared the stage. The moderator tried to regain order in the arena. Asad and Gary continued their shouting match as they both were rushed to the nearest dressing room.

"Have you lost your fucking mind?" Gary shouted to Asad and grabbed his face. His younger brother put a quick beating on him, and Gary was stunned by the altercation.

"How the fuck could you do that?" Asad yelled out, struggling with the security men.

The mayor looked around the dressing room. He pointed to Didi and his security team.

"Let him go and everybody get the fuck out of here…!"

Gary yelled.

The security men gave the mayor a strange look. "I don't think that's a good idea, Mr. Mayor," one of the security members said.

"Did you just hear what I said?" Gary shouted louder. "Let him go…we're okay…that's my brother. And everybody else get the fuck out of here. I need to talk to my brother really quick. Let's go! Get the hell out…now!" Gary looked over to his younger brother.

The coldness in his eyes put Asad on notice. There was something in the mayor's glare that reminded Asad that Gary was still his elder sibling. Asad pulled away from the security men and stood still. Everyone slowly started to leave the room.

"Didi, buy me a few minutes," Gary shouted. "Tell them I will be right back out there."

Asad looked at his brother's face. Gary was serious as he wiped his lip. The mayor wanted to talk to his brother in private. Didi cautiously left the room and slowly closed the door. The brothers were alone.

"You must've bumped your fuckin' head!" Gary shouted at his younger brother. "What the hell has gotten into you? Do you know what you just did out there?"

"All of this…is over, Gary!" Asad yelled. "Enough with the lies."

"What lies?" Gary tightened his face. "Are you drunk or something?"

"I seen it." Asad pointed to the mayor. "I seen the fuckin' video, Gary. This time…I can't help you. This is over."

Gary closed his mouth and thought about his brother's words. There were no more secrets to keep. Gary's heart started racing, but his expression never changed. "You saw the video?" Gary quietly asked and turned away from his brother. "How much did you see?"

"I watched the whole thing, Gary." Asad felt himself becoming emotional as the images on the video replayed in his mind. "How could you do something like that?"

Gary turned around and looked at his brother. Asad stared at Gary like he couldn't recognize him. The mayor didn't know what to say to Asad. A rush of compassion and remorse came over Gary. He thought about the video and shook his head. Gary was tired of lying. He loved his younger brother, and realized that Asad deserved an answer. He decided to come clean with his brother. Gary's hard expression finally cracked and he slowly rubbed his forehead.

"We all got demons, little brother," Gary whispered as he spoke. "What you seen was a terrible mistake. I fucked up."

Asad tightened his jaw. He sensed the honesty in his brother's words and shook his head.

"But why the fuck did you try to cover it up?" Asad quickly asked.

"What do you mean?" Gary responded.

"My best friend...Dante...didn't kill Lexi Hamilton," Asad slightly raised his voice. "Dante wasn't built like that. I knew he didn't do that shit." Gary didn't say a word. "How could you murder my best friend and blame Lexi's death on him?" Asad covered his chin with his fist and tried to hold back his anger. Gary never opened his mouth. "I know it was you, Gary. Who else could've set up that shooting in the park? Those shooters were never gunnin' for you. They were there to kill Dante that whole time. And you set that shit up Gary. Don't say you didn't."

"That's bullshit, Asad!" Gary shouted.

"No...Gary...that's real!" Asad fired back. "You and Didi agreed to hire Dante just to get him killed to cover your own tracks. You knew the city wouldn't blink twice once you accused Dante of killing Lexi. Tell me I'm lying!"

Gary felt cornered as his brother continued to shout at him. Gary tried his best to keep his composure, but his web of lies was quickly coming undone.

"You really fucked up this time, Gary," Asad dropped his voice. "And I can't help you on this one."

"Asad...listen to yourself." Gary moved closer to his

brother. "Do you realize what we have here? Let's say you're right. Let's say…I did all of that shit you accusing me of…so what?"

Asad didn't respond to Gary. He closed his mouth and continued listening to the mayor as he tried to defend himself. "Those people out there turn a blind eye to corruption every day," Gary lowered his voice so only Asad could hear him. "Yes…I fucked up…okay. I got demons just like the rest of us. You want me to be perfect. Well…I got some bad news for you…I'm not perfect. I got flaws. You want me to be an angel, and I can't do that. I can't be an angel in the middle of hell. I can't do it."

"What the fuck are you talking about?" Asad slowly shook his head. "You're delusional. This is not hell."

"Oh no…?" Gary sarcastically said. "Look around little brother. People don't care about shit. They barely care about themselves. Kids are being slaughtered every day…wars. . .mass famine…senseless violence…it's everywhere. The world is burning, Asad. But people…are so busy running around smelling they own ass…they can't smell the smoke in the air. You better get used to it. We are burning, Asad… believe me."

Asad walked away from his brother. He headed to the other side of the room. The mayor's words hit him heavily. Asad knew his brother was in a dangerous state of mind. He felt remorse for a man he looked up to for so many years.

"Asad…listen. We can get past this," Gary whispered and walked over to his brother. "I apologize about your best friend. I had to do it. I had to protect what we had. But let's move on from this. We have a chance to have something great here. The Banks' name will live forever out here, and we can only get bigger. All we have to do is get past this."

Asad turned around. His emotional expression was hard for Gary to look at. Asad's eyes became glassy as he looked at his older brother. "Gary…you disgraced our name," Asad said. "You disgraced the Banks' name. Our father's name. I will never forgive you for that."

Before Gary could respond, there was a frantic knock on the door. Gary turned around just in time to see Didi rushing into the small dressing room.

"We need to get out of here," Didi shouted.

"What's going on?" Gary looked at her frightened face.

A loud commotion erupted backstage. People were yelling and cursing as the uproar became louder. Gary's heart dropped. He ran to the door and peered out into the hall. He noticed a group of police officers were rushing toward him. Didi tried to move by him, but Gary was unknowingly blocking the door.

"Gary Banks….you are under arrest," an officer yelled out.

A second police officer grabbed the confused mayor and spun him around against the wall. Didi tried to flee, but was tackled by another officer.

"What the hell is going on?" Gary yelled out as the metal handcuffs were placed around his wrists.

Asad slowly emerged from the dressing room. His troubled face grabbed Gary's attention.

"What the hell is goin' on, Asad?" Gary shouted again.

"I'm sorry, Gary," Asad uttered and pointed to a television monitor in the hall.

The mayor looked up to the screen and nearly broke down in tears. The video of Gary and Didi played on the television monitor, along with every screen in the large arena. The images were grainy, but people could clearly see a younger Gary Banks and Didi having sex with sixteen year-old Lexi Hamilton. The mayor was forcing himself inside the teen from behind, while Didi held a long leather choker, which was wrapped tightly around the young girl's neck. After a few minutes, the disturbing sexual act tuned violent. Gary was humping the teen like a soulless animal and grabbing Lexi by the neck, while Didi relentlessly pulled on the choker. The teen was screaming and begging for them to stop choking her. Lexi was reaching behind her body, desperately trying to get away from the sadistic duo. The frail girl was too weak to fight them off, and she suddenly collapsed to the floor. Lexi was unresponsive for a few minutes before Didi and Gary discovered something was wrong. They seemed to panic when Lexi was not responding to their pleas to wake up. Apparently, the choking had cut off her air supply for too long. Lexi Hamilton died on his floor.

The entire arena had just witnessed a murder caught on tape.

"Oh my God..." Didi cried like an infant. "It was a mistake...please God...listen to me...it was a mistake!" Didi screamed to the aggressive police as they rustled her down the hallway. She knew her life was over.

Gary dropped his head in shame. He wanted to crawl in a corner and die. The police held back the angry crowd that quickly began gathering in the hall. Everyone wanted to get a piece of the mayor.

Asad felt a strange calm in the middle of all the chaos. He looked at his brother's face. Gary knew he would soon be condemned. Asad hated to expose his brother, but he knew the truth needed to be known. The lies and deception needed to be unmasked in order for both the brothers to find inner peace. As the Newark police led Gary away in handcuffs, Asad couldn't help but believe that somewhere deep inside, Gary finally felt free.

Chapter 37

Tuesday, October 29
7:25 pm
Newark, NJ

Heidi's vehicle violently screeched to a halt. She glanced at the red light and banged her fist on the steering wheel. Heidi was a half-mile away from her mother's house. Her eyes were blood shot red, but she wasn't crying. Her face was too hot for tears. The rage she felt deep inside was unlike anything she had ever experienced.

For the past few years, the emotions of betrayal, treachery and revenge were bottled up inside her heart like a pressure cooker. She was ready to explode. Hearing Aaron on her mother's phone had made Heidi's stomach burn. She was beyond ready to confront the man who had tried to kill her. Heidi's mind was thrust back to the night she almost died at the hands of Aaron. She could still feel the angry bullets tearing through her flesh. Tonight there was something different about her memories. She wasn't scared anymore. A cold chill flowed through her body. For a moment, Heidi felt like an empty shell. She didn't know what to expect once she got to Pearl's house.

Aaron's cold-blooded voice echoed in her mind. Heidi knew there was a possibility that she wouldn't survive tonight. She shook the thoughts of dying. She refused to dwell on her own demise. She knew she needed to stay focus. She needed to get her mother away from Aaron, and she had to repay him for the absolute wrong he'd inflicted upon her. Knowing Aaron was responsible for the death of her first fiancé only added to her fire.

Heidi took a deep breath. Tycen's face came to her mind. She looked at her phone and felt sick to her stomach. Her battery was about to die, and Heidi didn't have a phone charger. She thought for a moment and decided to call Tycen. She quickly dialed his number. His phone continued to ring with no answer. Heidi waited for the voicemail to activate and took a moment to speak. "Tycen…I really needed to make this phone call before my battery died," Heidi whispered into the phone. Her voice sounded troubled. "I just wanted to… apologize for everything these past few weeks. You know I've been dealing with a lot of things, and I had no idea of how to handle them…emotionally…I just…wanted to say I'm sorry. And…umm…I'm heading to my mother's house right now. Aaron is there. He found me. He's in Newark. And…Tycen…I don't know what's going to happen. But I just wanted to… say that…ummm…I love you—" Heidi's phone disconnected. She looked down and noticed that her phone was completely dead. "Shit…!" Heidi huffed. Heidi put her phone down and looked up. She never noticed she was sitting at the light for nearly five minutes. Heidi punched the gas and sped away en route to her mother's house.

Back at the Prudential Center, the crowd was still in shock about tonight's events. Media teams were scampering about, trying to get any interviews and news stories they could spin from the wild debate. A few people took to the streets and a small protest spontaneously emerged in front of the arena. Gary Banks and Didi were now arrested, and the news sent a major shockwave through the city of Newark.

Tycen and Lawrence were still backstage. Tycen was finishing up a small interview with a local news network and Lawrence was looking on.

"Okay guys…I really have to go now," Tycen politely said.

"Please speak to my campaign manager for more interview requests." Tycen smiled and walked away from the small group of reporters.

"Good job, Tycen." Lawrence nodded as his client approached him. "I just got a text message from my contact at CNN. They have a broadcast set in the arena, and they want to interview you now. It's live and it's national." Lawrence nodded his head with confidence. He was thrilled about the news coverage. The interview would give Tycen the much-needed exposure to help his campaign. Lawrence couldn't hide his excitement.

"Okay…that's fine." Tycen quickly nodded. "I just need to make a call."

Lawrence gave Tycen a strange look. He was reluctant to give him the phone back.

"Tycen…you can't make that call after the interview?" Lawrence asked.

Tycen glanced at his campaign manager. He instantly recognized Lawrence's expression.

"Just two minutes." Tycen shook his head. "I just need to let her know that I'm okay. I'm sure she's heard about this craziness."

Lawrence hesitated for a moment. He didn't want to give Tycen the phone, but he went against his better judgment.

Tycen quickly grabbed the phone and flicked on the display. His face turned serious when he noticed Heidi had called him over ten times. He frantically dialed his voicemail and listened to his messages. "Shit…!" Tycen blurted as the last message played in his ear.

"What's wrong?" Lawrence grew concerned.

Tycen looked to the nearest exit. His heart started racing.

"Tycen…what the hell is the matter?" Lawrence raised his voice.

"I need to go," Tycen quickly responded.

"What? Now…? No…wait…!" Lawrence stuttered.

"I have to…" Tycen moved toward the exit and Lawrence

followed close behind.

"Tycen…are you nuts?" Lawrence grabbed him by the arm. "This is an amazing opportunity for you right now. This is it! Gary is toast! We got this!"

Tycen shook his head. He looked down at the phone and thought about the CNN broadcast.

"Tycen….listen…just do this quick interview…that's it. Everybody is watching now. This will put you in the driver seat. Believe me. Do this interview…and then you can go," Lawrence tried to plead with his client. "The mayor's seat is all yours, Tycen…can't you see that… You can't leave, Tycen… you have to do this!"

Tycen thought about Lawrence's words. His campaign manager was making sense. Tycen reflected on his lifelong dream to be the leader of Newark. The winds of change had blown in his direction and gave him a clear advantage. Tycen dropped his head. An image of Heidi's face flashed in his mind. The look in her brown eyes put his entire world in perspective. He glanced as his campaign manager and slowly shook his head. "I'm sorry…I have to go…" Tycen uttered. "You don't understand…without her…none of this….even matters."

Tycen closed his mouth and never said another word. He turned around and rushed toward the nearest exit. The campaign was the last thing on Tycen's mind. He bolted through the doors. A heavy feeling came over him. Something deep within made him feel like he needed to get to Heidi fast. Tycen didn't waste another second as he sprinted to his vehicle.

A few miles away, Heidi's car slowed down to a crawl in the quiet neighborhood. She peered through her window and looked at her mother's house as she parked her vehicle. Heidi was edgy. The house was dark, and she could only imagine what was waiting for her inside.

Heidi reached behind the passenger seat and carefully pulled out a small shoebox. She put the box in her lap and took a deep breath. Heidi flipped the top off and stared at a gun she hadn't seen in years. She grabbed the pistol and firmly squeezed it. The cold steel sent her mind to another place. She thought about Pearl and jumped out the car. There was no time for a plan, and Heidi knew she was racing against precious seconds.

Heidi moved swiftly though the dark like a criminal. She approached her mother's house and stopped on the porch. The front door was partially opened. Heidi's face tightened. She gripped her pistol firmly and carefully stepped into her mother's home. Heidi checked behind the door and closed it shut. She kept her eyes wide open for any surprises. She hit the lights, but none of them were working. Heidi started breathing heavy as she moved through the dark house with her gun raised. There was no sign of Aaron or her mother. Heidi felt something wet under her feet and looked down. She never realized she was walking through a puddle. Heidi heard a subtle noise come from the rear of the first level. Her heart started beating faster. Heidi raised her gun and entered the kitchen.

"Baby…thank God, it's you! Heidi….please help me…!" Pearl cried out.

Heidi rushed in. The dimly lit kitchen was in shambles. Heidi couldn't believe her eyes. Pearl was tied to the large steam radiator in the corner. She was crying and sitting in a large puddle of water. Heidi quickly scanned the kitchen. Her face turned to anger the moment she laid eyes on Aaron Smith. He was standing on the opposite side of the kitchen near the back door. Aaron calmly lit a cigar and blew out the smoke.

Heidi looked into his eyes and a heavy feeling of rage rushed through her body. She raised her gun and pointed it directly at Aaron's face from across the kitchen. The vengeance that once confused her was now keeping her focused. She was ready to end Aaron's life.

"Heidi…wait…don't shoot him…please…!" Pearl cried out again.

Heidi heard her mother's voice and paused. Her finger was

on the trigger and Heidi was ready to pull it.

"Don't do it Heidi…that's what he wants you to do," Pearl frantically screamed. "He wants you to kill us all."

A crooked grin came to Aaron's face. He took another long pull of the cigar. The amber tip illuminated his face. Heidi looked around and thought for a moment. She glanced at the floor and noticed the water was strangely reflecting rainbow colors. Heidi stepped back and looked at her feet. She wasn't stepping in water after all. Aaron flooded the house with highly flammable kerosene. He looked at Heidi and smiled when he realized her revelation.

"You sure you don't want to shoot me, Heidi?" Aaron whispered with a twisted grin and showed her the lit cigar. "Go ahead….let's end all of this right now."

Heidi kept her gun on Aaron. She looked at Pearl's terrified face. Heidi's hands started shaking. "What do you want?" Heidi whispered in anger.

"You…could never give me what I want," Aaron's harsh voice echoed in the kitchen.

"Let my mother go…you son of a bitch," Heidi shouted. "Keep my mother out of this. Motherfucker…this is between me and you. She has nothing to do with this."

"See….that's where you're wrong." Aaron switched the cigar to his other hand. "It's never been about me and you. You are so fuckin' blind…Heidi…you never realized that."

Heidi closed her mouth. She didn't know how to respond to Aaron.

"It has always been about me and Pearl…ain't that right?" Aaron sadistically said and looked at Pearl.

Heidi glared at her mom. Pearl turned away, and her face seemed to break down into more tears. "What the fuck are you talkin' about?" Heidi raised her voice again.

"Yes…what the fuck am I talkin' about, Pearl?" Aaron yelled in the kitchen.

Pearl never answered. Her body started shaking against the radiator. Aaron moved closer to Pearl.

"Don't you fuckin' touch her!" Heidi yelled and kept her gun on him.

"Don't be shy now, Pearl....tell her," Aaron uttered with a hellish grin.

Heidi felt confused. The look in her mother's eyes scared her. Aaron continued to antagonize Pearl and there was nothing she could do. With one mistake the entire house was going to explode in flames.

Aaron turned to Heidi and shook his head. "Fuck it...since she's not goin' to tell you, I'll just show you," Aaron said. He reached into his pocket and pulled out the gold locket that Pearl had been looking for. Heidi's eyes grew wide when she glanced at the gold chain. Pearl cried again and buried her face in her arms against the radiator. "Catch...!" Aaron yelled out and tossed the locket to Heidi.

Heidi caught the chain against her body. She gave Aaron a suspicious look and turned her attention to the locket.

"Go 'head...open it." Aaron pointed to the chain.

Heidi moved slowly. She looked at her mother, but Pearl never faced her. Heidi's heart was beating out of control. She slowly opened the locket. "Mom..." Heidi quietly stuttered.

Pearl's body started rocking as the thoughts of her past consumed her. Heidi's face cracked with emotion. She looked at the picture in the locket. The photo was over twenty-five years old. It was a picture of Pearl and Heidi's father posing with three very small children. Two boys and one girl. Heidi had never seen the image before. She recognized herself in the photo and recognized her brother Lamar. She had never seen the other boy before.

"Do you know what it's like...to be abandoned as a child?" Aaron coldly said from the other side of the kitchen.

Heidi looked up to Aaron. The house fell silent. Heidi couldn't believe what she was hearing. Her mouth fell open. She froze like a statue.

"I tried to find y'all for years," Aaron's voice trembled. "I can't believe she kept running from me. Do you know...what the fuck…that feels like?" Aaron yelled out. "She gave me away like a bag of old clothes. No remorse…just left me!"

Pearl never looked up. She cried. Heidi's heart felt heavier than a cinderblock.

"It took me a hundred fuckin' years…but I found y'all…" Aaron cursed at Heidi.

"You need to stop…fuckin'…lying right now." Heidi raised the gun again toward Aaron. Her eyes bubbled with tears. Heidi thought back to the conversation with her mother at the kitchen table. Learning of Pearl's indiscretions was coming full circle. Heidi wanted this night to evaporate in thin air. What was unfolding in front of her was surreal.

"Look at me, Heidi…!" Aaron yelled at her. Heidi tried her best to resist, but she needed to look at him. His familiar eyes made her even more emotional. "Look at me!" Aaron yelled again. Heidi started breathing heavily. Her chest burned. Aaron stepped away from the wall. He held the cigar tightly in his fingers. Heidi unconsciously took a step back. "Look at me, Heidi…," Aaron dropped his voice. "I'm your brother."

"No!" Heidi cried. She kept her eyes on him through the tears. She gripped the gun tighter. "Don't you fuckin' say that!" Heidi looked down and saw her mother crying uncontrollably. She could tell by the shameful look in Pearl's eyes that Aaron was telling the truth. "You are a fuckin' monster!" Heidi yelled at Aaron. "You tried to kill me."

"I hated you, Heidi!" Aaron shouted back. "I still do! You have no idea…what it feels like to ask…where is your fuckin' mother, and no one has an answer. And then I find out she gave up on me before she even knew what I was like."

Heidi's eyes grew wide. Aaron's angry voice made the hairs on the back of her neck stand up. For the first time tonight, Heidi grew scared.

"So did I hate you? You fuckin' right I hated you, Heidi," Aaron shouted. "It wasn't a day that went by that I didn't want to destroy everything you touched. I couldn't wait to find you. And when I did, I wanted to crush every dream you had. I got

Jayson...I got Lamar....and now it's time for all of us to go!"

"You are a fuckin' monster," Heidi repeated and pointed at Aaron.

He took another long pull of his cigar. He cut his eyes to Pearl, and his face grew serious.

"Bitch, you haven't seen a monster yet," Aaron coolly said, then looked down at the kerosene on the floor.

Heidi looked at Aaron's eyes. He was suddenly emotionless. Heidi turned to her mother and her mind started racing.

"You should just put the gun down right now, Heidi," Aaron mumbled. "No one is leaving this house alive tonight."

The threat gave Heidi pause. Aaron's eyes were not lying. He was serious. Heidi looked at the dangerous cigar in his hand. She sized up the kerosene on the floor, and felt her heart thumping through her chest.

Pearl cried out knowing there was a strong chance she wouldn't survive. Heidi heard her reciting the Lord's Prayer. Aaron took another pull, and then showed Heidi the red-hot tip. Heidi looked into his suicidal eyes, and knew she needed to do something fast. Heidi quickly wiped her eyes so she could see straight. She started to recite the prayer quietly with her mother. Heidi calmly stepped out of the puddle and looked to Aaron.

"Heidi, I'm only goin' to tell you this one more time..." Aaron pointed to her. "Put the fuckin—"

Before Aaron could finish his last statement, Heidi let off two thunderous gunshots toward him. The hot bullets viciously caved his chest in. Aaron flew backwards. The cigar dropped to the floor. A huge blaze erupted in the kitchen, and the fire started to ignite the kerosene all around. Aaron fell into the scorching flames, and started screaming from the unbearable pain.

"MOM....COVER YOUR FACE!" Heidi yelled out.

Pearl screamed as the blaze sped toward her. Heidi quickly pointed at the steam radiator and blasted four shots into the metal pipes. Two large torrents of white thick steam blasted from the radiator. The flowing hot vapor momentarily slowed down the fire around Pearl. Heidi fired another shot and created another hazy stream.

"Oh Jesus...please...help me Heidi!" Pearl screamed to the top of her lungs.

Heidi tossed the gun and rushed to the other side of the kitchen. She grabbed a knife from the drawer, and then rushed to her mother. Half of the kitchen was in flames now. The kerosene was quickly igniting all around them. "Mom!" Heidi yelled and grabbed Pearl. She reached into the piping hot steam and desperately cut her mother loose. She heard a loud crash and saw the fire had spread to the living room.

"We got to get out of here...," Pearl cried out.

Heidi frantically snatched up her mother. Pearl put her arm around Heidi's neck, and they rushed toward the burning living room. Heidi felt the flames on them, but she needed to get her mother to safety.

Aaron yelled in pain from the kitchen floor. Heidi spun her head around and saw Aaron's legs and mid-section were on fire. But Aaron wasn't done. He seemed to be possessed. Aaron was crawling toward the gun that Heidi had tossed. For a moment, she thought she had seen the devil in his eyes. She pulled on her mother's limp body, trying to move as fast as she could. Her heart pounded uncontrollably. She heard two loud gunshots blasting off from the kitchen, but Heidi never turned around. She rushed her mother outside, as the blaze seemed to engulf the large home in a matter of minutes.

"Mom...are you okay?" Heidi yelled as she continued to struggle with her mother.

"Yes...I'm fine," Pearl quickly responded and coughed from the smoke.

Heidi continued to move her mother to the middle of the street. The large fire crackled behind them. The house started collapsing inside as the fire relentlessly chewed up the old structure. Heidi turned around, with her mother draped around her neck. The blaze lit up the dark neighborhood. Heidi couldn't believe how fast the house was burning.

"My....God..." Pearl uttered and suddenly fell to the concrete.

"Mom!" Heidi yelled out and crouched over her. "Are you okay?"

Pearl was lying flat on her back. She was in obvious pain. Her eyes were wide. She was having a hard time breathing.

"Mom...are you okay?" Heidi frantically repeated. "Talk to me...what's wrong? Are you okay?"

Pearl tried to speak, but it was hard for her to get out a word.

Heidi's face exploded into tears when she noticed her mother crying. "Mom!" Heidi yelled. "It's okay... You can tell me. What happened? What's wrong?"

Pearl's looked at her daughter. There was fear in Pearl's eyes. She slowly moved her right arm and pointed to her lower back. Heidi wiped the tears away from her eyes, and then gently rolled Pearl onto her side. Pearl shrieked in pain. Heidi's face flushed with emotion. She noticed a bullet wound in Pearl's back, and nearly died from the sight. Aaron's final shot to destroy her family had connected with deadly accuracy. Heidi let out a primal scream, realizing her mother was gravely injured. She carefully rolled her mother back onto her back, and then looked at her.

"You're goin' to be okay." Heidi tried to keep her composure. "It's okay...we are goin' to get you some help. Mom...please stay with me."

Pearl cried the moment she looked into her daughter's eyes. She sensed her injury was severe. She could feel her body reacting to the gunshot. Heidi grabbed her mother's palm and held it tight.

"Somebody... HELP!" Heidi yelled out to anyone who was in earshot. Pearl tried to speak to her daughter, and Heidi looked at her. "It's okay, Mom," Heidi whispered. "You're going to be okay." A large SUV quickly pulled up to the house. The bright lights almost blinded Heidi. The truck pulled over to the other side of the street. Heidi looked up and saw Tycen jumping out of his vehicle. She yelled at him. "Call an ambulance!" Heidi screamed. "Please!"

Tycen turned around and grabbed his phone from his truck. Pearl tapped her daughter's hand to get her attention.

"Mom…we are going to get you some help," Heidi whispered.

"Baby," her mother mumbled through the pain. Her tears were flowing heavy now. "Baby…."

"Yes…Mom…I'm here," Heidi spoke softly and moved closer to her mother's face.

"Please…" Pearl mumbled. "Please forgive me…for your brother. I'm…sorry. Please…forgive me."

Heidi cried uncontrollably. She nodded her head and squeezed her mother's frail hands.

"I forgive you, Mom. I do," Heidi whispered. "I forgive you."

Pearl gave her daughter a gentle smile. Heidi collapsed over Pearl as she closed her eyes. Heidi wept for her mother as she felt her grip becoming weaker. A few minutes later, Pearl was unresponsive.

Epilogue

Tuesday, October 5
1:29 pm
Brick, NJ

THREE YEARS LATER

"News 12 New Jersey has learned that former Mayor of Newark Gary Banks plans to appeal the guilty verdict handed down just a week ago. In a long and drawn out trial that polarized the state, Gary Banks and his former Chief-of-Staff, Deanna Dickson, was found guilty of involuntary manslaughter for their participation in the death of Lexi Hamilton. The former mayor could face up to fourteen years in prison if the verdict stands. Please stay tuned to News 12 for more updates on this and other breaking news stories."

Kimi Moore quietly stood behind the front counter of a small flower shop. She was reading over the receipts from the week's sales, and never paid attention to the news story on the television. Kimi smiled at her financial records. Her new business venture was doing well.

After a wild few years, she needed a drastic change in her life. She'd invested the money she earned from selling her old business and opened a quaint flower shop nearly sixty miles from Newark. Her lifestyle had slowed down tremendously. The charming and old-fashioned neighborhoods of her new city were just what she needed. As her small business started to grow, Kimi started to feel more at home.

The loud bell on her front door sounded off as another customer walked into the store. Kimi never looked up from her notes as she wrote down her final figures. "I'll be right with you in a minute," Kimi sang out as she tallied the numbers.

"I knew I would find you," a familiar voice blurted from the middle of the store.

Kimi's hands froze when she heard the voice. Kimi slowly looked up, her heart raced when she glanced at the familiar face. Asad Banks. Kimi smiled. "Oh my God!" Kimi laughed and walked around her counter.

Asad smoothly approached and embraced Kimi. He was clearly excited to see her.

"Damn....Asad...look at you..." Kimi gasped and shook her head. She looked him up and down. Asad looked good.

"Wow, Kimi...no look at you." Asad flashed his pearly whites to her. "A flower shop?"

"Yeah." Kimi took a deep breath and looked around at all of the colorful plants and flowers. "I figured I'd been around death for too long. It was time to put some life around me."

Asad nodded his head. Kimi had matured so much and her beautiful face warmed his heart.

"So how have you been, Mr. Banks?" Kimi smiled. "I'm so sorry to hear about your brother, Gary."

"No, it's okay. Really." Asad nodded. His facial expression never changed. "It's the best thing that could have happened to our family. We all needed closure. He'll be fine. We all... will be fine."

Kimi looked at Asad, and could tell he was hurting over his older brother. She reached out and gave him another long hug. "You are such a sweetheart, Asad." Kimi smiled. "I always said that about you. You are such a sweetheart." Kimi looked into Asad's eyes. They both shared a peaceful moment. "So what brings you down this way? You need some flowers?" Kimi asked and winked at him.

"Actually, I came down here for you..." Asad whispered and gave her a serious glance.

Kimi stopped. She looked at him. Asad's eyes grew warm and she smiled. "Me...?" Kimi asked.

"Yea...I know that sounds crazy. . .and I'm sorry...for just popping up on you like this." Asad cleared his throat. "But it's just that... I never got a chance to say goodbye to you."

Kimi looked up to Asad for a moment. She loved the way he looked at her. It had been years since a man made her feel beautiful. She thought about how much she secretly missed Asad. The shop fell silent for a moment. Asad tried to read her eyes.

"So...is that...what you want to say to me?" Kimi quietly asked. "Goodbye?"

Asad smiled at Kimi. He was hoping he was reading her signals correctly. Asad glanced down to her arm and saw she was still wearing the Shamballa bracelet he'd given her a few years back. Asad slowly shook his head. "No...Kimi...I don't want to say goodbye..." Asad's face grew serious. "Not for a long time."

"Then don't." Kimi gave him a flirtatious glance and gently grabbed him by the hand. "It's good to see you, Asad."

"Kimi...you have no idea." Asad squeezed her hand and looked into her gorgeous eyes.

"Come on Mr. Banks..." Kimi smiled and turned around. She kept a warm grip on Asad's palm. "Let me show you around the shop."

Back in Newark, Tycen's vehicle drove through the enormous gates of St. Mary's Cemetery. The mood in the large SUV was somber. Heidi held on tight to Tycen's hand as they slowly drove by thousands of headstones and tombs. She looked out the window and held back her tears. Her world had changed dramatically during the past three years. The violence in her life had aged her beautiful face, but the coldness in her eyes had finally disappeared. There were no more nightmares and no more demons to run from. Heidi was a changed woman.

The SUV slowly made it over the quiet hills of the cemetery. Heidi looked over to Tycen. His handsome face made her smile. "You ever miss it?" Heidi asked.

"Miss what?" Tycen's voice echoed in the car.

"Being a politician....the campaigning...the interviews?" Heidi quietly asked.

"Sometimes," Tycen honestly replied and glanced over to Heidi.

"You know...I never want you to feel like you have to do this for us," Heidi uttered. "You know I never got over you dropping out of that campaign."

Tycen smiled. He slowly squeezed her hand tighter and pulled it up to his face. He kissed Heidi's wedding ring and gave her a pleasant expression. "There will always be another campaign and another opportunity to be mayor somewhere." Tycen squeezed Heidi's hand. "But there will never be another you. Those people out there needed a leader that could be focused on them. And I knew I couldn't do that just now. It's three hundred thousand people in this damn city...but I swear it's only two that matters to me the most right now."

Heidi smiled at her husband. No words could express how much she appreciated having him in her life. Tycen looked into the rear view mirror and took a glance at a marvelous sight.

A two-year old beautiful angel sat quietly in the back seat. It was their daughter, Faith Wakefield. The precious girl beamed when she saw her father making funny faces at her.

Tycen turned onto a small patch in the cemetery and turned the truck off. Heidi turned around and looked at her daughter.

"Faith...baby...you ready to see grandma?" Heidi quietly asked. The question was bitter sweet. The little girl put down her toys and nodded her head. Tycen looked over to his wife.

"You sure you want to do this," Tycen quietly asked.

Heidi wiped away a few tears and nodded. "Yes...I have to," Heidi uttered.

Tycen got out of the truck. He walked around to the

passenger side and made sure the women in his life got out safely. The cool air was calm. Heidi took a deep breath and prepared herself. Tycen hugged Heidi as they walked through the bright green grass and slowly made it over a small hill. Tycen held his wife tighter with each step.

"Grandma!" the little girl yelled and broke away from her mother's grip.

Heidi watched her daughter as she rushed over to an elderly woman sitting quietly in front of a huge gravestone. It was Pearl.

"Oh my goodness....look who it is." Pearl smiled as the little girl rushed into her arms. "I missed you so much, Faith!"

The little girl smiled at Pearl, then squeezed her like she hadn't seen her grandmother in one hundred years.

Pearl slowly stood up and looked over to Heidi and Tycen. She smiled when she laid eyes on the happy couple.

"Hey Mom..." Heidi calmly smiled and hugged Pearl. "I'm glad you could make it."

"Every year that the Lord blesses me with life...believe me...I will be here." Pearl smiled.

Tycen embraced his mother-in-law. The small family hugged each other and turned to the gravesite. Heidi read Lamar's name on the headstone and slowly nodded her head at the inscription. She missed her brother, and every year she promised to visit him on his birthday. Heidi put one arm around her mother and the other around her husband, Tycen. She knew her brother Lamar was smiling down on them from heaven. The family squeezed in tight and said a short prayer over Lamar's peaceful grave.

THE END

Book Club Question and Discussion Topic

What would be your perfect cast for The Final Kiss movie?

Heidi Kachina ______________________________

Tycen Wakefield ____________________________

Pearl Kachina ______________________________

Aaron Smith _______________________________

Kimi Moore ________________________________

Niko Stanton _______________________________

Asad Banks ________________________________

Mayor Gary Banks __________________________

Dante Harper ______________________________

Bethany "Dirty Betty" Stanford _________________

Rojo Marquez ______________________________

Deanne "Didi" Dickson ______________________

Shayla "Skittles" Johnson ____________________

Feel free to email your ideas and thoughts to:
movie@thefinalkiss.com

Name: ______________________________

Address: ______________________________

City/State: ______________________________

Zip: ______________________________

Institution info* ______________________________

QTY	TITLE	PRICE
	From Poverty To Power Moves ISBN-10: 0-9800154-1-3 ISBN-13: 978-0-9800154-1-6	$15 USD $19 Canada
	Kissed By The Devil ISBN #: 0-9800154-0-5 EAN #: 978-0-9800154-0-9	$15 USD $19 Canada
	Kissed By The Devil II ISBN #: 0-98001-5421 EAN #: 978-09800-1542-3	$15 USD $19 Canada
	Messy Sheets ISBN #: 0-9800154-8-0 EAN #: 978-0-9800154-8-5	$15 USD $19 Canada
	The Final Kiss ISBN #: 0-9800154-5-6 EAN #: 978-0-9800154-5-4	$16.95 USD $20.95 Can
	*Shipping & Handling (2.95 per book)	

TOTAL $ __________

Send check or money order to:

Next Level Publishing PO Box 83, Newark, NJ 07111

Wholesalers and Credit Card Orders, please call 973.634.8421 or email info@nextlevelpublishing.com

*Please allow 5-7 Business Days for Shipping and 2-3 Weeks for All Institution Orders.

For Booksignings and Appearences
Contact Aleasha Arthur - aarthur@nextlevelpublishing.com
Office: 301.213.1599

The Final Kiss

The Final Kiss